Normal Functioning Adult

Printed in Australia
Cover design by Shawline Publishing Group Pty Ltd
First Printing: May 2023

Shawline Publishing Group Pty Ltd
www.shawlinepublishing.com.au

Paperback ISBN 978-1-9229-9303-8
eBook ISBN 978-1-9229-9310-6

Distributed by Shawline Distribution and Lightningsource Global

A catalogue record for this work is available from the National Library of Australia

More great Shawline titles can be found by scanning the QR code below.
New titles also available through Books@Home Pty Ltd.
Subscribe today at www.booksathome.com.au or scan the QR code below.

Normal Functioning Adult

a novel by

SAMANTHA L. VALENTINE

For every minority voice who struggles to be heard.

Contents

Chapter One

I stare at the glass doors of The Psychology Centre. I've been coming here since my wife died, since my soul cracked and shattered, but only for occasional one-on-ones with my psychologist. Now he's put me into a group therapy program that starts today, and the thought of reliving Mel's death for strangers makes my pulse thump.

A knock to my shoulder jolts me forward. 'Jesus!' I shout.

'Watch it, love,' grunts a man in a suit striding past.

I'm about to call him an arsehole when I realise I'm the arsehole blocking pedestrians by standing in the middle of the footpath. I take a deep breath and walk through the sliding doors. My skin welcomes the cool air – a reprieve from the blistering January heat. A few people are scattered in the waiting area flicking through magazines or watching the morning news on the wall-mounted TV.

A gentle voice greets me as I slide my sunglasses into my handbag. 'Hello, Amy. I could see you out there. Wondered when you'd come in.'

The familiar face behind reception diffuses the tension in my shoulders. 'Hi, Barb. Just trying to psych myself up. I'm here for the group session.'

She gives a warm smile. 'It's in the end room on the left.'

I thank her and head down the corridor. Large black-and-white photographs of Brisbane landmarks decorate the walls: Story Bridge; Mt Coot-Tha; City Hall. The consulting room doors are all closed with the 'do not disturb' signs on display. Do not disturb the disturbed. I scoff at the absurdity. My phone buzzes in my bag, and I dig it out to find a message from Caroline, my best mate and colleague.

good luck chat later x

I reply with an 'x' and slowly open the therapy room door. Morning sunlight streams through a large window on the far wall. A few people are gathered in the middle of the room on lime-green sofas, the low murmur of their voices breaking the silence. I pick up a couple of pamphlets that are neatly stacked in a tall display rack by the doorway. The headings *Understanding grief* and *Coping with loss* make that constant pang in my chest burn. I quickly replace them and move towards the group, recognising a delicate floral scent as I get closer. My skin prickles. Oriental lilies. Mel's favourite. I want to believe they're a sign, but in reality they bloom year-round and are in every bouquet. I can't escape them.

I take a seat and the man opposite acknowledges me with a nod. Such torment in his eyes. Beside him is a young woman who's so vibrant I can only assume she's not one of the clients. Either that or she's dealing with the death of her spouse better than I am. Her bouncy, blonde curls frame a petite, youthful face, and her floral-print dress and bubble-gum pink nail polish fit perfectly with the brightness of the room. I attempt to smile but suspect the caustic taste she's left in my mouth plays out on my lips.

She does a quick headcount. 'Good, we're all here. Hello, everyone. I'm Kylie. I'll be your therapist for the program.' She gives a sympathetic frown. 'I know this is difficult, but you've taken an important step in your recovery by being here.'

My psychologist, Dr Sachdev, is the one who wants me to be here. I'm too *introspective* and *bitter*, apparently. Not progressing as I should. Attending group therapy will allow me to be with people who can understand. I had the urge to shove him off the chair when he'd said that. I don't know anyone who's lost their partner tragically. Not at this age. Now here I am on the Good Ship Lollipop with Shirley fucking Temple for a therapist. I cover my mouth and silently snigger at my own joke. I picture Mel rolling her eyes and saying, 'Get some contemporary references, will you. You're so un-relevant.' Then she'd laugh and touch her finger to my nose and say, 'But you're very cute.'

Kylie continues. 'As your psychologists explained to you, this group is for people who are experiencing...' Her voice takes on a sage tone. 'Complicated grief.' She pauses, clearly pleased with herself. 'Of course, there's no time limit on grief, but when certain symptoms persist beyond twelve months it puts you at risk of developing serious mental, social and physical complications.' She pauses again as though we need time to allow her words to sink in. 'Complicated grief therapy will complement your psychology sessions and help you connect with others who might feel the same.'

I cross my arms and focus on the lilies, willing myself to believe they're a sign I'm where Mel wants me to be.

Last week, Dr Sachdev spent our entire session on complicated grief. He told me about the symptoms and treatments and explained how some of my behaviour isn't healthy, such as my fixation on Mel's death, my belief I could've done something to prevent it, and my persistent yearning for her. But I hadn't been completely honest with him about my lifestyle over the past few months, so when he explained that not dealing with certain behaviours can lead to anxiety, sleep disturbances, difficulty at work and alcohol dependency, I told him he should be a psychic. He told me I had complicated grief disorder and that I needed group therapy, as well as weekly sessions with him.

'Let's start with introductions.' Kylie's melodic voice brings me back and her gaze lands on me.

I raise my hand to wave, but quickly drop it and cross my arms again. 'Hi. I'm Amy.'

'Welcome, Amy,' Kylie says and looks to my left.

The woman beside me has cropped silver hair and gives off a strong maternal vibe that makes me wish she was the therapist. 'Hello, everyone. I'm Trish,' she says, pushing black-framed glasses up the bridge of her nose.

'Hello, Trish,' Kylie says and turns to the man sitting beside her.

He pulls the fingernail he's been chewing from his mouth. 'Um, I'm Steve.' He has messy blonde hair, and the dark circles under his eyes are prominent against his pale skin.

I'm surprised to see someone so young here – he must only be late twenties.

'Hi, Steve. Nice to meet you.' Kylie turns to the final person in the group – the man opposite me with the tormented eyes.

His dark brown hair is lightly peppered with grey, and his skin is tanned, like he spends most of his time outdoors. I wonder if the fine lines around his eyes and across his forehead have deepened since he lost his partner. He rubs his hands up and down his thighs. The rustle of friction between his palms and the material of his shorts jars in the stillness. 'I'm Luke. G'day.'

'Welcome, Luke.' Kylie clasps her hands around a crossed knee. 'So, the sessions will run for an hour and the program lasts for six weeks. I haven't planned anything specific today because I'd like you to share your stories.' She tilts her head. 'If you feel comfortable that is. There's no pressure.' She gives us a kind smile and continues. 'Over the course of the program, we'll talk about grief in more detail and look at strategies and resources that can help. For now, we'll try and get to know each other a little bit and understand why you're all here.' She turns to Luke. 'Would you like to start?'

He stares at her. 'Oh… erm…' And after a few seconds, he says, 'I don't know what to say.'

'Tell us about your wife,' Kylie says softly.

'My wife. Right. She, Sarah, passed away just over a year ago. In a car accident. A drunk P plater ran us off the road. A fucken P plater!' He holds up a hand. 'Sorry.'

'That's alright,' Kylie says. 'Go on.'

The room is so quiet his swallow is audible. 'We'd been together almost twenty years when it happened. We were coming home from a New Year's Eve party.' He rests his elbows on his knees and twists the gold band on his ring finger. 'It's really bloody hard for me and the kids without her.'

When the silence extends and it's clear he's finished, Kylie asks if I'd like to speak. I don't want to because telling strangers what happened makes my insides twist, but at the same time, talking about Mel feeds my desperate need to keep her alive.

I give her a nod and begin. 'My wife, Mel, passed away twelve months ago. Twelve months, two weeks, and four days, to be exact. She went to Melbourne for work, got drunk, took...' I swallow. 'Took stuff and was found by hotel staff the next morning.' I grasp my wedding ring, which hangs on a fine gold chain around my neck. A chain Mel gave me for my thirty-fourth birthday, seven months before she died. 'We were together for nine and a half years but only married for one.' I glance at the faces peering back at me. All I see is compassion, so I continue. 'I have these huge highs and lows. Some days I can get on with life. Other days I can't get out of bed.' A tear escapes and I wipe it with the back of my hand.

I fall quiet then and after a minute or so, Kylie asks if I'd like to keep going. Although I've barely spoken, I shake my head. Luke catches my eye and gives me a tiny, encouraging smile.

The rest of the session is a blur. Voices drift, sad stories and circumstances. The air is heavy with sorrow, and it smothers me. I have no space for anyone else's grief or tragedy.

When Mel died, I descended into a dark well. After a few months,

I managed to crawl out and sit on the edge, legs dangling. I went to work. I smiled. I did what I had to do. But towards the end of last year, as the date of our second wedding anniversary approached, along with the anniversary of Mel's death, I slipped. A constant bitter taste in my mouth. Hazy mind from little sleep. Extra wine bottles in the recycle bin. More sick days from work. My friends and family caught me sliding, hauled me up and dragged me straight back to Dr Sachdev. That was three weeks ago. Since then, I've had several sessions with him and I can see the top of the well again, although I can't quite grasp the edge.

Kylie ending the session brings me back to the present, and I leave with barely a goodbye. The Brisbane CBD is bustling with people making the most of their lunch break. I walk close to the shopfronts to take advantage of the small amount of shade the awnings offer from the midday sun. I can't face work straight away so instead decide to stop at my regular café.

'Hey, Amy,' Evan says over the whirr of the coffee machine.

This café is nothing flash. Cheap pine furniture and a simple menu – sandwiches, burgers, all day breakfasts, that sort of thing. The food is always fresh and cooked perfectly, and the coffee is great. Evan owns the place and has served me for years.

'Hi, Evan. How's things?'

'Can't complain. You?' He withdraws the milk jug from the steamer and pours two coffees.

'I can complain; but I won't.'

He gives an understanding smile; he's used to my misery. 'You want your usual?' He hands the two takeaway cups to a waiting customer.

The rousing smell of crushed coffee beans and the scent of bacon wafting from the kitchen cause my stomach to growl, reminding me I haven't eaten today. I scan the menu on the blackboard behind him but decide having something different is too much effort. 'Yeah, ta.'

I pay for my flat white and ham, cheese, tomato toastie and head to my regular table in the back corner. As soon as I sit, I sweep my hair to the side. The cool air from the vent directly above caresses the back of my neck.

Not only is this the best spot for air conditioning, it's also where Mel and I used to sit. She was an employment lawyer and worked for a small firm around the corner near Central Station. She didn't have lunch breaks often, but when she did, we'd come here. I thought I'd be okay the first time here without her. But as soon as I sat down my throat tightened and I struggled to breathe. Evan was by my side in minutes and guided me to his office, where I spent the next half hour taking slow, deep breaths while he brought me wet napkins for my face.

Now I sit and think about the way Mel would watch me as she sipped her coffee, or the way she'd wink and run her hand up my thigh when she thought no one was looking.

Evan appears and sets down my flat white. 'There you go. Enjoy.'

I take a sip and sigh at the first hit of caffeine I've had since yesterday. I pull my phone from my bag to find a missed call from Mum. I told her I'd call after the session, although discussing it with her is the last thing I want to do.

I dial. 'Hi, Mum.'

'Hello, darling. I was wondering when you'd call. How was it?'

I shrug even though she can't see me. 'You know.'

'No, I don't. That's why I'm asking.'

I huff. 'It was hard and uncomfortable and I'm not sure I want to talk about it.'

'No need to get snappy.'

'I'm not get—'

'What about the others? What were they like?'

'It was a small group. Two men, another woman and me. One guy lost his wife in a car crash caused by a P plater.'

Mum gasps and I picture her clutching her chest. 'Oh dear, that poor man. That is heartbreaking.'

'Yeah. Really sad. The other stories are a blur. It was hard to focus.'

'When's the next session?'

'Every Friday morning for six weeks. Dr Sachdev wants me to go. Says it will help with my one-on-one sessions.'

'Well, that's good, darling. He must think it will help. Is your boss okay with this? He's supporting you?'

I shift in my seat. 'Er, yeah, he's fine.'

Evan places my toastie on the table. I mouth 'thanks' and take a quick bite.

'Good. Try and stick with it. It will get easier.'

'Maybe. Anyway, better go. Gotta get back to work.'

'Why don't you come over for lunch on Sunday? Your brother might come, too.'

'I'll think about it.'

She falls silent for a moment. 'Don't push your family away, darling.'

I close my eyes and take a deep breath. 'I'm not pushing you away, Mum. I just can't think straight right now. It was a tough morning and I need to go back to work. I'll call you on the weekend. Say hi to Dad.'

'Okay, have a good afternoon. See you Sunday.'

'I said I'll thi—'

But she's already hung up.

I take my time eating my lunch while I scroll through Instagram, inevitably ending up on Mel's profile. The last photo she posted was of her and Maddie, her best friend since primary school and one of my closest friends. They were out for lunch by the Brisbane River on New Year's Day. Eight days before she died. A powder blue sky hangs above them and tiny beads of sunlight skate across the water. Mel's caramel-coloured hair shines and her dark-blue eyes twinkle at the camera.

Her cheeks are flushed from wine and her mouth is fixed in a wide grin. That familiar, painful lump forms in my throat and I quickly close the app at the same time my phone buzzes with a message.

How was it? Coming back to work soon?

I'm about to reply to Caroline when Evan appears. 'You finished, Amy? I don't want to kick you out, it's just that people are waiting for tables.'

'Oh, sorry.' I jump up.

'No worries. See you next week.'

Outside the sun beats onto the footpath and I fish my sunglasses out of my bag. Traffic fumes stick in my throat as I walk along Edward Street adding to my discomfort. I pick up my pace, eager to see Caroline. The antidote I need to soothe this burning pain.

Chapter Two

It's the following Friday, and I blink at my monitor trying to remember what I'm supposed to do, but my brain has a murky lake quality about it today.

'Hi, Ames.'

I spin at the sound of Caroline's voice. 'Morning.'

She perches on the edge of my desk. Her long legs stretch out in front of her, and the sunshine filtering through my office window makes her blonde hair gleam.

We met in Melbourne sixteen years ago, both in our first year of university, and bonded over being from Brisbane and our emerging sexuality. We've also worked together at Australian Airlines for the past four years, although I've been with the company almost ten. I manage client services while she runs employee relations on the floor below.

'Ooh, had your colour done,' she says, giving me a once over.

'Oh, yeah.' I run a hand through my hair. 'Did it myself last night.' A few years ago, my hairdresser talked me into going from 'dull brown to rich chestnut'. Mel loved it. She said it highlighted the green in my eyes. Now I can't bring myself to change it. 'Look okay?'

Caroline nods. 'It's nice.' She glances at her watch. 'Don't you have your group this morning?'

I slump. 'I don't want to go.'

Irritation flashes in her eyes. 'Why?'

'Why?' I sit up. 'Because the therapist is twelve. I doubt she's even grieved a goldfish. How's she going to help me?'

She laughs. 'You don't know anything about her. I'm sure she's experienced, otherwise they wouldn't let her look after such a vulnerable group.'

'It's a community mental health centre, Caz, they're hardly rolling in cash to pay top therapists. I reckon they whipped down to the local high school and pulled out one of the year seven kids to do the job.'

'You're being absurd.' She crosses her arms.

I pick at the vinyl strip on the edge of my desk. 'And it's hard.'

'Oh, Ames. I know, but you need to give it a go. You've only been once. And remember what Paul said – he's happy for you to take the time for this if it's going to help.'

Paul. My hands clench at the sound of his name. He's the company's human resources director and our boss. Before I started seeing Dr Sachdev again a few weeks ago, Paul had been pushing me to 'do more to move on', as though my grief is something a few simple life hacks can fix.

'What the hell does he know? I'm surprised he hasn't emailed me a wikiHow link to "seven simple steps to overcome your grief – with pictures." Anyway, I'm here, aren't I? Working and doing all the crap he can't?'

She gives me a wry grin. 'You're in fine form this morning. Come on. Up.' She pulls me to my feet. 'I'll walk with you. I want to get a coffee anyway.'

'Alright,' I groan, swooping up my bag and tossing in my phone.

We cut through the open plan area outside my office. Sunlight peeks through the gaps around the lowered window shades, and the HR team tap on their keyboards or chat across the aisles. I stop by Daniel's desk, my assistant manager, to tell him I'm going out, and catch the enticing scent of hot cinnamon and sugar from the box of fresh donuts on the table beside him. I crave one, but the tide of anxiety that ebbs and flows in my stomach stops me.

Daniel follows my gaze. 'Don't worry. I'll save you one.' He gets my sugar addiction.

I point at him. 'Showing initiative. I like it. You'll go far in this job.'

He grins his big toothy grin and turns back to his computer.

'Didn't you have a meeting this morning?' I ask Caroline as we continue to the lift, past the row of large potted plants that partition a bank of desks.

She jabs the down button. 'Meeting's over. That's why I need to get out. This dispute is going from bad to worse. Julia's got the union involved now because Scott tried to bloody sack her. Fucking nightmare.' She presses her fingers to her temple and screws her eyes shut as we enter the lift. 'And this woman from the union – Rachel – is seriously testing my tolerance levels.'

I'm aware of the case because Daniel's been working on it, but he hasn't mentioned the union rep.

Caroline leans against the handrail and I take in her outfit. Black tailored pants, nude heels that I haven't seen before, her very expensive cream chiffon blouse and the statement-red lipstick she pulls out for certain meetings. The suit jacket will be on the back of her chair. 'Wondered why you had this look going on today. You're telling the union rep who's boss.'

'Too fucking right I am.' She strides from the lift and across the foyer.

I trot to keep up. 'Well, if anyone can handle her, it's you,' I say, and I mean it. In all the years I've worked in HR, I've never met anyone who manages employee disputes like Caroline. She used to spend hours discussing employment legislation with Mel, while Maddie and I drank wine and cyberstalked celebrity lesbians – or those we hoped were. Someone had to be across the important stuff.

The minute we're outside, beads of sweat form along my hairline, and my underarms become sticky. 'Yuck, it's revolting out here.'

Caroline grunts and brushes the hair from her face. 'I'm boiling in these pants.' She raises her voice to be heard over the car horns and the number 328 bus that's pulled up beside us. 'And it doesn't help that Rachel's hot. I stare at her and think, "How can you be so attractive but such a pain in the arse?"'

'Ooh, that definitely makes things more interesting. Maybe I'll find a reason to come to your next meeting.'

We weave through traffic to the hole-in-the-wall café on the corner of Queen and Edward. Their coffee range spans the globe, and they have the sweetest chocolate croissants in the city. Caroline comes here every morning to perform a ritual of choosing a caffeine intensity to match her mood and work schedule. Sometimes she chooses for me, too.

She orders a triple shot macchiato and croissant for herself, and a single shot flat white for me, and returns to work talk. 'Anyway, this dispute is giving me brain ache. I could use more than a coffee right now.'

'I always need more than a coffee. That's my life now.'

She frowns in sympathy. 'Hey, what are you doing tonight?'

She asks that question like she expects me to have plans. 'Sobbing into my wine glass and alternating between a movie and my phone, like I do most nights. I might even put on my wedding dress since it's a Friday.' She knows I'm not joking; she's found me crying in my wedding dress before.

'You wanna come over? Maddie's cooking.'

'Maddie's cooking for you? Sounds like I shouldn't interrupt.' I nudge her with my shoulder. 'Getting back together maybe?'

She shakes her head. 'No. Sorry to disappoint you. Besides, I think she's met someone. Or is sleeping with someone. Or, knowing Maddie, several someones.'

Although I'm happy Maddie's making the most of being single, my heart twinges that a reconciliation isn't possible. They'd become a couple when Maddie visited from Melbourne years ago and split six months after Mel died. Another ending, another life change we had to deal with. Or that I had to deal with – they were okay with it.

'Oh, that's a shame,' I say.

Caroline wrinkles her nose, the delicate lines around her eyes visible in the sunlight. 'You need to let it go, Ames. We're done.' The barista calls Caroline's name and hands over our order. 'We're great friends, though, and that's what matters, right? You still have both of us in your life.' She sips her coffee and groans. 'Oh, god, perfect choice. I'll be ready to kick Rachel's arse after this.'

I smirk. 'Sounds like you might want to do something else with Rachel's arse.'

She laughs. 'That would be painful. She'd quote me chunks of legislation while I'd be getting sexy.' She adopts a husky voice. 'Ooh, Rachel, read me Subdivision 1 of the *Industrial Relations Act* while you undress me.'

I chuckle and tilt my head in the direction of the centre. 'Better go. Might see you tonight.' I'm about to walk off when something occurs to me. 'Oh, Zoe won't be there, will she?'

Caroline shrugs. 'Maddie didn't mention it and I haven't spoken to Zoe this week, so I doubt it.'

Zoe works at Maddie's architecture firm and has become part of our circle over the past few years. She's also the woman I had a brief but intense six-week relationship with a little while after becoming a widow. I finished it, but it didn't take long for a friends with benefits arrangement to start. An arrangement I've been trying to end. It's not going well.

'Okay. Ta for this,' I say, holding up the cup.

She gives me a quick hug. 'You'll be fine. Give therapy a chance, hey?'

I swallow back the emotion that's inching up my throat and nod. 'See ya.'

As I cut through Queen's Plaza, I'm momentarily side-tracked by the diamonds in the Tiffany's window, but they don't sparkle like they used to. The vintage-style ring on display reminds me of Mum's and also reminds me I haven't called her for a few days. I pull out my phone, set a reminder and continue through the arcade.

My family has been incredible since Mel died, but Caroline and Maddie have been the force behind me. Caroline in particular. She made sure I ate, dragged me to therapy, held me while I cried, sorted out a return-to-work plan, and eventually made me smile again. She did it all for Maddie, too, who was as broken as me over losing her oldest friend. My dad is one of Caroline's biggest fans. 'She'd stay upright in a cyclone, that one,' he always says. My resilience used to match hers, and I've carried her through devastating times, but like so many other things, grief has stripped me of that trait. I question whether I'll ever get it back.

As I near the centre, the heart palpitations begin. I lean against the wall and close my eyes. What did Dr Sachdev say to do? Count to ten. Slowly. It will pass.

'Morning, Amy,' Barb says when I finally enter. 'Wasn't sure I'd see you today.' She's come to know me well over the past year, given the number of appointments I've cancelled.

'You almost didn't. Caroline forced me.'

She gives a knowing smile. 'Well, I'm glad she did.'

'Yep. Pretty useless without her kicking my bum.' I point towards the corridor. 'Better get in there.'

'Oh, before you go, Dr Sachdev asked me to book you in for next week.'

'Right. Um, I—'

'He said he explained that the one-on-one weekly appointments are part of the program?'

'He did.'

'How about Wednesday at five? Does that suit you?'

'I guess so.'

'Good. I'll pop you in for then.' She keys the information into the computer. 'You'll receive an automated reminder the day before.'

I nod, accepting that there's no getting out of these appointments. 'Thanks.'

Trish, Steve and Luke are sipping from polystyrene cups when I walk in. Sunlight bounces off the lime-green sofas, the brightness causing me to squint. Then I catch the soft perfume of the lilies and my breath hitches. They're in full bloom today with the powdery yellow pollen surrounding the base of the vase. My first thought is that the pollen is going to stain the white coffee table and it reminds me of arguments with Mel. She'd bring lilies home; I'd tell her off, then she'd kiss me and say, 'They're a symbol of beauty, just like you,' and I'd turn to liquid.

Kylie arrives, smiling brightly. Her curly hair is pulled back into a loose pony, making her eyes appear rounder and more child-like. She's wearing canary-yellow earrings teamed with a hot-pink linen dress and beige sandals. I find myself thinking how surprisingly well the colour combo works and I hate myself for it. I smooth down my black dress as a reminder of my usual sombre mood.

'Sorry I'm late. How is everyone?' she asks, positioning herself between Luke and Steve.

We all mumble and shrug. That's all she's going to get from four people who'd rather tattoo their own eyeballs than sit in a room with strangers dealing with their perpetual grief.

She nods slowly, but that smile doesn't budge. Nothing penetrates this woman's positivity. 'Good. I'm so pleased to see you all again. I know last week was tough. This week, if you can, I'd like you to open up more, tell us how you're feeling, what you're thinking. Would you like to start, Trish?'

Despite Trish's calm air, her hand trembles as she sips her tea. She tells us about her wife who passed away fourteen months ago from brain cancer and how hard it's been adjusting to life on her own after thirty-one years. She has no children, her parents have passed, and her sister lives in Perth. An image of Trish moving through life alone forms in my mind. Long, gloomy days with no one to confide in, to hold, to laugh with. My chest tightens and I want to give her a hug.

Once Trish is finished, Kylie turns to me. 'Amy? How about you?'

I grip my wedding ring so tight that my fingernails dig into my palm, and I have to be careful not to snap the chain. Dr Sachdev's voice has been on repeat in my head all week telling me how important it is to be honest with the group. 'I left a bit out last week,' I blurt, my voice shaky. 'What I didn't say was that Mel overdosed because she mixed opioids with alcohol. She didn't have a lot, just enough to...' I fall silent. I don't need to finish that sentence; they know how it ends.

Kylie gives me an encouraging nod, and I continue. 'I think it was an accident. I want to believe it was. She got hooked on painkillers after an incident at work. I did everything to get her to stop. And she was getting there. Down to one a day. I know that because I only let her take one a day.' I screw my eyes shut to trap the tears, but it doesn't work and my sobs echo around the room. Saying those words is a reminder that Mel's addiction was potent – so strong that it overrode her love for me. I bend forward and clutch my chest as though that will stop the agony.

When I sit back, I grab a tissue from the box in front of me and dab my eyes before continuing. 'I constantly question myself. What if she'd taken one less pill, would she still be here? Why didn't I make her stop? I knew what she was like. I should've made her stop.' I gasp for air as I keep talking. 'Are the two painkillers I gave her to take to Melbourne the ones that killed her?' I dip my head. I can't go on. All I want to do is curl up, go to sleep and never wake up.

Kylie gives me the space to allow my tears to ease before she moves to Luke. His eyelids are heavy today. I guess lack of sleep is one of his symptoms, too.

Like me, he reaches for his wedding ring. 'Um, like I said last week, Sarah died in a car crash.' His voice is deep and gravelly. 'We were coming home from a party. She was driving because I'd been drinking. She didn't even want to go, but I talked her into it.' He pauses. 'That goes around in my head all the time.' He shakes his head. 'I talked her into going. And I can't stop asking myself why I did that. If I'd just bloody listened to her.'

Our eyes meet, the torment of those unanswered questions forming a thread between us. He averts his gaze. 'It was late. We were on that stretch of the Bruce Highway as you come into North Brisbane. You know that section? It's two lanes and it's pitch-black.'

Steve and I nod.

'Yeah, that bit. We were in the left lane. This car came flying up behind us. Sarah was so scared. She slowed so they'd pass, but this kid driving sat on our tail flicking his lights.' He closes his eyes briefly. 'When he changed lanes, he clipped us. Sent both cars spinning off the highway. I remember Sarah screaming. I don't remember anything after that. I woke up in hospital, sore and bruised. She…' He clears his throat. 'Our car had slammed into a tree on the driver's side. She died instantly. That kid died, too.' His jaw clenches and his eyes turn cold and black. 'And I'm fucking glad.'

Oh, god. A chill settles over my skin. The eerie presence that sweeps the room must also affect Trish, because she rubs her forearms like she's trying to warm herself up. Kylie has a hand to her throat and seems to need a moment to recover before she moves on to Steve, but he keeps his head down and doesn't want to speak today. Instead, Kylie discusses resources and strategies for the rest of the session and checks that we've all booked appointments with our psychologists for next week.

Afterwards, I'm still seated with my eyes closed waiting for my heart rate to slow when a deep voice says, 'I'm sorry to hear about your wife, Amy. Must be tough going through that.'

My lids fly open to find Luke standing at the end of the sofa. He's taller than I realised. 'Oh, hi. Yes, it was… it is. But your situation doesn't sound much better. Just as hard.'

He frowns. 'Yep. Anyway, better get back to work. See you next week?'

'Yeah. Bye.'

I watch him leave, curious about the life he's returning to, then take a long sniff of a lily before scooping up my bag and trudging back to the office in the searing heat, heavy traffic and construction drills reverberating in my ears. It's busy at my regular, and my table is taken, so I opt for takeaway and make small talk with Evan while I wait.

Twenty minutes later, I sit down at my desk and unwrap my toastie when my brother's name flashes on my phone. He usually sticks to messages, and it ignites that ball of fear that lives in my gut.

I snatch up my phone. 'Josh? What's up?'

He sighs dramatically. 'Why didn't you come for dinner on Wednesday night?'

'What?'

'At Mum and Dad's. Mum said she spoke to you about it.'

Now it's my turn to sigh. 'Jesus. I thought something serious was wrong. She didn't speak to me; she sent a text and I said *maybe* I would go. Then I forgot. You know what I'm like at the moment, why didn't you call?'

He tuts – just like Mum. 'Bloody hell, Amy. Could you make a bit more of an effort? She made a huge roast pork. You didn't come on Sunday either, she was really upset. So was Dad.'

Typical of Josh to do their dirty work. The golden boy. 'It was a bloody roast, Josh. It's not the end of the world.'

'They're worried about you; you know that. You need to visit them more. Or invite them to your place. Just something.'

Guilt takes hold and I soften. 'Sorry. I'll try harder.'

'Can you come this Sunday? It's Sophie's birthday. They want to do something.'

He's right that I need to make more of an effort, and I like my sister-in-law, so I scribble, 'Soph – Sunday' on a Post-it and stick it to the bottom of my monitor. 'Yeah, Sunday's good.'

'The boys will be there, too. It's a surprise so don't tell Soph.'

'Ollie and Finn are here?'

'Not yet. I'm picking them up from the airport later.' He must detect the hurt in my voice because his tone warms. 'Don't worry; they've already planned to spend time with you.'

A shred of joy breaks through my deadened spirit. I've always been close with my nephews, but after Mel died, they lived with me for a few months tasked with watching over me and keeping me company. It strengthened our bond and made me appreciate them as young adults, rather than my little nephews. They moved to Sydney a few weeks ago for university, and I miss them.

'Can't wait to see them. Anyway, I've got loads of work to do,' I say.

'Make sure you're there on Sunday.'

'I will be. See you later.' I hang up, unlock my computer and find an email from Paul. At the same time, Daniel walks into my office and places two donuts on my desk.

'As promised.'

I groan and take a massive bite of one. 'You're the best.'

'And Paul's been looking for you. He's gone to a meeting but said he'll be back at four.'

I roll my eyes. 'He's emailed me.' I turn back to read the message and hear Daniel shut the door as he leaves.

Amy, send me the monthly compliance report when you're back at your desk. Paul.

Damn. I knew there was something I needed to do today. The second month in a row I've missed the report deadline.

I shovel in more donut, followed by my sandwich while I get to work. After ignoring an email and phone call from Paul, plus messages from my team about signing a leaving card and next week's lotto syndicate, I finish two hours later.

Sorry, Paul, here you go.

As soon as I hit send, my temples throb and the sharp pain that lodged itself in my chest during the session disperses and races around my body. I slump onto the desk. Only a few hours to go before I can spend the night with my best mates and the weekend with my family. The oxygen I need to keep breathing.

Chapter Three

'You made it,' Caroline says as she opens her front door. It's a warm, sticky evening and she's changed from her work clothes into shorts and a T-shirt.

'I didn't think I had a choice.' I hold up a small overnight bag. 'And I brought this.'

A smile spreads across her face. 'Sleepover. Good.' She takes my bag and drops it down in the hallway. 'And no, you didn't have a choice.'

The minute I'm inside, the tranquil ambience that's a permanent fixture of her home penetrates my skin, and my muscles loosen. This house is modern with neutral shades on the walls and dark, timber floors. Large, colourful rugs and oil paintings are scattered throughout breaking up the natural tones, and the furniture is stylish and practical. Caroline bought it when she moved back to Brisbane a year after we graduated, when prices in Clayfield were still affordable. Maddie designed extensions and together they spent years renovating it. After they split, Caroline stayed, and Maddie bought a new place a few streets away.

'Sorry about the quick texts this arvo,' she says, leading me through the lounge to the kitchen. Music and a sweet, buttery aroma float through the house. 'I wanted to call but I was in meetings. How was it this morning?'

I grunt. 'Horrible. So hard.'

'Oh, Ames. Come here.' Her arms wrap around me, and I breathe her in to absorb the oxygen fix I've been craving all afternoon. I also catch her familiar scent of vanilla shampoo and coconut soap, and it soothes me. 'We'll cheer you up.'

In the kitchen, the ceiling fans are on high and the large bifold doors that access the back deck are open, although it does little to offer relief on such a humid night. The bulk of their renovation budget was spent in here, so it looks like it's straight from *Home Beautiful*. Natural stone splashbacks, top quality appliances and fittings, marble benches.

'Ames, hi,' Maddie says, wiping her hands on an apron before opening her arms for me.

I squeeze her tight. 'Hey, Mads.'

'You're hurting me.'

I loosen my grip. 'Sorry.'

She laughs and lightly cups my cheek. 'You okay?'

'Yep.' The cooking scent is stronger now and I moan. 'That smells incredible.'

'It's just ghee and onions. I haven't put any other ingredients in yet.'

'You know it doesn't take much to impress me.' The only reason I eat as well as I do is because Maddie and Caroline cook for me. I'd live off Promite on toast and sugar otherwise – washed down with coffee and wine.

I sit on the leather stool on the opposite side of the bench to where Maddie is preparing dinner. The industrial style pendant lights that hang above cast a soft glow on her cropped black hair as she crushes spices using a pestle and mortar.

'Caz said you didn't want to go to your session today.'

I screw up my nose and take the wine Caroline hands me. 'Nope. It's hard having to relive it all again for people I don't know. It's like all the crap inside comes to the surface and sits here with nowhere to go.' I rub my hand over my chest. 'And the others. God. Their stories.'

Caroline places some cheese, crackers and olives on the bench and sits on the stool beside me, concern on her face.

'That sounds rough,' Maddie says, reaching over to pat my hand.

'It was. And group therapy is supposed to help?'

Caroline gives my back a quick rub. 'It will. It's just going to take some time. If you stick with it, keep up your other appointments, I reckon it'll make a huge difference.'

Maddie slices into a zucchini and tilts her head towards Caroline. 'She's right.'

They both threw themselves into therapy after Mel died in a way I couldn't manage. Maddie was at the bottom of that dark well with me for a while, but she's bounced back over the past six months, and I love her even more for it. But that's Maddie – positivity is in her blood. I don't mean Kylie-like positivity that's all chirpy and in your face, more of a cool, understated confidence. Her entire family are the same and they rearranged their lives to get Maddie back to a place I can't ever imagine being. She looks great at the moment, too. Her brown skin shimmers, and a contentment has returned to her dark eyes that I haven't seen for a long time.

The downside for her is that she has to help Caroline keep me afloat, and I think I'm getting heavy. But losing them will be the end of me, so although I struggle with the idea of getting through the six-week program plus additional psychology sessions, I'll continue to push through the pain. If not for me, then for them.

I force myself to smile. 'I know she is.'

'You can start running with me, that will sort you out,' Maddie says.

I curl my top lip. 'Why would I do that?'

'Because it's good for you. Release some endorphins. Get you off the couch. And away from that bloody thing.' Maddie points the knife at my phone, which sits on the bench in front of me.

'Sounds like a lot of effort.' I bite into a chunk of cheese and wash it down with a gulp of white wine.

'That's a great idea,' Caroline says. 'You used to be super fit. When's the last time you did something physical?'

I give them a sly smile. 'I get physical when Zoe comes over.' I wink at Maddie. 'She keeps me fit.'

Maddie laughs. 'I bet she does.'

Caroline shakes her head and grins. 'Not what I meant.'

'And are you going to run with us?' I ask Caroline.

'Nope. Not my thing. I'll stick with swimming. You can do that instead if you like. That's your choice. Swim with me or run with Mads. Up to you.' She pops some olives into her mouth and peers at me, waiting for my reply.

If I don't agree, they'll hound me until I do. I sigh. 'Fine. I can't take my phone into the pool, so looks like I'm running.'

Maddie beams. 'Excellent. We'll start next week.' Her phone buzzes. She drops the knife and heads for the back deck to take the call.

'How was your afternoon?' I ask Caroline. 'Still busy with that dispute?'

She groans. 'I spent all day on that. Bloody Rachel. Emailed twice quoting me sections of *our* enterprise agreement – the very sections I wrote myself. Like I don't eat that fucking thing for breakfast every day.'

I bristle on Caroline's behalf. 'What's her issue?'

Caroline shrugs. 'Dunno. Did you manage to get much done after the session?'

'A bit. Paul was a prick. As usual.'

She grins. 'It's his superpower. What did he do this time?'

'Hassled me about the compliance report.'

'You mean the report you were supposed to do on Tuesday?' She raises her eyebrows. 'That one?'

'Yes. That one.'

She laughs. 'Then do your reports on time.'

I poke her shoulder. 'You're supposed to be on my side. Seriously though, there's something about him lately. I can't work it out. His tone, his emails. Really short with me.'

'You sure?'

I nod. 'I know I've had loads of time off but his attitude towards me has changed. I mean, he's always been an arsehole but now it feels personal.'

Maddie returns, cutting our conversation short.

'Who was that?' Caroline asks.

'Just a friend.' Maddie scratches her forehead, but it's a weak attempt to hide the wide-eyed look she gives Caroline.

'I saw that, Mads. What's going on?' I ask.

She winces. 'Sorry.'

'Oh god, what?' Caroline says.

'Zoe's on her way over.'

I choke on my wine. 'What?' I face Caroline. 'I asked if she was going to be here, and you said no.'

'I said I doubt it.' She glares at Maddie. 'Why is she coming? I didn't invite her.'

Maddie holds up her hands, a large knife in one of them. 'This morning she asked what I was doing tonight, so I told her to come over. Then I was with a client all arvo and forgot about it.' She slices into a red capsicum. 'I didn't think she'd actually come. She usually does her own thing on Friday nights.' Her eyes flick to me. 'If she's not doing Amy, that is.' She chuckles and throws vegetables into the pot.

'You're very funny,' I deadpan.

'Of course she's going to come over. She'll assume Amy's here,' Caroline says.

Maddie shrugs. 'Sorry. I didn't think.'

I drop my head into my hands and groan. 'You know I'm on the no-Zoe diet. Do you know how hard it is to stick to?'

When I first started seeing Zoe, I was a fragment of my former self – a single jigsaw piece lost in a dark corner never to be matched up with its original puzzle again. I wasn't capable of a relationship, but she was interested, and I took advantage of that. After six weeks, she started pushing for something more serious, so I ended it. But after having human touch again, I craved more and started calling her for sex. The calls are becoming less frequent, but I need them to be non-existent. My current record is strong, though – sixteen days. Not that I'm counting.

'Sorry, Ames, I had no idea,' Caroline says.

'Anyway, what's the go with you two?' Maddie says, reaching for a cracker and some cheese. 'You sleep with her often enough. And she's fucking hot. You could do a lot worse.' She pops it in her mouth and watches me, a mischievous glint in her eye. She's fishing and it makes me laugh.

'There's no go with us. She's as needy as me. I can't be in a relationship with someone like that. We'd combust. And yes, I know she's hot, that's why it's so hard sticking to the diet.'

Caroline gives me the cocked brow treatment.

'What? Sometimes I just want sex and I want someone to be there.' I turn to Maddie. 'Sometimes I need a little sugar in that diet.'

Maddie shakes her head and grins.

I face Caroline. 'Is that so wrong?'

'Not if the other person wants that, too, but you know she wants more. You're leading her on.'

'I've told her the deal, and she keeps coming back.'

'You keep making her come back,' Caroline says. 'Stop using her for sex if you have no intentions of anything else. You're messing her up. And you're messing yourself up.'

I take the opportunity to wind her up. 'But it's soo goood.'

She presses her lips together, but her dimples give away the smile.

27

Maddie laughs. 'I get it, Ames, but she is getting a bit screwed up by it. Either give her what she wants or turn off the tap.'

I wash down the guilt with a large swig of wine. I didn't realise Zoe was getting so messed up over this. Or maybe I did and had ignored that detail. I care about her; I just can't deal with the intensity. She indulges me and wants too much. It sucks me dry. 'I have turned it off. I haven't seen her for two weeks.'

'That's only because you don't trust yourself, not because you've ended it,' Caroline says, walking out to the deck to sort out the table for dinner.

'That's not true,' I say. It is true, but not verbalising it somehow makes it more believable.

The doorbell sounds and my stomach lurches.

Maddie points at me. 'Behave. And be nice.'

'I'm the nicest friend you have,' I call after her.

'Don't be too nice.' Caroline walks up behind me. 'That's the problem.'

I hold out my glass. 'I'll need more wine for this.'

'You sure? You know what happens when you drink too much and Zoe is around.'

'Maddie has given me strict orders to behave.'

'Promise,' Caroline says.

'What?'

'You've got to promise.'

A few months after we met, Caroline pinned me down on the old, beaten-up couch in my flat and tried to make me swear I wouldn't sleep with the girl in our international relations lecture that she was desperately in love with. When I refused, she tickled me until I couldn't breathe and wouldn't stop until I agreed. Turned out that girl only liked boys, so it was never an issue, but to this day Caroline makes me keep promises.

I laugh. 'How old are you?'

She chuckles and tops up our wine as Maddie and Zoe appear in the doorway talking about a work issue. Zoe's caught up in the conversation and hasn't noticed me across the kitchen. She's dressed in a tight vest top that clings to her incredible breasts and a short denim skirt that hugs her shapely hips and thighs. Her dark, wavy hair is loose and brushes her shoulders. I'm amazed she didn't get arrested on the way over for being too damn sexy. A soft sigh sounds in my ears, and it takes me a second to realise it came from me. I run my eyes up her smooth, brown legs remembering the last time they were wrapped around me and—

My phone buzzes. I cast my eyes down to find a message from Caroline.

you're drooling

I bite my bottom lip to stop myself from laughing and casually lift my hand to my mouth to check because Caroline's possibly right. My skin is hot, blood is surging through my body in all the right places, and the room is even warmer than it was before. I look upward to check the fans are still on and pull my hair back into a pony, securing it with the hairband around my wrist.

Zoe stops mid-sentence and whips her head towards us. 'Amy! I had no idea you were going to be here.' She strides across the kitchen.

'Hi, Zo.' I stand to hug her and catch the fresh citrusy scent of her Jo Malone perfume. It reminds me of the last time she was in my bathroom getting ready for work. Naked. Sixteen days ago.

'I haven't heard from you,' she says, her soft hands lingering on my wrists. 'You didn't return my calls the other day.'

She left a couple of messages earlier in the week asking if I wanted to meet up. I did, but the same thing always happens when we're together – she wants to know how I feel, so I talk about Mel and my shattered heart; she lets me cry and wallow, and I initiate sex so I can feel better. Afterwards, she wants to talk about 'us', which turns me cold because I can't give her what she wants.

I loosen myself from her grip. 'Sorry, Zo. I've had a lot on with work and… other stuff.'

Her dark eyebrows pull together, and her eyes search mine, like she's trying to see into my soul. I wouldn't bother if I were her; it's dark in there. She takes the glass of wine Maddie hands her. 'Are you okay?'

'Yeah. Thanks.' I spot Maddie from the corner of my eye shaking her head at Zoe, presumably to indicate she doesn't think I'm okay. 'I'm fine, Maddie.' I turn back to Zoe. 'I've started a new therapy program and it's brought up some stuff, that's all. It's been a tough week.'

She nods. 'Of course.'

As she gazes at me, I think how easy it would be to jump into a relationship. To have someone there all the time again. We could grow to love each other, have more to us than sex. But then Dr Sachdev is in my head, *could you be using Zoe as another coping mechanism?*

Caroline jumps off the stool. 'Let's go outside for dinner and try out some of this wine I had delivered today.'

I almost sigh with relief I'm so grateful for the distraction. 'Great idea!'

On the deck, citronella candles burn to keep the mosquitos away, and the underwater pool lights create a warm glow that hovers over the surface of the water. Caroline has turned the music up slightly, but the crickets' high-pitched voices still take precedence. For the next two hours we chat, laugh, drink more wine, and eat Maddie's amazing vegetarian Madras with dahl and homemade roti that makes us slump in our chairs and rub our bellies. My spirit is a mix of love and gratitude for what I have and longing and sorrow for what I don't. Mel sitting beside me enjoying moments like these filters into my mind, but I try to focus on the beautiful people in front of me and what I still have.

By the end of the night, I've had enough wine that I farewell Zoe with a brief kiss. The scorching look she gives me as I pull away makes my groin twinge. A night with her would take the edge off – a sweet end to a sour day – but I force a goodnight and walk away before I can take things any further.

After cleaning my teeth and changing for bed, I find Caroline and Maddie in the lounge. 'Thanks for tonight,' I say, before noticing how close they are on the couch. 'Oh, sorry. I'm interrupting.'

'No. You're good,' Caroline says.

'It's fine. You're not.' Maddie jumps up and gives me a hug. 'I was about to leave anyway. See you both soon,' she says and lets herself out.

I drop beside Caroline and hold my stomach. 'I've had too much good stuff.'

She yawns and stretches. 'Me too.'

I pull my legs up onto the couch and face her. 'I was in the way, wasn't I? Do you and Maddie want to get back together?'

She shakes her head. 'We were just talking. We're better friends. You know that.'

I do know that, but I'm desperate for something from my old life. 'Can't you work it out?'

She gives me a sad smile. 'There's nothing to work out. It's just the way it is.'

I nod and wrap my arms around my knees. 'Zoe. That was bloody hard.'

'I bet. You did well. Kept your promise. Might take you out for breaky tomorrow for that.'

'Breaky? I gave up hot sex for a free breaky? Where's my phone. I'm calling her now.'

She laughs and whacks me with a cushion. 'Shut up.'

'It would be easy, right?'

Her brow creases. 'What? Something with Zoe? You don't mean that.'

I shrug. 'Maddie's right. I could do a lot worse. And she's smoking hot.'

Caroline grins. 'She is.' Her smile fades. 'Is that what you want? Someone to be there for the sake of being there? Don't you want to be in love? Feel some passion?'

The cut in my soul wedges open and fresh pain seeps out. 'I'll never find that again, Caz. What I had was a once in a lifetime love. Maybe I need to lower my expectations.'

She considers me a moment. 'You don't know that. And anyway, I wouldn't let you fall into a relationship like that. It wouldn't be good for you, and it wouldn't be fair on Zoe. She's a good person.'

I sigh. 'You're right.'

'You'll see things more clearly tomorrow.' She hops up and heads into the kitchen, returning a minute later with a large glass of water. 'Here you go.' She hands it to me. 'I'm going to bed.'

Once I hear her bedroom door close, I grab my phone and scroll through the contacts until I reach Zoe's number. My finger hovers over the message icon but Caroline's words are loud in my ears. *Is that what you want? Someone to be there for the sake of being there? It wouldn't be fair on Zoe.*

I huff, throw my phone to the other side of the couch and head to the spare room.

Chapter Four

Eleven years ago, my world changed overnight when I met Mel. The woman with the dark-blue eyes and brazen smile that I saw in a bar. I was twenty-five; she was a year younger.

Caroline and I were at a human resources conference at the Savoy Hotel. Caroline had moved back to Brisbane but was in Melbourne for the week. Because I was on the conference organising committee and lived on the other side of the city, I was staying at the hotel for a couple of nights, too.

It was early evening in mid-winter, and the sun had already set over Port Phillip Bay. The bar was crowded, and the murmur of voices, clinking of glassware and a sense of relaxation filled the air. We grabbed a small table by the window and settled in for the evening with our wine and variety of bar snacks – olives, cashews, salted chips. Caroline was gushing about her new girlfriend Tessa, while I was slating an ex who'd tried it on when I'd run into her at a club the weekend before.

We were on our second glass of wine when Caroline said, 'That woman at the bar – the one in the black top and grey pants – keeps checking you out.'

I leant forward. 'The one with the light brown hair?'

Caroline nodded and sipped her wine, casually glimpsing the bar.

'She's hot. I saw her at some of the sessions today, but couldn't get close enough to read her name badge. You think she's with that woman?' The woman beside her was attractive with cropped black hair, brown skin and round, dark eyes. They were similar height and had the same small build.

Caroline narrowed her eyes as she assessed them. 'They're both hot. Nuh, they're not together. Not the way grey pants keeps looking at you. And they're not acting like a couple would.'

'I need the bathroom. Do I look okay for a walk by?' I asked.

Caroline gave me a quick once over. 'Yep, gorgeous.'

'Anything on my teeth? Lipstick? Food?'

She squinted as she took a closer look. 'Nuh.'

'How's my hair?' I said, feathering my fingers through it.

'It looks good.'

'Maybe I should put more lipstick on?'

'Don't. It'll go all over her face when you pash.'

'Bit presumptuous, Caz, I haven't even met her yet.'

'Oh, it's on. I can tell.'

I gave a little squeal. 'Back soon. I'll grab more drinks while I'm up.'

I wove my way through the crowd and sensed this woman's gaze follow me. I tried to play it cool, but some imaginary force tethered me to her, causing me to stare. As I passed, our eyes locked until I came to an abrupt halt when I stumbled over a bar stool. A fire raced up my neck and spread across my face. I spun around to find her walking towards me, a tiny smile on her lips.

'You okay?' she asked.

'Yeah. Thanks.' My skin still burned, but I was lost in the most alluring eyes I'd ever seen. They reminded me of a twilight sky, the deep blue before fading to black.

'Can I buy you a drink...' Her eyes flicked to my chest and back up. 'Amy?'

My head inflated a little knowing she must've asked about me. 'You know my name?'

'You've still got your name badge on.' She glanced down again. 'Amy Campbell from the department of public affairs.'

Thankfully, I was still flushed from the stumble. 'Oh. Right.' I stripped off the lanyard and shoved it in my pocket. 'Probably should take that off now.'

She smiled. 'I'm Melissa – Mel. So, how about that drink?'

A different kind of heat flooded my body. 'That would be nice.'

She gestured to Caroline. 'What about your friend over there, does she want to join us?'

Caroline was tapping at her phone, a stupid dreamy expression on her face. 'Yeah. I'll tell her to come over.'

'What can I get you both?'

'I'll have a sav blanc; Caz will have a pinot.' I pointed to the bathroom. 'I need... I'll be back in a few minutes.'

One side of her mouth curved upward. 'Don't be long.'

My mouth turned dry. 'I won't.'

As soon as I reached the bathroom, I texted Caroline.

She's buying us a drink come to bar

She replied within seconds.

I knew it!

I checked my teeth, applied a touch of lipstick, fluffed my hair upside down to create volume and then smoothed it down like I hadn't touched it.

Five minutes later, Mel handed me a glass of wine and passed the pinot to Caroline. 'You must be...' She glanced at me. 'Caz, did you say?' She turned back to Caroline and flashed a smile. That's all it took for Caroline to like her.

After our round of introductions – her friend's name was Madeline, Maddie – I sat on the stool facing Mel.

'So, Amy Campbell, what brings you to this conference?'

We talked about our jobs, our families, our shared love of old movies and theatre. She was an employment lawyer and Maddie an architect. They shared a flat in Brighton East and had been friends since they were ten years old. Mel told me she'd noticed me through the day and watched me come into the bar. I confessed to noticing her, too. Other than occasionally glancing at her full, pink lips and imagining what they'd be like to kiss, my eyes stayed fixed on hers. When she tore herself away from me to go to the bathroom, I peered at Caroline, but she seemed happy in conversation with Maddie.

An hour later, Caroline cut in. 'I'm going up to my room. I need food.'

I looked at my watch, not realising how quickly the time had passed. 'Do you want me to come with—'

'No, you stay. I'm going to get some room service and watch telly.' She faced Mel. 'Nice to meet you, Mel. Thanks for the drinks.' She glanced between us with a sly smile. 'Enjoy your night.'

'We will,' Mel said, gazing at me, eyes smouldering.

A blistering urge exploded in my stomach and raced through my body. I was still staring at Mel when Maddie interrupted a few seconds later.

'I'm off. See you later, Mel. Good meeting you, Amy. Caz, too. I rarely meet people who love food and cooking as much as me.'

'Oh, that's her thing,' I said, relieved Caroline's night wasn't ruined.

Maddie smiled, her dark brown eyes warm and friendly. 'Mine, too.' She held her hand up and wiggled her fingers. 'Bye. Have fun,' she said and left.

Mel leant in so that her face was only inches from mine. Her eyes burned bright against jet-black lashes, and her caramel-coloured hair swept softly across her forehead brushing her dark eyebrows. She placed her hand on my knee, and I could feel the heat through my pants where it landed, like she was branding me. In that moment, I had never physically wanted anyone as much as I wanted her.

'Do you want another drink?' she asked.

I shook my head.

Desire flashed in her eyes and a satisfied smile pulled at the corners of her lips.

'Let's go,' I said.

In the lift, Mel stood so close that I could feel her body heat. She pushed my hair to the side and brushed her lips against my neck, her tongue grazing my skin.

'Oh, god.' I grabbed the handrail as every nerve in my body vibrated.

'You like that?' she whispered, her breath hot on my ear, her fingers slipping under my shirt and skimming my lower back.

I tried to answer but all that came out was a whimper.

Inside my room, a soft bluish hue from the moon shone through the open curtains. I was about to switch on a lamp and ask Mel if she wanted a drink when she gently pushed me up against the wall, her musky perfume lingering between us.

She tilted her face closer, her warm breath soft on my lips. 'Gorgeous,' she said before our mouths met.

Satisfied moans escaped from both of us, and my limbs weakened when her tongue pressed against my own. She tasted like sweet, red wine and desire. We hurriedly stripped off shirts and bras, a shiver running over me as her soft palms skimmed my breasts. I reached down to undo her pants, and we stumbled across the room exchanging urgent kisses and removing the rest of our clothing.

I fell back against the bed, but instead of joining me, she stood and slowly took me in. The moonlight was soft on her face and her eyes travelled up my body as my own gaze roamed her small frame.

Mel gave a breathy sigh and knelt on the bed, peering up at me with heated eyes as she bent down and brushed her lips against my hipbone, making me gasp. She pressed her mouth to my stomach, then between my breasts flicking her tongue out to taste my skin. When she lay on top of me, we both sighed at the sensation of skin on skin and her mouth met mine in a slow, deep kiss that made my body throb. Our breaths became more ragged as she tangled her hands in my hair and pushed her pelvis against me.

I wrapped my arms around her waist and flipped her onto her back.

'Okay, you want to be in control,' she said, with a laugh.

I smiled and dragged my lips down her chest, gazing up at her. Her eyes flashed with want, and she took a sharp intake of breath as my teeth grazed her nipple. My hand slid down the velvet skin of her stomach to the warmth and softness between her legs. She moaned, low and husky. As her pelvis rocked against my hand, my mouth moved over her breasts, her neck, her face, and my chest burst with new emotions. The taste of her skin on my tongue, and the heat of her body under my fingertips left me dizzy.

She guided my mouth back to hers, her teeth catching my bottom lip as her breath quickened. Her hand clutched my face, her groans vibrated against my lips and she shuddered underneath me.

As her body slowly stilled, she sighed and smiled up at me. 'And to think I wasn't going to bother coming to this conference.'

I grinned and kissed her, desperate to taste her lips again. 'I'm glad you did,' I murmured.

She rolled onto her side and traced her hand along the curve of my body, dipping her head to slide her tongue over nipple. My body sparked and I shifted onto my back, an ache between my thighs. Her hand trailed my stomach and slid between my legs making me moan with pleasure. My hips rose against her as she kissed me deeply and her hand worked in time with my body.

It wasn't long before heat surged through my veins, and the pressure in my pelvis intensified. She rested her mouth on mine and whispered, 'You're so beautiful,' just as my back arched and my legs tensed. With my pulse thumping and a tingling sensation sweeping my skin, I released a loud groan before my body finally wilted.

My eyes were closed savouring the luscious satisfaction when Mel lightly kissed me and brought me back to the room. 'Intense,' I said.

I could hear the smile in her voice. 'It sounded like it.'

In that moment with her sweet breath on my lips, a pounding in my heart and a flutter in my stomach, I felt our souls fuse. I kissed her, and she returned my kiss with a longing that told me she felt that, too.

*

The following morning, the biting wind that blew off the sea ripped through my skin like shards of ice, and I tucked my hands deep into my jacket pockets. Wellington Street buzzed with commuters – trams hummed up and down, cars and bikes whizzed by, and pedestrians scurried past, scarves wrapped tightly around their necks.

Mel pointed towards Victoria Street. 'There's a good café around the corner.' She linked her arm in mine and huddled close. 'And it's too cold to walk any further.'

The minute I stepped inside, the warmth and intoxicating smell of fresh coffee soaked into my bones. We chose a table at the back, away from the icy wind that drifted inside every time the door opened.

After we placed our order, Mel said, 'I'm starving now.'

I held out my hands and splayed my fingers. 'Still shaking.' Earlier, when I was dressing, Mel had emerged from the shower and tried to delay me with activities that would've been far more satisfying than food, but I had showed her my quivering hands and said I needed to eat before I passed out.

She leant across the table and wrapped her hands around mine. 'They're fast here. It won't be long.' The tenderness of that gesture and in her voice made my heart soar. She kept her hands on mine and said, 'I'm very glad you were at the conference yesterday. And in the bar last night.'

'Me, too. Very glad.'

She averted her eyes and gave a shy smile. It was the first glimpse of vulnerability I'd seen from her, and I liked it.

Our meals arrived, and I tucked into my cheesy omelette as Mel took a big bite of poached egg and avocado, and we both gave a little groan of satisfaction as the food hit our stomachs. As we fell into easy conversation, the space between us sparked with lust, like, curiosity, and hope. I thought I'd been in love before, but I'd never experienced such an aching thump in my chest after meeting someone for the first time. It was like something tangible had formed between us and had knotted us together.

Mel pushed her plate to side. 'I can't eat any more.'

'Me neither.' I peered at my watch, disappointed the time had passed so quickly. 'And I have to be at the conference by nine.'

Mel nodded. 'And I should get to work.' She rested her forearms on the table. 'So.'

I narrowed my eyes. 'So.'

'It would be nice to see you again...' She paused. 'Amy Campbell from the department of public affairs.'

Relief flooded me, but it didn't stop the fireworks going off in my stomach. 'I'd like that.'

'How about Friday night?'

That meant waiting only one night before seeing her again. 'Perfect.'

She flashed that cocky smile, but it didn't detract from the delight and sensitivity in her eyes.

Outside, Mel pointed to the tram stop. 'I'll jump on a tram here. Goes right to my place.'

I walked with her to the stop, where we exchanged numbers and organised a meeting place in the city. She leant in to kiss my cheek, but I turned to taste her lips once more. They were like a hot fire on a wintery night. I rested my forehead against hers and reached for her hand. I wasn't one for public affection, but she was so divine I didn't care.

She cupped my cheek, the wool of her gloves soft and warm against my skin. 'See you Friday,' she said, as the hum of the tram grew louder.

I tore myself away, our fingers only parting when we couldn't physically hold on any longer. I looked back to find her still watching me. Then she threw me one last grin before disappearing onto the tram.

Chapter Five

When I was eleven, my science teacher spent an entire lesson talking about Venus flytraps. Mrs Miller explained that the leaves snap shut for five to ten days once a fly is trapped, because that's how long it takes the food to be digested. But when something inedible lands, like a twig or a raindrop, the plant knows it needs more to survive, and the leaves open in less than twenty-four hours. With childlike wonder, I imagined flytraps were sentient, and the nectar that oozed from their open leaves were tears because they were lonely and in need of love and nourishment.

That's how I think about the deep cut in my soul. It opens and closes depending on what I trap. When I catch something that feeds and sustains me, the cut closes while my spirit absorbs and digests the goodness. But when I trap a twig or a raindrop, it opens and leaves me exposed and starved until something more substantial lands.

This has been my life over the past two weeks. The cut closed while I had a nice weekend with my family. Opened again when I was alone. Closed when I spent time with Caroline and Maddie. Opened when I saw Dr Sachdev and in group therapy last Friday. While it was closed, I lugged around the dull pain and participated in life as best I could. I functioned at work most days, visited Mum and Dad a few times, slept, didn't drink every night. I even managed two runs with Maddie, where she pushed me until my muscles screamed for respite.

But some days it remained wedged open. Particularly after the appointment with Dr Sachdev on Wednesday afternoon, where we talked about Mel's addiction and the profound regret that consumes me over letting her take painkillers. Dr Sachdev reminded me that I couldn't control her addiction, and although the rational part of me knows that, the grieving part can't let it go. That evening the debilitating darkness of grief crept up on me, sleek and black, like a panther hunting its prey. I spent the night in bed with Mel's ashes clutched to my chest while I scrolled through old photos and clips, the searing pain carving up my insides.

And I drank.

Yesterday, nausea and a puffy face prevented me from going to work. I lay on the couch drifting in and out of sleep, the unmistakable stench of stale wine and shame seeping from my pores. By the evening, the cut had been open too long, and I needed nourishment. I called Zoe and today I can function again.

I wanted her to leave before Maddie arrived this morning, but in typical Zoe fashion, she took her time getting ready.

She wandered into the lounge and ran her eyes over me as a knock sounded at the door. 'Going somewhere?' she asked.

'It's Maddie. She's making me run.'

She bent down to strap her sandals. 'Wow. Maddie can make you do something? I'll have to ask what her secret is.'

I rolled my eyes and answered the door.

'Morning,' Maddie said, stepping inside. 'Hello, Zoe. Saw your car in the driveway. Don't want to come running with us?'

'Sorry. Dressed for work now.' She swung her handbag over her shoulder. 'And I had a vigorous enough workout this morning, thanks.' She smiled.

Maddie turned to me with a bemused expression.

'Goodbye, Zoe,' I said, with a peck to the corner of her mouth.

'So, we'll do something on the weekend?' she asked.

'Um.' I rubbed the back of my neck. 'Maybe. I'll call you.'

She shot me that familiar displeased look and huffed. 'Fine. Bye.'

I peered through the shutters as she jumped into her car. 'She's not happy with me.'

'I'm not surprised,' Maddie said. 'And now you're going to have to run extra hard since you've broken your no-Zoe diet.'

So, at 7:00 a.m., with the scorching February sun burning my skin, and the noisy miners screeching in my ears as they darted between the paperbarks, I ran around Kalinga Park. Maddie added to my sensory overload by yelling, 'step it up!', 'move that arse!', 'too much sugar in your diet!'. After thirty minutes of torment, I was sprawled on the grass, drenched in sweat, heart rate off the chart. Lactic acid pooled in my muscles preparing for tomorrow's agony.

Maddie dropped down beside me, barely a drop of sweat on her, and slapped my thigh. 'Good job. Don't break your diet again and I won't push you so hard.'

If I was able to speak, I would've told her what she could do with that comment. She allowed me a five-minute recovery before she jumped up and held out her hand for me. We walked back to my place where she made poached eggs and downloaded some meditation apps on my phone. When she told me to listen to them on the way to work, I scoffed.

'I'll call you later to check. If you can't tell me anything about those apps, next time we run, you'll think today was easy.' This time I was able to speak and told her what she could do with that comment. She laughed, gave me a quick hug on her way out and said, 'Speak to you later.'

Now I'm sitting in my office, and despite engaging in some healthier living this morning, my gut agitates about group therapy. The string of demands Paul emailed me yesterday while I was off doesn't help.

I glance at the clock above my desk. I have strict orders to be in Caroline's office at 9:45 so that she can check in with me before my session. I scoop up my bag and head downstairs.

When I walk in, she's swearing at the computer.

'Morning, Caz.' I roll one of the meeting chairs over to her desk. Her office is more appealing than mine – bigger space, nicer artwork and a great view of Edward Street. I'm on the other side of the building with a view of city roof tops.

She spins round. 'Oh, hi. Didn't hear you come in.'

I'm about to ask her what's going on, but she jumps in first. 'How are you?'

'Okay, I think.' I don't mean to sound so uncertain and morose.

Her eyes pool with concern. 'Anxious about your session?'

I shrug. 'A bit. It's been a good morning, though. Ran with Maddie. Ate breaky.'

She smiles. 'Maddie told me. I'm impressed.' She pauses for a beat and then tilts her head. 'Do any other workouts this morning?'

I stare at her open-mouthed and then shake my head. 'Maddie has a big mouth. She told you about Zoe.'

'You know we have no secrets.'

I wait for the people walking by in the corridor to pass before I speak. 'Yeah… Zoe.' I scratch my head sheepishly. 'I tried not to call her, but the past two days have been awful. I was in such a bad place yesterday. And so lonely. I needed… someone to be there.'

She gives an understanding nod. 'You can call me or Maddie when you feel like that.'

'You both do so much already. I weigh you down and—'

She grips my shoulders and looks at me intently. 'Don't ever think that. We're here for you. Always.'

Emotion edges up my throat and my eyes water. 'I know you are.' I try and lighten the mood to stop myself from crying. 'But you and

Maddie won't have sex with me.'

She laughs and releases her grip. 'When you put it like that.' After a couple of seconds, she adds with a sly smile, 'Tried that, we weren't good enough for each other.'

I give her a light shove. 'Shut up.'

When we first met at university, we were confused about our feelings. After a few weeks of seeing each other, we both thought we made better friends and called it off. We also agreed that there were too many people at uni to be tied to one. A few years later, we fell into that territory again – for a night. It didn't turn out how I wanted it to at the time, and once I got over the rejection, we never really spoke about it again, apart from the odd joke between us now and then.

'Anyway. I don't want to focus on Zoe. Or think about therapy until I get there. Apparently, it helps to keep busy beforehand, so the crap doesn't build up. I'm trying to stay distracted. The only reason I agreed to a 7:00 a.m. run.'

'Yeah? Who gave you that nugget of wisdom?'

I roll my eyes and adopt a mocking tone. 'Kylie.'

She grins. 'The twelve-year-old therapist? She knows something?'

'Well,' I sniff. 'She had a birthday last week so she's thirteen now. She knows a bit more.'

Caroline laughs, then softens. 'Proud of you.'

I give her a playful kick. 'Aw, thanks, Caz.' But the comment makes something warm and lovely flow through me while simultaneously causing the pain in my heart to flare. My eyes sting again, and I take a deep breath. 'Enough of that. Distract me. Why were you swearing at your computer?'

She throws her head back and groans at the ceiling. 'Rachel. She keeps fucking emailing me with all this shit I already know.'

My protective armour clicks into place. 'Serious? Who is this woman? And why haven't I dealt with her before? Have you checked her out on socials?'

'She's only been with the union for a couple of months. No, course I haven't checked her socials. You know I can't be bothered with that.'

I hold out my hand. 'Give me your phone. What's her last name?'

She sighs, unlocks her phone, and passes it to me. 'Burley.'

I type 'Rachel Burley' into Instagram's search function and scroll through the images until Caroline recognises one.

'Oh, that's her, I think,' she says.

I open the profile of a woman with long, brown hair. Smiling. Attractive. Very attractive. I read her bio. 'Okay, yep, I see what's going on here.'

'What?'

'Lesbian.'

'Get lost. You don't know that by looking at her photo.'

'I do. It's my special skill. And the rainbow flag emoji, "lesbian" in her bio, and photo of her kissing a woman are also a giveaway.'

'No way!' Caroline snatches the phone. 'Shit. Didn't pick that up.'

'Your lesdar faulty? Now I know why she's hassling you.'

'I'm sure that's not the reason.' Caroline squints at the profile picture as though that will help her see it more clearly. She taps the image.

'Don't do that!'

Her eyes widen. 'Why? I was trying to make the photo bigger to have a better look.'

'You can't zoom profile pics on Insta. And if there's a pink circle around it when you tap, you get directed to their story.' I point to the phone. 'See, she posted a story, and now you're viewing it.'

Her brow creases. 'So what? I'm allowed to look at someone's story, aren't I? That's why people post them, right?'

She really knows nothing about the secrets of cyberstalking. 'Sure. If you don't care about them knowing you've looked.'

She swallows and her cheeks turn pink. 'People can't tell if you've looked at their profiles?'

'Profiles, no. Stories, yes.'

'Fuck. So she'll know I've looked?'

'If she checks. Yeah.'

Caroline drops her head into her hands. 'Nooo.'

I can't help but laugh. 'She might not look.' I check the number of followers Rachel has – it's low, so she'll probably notice who views her stories, but I keep this to myself. 'Even if she does, she might not realise it's you.'

Caroline's hands cover her eyes, and she separates her fingers to peer at me. 'My username is my name. My profile pic is me.'

'Then you shouldn't stalk people on Insta. What are you doing?' I say, still laughing.

She picks up a document and slaps my arm. 'This is your fault. You and your bloody social media obsession.'

'Seriously. She won't even notice. Don't worry about it.'

She throws her phone into her bag. 'Come on. I'll walk with you. Keep you distracted. You can buy me a coffee on the way for humiliating me.'

*

Barb greets me with a kind smile when I walk into the centre half an hour later. 'Morning, Amy. How are you?'

'Hot and sweaty.' I pour a cup of water from the dispenser and down it in one. 'Horrible out there.' I rest my arms on the counter. 'Other than that...' I shrug. My pulse is beating faster than normal, and anxiety swirls around in my gut, but she doesn't need to know that.

She tilts her head sympathetically. She must tire of doing that for every client. 'I've made you an appointment for next week. Wednesday at five again. Does that suit?' She doesn't let me off the hook anymore; there's no point even trying.

'That's fine. Thanks.'

I head down the corridor and notice Dr Garcia's door ajar. She's Luke's psychologist. I peer inside as I pass and see her tapping at the computer. I'm curious about what Luke tells her. Does he talk about how much he blames himself? Does he tell her he wishes he died instead of Sarah?

Steve and Luke are on the sofa when I walk in, and Trish is making herself tea. After three sessions, I feel a connection between the four of us – a shared longing for our past and hope for our future gluing us together in a way that's different to the connections I have with friends and family. Dr Sachdev and Kylie said this would happen, but I doubted them. Last week Kylie encouraged us to exchange numbers and talk outside the group, so Trish and I went for coffee after the session. We chatted about support groups she wants to join, and I was surprised to hear myself give encouragement and advice. It sounded like the old me. It was nice to hear from her.

After the four of us make small talk for a few minutes, Kylie arrives. She's wearing her usual combo of bright colours – mint green and cobalt blue today – but it doesn't smack me in the face like it did the first time. Instead, it triggers a desire to pull out the colourful clothes in my wardrobe I haven't worn for a long time and see what I still like.

'Morning, everyone. How are you all?' Kylie sits and glances expectantly between us.

We all mutter unenthusiastic okays.

'Right. Well, I hope you've been able to tap into some of the strategies we talked about last week and went along to your weekly appointments.' It's not really a question, but she pauses as though she wants someone to answer. When we all nod, she continues. 'Great. Let's get started. I think it would be good to talk more about some things we touched on last Friday. It's important we keep exploring those particular aspects of your grief.'

Last week, we spoke about anger and guilt and how we all share those feelings in varying degrees. Kylie asked us to do an exercise where we had a conversation with our spouses telling them how we feel. Bitterness poured out of me like floodgates releasing water from a dam.

I suspect Kylie has worked out the dam isn't empty and right on cue she says, 'Amy, would you like to go first?'

I take a sip of water and nurse the plastic cup in my hands. My mind recalls the session with Dr Sachdev on Wednesday – how I struggled to talk because the fury inside made me want to scream. He said that I need to keep talking until I don't feel like screaming any more.

Kylie gently probes me. 'Last week you told us how angry you feel. Did you want to talk more about that?'

I nod. 'I'm still angry. I'm angry at Mel for doing this to me and for letting that addiction control her.' My voice shakes. 'And I'm angry at myself for not making her stop. For not being tougher with her. For believing she was over her addiction.' My tone turns bitter. 'And I can't forgive either of us because that means I'm accepting what happened and saying it's okay. But none of this is okay.' I pause to catch my breath. 'I want to scream and tear myself open so everything can pour out.'

I squeeze my eyes shut and hold my wedding ring. 'I can't stop thinking about her being alone the night she died,' I say, almost a whisper. I bring my wedding ring to my lips, see Mel slipping it on my finger, the summer sun warming our skin, the ocean breeze gently blowing her dress. The vision is immediately replaced with the image I've created of her gasping for air in her final seconds. I open my eyes to see Trish wipe away a tear and Kylie's eyes filled with compassion. Steve has a pained expression, but Luke is gazing at me with a look of recognition, like he understands exactly how I'm feeling.

'Was she scared?' I continue. 'Did she call out for me? The autopsy said she died of respiratory failure. What does that mean? Did she struggle to breathe? Or did she just go to sleep?'

The searing pain in my throat prevents me from going on. I put my head down, fold my arms across my waist and let out a strangled cry. Trish slides an arm across my shoulders, maternal and comforting, and I lean into her. After what feels like hours, but is only a few minutes, my tears ease. Kylie asks if I'd like to go on. I decline, and she moves to Steve.

He talks about his wife's ovarian cancer. I want to listen, want to support him, but his words don't register. There's a thumping in my ears and my limbs ache like I'm coming down with the flu. I lie my head back on the couch and close my eyes, Steve's voice drifting in and out. Was a full-time carer for his wife and the kids. She's no longer in pain. Guilt eats away at him.

By the time he finishes speaking, the ache has passed, and my mind returns to the room as Kylie asks Luke to share. Last week he talked about his remorse over the accident and how he blames himself for the kids losing their mum.

He releases a heavy sigh, like he does every week before he talks. 'Um, yeah, had a tough week. Felt... I dunno, down, I guess. And drained. Just really exhausted. I miss Sarah so much. Some weeks I can manage, but others are hell.' He pauses as he gazes across the room, like he expects her to be standing there. 'Everywhere I look, she's there. Can't get away from it. The only time I can escape is when I'm working. Digging in yards, pulling up trees, slashing hedges.' He rotates his wedding band slowly. 'I question whether the kids lost the wrong parent. Sarah would've been able to deal with this much better than me. She was strong and independent. She would've pushed through. Got on with it. And I don't know why I can't do that. The kids have lost their mum because of me and now they're stuck with me, but I'm not sure I'm doing such a great job.' His voice cracks and his eyes are glassy, but the tears don't flow.

It occurs to me that he hasn't cried in any of the four sessions. I wonder if he cries when he talks to Dr Garcia.

The silence stretches as we all allow Luke the space to continue, but he shakes his head to indicate no more. Trish speaks for a while, and then Kylie fills the rest of the session discussing our support networks and coping strategies, such as working on finding joy in everyday moments, focussing on the people around us and the importance of self-care.

Trish and Steve stand to leave, but I'm not ready to face the outside world yet, so I say goodbye and stay seated.

'You okay?' Luke asks.

I shake my head. 'No. This is fucking hard.'

He nods, his mouth set in a grim line. 'Yep. You heading back to work?'

'Eventually. I can't handle it straight away. You?'

'I've got a job to get to soon, but I've got a bit of time if you want to grab a coffee? Apparently, we should talk outside the group, so...' He shrugs.

'Oh. I'd like that.'

He points to the drinks station. 'And the coffee here is shit. I need a decent one.'

I dab at my nose with the tissue and give a weak laugh. 'It really is.'

We leave the therapy room and head to the café next door. Luke orders and I grab the last free table by the window. While we've been in the session, the humidity has increased due to a pending storm that's visible in the distance. Moisture forms on the back of my neck and my shirt sticks to my armpits. I pour two glasses of water from the carafe that's just been delivered to the table.

'So, what do you do for work?' Luke asks as he sits opposite.

'I work in HR. For Australian Airlines on Edward Street. What about you?'

'Got my own business, so I can give myself time off.'

'That's your business?' I point to the logo on his work shirt that says *Sandgate Gardening and Landscape*.

'Yep. I usually start early, break to come here, then get back to it. Don't always have time to go home and change.'

'You must be busy. Between that and your kids.'

He takes a sip of water. 'Sure am. There's always stuff going on.'

'How old are they?'

He brightens. 'Jenna's just turned seventeen – desperate to be an adult. Cody's fifteen. I think he's trying to work out who he is.' He turns pensive. 'Definitely seen a difference in them since...' He takes another sip of water. 'They were such happy, confident kids before, and now, Jenna is more... angry, I suppose. And Cody keeps to himself a lot. I worry about them.'

We're briefly interrupted by our coffee being delivered.

'That must be hard,' I say, ripping open a couple of sugar packets and pouring the contents into my flat white. 'I'm not sure I would've coped with kids going through this. I can barely look after myself.'

He places his mug back on the table and smiles. The lines around his eyes crease, and I catch a fleeting glimpse of what he must've been like before. He's attractive with his strong jaw and dark brown eyes, but more so when he smiles. He's got a tiny gap between his two front teeth, and it suits him.

'What do you think about the group?' I ask.

'Dunno. It's tough. I'm not one for talking about my feelings. Hard to be so open about something so personal.'

'You think it helps?'

He peers at me. There's something in his eyes – relief that he's met someone whose pain mirrors his own perhaps – and I feel that thread of understanding that's formed between us tighten. 'Does anything help?' he says.

I glance out the window for a few seconds before turning back to him. 'No.'

We finish our coffee and chat more about our jobs before Luke says he needs to get to North Brisbane.

We step out to the busy lunch crowd on Adelaide Street. The sky has turned dark grey as the storm draws closer, and I flinch as a crack of thunder explodes above us.

Luke looks up. 'Didn't realise this was going to hit so soon. Might be early knock off for me.' He points towards the centre. 'I'm heading this way. See you next week?'

'Yeah. Thanks for the coffee.'

He flashes that appealing gappy-toothed smile. 'No worries.'

As he walks away, I lean against the brick wall and fold my arms, watching him until he disappears into the car park. 'Huh. Interesting,' I murmur, then turn in the opposite direction and head back to work.

Chapter Six

Today is the last day of summer. The oppressive humidity that adds to my sense of heaviness will be gone soon, and that is something to look forward to. It's also the last day of group therapy. The thought of exposing my raw emotions still simmers in the pit of my stomach, but the bond I've formed with the others helps. I'm going to miss them.

The leaves of my internal flytrap have worked hard again the past two weeks. Opening and closing, good days and bad. Pros – I've only had one sick day and I'm still running with Maddie. Cons – after a week of calls from Zoe, I told her that I couldn't do it anymore because it's not good for either of us. It stung to hurt her like that, but she deserves so much more than what I can offer. That was on Wednesday afternoon before my session with Dr Sachdev, and afterwards, I slipped into that dark place. I called Caroline, and she and Maddie did a split shift to watch over me. I emerged in a couple of days and I'm functioning again, but I never know how long it will be before I fall.

Now, it's early morning, and I'm at my desk staring at the pigeons waltzing around on the city rooftops while I breathe fire over the relentless demands Paul sent me yesterday.

Amy, where's that report?

Amy, what's happening with that complaint?

Amy, attend this meeting on my behalf.

Amy, have you finished writing the recruitment strategy?

And on they go, with a new one arriving five minutes ago about the departmental budget. Paul's only been with the company a few years, and I'm not sure he remembers how much experience I have in this game, so I play along for now because I don't have the brain capacity to deal with this on top of everything else. Instead, I plough through as much work as possible and delegate what I can to Daniel, who's been a gem in stepping up.

I decide a cup of tea is warranted before I start a new task and head for the kitchen. The open plan area is quiet with only a few of the HR team in at this hour.

'Morning, Daniel,' I say when I reach his desk.

'Hi.' His focus doesn't shift from the screen, and his face is tight with stress.

'What's up?' I ask.

He releases an exasperated sigh. 'I've got Julia's meeting with the union at nine. We need a prep meeting first and my bloody PC is stuck on these updates.' He jabs his finger accusingly at the monitor. 'Everything I need is on here *and* I've got to get this to Caz.' He snatches up a document and waves it in my face.

'Okay. No big deal. Can I access the meeting docs for you? Where are they?'

He sighs again and brushes his floppy ginger hair from his eyes. 'No, they're on my desktop. I was working on them late yesterday, so I saved them there.'

'Daniel...'

He holds his hands up. 'Stupid, I know. And Rachel's already in the meeting room. They're ready to go.'

'Rachel's here?' I'm suddenly more interested in this case.

He looks at me, puzzled. 'Yeah, she's Julia's union rep. Course she's here.'

'She's in the meeting room?'

'Yes. They're waiting for me.'

Is that so. I grab the document from his desk. 'I'll drop this down to Caz. You call IT and get your PC sorted out. Which room?'

'Oh, thanks. The one downstairs across from the lift.'

I rush back to my office, switch my sensible flats for the uncomfortable spare heels in my desk drawer and head downstairs. I can't have Rachel towering over me. Not that I have any idea how tall she is, but still.

Caroline is bent over the audio system in the far corner when I walk in, no doubt trying to figure it out. Technology is not her strength. Rachel watches on from the opposite corner, and if she thinks I didn't notice her leering at my friend's arse like it's a prize piece of beef she wants to sink her teeth into, she can think again. Rachel whips round to face me. By the crimson that splashes her cheeks, I think she knows she's been caught out.

'Hello.' My own soul shrivels at the ice in my greeting, so goodness knows what effect it has on her.

Caroline spins around. 'Oh. Amy. Hi.'

I'm rattled by how preened Caroline looks. She's smartly dressed in a suit, which isn't unusual, but she's wearing a softer shade of red lipstick that makes her blue eyes pop, and her choppy blonde bob is styled with casual waves. Although I know how long it takes her to create that look and those waves aren't so casual.

'Daniel's having IT issues; he'll be a few minutes late.' I slide the document across the boardroom table. 'He said you needed this.'

Caroline eyes me suspiciously. 'Thanks. Do you think he'll be long? We need to get started here.'

'No. His PC fired up as I was leaving. He should be down in a few minutes.'

I face Rachel. Her eyes are an unusual colour. A kind of frosty grey. Like dirty snow. Her long brown hair falls in a tousled style and her skin has a dewy Insta filter finish. The realisation that she's as attractive as her Instagram photos causes a jealous prickle to ripple through me.

She gives me a once over and some killer resting bitch attitude settles on her face.

Oh, throwing me some shade. She's messing with the wrong person. I can throw so much shade this city wouldn't see sunshine for a month. I cross my arms, raise my chin and narrow my eyes just enough to send a message.

A contrived smile emerges as she extends her hand. 'I'm Rachel Burley. AA's union rep.'

I step forward to shake. 'Amy Campbell. Client services manager.'

Her hand is cold, and the shake is limp. 'Nice to meet you, Amy. You've got a good reputation in our office.'

'Oh. Glad to hear it.' I cross my arms again. 'We haven't dealt with each other before. Are you new at AANU?' I catch Caroline in my peripheral shaking her head, eyes closed.

'Yes, I've only been there about three months,' Rachel says, the smile sticking, but her frosty gaze is replaced by a fiery glare.

'Thanks for dropping off the file, Amy,' Caroline interjects. 'I appreciate it.'

I don't take my eyes off Rachel. 'No problem.'

Daniel bursts through the door, his pale skin flushed pink. 'Sorry. IT issue. All good now.'

Caroline groans. 'Great.' She points to the audio system. 'Would you mind sorting this out, I can't get it to work.'

He races around to the other side of the table. 'No worries.'

'Thanks, Amy,' Caroline says. Her tone is polite, but her jaw tightens, and she widens her eyes at me.

'Let me know if you need anything else,' I say.

'We're good. I think Daniel can take it from here,' she replies.

Daniel's oblivious, his lanky frame bent over the audio system jabbing buttons like he's a little kid who's been given a phone for the first time.

I focus my attention back on Rachel. 'Bye, Rachel. Nice to meet you.' I'm amazed my words don't freeze in mid-air they're so cold.

'And you,' she says, with a little artificial sweetener. Always leaves a terrible taste in your mouth, that stuff.

In the corridor, I pull out my phone and message Daniel.

Can you update me after the meeting? Want to stay in the loop on this one.

Within seconds I receive a reply that doesn't surprise me given I've shown no interest in this case to date.

???

I ignore it and head back upstairs to my office. I can't shake the image of Caroline. The fact she's gone that extra mile with her appearance makes my chest boil. She'll get herself in all sorts of complications blurring work and personal boundaries. She's done it before and I'm the one who has to put her back together when it all goes wrong. My cheeks burn, and a thunderous mood grips me. I swap back to my sensible flats and try to focus on the job I was doing earlier. The buzz of my phone interrupts with a message from Caroline.

WTF was that?!

I huff and throw the phone into my bag. As I fire up my PC, a sharp rap sounds on my door. I spin to see Paul and my insides turn cold.

'Amy,' he says, leaning against the doorframe and crossing his legs at the ankle. 'How's that recruitment strategy? Will I have it today?'

'I'm working on it. And you asked for it by next Thursday,' I say, through clenched teeth.

He arches a thick eyebrow. 'Pretty sure I said I wanted to see a draft today.'

I stand. Now is not the time to take me on. 'If you look back at your email, you'll see you asked for it by Thursday.'

The flare of his nostrils is so fleeting I almost miss it. 'In email, yes, but when we caught up the other day, I asked for a draft by today.'

Although I'm almost certain he didn't, the tiniest doubt plants in my mind. I have been more forgetful the past few months, but I won't give him the satisfaction. 'No, you didn't. We discussed the diversity policy, which I finished and sent you on Tuesday.'

He pushes off the doorframe, shoves his hands into his pockets and adopts the man-spread. 'Right. Must be my mistake then.' He stares at me like he's waiting for me to tell him it's not him – it's me.

I cross my arms and glare back.

His mouth forms into a tight line and he turns to leave. 'Thursday,' he mutters as he strides away.

As soon as he's gone, I swing my door shut and drop onto my chair. My temples throb, and my hands shake as I grab a couple of paracetamols from my bag. I tie my hair back into a pony, place my cool palms on the back of my neck and wait for the rage racing through my veins to slow.

*

An hour later, I walk into the centre. I listened to Maddie's meditation app to try and dissolve the earlier rage, but it did nothing to slow my heart rate. I'm also bruised that Caroline didn't ask how I was before my last group session.

Barb greets me with her usual warm smile. 'Morning, Amy. You made it. Last session today.'

I rest my arms on the counter. 'Yep. Made it all the way through.'

'How are you feeling?'

I shrug. 'Anxious. Sad. But kind of glad to get my Friday mornings back.'

'Well, you'll still see me when you come for your weekly sessions with Dr Sachdev.'

I smile. 'Thanks for that not-so-subtle reminder I need to keep my appointments.'

She laughs. 'It's what I'm here for. And yes, I have booked you in for Wednesday afternoon.'

The fact that she cares so much for my wellbeing warms my spirit. 'Thanks.' I point in the direction of the therapy room. 'Better get in there.'

When I walk in, Kylie's already perched on the edge of the sofa sipping from a mug. Trish is beside her, polystyrene cup of tea in hand, her silver hair perfectly styled. They both brighten when they see me, but before I have a chance to say hello, my eyes are drawn to the bouquet in the middle of the coffee table and goosebumps prick my skin. Pink lilies today. Nothing else. Just four pink lilies in full bloom. There's a dusting of yellow pollen around the base of the vase and the delicate perfume wafts under my nose. No one here knows they were Mel's favourite, so it's more poignant that they're here. I don't believe in the afterlife, but it feels like a message straight from her. A goodbye of sorts since I won't be back in this room. The thought makes me ache. I sit slowly, moisture building in my eyes.

'Beautiful, aren't they? They match my nail polish.'

I blink at Kylie. 'Sorry?'

She gestures to the bouquet. 'The colour of the lilies, it's the same pink as my nail polish.' She wiggles her fingers at me.

I close my eyes for a second to catch the tears, and all I can think about is how funny Mel would find that comment. I nod and give Kylie a small smile. 'It's a beautiful colour.' I feel like Mel has played a joke on me, told me to lighten up, and my heart swells with longing.

Luke and Steve wander in a few minutes apart. Steve looks a touch brighter this week – I think he might've even brushed his hair. But Luke's mouth is set in a frown, stress marks his forehead and worry fills his eyes.

Kylie starts the session by discussing the resources and support we can tap into after the program finishes and asks about our recovery plans. Steve is starting another group that's specifically for widowed dads. Luke isn't going to join that one, he says his business keeps him too busy, but he'll keep his regular appointments with Dr Garcia. Trish has joined several groups in the past couple of weeks, both grief-related and social. I don't want another group either, but I commit to my weekly sessions with Dr Sachdev. The four of us exchange numbers, and I arrange to meet Trish next Friday at Evan's for breakfast.

Then Kylie asks us to share one last time. Trish and Steve both talk for around ten minutes each. It's raw, but there's a hint of peace in their voices that gives me hope, and they don't have that same bitter edge that Luke and I have. It makes me wonder if I would've handled things differently if Mel died from an illness and we had time to prepare for it – whether I would've been more accepting of what life served me.

'Amy, would you like to talk today?' Kylie asks.

I nod. Last week, I talked about anger and guilt for the third week in a row, but I can't do that today. It drains me and I'll have to revisit it at my session on Wednesday. 'I've been thinking a lot this week about my life and my future. I've carried this feeling for the past year, but I haven't been able to articulate it until now. I think all the therapy lately has helped me work it out.'

A proud smile spreads across Kylie's face.

I reach for the water on the coffee table and take a sip before I continue. 'I'm so confused about who I'm supposed to be now. With Mel, I knew exactly who I was. I loved being her partner, and I loved it even more when I became her wife. It was such an important part of my identity.' I put the cup down and grasp my ring. 'And now that she's gone, a huge part of my identity has gone with her. And that makes me scared for my future because I don't know how to be me anymore. How am I supposed to be in a relationship with anyone again? How can I ever love someone like I loved her? And I'm so frightened, because what if I meet someone and fall in love and this happens again? Who's to say this won't happen again?' I look at the mournful faces staring back at me, uncertain if they're sad for me or whether they hold the same fears.

Kylie gives me an encouraging nod and the space to continue, but after a couple of minutes, I shake my head, the weight of what I've said silencing me.

'Thanks, Amy.' She turns to Luke. 'Would you like to share today?'

He looks like he barely has the energy to lift his little finger, but he nods and rubs his thumb and index figure along his stubble. 'Not sure I've got much to say. Things have been tough this week. I've got loads of work on and the kids are giving me a hard time, saying I'm never home. Cody's got stuff going on at school that he won't tell me about and Jenna's...' He scratches his head. 'I dunno. Pissed off all the time. And so much bloody attitude. It worries the hell out of me.' He hesitates like he wants to say more about Jenna, then says, 'Anyway. That's what's going on.' He slumps back on the sofa and lets out a long, dejected sigh.

Kylie thanks him and wraps up the final session. I hug Trish and Steve goodbye, but Luke is busy tapping on his phone. I wait for him to finish and then say, 'You okay? You seem distracted today.'

He looks up. 'Oh, hi, Amy. Just a lot on my mind with work and the kids. And I've got a big job I need to finish today. The boys can't get the materials they need.' He huffs. 'Bloody hassle.'

'Sounds like you don't have time for a coffee?'

He shakes his head. 'Not today. Sorry.'

'Okay. Maybe we can catch up again sometime? Or maybe I'll run into you here?'

'Yeah. We've all got each other's numbers now, so...' He glances at his watch. 'Sorry, I've gotta go.'

'Oh. No worries. Um, see you later then.'

'Yep,' he says, before striding out.

I stare after him wanting to call him back. I'm not sure what for, but parting like this doesn't feel right. I tap a reminder into my phone to call him in a few days and check in. I sit back down and take one last look at the lilies, then close my eyes and breathe in the sweet scent. I can sense Mel. Her warm presence. Her musky smell. My skin tingles. It's like she's sitting beside me. Watching me, smiling. I can almost feel her fingertips stroke my face.

'I love you,' I whisper and brush away my tears.

When I'm ready to leave, I snap a photo of the flowers. Then, on a whim, take three of them and rush back to work so they don't wilt in the scorching heat.

Chapter Seven

Later that afternoon, I'm bashing at my keyboard when I hear Caroline's voice.

'Hey, you.'

I spin round. 'Hi,' I say cautiously.

She perches on the edge of my desk. 'That was an interesting little performance you put on this morning.' Her soft tone signals she's no longer annoyed.

'Just looking out for my mate.'

She crosses her arms. 'I'm a big girl. I can look after myself.'

'I thought you might need a bit of help.' I pause. 'And I wanted to check Rachel out,' I add sheepishly.

'Oh, I know exactly what you were doing,' she says, with a half-smile.

'Well, do you blame me? She hassles you daily and it's getting to you. I wanted to see what she's about.'

'Alright. Thanks for sticking up for me, I guess.'

I run my eyes over her. 'You look good today. Your hair's nice.'

She shrugs. 'I like to make an effort for work.'

'Mmhmm.' I try to read her face, but it remains impassive. I take a different angle. 'You were right about Rachel – she's kind of hot.'

She frowns. 'I suppose. But she annoys me too much, so it's switched off her hotness.'

I quirk a brow.

'Okay. It hasn't switched it off entirely.'

'She was staring at your arse when I walked in,' I say.

'You're full of it.'

I'm not sure if Caroline's blushing, or if her fair skin has turned pink from the afternoon sun that makes my office too warm.

'I'm not. I caught her red-handed. Or red-faced, I should say.'

'Is that why you stabbed her with an ice pick?'

'What?' I say innocently. 'I'm protective of you. And there was something intense about her that I didn't like. Nor did I like the way she was eyeing you up like you were some kind of tasty snack.' I point. 'She was objectifying you.'

'Oh, really? Well, I don't have an issue with attractive women looking at my arse like it's a tasty snack.'

'Even if they're annoying and intense?'

'She's not. She's just a bit... full on with her job.'

I sigh. 'Fine. I'll be nice if I meet her again. Sorry.'

'Mmm, I'll let you off the hook this time. Anyway, I've been swamped all day, but I haven't forgotten it was your last session. How was it?'

The bruise from earlier instantly heals. 'It was okay. Not as tough as the other weeks. I'm going to miss the others.'

'You can stay in touch, can't you? Check in on each other?'

'Yeah. I'm going to meet Trish next Friday for breaky. And we've all exchanged numbers, so...' I shrug.

'That's great, Ames.'

'Oh, I have something for you.' I jump up, grab a lily from my meeting table and hand it to her. 'From Mel.'

She lifts herself off the desk. 'Mel?'

'The lilies were back today and...' I swallow. 'I felt she was there with me, so I wanted to take some.'

Her eyes moisten. 'Oh.'

'Kylie told me the colour matched her nail polish.'

Caroline chuckles. 'I think Mel might have sent you Kylie to add some colour to your life.'

I nod and wipe away a tear. 'I think so. I've got one for Maddie, too. I'll drop it off on my way home.'

'That's lovely,' she says, still gazing at the lily. She dabs the corner of her eye with her finger, and I grab a tissue from my desk to blow my nose. 'Hey, I'm sorry I can't hang out with you tonight,' she says. 'You going to be alright?'

It's her sister's birthday, so she's going out for a family dinner. She invited me, but I don't want to bring down the mood. Maddie and Zoe have a work function on, Josh and Sophie are busy, and I've kind of drifted apart from other friends since Mel died.

'I'll be fine. I'll watch a movie or something. Call Mum and Dad.'

'We've got that comedy festival show tomorrow night at the Powerhouse. We can go for dinner first if you like?'

'Yeah, let's do that.'

'I better go. I've got a few things to finish before I leave,' she says.

My being feels so fragile, like a feather could crush me, but telling her that will ruin her night. Instead, I pull her into a hug. 'Thanks, Caz. For everything.'

She returns the hug with her free arm. 'That's okay, but what are you thanking me for?'

I pull away and shrug. 'You and Maddie, you do so much. I'm lucky to have you both.'

Her eyes grow round with worry. 'You sure you're going to be okay? You can come. Or you can call me. I'll have my phone. I can come over afterw—'

'No. God, no. Sorry, I didn't mean to make you feel bad. I just wanted you to know that I appreciate you.'

She squeezes my hand. 'I know you do.'

I tilt my head towards the door. 'Go. Have fun. I'll see you tomorrow.'

She leaves and I return to the recruitment strategy. Ten minutes later, I'm interrupted by a call on my mobile. I stare at the name on the screen a second before I slide the answer icon.

'Hello?'

'Amy?'

'Yeah.'

'Hi. It's Luke.' A pause. 'From the group therapy.'

I chuckle. 'Hi, Luke. I know who you are. I just didn't expect to hear from you.'

'Right, yeah. Hey, I wanted to say sorry I had to rush off like that. It was rude. I was stressed about work and had to sort some stuff out quickly.'

'It's fine.'

'Um, I was wondering if you had any plans later? Maybe we could catch up or something? I could probably use someone to talk to if I'm honest.'

My heart warms that he's thought of me as someone he can talk to. 'I'd like that. What do you want to do?'

'I live in Sandgate. If you're close by, you're welcome to come over. My kids will be out for a couple of hours. I'll just be hanging around the house.'

I hesitate a moment uncertain about going to his house – that's moving into making new friends territory and I'm not sure I'm up for that. But then I remember Kylie encouraging us to talk outside the group and share how we're feeling, and the alternative is spending the night wallowing or with my parents. 'I'm in Clayfield, so not far. What time? Seven? Can I bring anything? Food? Wine?'

'Seven's good. Erm… I guess you can bring some wine if you like?'

'Sure.'

He gives me his address and hangs up.

Now that I've committed to going, my spirit perks up at the unexpected invitation. I shut down my PC, keen to get out of here. As I say goodbye to Daniel, I remember he hasn't given me an update on the meeting this morning, but I decide I don't care.

Outside, it's still scorching as I walk up the slope on Edward Street to Central Station. The humidity is record high today and sweat drips down my back. It's almost like summer is intentionally going out with a bang before retreating for the cooler months.

On the train, I sit by the window and watch the northern suburbs whiz by. The striking orange flowers of the poinciana trees have disappeared, making the journey that little bit duller.

Maddie isn't home when I stop by, so I leave the lily in the laundry sink under the house and send her a message to explain. She replies with a string of heart emojis.

When I step into my house an hour after leaving work, the familiar wave of loneliness hits me. Even after fourteen months, I still expect to find Mel waiting to kiss me hello and ask about my day. I take a deep breath as I walk past the photos scattered through the lounge room to put the wine in the fridge and dump my bag before jumping in the shower.

Under the cool stream of water, I tilt my face upward and let the day's grime, emotion and tears wash away. I want to stand here until this new skin I've been forced to grow disappears, allowing the old me to emerge, shiny and clean.

*

I shut the door of the cab, check the address on my phone and peer up at the street sign. Yep, this is Flinders Parade and the right house number. A few cars pass, and the gentle sound of the ocean lapping the rocks carries from the beach across the road. In the front garden, solar lights illuminate immaculate grass, thriving plants and manicured shrubs – definitely the home of a landscaper. I walk up a couple of stairs, cross the large deck that wraps around the front and side of the house and press the doorbell.

Luke answers within a few seconds; the stress that plastered his face earlier is gone. 'G'day. Come in.' He's barefoot and wearing long shorts and a T-shirt with a faded surf logo. He's also clean-shaven and wearing glasses that I don't recall seeing before. He looks good. Very good.

'Hel-lo.' My greeting is more flirtatious than it should be. Thankfully, he doesn't seem to notice. I point to his face. 'Have you always worn glasses and I've just never noticed?'

He smiles. 'I usually wear contacts when I'm working.'

'Ah, that's good. I was worried that I'm more wrapped up in myself than I realised.'

His smile widens and he leads me into the house. It's two-storey with a large open plan area on the ground floor. The space is sleek and stylish with polished concrete floors, a long stone bench in the kitchen and a huge, L-shaped couch in the lounge with a flat screen TV mounted to the wall. The bifold doors leading out to the front deck are open making the space appear even bigger. Off the back deck, I glimpse a pool shimmering with lights.

'Wow. This is some house,' I say. 'My friends would love this place.'

'Yeah?'

'Uh huh, Maddie's an architect and Caz loves everything to do with nice houses. They did designs and renovations on their own place. Well, Caz's place now.'

He nods. 'Right.'

I hand him the two bottles of wine I brought.

'Thanks.' He peers at the labels and heads into the kitchen. 'It was an old rundown weatherboard when we bought it. We wanted it for the location and block size. Took a while to knock it down and rebuild but got there eventually.' He does a sweeping gesture with his hand. 'This was all Sarah, though. She had her own interior design business. I just did the landscaping.'

'She did an amazing job. It's beautiful.'

He holds the wine up. 'Which one do you want?'

I shrug. 'Don't mind, you choose.'

He pulls two glasses from an overhead cupboard and opens the Margaret River chardonnay. He hands me a glass. 'We can sit out on the front deck. There's a nice breeze. Enjoy the last night of summer.'

As we move through the house, I look at the canvases and frames that contain various images of Luke with a dark-haired woman and two children. There's a wedding photo at the bottom of the stairs featuring a much younger Luke and a woman who is obviously Sarah. She has long, black hair that falls past her shoulders in thick glossy waves and is decorated with tiny white flowers. Subtle make-up highlights her dark eyes, and her ivory wedding dress complements her olive skin tone. Luke looks incredibly handsome in a grey suit, his brown eyes brimming with hope for the future. They're both gazing into the camera laughing, and even through the still image I can see the love that flows between them. There's a pang in my chest knowing he sees this photo every night before he ascends the stairs to bed. What that must do to him.

I tear myself away and follow him outside where a soft sea breeze sweeps my skin, and a salty ocean smell lingers. It's a welcome change from the heat and humidity of the city and inner suburbs. I take a seat opposite at the table. 'That breeze is lovely.'

'Mmm,' he says. 'Beautiful out here in the evening.'

There's an awkward lull before we both try to speak at once.

Luke laughs. 'You go.'

'I was going to say that it was nice to hear from you this afternoon. Kind of warmed to everyone in the group after a while.'

'Me too. And I'm sorry about this morning. I was panicked thinking we wouldn't get that job done, but all good in the end.'

'No problem.' I consider him for a few seconds wondering whether it's okay to probe. 'You were distracted in the session – with non-work stuff, I mean.'

He strokes his chin. 'Just wasn't in the mood. Things on my mind.'

I nod. 'Anything… in particular?'

He screws up his face and takes a sip of wine, then gazes at me like he's trying to decide if he should open up. 'Before I left for work, I found an email with Jenna's appointment to go for her learner's permit.'

'Oh.'

'She didn't tell me about it. She left her emails open on her laptop and I saw it. It made me feel…' He swallows. 'You know.'

I do know. The last thing he'll want is his kids out on the road after what happened.

'Thing is, she's seventeen. I can't stop her growing up. And I know it's ridiculous to not want her to have her licence, but…' He shifts his gaze to the sea. 'God, if I lost her. Or Cody.' His voice cracks. 'Ah, shit. Sorry.' His eyes are a little glassy, but like in the sessions, tears don't escape.

'Don't apologise. I can't image how hard that must be.'

He gives an appreciative nod before he continues. 'Jenna reckons she didn't tell me because I'm at work all the time so I'm not around to talk to. And that I'd lose my shit.'

I smile. 'Sounds like a perceptive girl.'

'She is. Like her mum.' He shakes his head. 'Anyway. I have to trust she'll be okay.'

I don't know what to say. If there's anything to say, so I sit quietly allowing him the space to talk.

He picks up his glass. 'I sit out here a lot, especially when I've had a bad day. Look at the ocean. I feel close to Sarah when I'm out here.' He points across the road. 'We scattered her ashes over there.'

I peer through the darkness, hear the gentle ebb and flow of the water.

'She loved this house. This area. We never talked about what would happen if... it seemed right, so...'

'That's lovely,' I say.

He clears his throat. 'Sorry. I didn't mean to get into all of that. Treating you like a therapist now.'

'Ha, I don't think I'd make a very good one. I could never be as chirpy as Kylie.'

He grins. 'She's certainly that.'

'You weren't keen on joining the single dad group that Steve's going to?'

He breaks eye contact and glances around the deck. 'Nah. It's not for me. I only went to get my family off my back. I guess it's helped a bit, but I don't want to keep doing it.'

'Are you still planning to see Dr Garcia?'

He nods. 'My family will hassle me if I don't.'

'Mine, too. Even Barb's in on it now making sure I don't miss an appointment.'

'Same here,' he says fondly. 'Sounds like your friends and family are a great support.'

I had talked about them in the session last week when we discussed support networks and coping strategies, and again when Luke and I had coffee afterwards. 'The best. Can't imagine where I'd be without them.'

'That's great.' He peers down at my chest. 'You wear your ring on a chain.'

I grab it. 'Oh.'

He gives a regretful sigh. 'Sorry, that's personal. I—'

'No, it's fine. After Mel died, I couldn't eat and it started slipping off, but I didn't want to stop wearing it, so I put it on here.' I run my thumb across the row of smooth diamonds. 'It fits my finger again now, but I like this. It's close to my heart.'

He gives a sad smile. 'That's nice.'

I pick up my glass and down the last mouthful, then say, 'Tell me more about Cody.'

He brightens. 'He's a good kid. Sensitive. Smart. Cheeky. Loves acting and basketball. He's going to be in the school play. Although I forgot about that, too, Jenna told me this morning. That's where he is tonight, at rehearsals. Then he's going to the basketball with his mates.'

'And Jenna? Where's she?'

'Out with friends. Going to the movies, she said.' He points to my empty glass. 'Want another one?'

'Um. Sure. Thanks.'

His eyes linger on mine for a few seconds before he takes our glasses into the kitchen. I'm not sure how to take that look, but I'm surprised to feel my cheeks warm. I check my phone while he's away. Separate messages from Caroline, Maddie and Josh making sure I'm okay. I shoot off the same reply to all of them.

All good. Catching up with someone from the group x

Luke returns and gestures towards my phone with his chin. 'People checking up on you?'

'Yeah. They're all busy tonight. They worry.'

'I get that special treatment, too. They also hassle me about getting back out there and meeting someone,' he says. 'I liked what you talked about today. Sounded like me.'

I cast my mind back to this morning's session. Loss of identity. Not knowing how to be with someone else. Scared to love again.

He continues. 'I like the idea of meeting someone. Just can't seem to do it. To get my head around it.'

I nod. 'I get that.'

'I had a few dates about six months after Sarah died.' He gives a short laugh. 'Bloody disaster.'

He never mentioned this at therapy. Not that any of us talked about our post-loss love lives. 'Sounds interesting. What happened?'

'My mate Nick set me up with one of his wife's friends. We went out a couple of times, got on well. Things moved on and we tried to... you know.'

'Have sex?' I say, tickled by his embarrassment.

He grins. 'Yeah. It was a nightmare. I felt guilty and out of my depth with someone new. I couldn't...' He gesticulates his hand around his crotch.

'Get it up?' I ask, a smile pulling on my lips.

He laughs and points at me. 'Yep. And then I broke down. I can laugh about it now, but at the time, bloody embarrassing.'

I chuckle. 'Awkward. What did she do?'

The grin is still on his face. 'She said that maybe I wasn't ready and left it at that. I never saw or heard from her again.' He crosses his ankle over his knee and picks up his glass. 'What about you? You mentioned you'd been seeing someone?'

I briefly told him about Zoe when we went for coffee again last week but had left out the details. 'Wouldn't say I was seeing her. We had a very short relationship not long after Mel died. I broke it off after six weeks but struggled to end the physical part. It's difficult because she's in our circle of friends. I've ended it properly now, about a month ago,' I say with a convincing nod, although I'm not sure if I'm trying to convince myself or him.

His brows furrow. 'Right. Sounds...' I can see the cogs working in his brain as he tries to figure it out. 'Complicated.'

I laugh. 'Yep. That's lesbian love lives for you.'

'Maybe in the future you might be ready? Sounds like she's keen.'

I shake my head. 'Nah, I don't think she wants me. She just wants a relationship, but she always seems to go for the wrong people.

Besides, we're not right for each other. I mean, she's lovely. Smart, sexy. Very sexy.'

He nods slowly. 'Yep. Complicated.'

'Mmm.' I pause. 'And she lets me wallow in all my miserable crap. I don't like myself when I'm like that. I can't be with someone who lets me do that.'

'I understand that bit,' he says.

'Mel didn't put up with it. She'd give me a bit of time to wallow, but anything past a day and she'd say, "for fuck's sake, Amy, get over yourself." God, I miss that.' I close my eyes and let out a long, slow breath. 'Shit. Now I'm treating you like a therapist.'

He smiles. 'Sarah was the same. She whipped me into shape every day. I got away with nothing.'

Our eyes meet for a few seconds before he says, 'Hey, you hungry? There's a great Thai close by. We can order some takeaway.'

'Um...' I blink to recover from what I'm pretty sure was a moment. Although, admittedly, my sexy-man-radar is rusty. 'Yeah, I am.'

We order a mix of dishes that arrive within half an hour. We share chicken curry, coconut rice and satay sticks, and talk about shows we're streaming, movies, sport, our families. My body is less tense, and I feel strangely connected to him, like our shared grief is intertwined.

After we've eaten and I've helped him clear away dishes, I check the time on my phone. 'I should probably go. It's late and you said you have work tomorrow.'

He nods. 'Yep, got some turf to lay. Big job so probably should stop drinking. And the kids will be home soon.'

I order a cab as he walks me to the door and holds it open for me.

'Thanks for tonight,' he says. 'It was good to talk to someone.'

'It was, wasn't it?' I say. 'Maybe... we can meet up again some time?'

His lovely eyes search mine and before I realise what I'm doing, my lips are on his and I'm surprised by how soft they are. He stiffens but then kisses me back for a few seconds before pulling away and peering at me with a bemused smile.

My fingers fly to my mouth. 'Shit. Sorry. I…' My face burns. 'Bloody hell. Sorry.'

He adjusts his glasses. 'Don't be. I just didn't expect it. And I thought you were…' His brows knit. 'I didn't think I was your type.'

I nod. 'Yes. I don't know why I did that.' I attempt to lighten the mood. 'I'll try and control myself next time.'

He gives a short laugh. 'Don't worry about it. Not every day an attractive woman kisses you out of the blue.'

I blush again at his compliment and point to the car as it pulls up. 'Perfect timing.' I hurry along the footpath and sense him watching me as I jump into the back seat. He waves as the car drives off.

The streetlights whiz by as the car moves along the parade. 'What the fuck?' I whisper.

Chapter Eight

It's Saturday night and I'm in the beer garden of my local pub. I chose this venue because it's less 'on a date' and more of a 'friends meeting up' kind of place. It's busy tonight. Groups of twenty-somethings knock back drinks, talk to their mates or peer at their phones. Couples eat dinner, chat and occasionally glance up at the rugby league match on TV. A group of middle-aged women beside me drink champagne and cackle at each other's jokes. I watch a young couple in the far corner. The woman is talking to her partner, holding his hand across the table, but he simply nods and gazes up at the football.

It reminds me of coming here with Mel. As soon as the AFL started, I'd lose her. It wouldn't matter what I'd say, she'd respond with 'that's great, babe'. She was even less attentive when Maddie was with us. They'd grab their wine or beer and position themselves in the perfect viewing spot, leaving Caroline and me to entertain each other and fetch their drinks because nothing comes between Victorians and their Aussie rules. My dad and Josh became involved too. They both swore league was the only code worth watching, but Mel was so passionate and persuasive, she won them over. The four of them spent many Saturday afternoons together watching football, taking turns hosting at their respective houses arguing over Richmond versus Brisbane Lions. Mel didn't have a brother and wasn't close with her parents, so those afternoons were special to her. Dad still talks about how much he misses that. Maddie's kept up the tradition as much as she can, but it's not the same.

I'm so caught up in my memories, Luke's deep voice startles me. 'G'day, Amy.'

I touch a hand to my chest. 'Hi. Sorry. I didn't see you come in.'

He grins. 'Didn't mean to frighten you.' The dark stubble is back and he's wearing glasses again. He points at my almost empty drink. 'Looks like you're one ahead of me. Can I get you another before I sit down?'

'Sure. Just the house sav blanc. Thanks.'

I scan his body as he walks to the bar. His tight T-shirt and jeans highlight the benefits of being a landscaper – toned without the bulging muscles. I feel a twinge somewhere I wouldn't normally in this situation.

Luke returns with wine for me and a beer for himself. 'Rowdy in here tonight.'

'It is.' I hold up my glass. 'Thanks.' I lean forward so he can hear me over the band that's started inside the pub. 'How did you get here?'

'My brother and his partner dropped me off. They're on their way to the theatre in Southbank. They'll pick me up on the way back.'

'They like the theatre?'

He nods.

'Me too. I can sit in the dark and be transported to another world for a couple of hours. It's magical.'

He smiles. 'That's what Ben says.'

'What have they gone to see?'

'No idea. They're always there. Musicals, comedy, plays.' His eyes shine. 'They take Cody with them a lot. I think he secretly wants to be an actor. He plays it down, but he's excited to be in the school play.'

'Is he with them tonight?'

He takes a sip of beer and shakes his head. 'At a friend's house tonight.'

'And Jenna?'

'She's at a friend's too. Although she keeps talking about this boy at school, so I hope she's at her friend's. I worry.' He alluded to some problems he's having with Jenna when we spoke during the week.

'She sounds like a handful, like a lot of seventeen-year-olds. I'm pretty sure I was the same.'

He grins. 'I definitely was. That's why I'm worried.'

I return the smile, then we both glance around the beer garden awkwardly.

'Thanks for suggesting tonight,' he says quickly. 'I would've been at home moping around with the kids out.'

'Same. Caz is away with her family this weekend and Maddie is busy. I would've been in front of a movie or hanging out with my parents – never fun in your mid-thirties.'

He nods.

'Should we order some food?' I ask.

'Yeah, I reckon we should,' he says, picking up the menu.

We choose our meals and Luke insists on paying. He says he's old school like that, and while I want to object, I also kind of like it.

I check my phone while he's at the bar to find a message from Caroline. I haven't told her or Maddie where I am tonight. I wouldn't normally keep something like this from them, but when I told Caroline about kissing Luke, she fell silent and stared at me open-mouthed. I know she doesn't want me to fall into a Zoe-type situation again, and the silence was her way of trying to stay out of my business, but I still feel uneasy about telling her. I type out a reply.

All good with me. Hope you're having fun.

She'll be too caught up in her sister's baby to think about what I'm up to anyway.

Luke returns and we relax into surface-level chat about work over the past week, his kids and my nephews. Our dinner arrives, and as I eat pizza and Luke hooks into his steak, we make more small talk, mainly about our limited cooking skills and our reliance on takeaway or baked beans on toast. I intentionally don't mention our wives or therapy, not that Mel isn't always in the forefront of my mind, like Sarah will be in his. It's just that talking about her makes those flytrap leaves spring open, and I don't want to cry in the middle of a pub or turn this into a therapy session.

I watch him closely as he talks. There's something about him tonight – he's not as tense, and that worry frown that was often present in group therapy has vanished. It's as though he's relieved that he can be around someone who's been in that dark place, yet we don't need to talk about what happened. I feel that, too. I don't need to explain why I'm half a person now. He just knows.

We fit in a couple more drinks before the bell signals last call.

'Do you need to contact your brother for a lift?' I ask.

He peers at his watch. 'I didn't realise the time. They'll be home by now. I can get a cab. Sandgate isn't far. How about you?'

'I'll walk.' I wave my hand in the general direction of my house. 'I'm just down the road.'

He smiles. 'I'll walk you home then.'

'Oh,' I say, taken aback. 'Okay. Thanks.'

Outside, it's a warm evening and the humidity has eased off. We walk along the footpath to the sound of crickets singing and frog croaks. The dim streetlights do little to brighten the footpath, but headlights from the odd car that passes help my night vision. Although Luke and I spoke through the week, I hadn't mentioned last Friday and want to clear the air.

'I didn't apologise properly for last week,' I say.

He frowns. 'Did you have something to apologise for?'

'Yeah, you know, for being a bit too... forward.'

'Oh. That.' He chuckles. 'That's right; you kissed me.' Alcohol has obviously made him more relaxed, too.

I smile. 'Yeah, that. I'm sorry. Not sure what came over me.'

He shrugs. 'Wine, probably.'

I give him a sideways glance and nod. 'Yep, definitely wine.'

'And probably some emotions too, I reckon.'

I nod. 'Uh huh. That too.'

He takes a step closer and his arm brushes mine. 'I didn't mind.'

I like him being close like this. It's as though that part of me that feels so isolated in my experience of being a young widow has opened and drawn him in, and he easily slots into place beside me. I stop in front of my gate and face him. He smells fresh, like bodywash, but I can't place the scent. It's kind of earthy, different to what I'm used to.

'After you left, I realised how much I liked it,' he says.

The space between us is dense with attraction and curiosity. He leans forward, hesitating centimetres from my face, then our lips connect. His stubble brushes my skin, prickly and unfamiliar, but his mouth is as soft as I remember. His arm wraps around my waist and draws me in.

I start to relax and ease into the kiss, running my hands over his shoulders, when a loud voice shouts, 'Get a room!' We break apart as a car speeds past, a teenager hanging from the window. We look at each other and laugh.

I gesture to my house. 'This is me.'

He takes it in, nodding appreciatively. 'Nice.'

'Do you want to come up? I have wine, tea, water.'

'Think I've had enough alcohol. Cup of tea would be good, though.'

I lead the way upstairs, put the jug on and grab a couple of glasses of water.

He stands in the lounge peering at my photos that line a long cabinet. Mel's ashes are there, too, but he doesn't seem to notice them.

'Here you go,' I say, handing him some water. 'Tea won't be long.'

He takes the glass from me and picks up a photo with his free hand. It's my favourite. It was taken at a café in Vienna. Mel's looking straight at the camera laughing, and my lips are pressed against her cheek, my eyes closed. It sums up our relationship – in love and happy.

He looks up at me. 'This is Mel?'

I swallow. 'Yep.'

He glances at the photo again. 'You look good together. Happy.' There's a sadness to his voice, an understanding.

I clear my throat and head back into the kitchen. 'How do you have your tea?' I call.

'Milk and one sugar, thanks.' He walks up behind me. 'Sorry. That was rude. Helping myself to your photos.'

'It's fine.' I stir in the sugar and hand him a mug. 'Come on. We can sit on the deck.'

As I open the glass doors, geckos dart across the wooden beams, catching moths, chirping to one another. A half-moon bathes the backyard in a dull light, and a tawny frogmouth stares up at the house from the clothesline.

Luke walks over to the railing. 'G'day, mate,' he says to the owl.

That makes me smile. 'He's here most nights. We've had some good chats. At least I think it's a "he" because of all the grey fur.'

'Don't see them at my place.' He scans the yard. 'Look at the size of this. Gardener's dream.'

I sit on the outdoor two-seater. 'It's a great block. We bought it when we first moved up from Melbourne.' He faces me as I wave a finger across the deck. 'Maddie redesigned all of this, and she renovated the kitchen with Mel. My mum added all the indoor plants. She thinks it brightens things up.'

He crosses the deck and sits close to me. 'She's right about that. Beautiful house.'

'It is. The yard isn't great, though. Neither of us were into gardening.'

'From what I can see it doesn't look too bad. I could have a look some time if you like. Give you some ideas.'

'That would be great, thanks.'

I watch him as he sips his tea – the dark hair on his forearms, his T-shirt sleeves tight across solid biceps, the cut of his jaw firm and strong. Those chocolate brown eyes return my gaze, and my curiosity stirs and builds momentum.

He tilts his head. 'So. You... like guys too?'

The hope in his voice is sweet and I think about the best way to answer. I don't want to discuss the sexuality spectrum or where I sit on it. I don't dislike men; I just don't pay much attention to them. But he's different. We share something unique, and it makes me want to be close to him. It also sparks an urge to get back to that kiss.

'I like you,' I say. And that's the simplest explanation I can give him.

He pushes up his glasses. 'I like you too.'

I take his mug and place it on the coffee table, then lean in until our lips meet. His hand slides to the back of my neck, hot on my bare skin, and mine runs up his thigh, which feels as hard as it looks. The kiss deepens, our tongues mingle, and our breathing becomes heavier. He tastes good – salt and spice. The slow-burn desire that's been simmering through the night ramps up. I halt the kiss, stand, and hold out my hand. His brows draw together, but he takes it.

In my bedroom, a warm breeze floats through the open windows, and the ceiling fan whirs on low, circulating the sweet perfume of the frangipani flowers on the tree outside. Soft lighting flows from the kitchen along the hallway, giving the room a dim yellow glow.

I remove his glasses and place them on the chest of drawers. He pulls me close, kissing me harder this time. Our shirts come off and I tentatively run my hands over the hair on his chest. It's softer than I thought it would be. His hand finds my breast while the other runs up my spine. His palms are rough, but his touch is light and hesitant.

I undo his jeans and slip my hand inside. It's been so long since I've done this that I unexpectedly jerk my hand away for a second before I relax. Then it occurs to me I might've gone in too fast, but he groans softly, and he's obviously not having the same issue he had last time he did this.

'You sure about this?' His voice is low and gruff.

I can't believe he doesn't get the message from my body language. Or my hand on his dick. 'I'm sure.'

'I don't want to take advantage.'

I remove my hand, wrap my arms around his waist and kiss him gently. 'I'm thirty-five. I'm widowed. I'm slightly drunk and I'm turned on. Take advantage.'

He swallows. 'Okay.'

I pull him down to the bed. After a minute, he stops kissing me and sits up.

Now what?

'Um, this is going to look bad...' He pulls his wallet out of his jeans pocket, opens it and takes out a condom.

'Oh. I didn't think about that.' It's been a long time since I've needed condoms.

'I don't carry them round or anything. I don't want you to think I had this planned,' he says, sitting on the edge of the bed waving the foil packet around.

I'm worried he's going to smack me in the face with it. 'Okay,' I say dubiously.

'My brother's a real smartarse. He shoved some in my pocket when he dropped me off. I... ah... told him about last week. I think he wants me to have sex more than I do.'

I sense his nervousness, so I take the condom and put it on the side table. 'Well, I don't have any, so that's good.' I pull him back down onto the bed. 'Ow.'

'Did I hurt you?' he asks.

'Your elbow is on my hair.'

'Oh.' He moves it. 'Better?'

'Yeah.'

He lies down and presses against me. I like the feel of his hard body against my soft curves. It's new and different. I want new and different. I need new and different. We remove the rest of our clothes, but it's more perfunctory than passionate, and he fumbles with the condom.

'Been a while since I've used one of these,' he says, finally managing to get the packet open.

'Don't ask me for any tips.'

He moves back on top of me, inhaling sharply. 'Ah. Shit.'

'Are you alright?' This isn't going well. A sign maybe? No. I don't believe in signs.

'Just my hip. It's a bit buggered from years of gardening. I'll be right.'

I need him to shut up now. My body is pulsing, and I want this to happen. I wrap my arms around him and intertwine my legs with his. He responds, his hardness against me and then inside me. We both moan softly as our bodies move together, slowly at first, but the pace soon quickens. The skin on his back starts to get clammy under my grip and his breath is hot on my neck. I'm starting to get into a rhythm, feel my own body heat up, when he groans low in my ear and thrusts harder.

His body tenses. 'Oh, god,' he breathes.

I don't know whether to laugh or cry.

'Shit. Sorry.' He lies on me for a minute before he props himself up and looks down at me. 'Not *as* embarrassing as last time.'

My body feels like a hand grenade that failed to go off.

'I take it that was a bit quick for you and you didn't... or did you?' he says.

He can't seriously think I had an orgasm. 'Um. No. I didn't.'

He slowly rolls off me. 'Erm, do you want me to... you know?'

'What? Give me a happy ending?' I say with a laugh.

He laughs, too. 'Yeah, I guess.'

I prop myself up on my elbow. 'I'll survive.'

'Haven't had a lot of practice lately.'

I kiss him briefly. 'Reckon we both need more practice. I need some water. You want some?'

He yawns. 'Yeah. Ta.'

I swing my legs out of bed and sit on the edge a moment while the tingling in my body dissipates, then pad out to the kitchen and pour two glasses of water. As I head back to the bedroom, across the lounge, I glimpse the photo of Mel and me and my heart squeezes. I place the water down and walk over to pick up the frame, running my thumb over her face. She gazes back at me, her face bright with happiness. 'I miss you so much,' I whisper. 'I don't want to be here with anyone else, but he understands.' I quickly replace the photo knowing that if I stare at it any longer, I'll crumble.

By the time I return to the bedroom, Luke is on his side and covered with the sheet. 'Here you go.' I place the glass on the side table, but his breathing is low and steady. It's a change from the deep, emotional discussions Zoe wants to have afterwards when all I want to do is sleep.

I close the shutters and lie in the dark. My usual bedtime memory emerges – the last night in the house with Mel. Her naked body pressed behind me in the spoon position. Her arm slung across my waist. Her sultry voice whispering, 'I love you' in my ear before we drifted off.

And now Luke lies here. He somehow gives me breathing space, like he takes half the load, so I don't have to carry it alone. There's been no earth-shattering moments tonight, but he comforts me and there's an affection growing in my heart.

I scoot closer and kiss the skin between his shoulder blades. 'Night.'

Chapter Nine

The Wickham Hotel slowly fills with an after-work crowd. Piped music plays, but it's only audible when there's a lull in conversation. The strong smell of beer and wine mingles with occasional plates of hot wedges or beef burgers that pass us on the way to people's tables.

Caroline returns from the bar with a bottle of sav blanc and three glasses. A scowl has been stuck to her face since we arrived, and she's been short with me all day. She pours the wine and takes a slow sip, fixing me with a glare over the rim of her glass before placing it on the table. 'So, you're going out with this bloke now?'

I have the glass halfway to my mouth and my hand pauses mid-air. 'No, Caz, we're not going out. We went to the pub for some dinner, and we spoke through the week.' I take a swig, her vibe robbing me of the enjoyment I get from the first sip of wine on a Friday evening.

'And you're seeing him this weekend?' she says.

'Yeah. So?'

She breaks eye contact. 'Seems cosy.'

I look at Maddie for support, but she just smirks. Typical. She thrives on hook-up drama.

'So, you're straight now?' Caroline asks. She shifts so that her back is against the wall and she's facing the bar. And now I know for certain she's pissed off because this is what she does – positions herself so that she can control the eye contact.

'For goodness' sake, we've seen each other a couple of times outside the group.'

'Don't forget the kiss,' Maddie chimes in.

I shoot her a look. 'Yes, Maddie, thank you.' I turn back to Caroline. 'And that doesn't make me straight. People can be bi. Or pan, queer, sexually fluid, whatever. They don't have to be one thing. And they don't have to be labelled.' I snatch up my glass. 'Plenty of our friends are bi, including Zoe, so what's the issue?'

'They're not you,' Caroline says.

'What does that mean?' I ask, incredulous.

She rolls her eyes and faces me. 'Since when are you bi? Or pan? Or sexually fluid? I've known you for sixteen years and you've called yourself a lesbian since the first day we met. You've hardly ever talked about men in that way, other than the occasional "he's hot" over a celebrity or some bloke walking down the street.'

'I had a boyfriend when I was young and hooked up with guys at uni, you know that.' I shrug. 'Men haven't been in my life for a long time because I was with Mel.'

Caroline wrinkles her nose. 'One boyfriend for five minutes when you were eighteen, and you hooked up with two guys in your entire degree.'

'So my men history isn't extensive. I might've hooked up with a bloke more permanently if I was single. Who knows?'

Caroline shakes her head. 'No way. You like women too much.'

I peer at Maddie, who shrugs, before I turn back to Caroline. 'I do prefer the ladies, actually, and I still think of myself as a lesbian, but that doesn't mean I can't find a man attractive. There are no rules. And who are you to judge anyway? You've slept with men.'

'She's got you there,' Maddie says.

'That was a long, long time ago,' Caroline says.

'I remember the last one being after we graduated, so not that long ago,' I counter.

'You'll have to sleep with him if you keep seeing him. You'll have to touch it. You might even need to put it in your mouth. Have you thought about that?' Caroline's eyes are fiery tonight, and she watches me as she swills the wine around her glass.

I laugh. 'For god's sake.'

'Give it a rest, Caz,' Maddie says, shaking her head to indicate her own exasperation.

But she doesn't. 'Can you even remember what to do with one?'

'Yes, I can,' I say. 'And I don't think men are that bothered by technique. I'm pretty sure touching it is enough.'

Maddie snorts. 'Ha, yeah.'

I hadn't thought about the timing of when I would tell them about Luke, but an angry fire lights in my belly, and I want to shut Caroline up. 'Anyway, I've already touched it.'

Maddie chokes on her wine, and Caroline's eyes narrow as she assesses me.

'Well, well, well,' Maddie says, a sly smile spreading across her face.

'When?' Caroline asks.

'Saturday night,' I say, casually glancing around the bar.

Maddie leans forward and rests her forearms on the table.

'And you're only telling us now?' Caroline says.

I point at her. 'You were away for the weekend, and I've hardly seen you at work this week.' I point at Maddie. 'And you were with Zoe all weekend and I didn't want to say anything in front of her.'

'Aw, you do care about her. Sweet,' Maddie says sarcastically.

I stare at her, straight-faced. 'That's not fair. You know I do. That's why I keep away from her.'

Maddie pulls her chair forward and settles in with her wine, like she's about to watch a long-awaited movie. 'So, how was it?'

'For someone who isn't into men, you're very interested in what it's like to have sex with one,' Caroline says to her.

Maddie shrugs. 'I've never been there, have I?' She grins and fixes her gaze on me. 'Maybe I'm interested.'

'It was...' I peer upward while I search for the right word. Nice? Comforting? Frustrating? 'Different.' I pick up my glass.

'Different?' Caroline says, scrunching her face. 'Doesn't sound like it blew your mind.'

'Yeah, Ames, "different" doesn't sound too hot.' Maddie grins. 'Or did he get there too early?'

I scratch my forehead. 'He... ah... might have peaked before me.'

Caroline swipes up her glass with a satisfied smirk. 'Course he fucking did.'

'Give him a break. His wife's the only person he's had sex with in the past twenty years. And I'm not exactly experienced in the men department. It was fine. It's what we both wanted at the time.'

Maddie sits back, clearly disappointed. I guess she won't be giving that movie five stars. 'Sounds boring. And vanilla.'

'Erm, we were together for four years,' Caroline says to Maddie. 'Our sex life was vanilla by the end. Less than that. Flavourless.'

Maddie's eyes flame. 'And whose fault's that?'

Caroline's cheeks flush but her glower matches. 'Well, you fucked someone else, Maddie, so I'd say it's yours.'

Maddie's lips pinch before she shoots, 'And why did I fuck someone else?'

'Okay, you two, stop. I thought you'd dealt with this?' I say, motioning between them. I lean forward. 'Maybe Luke was really hot, and I'm leaving out the flavoured bits because it's none of your business.'

'Sure.' Maddie grins. 'It's hetero sex. I don't reckon it's that exciting.'

'Well, for a start you wouldn't know. And it's not hetero sex if I'm not hetero, is it?' I tilt my head and raise my eyebrows at her.

She grins. 'Fair point.'

Caroline runs her finger along the condensation of the ice bucket that sits in the middle of the table. 'So, you like this guy? Or is this another rebound?'

The comment stings and I glare at her before I answer. 'I like him. We understand each other.'

'You don't have to settle. Luke and Zoe aren't the only options you'll ever have,' Caroline says.

That sting cuts a little deeper. 'I'm not settling, Caz. This isn't serious. Jesus, what the fuck is wrong with you tonight?'

She shifts her gaze to the bar.

Maddie smirks. 'You know, Ames, if it's penetrative sex you're after, there's toys for that.' She takes a sip of her wine, eyes glinting.

I grin. 'I'm aware of that. And Zoe knows exactly where I keep them.'

Maddie laughs.

Caroline grunts and stands up. 'I need the bathroom.'

'Grab another bottle on your way back?' Maddie asks.

'Fine,' Caroline snaps before striding off.

It's busier in here now, And I lean forward so Maddie can hear me over the music and voices that have increased in volume. 'What's up with her?'

Maddie shrugs. 'Bad day at work?'

'That doesn't explain why she has such an issue with me being with a man.'

Maddie shakes her head. 'She doesn't care about that. She'll be worried about you and trying to figure it out. Think about it. You've spent your adult life with women, apart from the very occasional hook up with a guy. Caz has been there for all of that. You know she gets agitated with sudden change.'

I sigh and sit back.

'You have to admit, it's a bit out of left field,' Maddie says.

'Yeah, I get it, but it's confusing for me too. I don't need her giving me a hard time.'

Maddie places an elbow on the table, rests her chin on her fist and peers at me for a long moment. 'So, you're seeing him again this weekend?'

'Yep.'

'You know I don't care what you do, and I get why you've bonded with Luke, but is a sexual relationship with him what you want? Sometimes people do things out of the ordinary when they're struggling.'

Her comment rubs me the wrong way, but I don't want to argue with her as well. 'I don't know what I want. All I know is that we get each other.' I soften. 'And I'm okay, Mads. It's not a cry for help. We bonded, he's attractive and I was curious.'

She sits back and holds her hands up like some sort of peace offering. 'Fine. I'll drop it. We just want you to be happy and to look after yourself.'

I nod and give a weak smile.

Caroline returns and plonks another bottle of wine on the table.

'Thanks,' Maddie says, topping up our glasses. She points between Caroline and me. 'We all good now? You two going to play nice? Because if you don't, I'm going to talk to that woman over there who's giving me sexy vibes.' She jerks her head in the direction of the bar.

Caroline rolls her eyes.

I sweep the line of bodies perched at the bar. A woman with short auburn hair is casually glancing at Maddie. She is indeed giving her sexy vibes.

'You'll go and talk to her anyway,' I say.

Her eyes gleam. 'I will, but I won't ditch you two yet.'

The talk of her potentially picking up reminds me of something I've been meaning to ask. 'So, you and Zoe are spending a lot of time together.'

'We work together,' Maddie says dryly.

'I mean outside of work. Seems like every time I contact you lately, you're together. Something you want to tell us?'

Caroline widens her eyes at Maddie. '*You're* seeing Zoe now?'

Maddie sighs. 'I'm not seeing her.' She gives a nonchalant shrug. 'We hooked up.'

'What the fuck, Mads?' I say. 'That's all we need, a new thread in our lesbian spider web. Like we don't have enough.'

'We'd be letting the community down if we didn't spin new threads,' Maddie says, grinning. 'And she's hot.'

Caroline's still staring at Maddie. 'You're *sleeping* with Zoe?'

Maddie stares back. 'I've slept with her, yes. Will I sleep with her again?' She shrugs 'Maybe.'

'So, we're sharing her?' I snatch up my wine with a little more gusto than I anticipate, and a few drops splash onto my shirt. 'That's fucked up.'

Maddie looks displeased. 'You told her it was over weeks ago. And sounds like you've been busy anyway. What? You want to keep her handy just in case?'

I ignore the dig and dab my top with a napkin.

'I can't believe you're sleeping with Zoe,' Caroline says.

Maddie huffs. 'What am I supposed to do, Caz? Sit back hoping the perfect partner knocks on my door? It's nothing serious.' She glances towards the redhead.

'Oh, so you're picking up tonight? Zoe's available later then? Good to know,' I joke.

She smirks. 'I doubt she's available. We're not the only two people she's been sleeping with, you know.'

I didn't know. I take a sip of wine to mask my sulky pout. Caroline and Maddie are watching me, and their wry smiles tell me they've both picked up on it.

'Am I the only one not getting any?' Caroline says.

'Looks like it,' I say.

'And why aren't you? It's not like you'd have any trouble picking up,' Maddie says.

'Yeah, you're hot, smart, friendly,' I say.

'Passionate, feisty, caring,' Maddie adds.

'Okay, you two, enough,' Caroline says.

'What about that woman you went out with during the week for a drink?' Maddie says.

My head whips to Caroline, who's shooting Maddie daggers. 'What woman? So you can keep date secrets but I can't?'

Caroline sighs. 'It's nothing. It was just a drink.'

'She seems keen,' Maddie says. 'What's her name? Rachel?'

The boiling in my chest I had the day of that meeting is triggered. 'You are fucking kidding me. From the union? *That* Rachel?'

'It was a drink, Amy,' Caroline says sharply.

Maddie watches us open-mouthed, twisting her head back and forth slowly like she's one of those clowns in side-show alley, then realisation dawns. 'Oh, *that* Rachel. I didn't make the connection.' She sheepishly picks up her glass.

Things add up now. How preened Caroline was that day, blushing when I told her Rachel was staring at her arse. She was already interested. 'Did she message you on Insta to ask you out?'

Caroline nods but she doesn't look at me.

'You seriously like her? She's cold and intense, and you whinged for a month about how much she pissed you off,' I say, aware my voice is rising.

Maddie's eyes dart between us, a puzzled expression on her face.

'She's just passionate about her job, and yes, I do like her.' Caroline turns to me and spits, 'Is that alright with you?'

'Well, yeah. She doesn't seem your type, that's all.'

'And what's my type?'

I gesture to Maddie.

'I can have more than one type,' she snaps. 'In the same way that you can.'

She's always been a sucker for a pretty face and a hot body. She's become mixed up in bad relationships before this way. I shake my head. 'Thinking with your pussy again, Caz.'

Maddie snorts with laughter.

Caroline shoots me a filthy look. 'Oh, like that's not what you've been doing with Zoe for the past however long.'

'It's not actually. I happen to like her, which is why I ended it.' I point to my head. 'Thinking with this.'

She ignores me and addresses Maddie. 'And I don't know what you're laughing at. Like you don't do that with… oh, let's see…' She widens her eyes. 'Everyone.'

Maddie rolls her eyes and shifts her gaze back to the redhead.

I cast my mind back through the week. Caroline and I were messaging, and we spoke on Wednesday night, plus casual chats in the office. I can't think when she would've gone out. She would never normally keep something like this from me. She knows I'll give her a hard time because of the work connection. 'When did this happen?'

'I don't know, Amy, maybe it was around the time you were fucking Luke.'

'Caz! Jesus,' Maddie says.

She was away all weekend, so she's said this to deliberately stick the blade in. And it's worked because a darting pain shoots straight through my chest.

'I don't need your permission to go out for a drink,' she adds tartly.

I soften my approach. 'I know you don't. It's just that you're working with her on an employee dispute. These things can turn sour. It's unprofessional and it can go very wrong.'

A dark expression crosses her face. 'Says the woman who's had no boundaries for the past year.'

I gasp.

'For fuck's sake, Caz. Could you be any more of a cunt tonight?' Maddie says.

Caroline closes her eyes and releases a remorseful sigh. When she opens them, they're full of regret. But it's too late; the damage is done.

'Gee, Caz, I wonder why that is.' I squint to stop the tears. I need to get away from this conversation, and from her.

'Ames, I'm sorry, I...'

I stand and hold my hand up to halt her apology before barging my way through the crowd. In the bathroom, I lock myself in a toilet cubicle and press my palms to my eyes. I don't want to cry here and walk out with mascara streaming down a blotchy face. I take slow, deep breaths. Count to ten. Outside the door, I hear voices, laughter, taps running, the blast of hand dryers. I screw my eyes shut and block everything out.

After a few minutes, the tears retreat and my face cools. Caroline never acts like this unless something is wrong. I don't know what it is, but I can't function properly when we're out of sync. I emerge from the cubicle, splash some cold water on my cheeks and return to our table.

Maddie and Caroline are deep in conversation, and I can tell by the angry crease in Maddie's brow that she's giving Caroline a hard time. I sit and pour a drink.

'I'm sorry, Ames. I didn't mean it,' Caroline says, with genuine regret.

Maddie stares at her like she's waiting for her to continue. When Caroline doesn't speak, Maddie says, 'And?'

Caroline sighs. 'And I'm sorry for the comments about Luke. I don't have an issue with you being with him. It was unexpected, that's all. I just...' She shrugs. 'Worry and want you to be okay.'

I nod. 'And I have no right to lecture you about relationships or who you have a drink with. I'm sorry, too. Ignore me.'

She offers a tiny smile, but a sad aura surrounds her, and I feel like another little part of me has been chipped off.

The three of us make stilted conversation for another ten minutes or so before Maddie heads to the bar and Caroline says she's going home. She stands to leave and pauses by the end of the table. I could leave with her, share a cab, but I don't want to.

'I'm going to finish my drink,' I say. 'I'll call you on the weekend.'

She stares at me a second before she walks out. As soon as she's gone, the wine tastes sour and I don't want to be here. It's noisy and crowded, and I'm drowning in loneliness.

Maddie's already cosy with the redhead, so I send her a quick message to say goodnight. When I walk outside, Caroline is leaning against the brick wall, arms crossed. I settle beside her. 'Share a cab with me?'

She nods.

I slide my arm across her shoulders and pull her close. I catch a waft of the Chanel perfume I gave her for Christmas – jasmine and patchouli. It always smells great on her.

She rests her head on my shoulder and wraps her arm around my waist. 'I'm so sorry,' she says. 'I didn't mean it.'

'I know.' Some of the cogs that clicked out of place earlier slot back to where they belong, but something's still off. She tilts her face upward and I feel her warm breath on my lips. My mouth turns dry. I drop my arm and push off the wall. 'Let's get that cab, hey,' I say, stepping forward as one comes towards us.

There's a heavy sigh behind me, and she walks around the back of the cab to hop in the other side. We peer out our respective windows as the northern suburbs blur past and voices on a talkback radio station drone on about the day's news events.

'You wanna come up for a cuppa?' I ask when we stop at my place. 'Something to eat?'

She looks defeated and moisture forms in the corner of her eye. 'No. I'm good.'

'Caz?'

'I'm tired. Been a long day. I want to go home.'

I don't want us to end the night like this, but I know not to press her. 'Okay. Speak soon?'

'Yep,' she says, turning away quickly.

I jump out and stand on the footpath watching the cab disappear around the corner. *What the hell just happened?*

Chapter Ten

The dusk sky above Bramble Bay is a perfect blend of pale blue and burnt orange, turning the wispy blanket of clouds the same vivid pink as Mel's favourite lily. The salty air mingles with the scent of onions and sausages that Luke is cooking on the BBQ. Ben, Luke's younger brother, and his partner, Chris, are here along with Luke's kids. Cody is focussed on his laptop, and Jenna alternates between her phone and fixing me with hostile glares. The kids are more Sarah than Luke. They both have her black hair and olive skin, but Jenna has Luke's deep-set eyes, and Cody has his height and smile – even the same tiny gap between his two front teeth.

Despite Jenna's glares, this is the best I've felt all year. By best, I mean the flytrap is staying closed that little bit longer. I'm not as fragile or erratic as I was at the end of last year, and not as on edge as when I started therapy again in January. Luke and I have spent time together the past two weekends and we speak often during the week. Even the sex is better – less awkward, at least. He's kept his appointments with Dr Garcia, but when I ask about them, he changes the subject.

Caroline and I are both pretending that strange night at the Wickham Hotel never happened, but there's been a disturbance in our dynamic bubbling underneath ever since. The dispute she's been working on with Rachel is coming to an end, which means the personal side of their relationship is on, according to Maddie.

I glance across to the beach. It's still light enough to see the joggers, dog walkers and bike riders move along the esplanade. The tide is in, and the gentle swish of the water licking the rocks carries on the breeze. It's calming until the high-pitched screech of the rainbow lorikeets starts. Jenna's been muttering comments under her breath all afternoon. I can only assume they're meant for me since they accompany daggers in my direction, but she keeps her voice low and only does it when everyone is talking.

'Did you drive over, Amy?' Ben asks.

I'm about to reply that Luke picked me up, when Jenna says, still staring at her phone, 'Why are you here anyway, this is a *family* dinner.' Then her eyes, flaming beneath perfectly shaped black eyebrows, flick up to me.

Ben and Chris gape at her, but Luke doesn't seem to hear over the sound of the sizzling BBQ.

Cody, who I don't realise is listening because he's so engrossed in his laptop, says, 'Stop being such a bitch, Jenna.'

Luke spins around, tongs in hand. 'What's goin' on?'

'She's being a bitch, Dad. Someone has to tell her,' Cody says, eyes blazing at his sister.

'Fuck off, you little fag,' Jenna spits.

Time freezes while that comment hangs in the air. Cody ignores her, but his cheeks flush and he stares at his screen. I'm wide-eyed in shock. Ben and Chris' mouths drop open while Luke's face turns thunderous.

He calmly puts down the tongs, reduces the heat on the BBQ and walks over to her. 'What did you just say?' His voice is composed, but the fury in his tone is unmistakable.

Her cheeks turn scarlet, but she stands, looks Luke straight in the eyes and says, 'I said, "Fuck. Off. You. Little. Fag."'

Now Luke's face turns red. 'Don't *ever* use that word in this house. And I hope to god you don't use it anywhere.' His voice rises. 'Since when do you speak like that?'

'Well, he is one and he needs to fuck off.'

'Jenna! Enough! Do not speak to Cody like that. And you've been rude to Amy. Apologise to both of them, or I'll... I'll turn off that bloody Wi-Fi, and you won't be using the car to get your driving hours up.'

Jenna's face crumples, and she stares at Luke like she expects him to cave. He fixes her with a stern look and crosses his arms.

I take a sip of my drink and check what the lorikeets are up to.

Jenna races upstairs, a door slamming a minute later.

'Awkies,' Ben mumbles, with a wince in my direction.

Chris jumps up and takes charge of the BBQ.

Luke shakes his head, mutters 'teenagers' and sits beside Cody. 'You okay, mate? Why is Jenna saying stuff like that?'

Cody stares at his laptop. 'It's nothing.'

'It's obviously not nothing. What is it?'

'Nothing, Dad. Don't worry about it.'

'Cody,' Luke says firmly.

Cody picks at the faded print on his T-shirt. 'Just something that happened at school yesterday.'

'Alright. What?'

Cody brushes the thick, dark hair from his eyes. 'Some of the year eleven guys were hassling a trans kid. I didn't like what they were saying to him, so I had a go at them and told them to stop. Ever since, they've been calling me a fag.' He taps his keyboard.

'Oh. Right. Well, good on you for sticking up for him.' Luke pauses. 'This only happened yesterday, not before?'

Cody hesitates a few seconds. 'It's happened before, yeah.'

Luke sighs. 'Why didn't you say anything? I need to talk to someone at the school about this.'

'No, Dad. Don't. I can handle it.' He peers up at Luke. 'And you've got your own stuff to deal with,' he adds softly.

Luke closes his eyes and swallows back the knot I know will be lodged in his throat. 'Codes, you can't worry about that. You've got to tell me when things are going on. And it still doesn't explain why Jenna said that to you.'

''Cause she's hanging out with Noah and he's a fuckhead.'

Ben and I both suppress a laugh.

'Oi, language,' Luke says, turning to us and shaking his head. 'Noah?' Luke frowns. 'Hasn't Jenna been going to his place to study for the biology exam?'

I grimace. *Oh, Luke. So naïve.*

'They're studying *biology* alright,' Cody scoffs.

Luke closes his eyes again, his jaw tightening. 'Anything else you want to tell me? Any other reason Jenna is saying that?'

Cody shakes his head. 'Nuh.'

'You sure? Because if there is, it's okay.'

Cody's eyes flit around, then he glowers at Luke. 'I'm not gay, Dad, if that's what you're thinking.'

Luke holds up his hand. 'It's okay if you—'

'I know it's okay; but I'm not. God, you're as bad as the kids at school. Being friends with a trans guy doesn't make you gay. And he's not even gay.' Cody's voice starts to tremble. 'If people bothered talking to him, they'd know that. I just didn't like what they were saying to him.'

'I don't think... I'm sorry. I was just asking a question.' He ruffles Cody's hair. 'Proud of you.'

Cody pushes his hand away. 'Don't.' He snatches up his laptop and heads into the lounge.

'Codes...' Luke stares after him, then sighs heavily. 'I better go see

Jenna.' As he passes, he puts his hand on my shoulder. 'Sorry about this. I won't be long. Don't go anywhere.'

He looks so vulnerable and lost. I wish I could do more to help him, but I have no words of wisdom for dealing with teenagers who've lost their mum. I gently squeeze his hand. 'I won't.'

Ben reaches across the table and pulls the wine bottle from the ice bucket. 'God, the drama,' he says, and tops up our glasses.

Chris reduces the heat on the BBQ and joins us. 'And you love it.'

'I don't. I don't like seeing Luke dealing with this alone. Has he talked to you much about the kids, Amy?'

'Not really.' I glance inside to check that Cody is still watching TV and lower my voice. 'He said he thought something might've been going on with Cody at school. And that Jenna is angry all the time, but that's it.'

Ben nods. 'That's all he's said to me, too. Maybe he talks to his psych about it?'

'I'm sure he does,' I say for Ben's benefit, but I'm not certain I believe that.

'I hope so,' Ben says, jumping up. 'I'll set the table for dinner.'

I help Ben while Chris finishes cooking the meat. We chat easily; they don't ask about therapy or my circumstances, although Luke's told me he's spoken to them about it, and I'm grateful. By the time Luke returns, the sausages are well fired, and the steak is well-done.

Luke drags a chair over and sits close to me. He rubs my thigh. 'I'm sorry you had to be here for this. And sorry she spoke to you like that.'

'It's fine. I understand,' I say. I'm an adult still struggling with a loss after more than a year. I can't imagine what it must be like for a teenager.

'I know she's had support at school,' Ben says. 'But maybe you should take her to someone else – a counsellor? Or a psychologist?'

Luke nods. 'Yeah. Maybe.' He leans over and strips the cling film off the salads. 'Let's have dinner, ay.'

*

A couple of hours later, Ben and Chris have left, and Cody has retreated to his room. Jenna appeared briefly to make herself a sausage sandwich and went back upstairs.

Luke and I are still outside. It's been a balmy evening, but the temperature has dropped, and the breeze is cool on my skin. Luke pulls me close, and I bury my head in the crook of his neck. His earthy scent and the brush of his stubble are becoming more familiar.

'You cold?' he murmurs.

'Little bit.' I lift my head to kiss him. It warms me despite his nose and lips being cool.

'Oh, you want me to warm you up like that?' he says, smiling.

I give a low laugh. 'No. Not with the kids here. I'm worried what your family thinks. Must be weird for them – you having someone here.'

'Nah, you're worrying about nothing. Cody and Jenna… well, they're teenagers. Who knows what they think? And Ben and Chris don't care. I can tell they like you.'

'You think so?'

'Yep.'

He seems calmer now, so I take it as an opening to ask about earlier. 'You okay about what happened before? With the kids?'

He shifts his gaze to the ocean. He must torture himself every time he looks out there. After a few seconds, he says, 'Yeah. They're always at each other. Nothing new.' He rubs my arm and gives me a reassuring smile.

'Are you going to talk to someone at the school about Cody?'

He scratches the side of his face. 'Um. I'll speak to him more about it tomorrow.'

'Have you checked any of his social media?' I ask.

Luke's brows furrow. 'Oh. No. I didn't think of that. Should I?'

I nod.

He screws his eyes shut like it's all too much. 'I've got no idea where to start with all this stuff.'

My heart aches for how lost he is. I'm not entirely sure how to help him, but I am good at cyberstalking. I sit up. 'Do you know what social media he uses?'

He shakes his head 'You're into that stuff, can you look? And search Jenna, too? I'm worried what she's up to with this Noah kid.'

'I can, but kids these days use different platforms. They're unlikely to be on Facebook or Twitter. And they're usually smart enough not to post anything publicly on Instagram.' He stares at me like I'm speaking a long-lost language. 'Okay, I'll try.' I grab my phone and search for 'Cody Harris' and 'Jenna Harris' across various platforms but only find their Instagram accounts, which are the usual teenage selfies with mates. 'Not much here.'

'Righto. Thanks.' His eyes glaze over then, and he yawns.

I take that as a hint to leave and stand. 'I should go and let you get to bed.'

'What?' He pulls me back to him. 'Why? Don't go.'

'Well, I'm tired and you worked today. You must be exhausted.'

'I am, but you don't need to leave. Stay here with me.' He brushes his lips against my temple.

'I'd like to. I just don't want to make things harder for you and Jenna.'

He shakes his head. 'Don't worry about that. She'll come 'round. Besides, you probably won't see her tomorrow. She's got plans with her friends and Cody has a game on in the morning.'

I want to be with him and Saturday nights at home alone are tough. 'If you're sure?'

'Yep.' He stands and holds out his hand. 'Come on, let's go before we fall asleep out here.'

*

The following morning, Luke and I are on the way to my place in his work van. He's not working since it's a Sunday and has offered to look at my backyard.

'How was Jenna this morning?' I ask as we near my place. I didn't wake until nine, and Jenna and Cody had already left, but I wanted to build up to the topic.

Luke shrugs. 'She was talking to me. She kind of said sorry. As much as a sorry as I'm going to get.'

'You think maybe she needs to see someone?' I probe gently, revisiting Ben's comment from last night.

'Dunno. I mentioned it to her. She just shrugged it off and said it was her hormones. Time of the month or something. She knows I never have a comeback for that.'

I smile. 'Yep, I've used that more than once myself.'

We pull into my driveway, and he cuts the engine. I head for the stairs, but he starts walking around the side of the house straight to the backyard.

'Oh, you don't want to come upstairs first? Have a coffee or something?'

He tilts his head towards the backyard. 'I can have one out there, can't I?'

'Sure, I'll bring you one down.'

I head upstairs and dump my bag on the couch, taking a minute to run my hand over Mel's urn. My body relaxes as I feel that instant connection with her spirit. 'I'm home,' I say. I head to the kitchen, switch the jug on and watch Luke out the window. He has his hands on his hips and is glancing around at the various plants and weeds in the garden bed. I remember the therapy session where he said he only feels okay when he's at work, when he can dig and slash and pull, and I wonder if his eagerness to get into the yard is his way of coping.

I make his coffee and take it downstairs. 'So, what do you think?' I ask, passing the mug.

'It's not too bad.' He motions his finger along the garden bed in front of him. 'You've got some nice plants here you should keep.' He points to a bare area along the back fence. 'Over there would be a good place for some small plants. I can get you some low maintenance ones, like bottlebrushes and succulents.' His eyes are alive in a way they weren't earlier. 'I can set up a reticulation system for you, too, so you don't have to think about how often to water everything.'

'Great. I never know when I'm supposed to water, so go for it.' I fold my arms. 'Hang on. I reckon you'd be expensive. How much is all this going to cost?'

He grins. 'Reckon I can give you a hefty discount. Or you can always pay me in kind.' He winks.

I smirk. 'You're pimping yourself out now? Or are you pimping me out? I'm confused.'

He laughs and looks around me to the driveway. 'I think you've got a visitor.'

I spin around to see Maddie's RAV. 'Oh, it's Maddie. Back in a minute.'

As I approach the car, I notice that Caroline is with her.

'Hi,' Caroline says as she hops out.

Maddie hits the lock button on the key fob. 'Hey, Ames.'

'Hi. Why are you here?' I look between them. 'Together.'

'We're not back together if that's what you're thinking,' Caroline says.

Maddie smiles. 'Caz's new *girlfriend* has let her loose for the day and she's helping me with renos. We need more paint. Saw your car and thought we'd stop in.'

'Shut up, Maddie. She's not my girlfriend. And I'm allowed to do what I want.'

'If you say so,' Maddie says.

I don't like what I'm hearing, but Caroline's dour expression sends a clear message that this is a no-go topic. Instead, I say, 'You saw my car? You didn't notice the work van?'

They both shrug.

'You're not here to see me. You're here to check out Luke. Come on, he's out the back.'

Luke's sipping his coffee and assessing the weeds, deep concentration on his face.

'Well, well,' Maddie says, her voice low. 'Who's a hottie then?'

Caroline squints as she assesses him. 'He's alright, I guess.'

'Hey, Luke,' I call.

He flashes us a smile. He looks rugged and handsome in his tight T-shirt, shorts and work boots.

'This is Maddie and Caz,' I say, pointing out who's who.

'Hi, Luke. Nice to meet you,' Caroline says, sticking out her hand. Her pleasant tone and relaxed body language immediately put me at ease.

'And you,' he says, shaking her hand.

'And I'm Maddie.' She gives him a friendly smile and shakes his hand.

'G'day, Maddie. I've heard a lot about you both. Amy's always telling me what good friends you are.'

'Aw, that's sweet,' Caroline says.

'We love you, too, Ames,' Maddie says and then addresses Luke. 'So, is it beyond repair out here?' She jerks her thumb in my direction. 'She's pretty useless in the garden.'

Luke shakes his head. 'Nah. The lawn is good. Just need to sort out these garden beds. Maybe put a few new plants back there.' He points to the back fence.

Maddie nods. 'Right. You know, I could do with some work at my place. I might get your details and set up a time?'

'Great,' Luke says.

'Watch him, his payment terms are dubious,' I say.

Luke grins. 'Reckon I can sort something standard for Maddie.'

Maddie's brows draw together in confusion, and Caroline's eyes dart between Luke and me.

'Do you want to stick around for lunch?' I ask them.

Maddie shakes her head. 'No, thanks. Want to get this painting finished today. We'll leave you to it.'

'We just wanted to say hi,' Caroline says.

They say bye to Luke, and I walk them back to the car.

'He's nice, Ames,' Maddie says.

'Yeah, he is.'

I wait for a similar comment from Caroline, but one doesn't come.

She jumps in the passenger seat and slides down the window. 'See you at work tomorrow.'

I peer at her trying to work out what she's thinking, but she's a pro at keeping emotions in check. 'Let's go for lunch or something,' I say.

She nods. 'Sounds good.'

As Maddie's car disappears around the corner, a sudden wave of longing for the life we all used to have hits me, and I have to stop myself from running after them.

Chapter Eleven

I'm en route to my office when Vanessa, the assistant manager from finance, and Paul step into the corridor and head towards the lift, their backs to me. Vanessa adjusts the waistband of her pants while Paul strides ahead, like the pig that he is. It's the first time I've seen them together for months, and it triggers a memory I'd buried deep.

It was last December, and I was about to leave work when I realised I didn't have my phone. I headed to the meeting room, where I'd been with Paul and some staff from finance, and threw open the door to find Paul and Vanessa pressed together. Paul's face turned beetroot as he fumbled to do up his belt, and Vanessa sheepishly did up her top buttons. I grabbed my phone off the chair and fled. Vanessa cornered me the next day to ask me to keep quiet. I glared at her and said, 'My wife's dead, Vanessa. Do you think I care what you and Paul are up to?'

I can't believe I'd forgotten about their little fling. But I'd been drinking heavily in December and that time is hazy. I slip into my office and boot up my PC. I can't dissect this right now. I need to finish up and get to Mum and Dad's to see my nephews who are visiting for the Easter holidays. I'm about to return to the departmental budget when I hear Caroline's voice.

'Hey.'

'Hi,' I say, without looking at her. 'What's up?'

'I just need to know if you're presenting at the training on Monday. Or is it Daniel?'

My eyes stay fixed on the monitor. If I'm honest, I'm a little pissed with her. She cancelled our lunch on Monday, and I messaged her to come to my parents' tonight, but she didn't bother her arse replying.

Before I can answer, she says, 'How did you get that? I've asked Paul for my team's budget, and he keeps making excuses not to give it to me.'

I spin in my chair to reply, but don't expect her to look so fresh at the end of the day and my words stall. She's wearing that soft shade of red lipstick again, and her hair is perfectly styled. She's obviously going out, and my heart sinks because I know nothing about it. 'That's probably because I haven't finished working on it yet.'

She scrunches her face. 'What? Why are you doing it?'

I shrug. 'Paul delegated it to me, and I thought I shouldn't push back with everything that's going on.'

She shakes her head. 'Amy, this is a departmental budget. For all of HR. It's Paul's job, and Greg specifically asked him to do this himself. I was in the room when they were talking about it.'

Greg is the company's CEO.

I huff. 'Well, I've nearly finished now.'

'He's taking the piss, getting you to do all his work.' She puts her hands on her hips. 'This is what he used to do. You're not his exec assistant. You're a senior manager with your own operations to run.'

Mel used to tell me off for the same thing. I throw my hands up. 'What am I supposed to do? I say no and he says I'm not cutting it.'

'He's giving you all of his work, though. That's not on. You've carried him for too long.' Caroline waves her finger and nods slowly like something has just occurred to her. 'This is why he's being an arse. You haven't been doing his work as much as you used to. I wondered why Greg was making a point of him doing stuff himself.' She grins. 'He must be slipping.'

'You think that's it?'

'Yep,' she says.

'Well, that and the thing with Vanessa,' I say.

'Ugh.' She rolls her eyes. 'Is that still going on?'

'Uh huh. I just saw them leaving his office. I forgot all about it. When I think about it, he started being an even bigger prick after I caught them.'

Caroline nods. 'That makes sense.'

I suddenly remember I'm annoyed at her. 'Daniel will do the training.' I turn back to my screen. 'I'm almost done here, and I've got to get to Mum and Dad's to see the boys.'

'Ollie and Finn are here?'

'Yep.' I bash at my keyboard.

'And you didn't tell me?'

I spin to face her. 'I sent you a message yesterday asking if you wanted to come tonight. You didn't reply.'

She frowns. 'I didn't get a message. Of course I want to see them.'

I narrow my eyes.

'Ames, seriously.' She pulls her phone from her pants pocket and scrolls. 'I didn't get that message.' She shows me the screen. 'See. This is your last message.'

I instantly soften. 'Oh. Sorry. I'm sure I sent it.'

'So, that's why you've been short with me today?'

'No.'

Her brows rise.

'Okay, maybe a bit. You want to come? Mum and Dad won't mind the late notice.'

She grimaces. 'I'd love to, but I've made plans with Rachel.' She glances at her watch. 'She's probably already on her way, so I can't cancel now.'

'Oh.' I turn back to my PC. 'Never mind.'

She pokes my arm. 'Hey, what about tomorrow?'

I shrug. 'Maybe.'

She leans forward so I have no choice but to look at her. 'You could all come over for a barbie or something? Maddie can come, watch the footy with your dad and Josh. The boys and Soph can swim. Your mum loves my cooking.' She pulls out the big, round puppy dog eyes and pouted bottom lip.

I push her away. 'Alright, get out of my grill.' But I get a little rush of satisfaction. 'That sounds nice. I'll check with them.'

'Great. Text me later and let me know what they say. I'd better go.'

'Um... have a nice time tonight.' The words are strained, and my throat is scratchy.

A corner of her mouth lifts.

'What? I'm trying to be nice here.'

'Uh huh. Then why do you look like you're in pain?'

I give her a shove. 'Get lost. I do not. Go on, get out of here. I've got work to do.'

But she doesn't move. 'Is... Luke going with you tonight?'

I scrunch my nose. 'It's a bit soon for "meet the Campbells."'

She shrugs. 'Is it?'

'No. I haven't invited him.'

She gives a single nod. 'See ya.'

'Bye.'

I stare after her, wishing she'd come back. I feel that I need to save her, like letting her go out with Rachel is feeding her to the wolves. Or maybe I don't like that our lives are changing, moving in different directions, and there's nothing I can do to stop it.

*

By the time I arrive at Mum and Dad's, I'm frazzled, and my muscles feel tight. I've been stewing about the Paul thing since I left work, and I can't shake the thought that Caroline chose Rachel over my family. Over me. I was already on edge after a week of juggling life – work, runs with Maddie, helping Luke set up fake TikTok accounts to check on the kids, and an uncomfortable therapy session with Dr Sachdev on Wednesday where he interrogated me about my new relationship – so I didn't need more stress today.

I put the wine I've brought on the kitchen table and wrap my arms around Dad. 'Hi, Dad.'

He pats my back as he returns the hug. 'G'day, love. How are you?'

'Okay. How's the back holding up?'

'Good. Plenty of life left in me yet.'

He keeps weeding despite complaining about pain daily, and Mum said he's been in agony the past few weeks, so I know this isn't true. 'You been to a doctor?'

'I am a doctor, love.'

That's Dad's answer to every ailment he has. He thinks because he's a retired GP, he never needs to see a doctor.

'Hmm, if you say so.' I head over to Mum who's peeling potatoes on the other side of the bench and hug her. 'Hi, Mum.'

'Hello, darling. Lovely to see you.'

I cling on a little longer than I normally would, my shoulders relaxing. I pull away and gesture to the table. 'Brought some wine for dinner.'

'Thank you,' she says, rubbing my upper arm. 'Caroline couldn't make it?'

'Nope. She's busy.' I pinch a carrot from the chopping board and crunch into it. 'Where's everyone else?'

'They're on their way from the airport,' Mum says, swatting my hand away as I reach for another strip of carrot.

'You need help?' I ask.

'No, I'm fine.' She smiles at me, which means I'm off the hook until dishes.

Dad's at the table eyeing up the wine. 'This looks a good-un. What's the occasion?'

I walk back over to him. 'No occasion, Dad, just thought I'd get something nice.'

'Too early to open it?' he asks.

Mum tuts. 'Will it kill you to wait until everyone arrives, Bob?'

'It might,' he says, giving me a wink.

He groans as he bends down to grab a couple of red wine glasses from the cabinet, and we settle ourselves at the kitchen table while Mum starts on the pumpkin.

There's a loud knock at the front door, followed by a scurry of voices and footsteps, before Josh, Sophie, Ollie and Finn appear.

I give a little squeal and smother Ollie and Finn with bear hugs and kisses. 'Missed you two.'

'Missed you, too, Aunty Amy,' they both say, trying to break free.

Sophie and Josh are only four years older than me, but they married and had the boys in their early twenties. We all thought they were too young at the time, but it's worked out well for them.

They all get their 'can I help' out of the way with Mum before they join Dad and me. Josh grabs some glasses from the cupboard, pours a white wine for Sophie and Mum, then helps himself to a large glass of the red I'd brought with me.

'Help yourself, Josh. Didn't you just walk in with beers?' I say.

'Yeah, but then I saw this beauty. Thanks, sis.' He gives me a cheeky grin and holds his glass up.

Mum peers over the top of her glasses and tuts. 'Use a coaster, Josh, you'll mark the nice tablecloth.'

Mum only uses this tablecloth for special occasions. She had her eye on it for ages before it finally appeared in a half-price sale. It's a top-quality white linen with an intricate pattern of birds and willow trees in navy. It blends well with the blues they have scattered through the tiles and artwork in here.

We talk for a while about the boys' lives at Sydney University and Mum and Dad's social events – cards, lunches, beach outings – and it's lovely. I can literally feel myself sink into the chair as the tension leaves me.

Ollie, my youngest nephew, who's nineteen, shifts off topic. 'Caz is on Insta a lot these days.'

'Is she?' I've seen the odd cute couple photo, despite it being very early days. All on Rachel's profile with Caroline tagged. They obviously haven't had the conversation about how much Caroline hates cutesy couple posts. I scratch my neck. 'Hadn't noticed.'

'Yeah. Her new girlfriend's hot,' Ollie says.

Sophie shoots him a disapproving look. 'Ollie.'

He shrugs. 'She is.'

'I hope you're not getting off on that, you little perv,' I say.

He screws up his face. 'As if. Caz is, like, forty or something ancient.'

Sophie shakes her head. 'She's thirty-five, hardly ancient.'

'Bro, that's weird,' says Finn, the twenty-one-year-old.

'What is?' Ollie says.

'You think Caz's girlfriend is hot, but she looks like Aunty Amy.' Finn chuckles. 'You can't tell me you haven't noticed?'

Josh laughs. 'No way. Give us a look.' He holds out his hand for someone's phone.

I grunt and grab my wine. 'We look nothing alike, thank you.'

Josh scrolls Ollie's phone. 'Yeah, she does. Hey, Soph, check this out.'

Sophie leans over, looks at the screen, then up at me, then back to the screen. 'Mmm. Maybe a bit, I guess.'

'We both have long, brown hair. That's where the similarity ends.' I remember my hairdresser's colour description. 'Besides, she's dull

117

brown. I'm rich chestnut.'

Sophie smirks.

Josh looks at the photo again. 'I dunno, your eyes are kind of similar.'

I huff. 'They're not. Hers are frosty grey. Mine are pure green, and you're colour blind anyway.'

'That's nice Caz has met someone,' Sophie says. 'What's she like?'

I swirl my wine. 'Not my cup of tea.' I take a swig. 'Or Maddie's,' I add quickly. I'm not the only one who has an issue with her.

'You don't sound too keen on her, sis. Not jealous, are you?' Josh says.

I curl my top lip. 'Why would I be jealous?'

He shrugs. 'Dunno. You just don't seem very happy about it.'

I sigh and opt not to bite.

'Anyway, not your type these days, ay?' Josh says, with a dumb grin. They know about Luke, but I haven't told Mum and Dad yet.

I fix him with a death stare, and Sophie digs him in the ribs.

'Dinner's ready,' Mum calls, saving me from further scrutiny.

We all jump up, serve our plates and settle back at the table. Dad tops up our glasses, Mum passes around the gravy and we tuck into our meal, listening to Josh and Dad drone on about the football tomorrow.

'Speaking of footy, I asked Caz to come tonight, but she couldn't make it—'

Ollie cuts me off. 'She's out with Rachel in the city. Saw it on Insta.'

My jaw clenches. 'How did you see it?'

He shrugs. 'I follow Rachel now because I thought she was Caz's new girlfriend. Didn't know you had beef with her.'

'I don't have beef with her. And she's not Caz's new girlfriend – they've just started seeing each other,' I snap.

Ollie widens his eyes. 'Geez. Sor-ry.'

I apply some pressure to my temple where a dull thud has developed. 'As I was saying, since Caz couldn't make it, she asked if you all want to go to her place for a barbie tomorrow arvo. Maddie will probably come – you can watch the footy, swim.'

'Sounds lovely,' Mum says. 'She can show me how she makes that watermelon salad.'

Dad beams. 'Caz has that big telly out on the deck.'

'Excellent,' Josh says. 'Beers, pool, footy, Caz's cooking. Bewdy.'

Sophie looks at him, unimpressed. 'You'll be getting off your arse to help, not being waited on with your feet up.'

He gives her a wink and rubs the back of her neck affectionately.

I grab my phone and shoot a quick message to Caroline to tell her we'll all be there tomorrow.

Mum brings the conversation back to me. 'So, how are you really, darling?'

I shrug. 'I feel okay.'

'How's the sessions with Dr Sachdev?' Dad asks. 'Still weekly?'

I nod. 'For now.'

'Are you...' Mum pauses and takes a bite of potato. 'Back on the scene. Met a nice woman, a potential partner?'

The shock of Mum's question makes me almost choke on my pumpkin. 'Since when have you been interested in my love life?'

She feigns surprise. 'Don't be silly. I've always been interested. I don't like to think of you being alone, that's all. Beautiful young lady like yourself. You've got a lot to offer.'

Josh is hooking into the roast beef, washing it down with my red wine, shaking his head and smiling.

Sophie winces.

'No, Mum. No woman on the scene. Thanks for asking.'

'What about that lovely one you were seeing a while ago? What was her name? Zoe? She's adorable.'

'She's adorable alright,' Finn mutters.

'Finn,' Sophie warns.

I stare at Mum. She has never referred to one of my partners as 'adorable', even Mel whom they loved and was actually adorable. 'Yes, she is, but we're not seeing each other.'

'Oh, why not?' Mum asks.

I cut into the beef. 'It just didn't work.'

'Think you might be barkin' up the wrong tree, Mum.' Josh shoves a roast potato into his big gob.

'Josh,' Sophie says sternly.

Mum looks confused. 'What do you mean the wrong tree?'

'Ignore him,' I say.

'Why don't you tell us why there's no woman on the scene, Ames,' Josh says.

'Don't be a dickhead,' I say.

'Enough, you two. You're like teenagers sometimes. What's he talking about, Amy?' Mum asks.

I sigh. 'I have been seeing someone.'

'Oh, but you said—'

'I'm seeing Luke.'

Dad turns to me, eyes wide.

Ollie and Finn look at each other with a grin and go back to their dinner.

Mum puts her hand to her chest. 'Luke? That's a man's name.'

'Yes. Luke's a man,' I say.

'I'm confused. Is he transgender?' Mum says.

Josh stares at her. 'What?'

'Mum! Don't throw assumptions like that around, and why on earth would you assume that anyway?' I say.

'Well, I don't know.' She throws a hand up. 'You're lesbian.'

'Oh my god, Mum!' I drop my cutlery and push my fingers into my forehead. 'That doesn't mean any man I'm with is transgender. That's not how it works.'

'Well, how can you be lesbian if you're seeing a man?' she says, with genuine confusion.

'It's very new. We like each other. He lost his wife, too.'

'He lost his wife? Oh, you've mentioned a Luke before, from the group. Is that him?'

I nod and continue eating.

She still looks perplexed. 'Well, how serious is it? Are you just very good friends?'

'It's not that serious, but we're more than friends.'

'More than friends?' she asks, dipping her head and peering over the top of her glasses.

Dad has his head down, rapidly scooping up his peas.

'Are you...' Mum clears her throat. 'Having sleepovers?'

The boys chuckle.

I screw up my face. 'Mum!'

'It's none of your business, Helen,' Dad says.

'Well, I'm trying to work things out here. I'm confused. How serious is it?' she says, exasperated.

I sigh. 'Yes, Mum. We're having sleepovers.'

Dad shakes his head. 'I think we'd better open another bottle of wine.' He hops up, grabs the second bottle I brought and tops up our glasses.

'But you're lesbian, darling,' Mum says as though it's something I've temporarily forgotten.

'Well, right now, I like Luke. It doesn't mean I'm no longer attracted to women or no longer a lesbian. I just happen to like this particular person at this point in my life.'

'But... I've joined a group,' she says, a touch of hurt creeping into her voice.

Dad rolls his eyes.

Josh laughs and Sophie covers her lips to hide her smile.

'What do you mean? What group?' I say, taking a sip of wine.

'PFLAG. Oh, sorry, PFLAG plus.' She tsks herself. 'I must remember the plus.'

I gag on my wine. 'PFLAG?'

'Yes, darling. It stands for Parents and Friends of Lesbians and Ga—'

'I know what it stands for. I don't understand why you've joined. Now. After I've been out since I was twenty.' My voice rises.

She looks offended. 'It hasn't been easy for us either. We loved Mel, too, you know. It's been hard watching you hurt so badly. I wanted to support you.'

'Oh, Mum,' I sigh. 'You can keep going to PFLAG and supporting me. I'm still a queer woman. I'm just seeing a man at the moment, that's all. It's not a big deal.'

'Queer. Yes. We talked about that term last week. A queer woman. Right.' She nods as though she's clarifying matters for herself. 'Well, tell us about Luke. Can we meet him?'

I push my plate to the side and pick up my glass. 'I'm not sure we're at the meeting parents stage yet.'

She holds her hands up. 'Fine. Can you at least tell us about him?'

'Um, I guess. He's forty-two. Lives in Sandgate. Runs his own landscape and gardening business. Sarah died in a car accident around the same time as Mel.'

Mum's hand flies to her chest. 'Oh, terrible shame.'

Dad gives my hand a supportive rub.

'He has two kids, Jenna and Cody.'

Mum's eyes widen and glow. 'He has children?'

Oh, god. Here we go. 'Yep.'

'How old?' Mum asks.

'Jenna's seventeen and Cody's fifteen.'

'You're going to be a stepmother? I'm going to have step grandchildren?'

I swear she's close to tears. 'For god's sake, Mum. I'm not their stepmother.'

I can see her thinking before a realisation settles on her face. 'Oh, my. You could have your own child. Your own biological child. You're only thirty-five.'

Dad cuts in. 'Bloody hell, Helen, talk about jumping the gun. She said it's not serious.'

'I'm not a stepmother, and I'm not having a baby with Luke. Besides, if I wanted my own biological child, I could have one without a man on the scene.'

'Oh, yes, I guess you could,' Mum says. 'Yes, we've talked about that at PFLAG. Sorry, darling, that wasn't very progressive of me.'

'Progressive? You?' I say.

She sniffs. 'Yes, me. I know about transgender and queers and rainbow families and pans and... oh.' She points at me. 'Maybe you're pansexual or bisexual, not lesbian after all.'

The tension in my shoulders is back and tighter than when I arrived. 'Why do I need to have a label?' I say through clenched teeth.

She places her palm against her chest. 'I'm not the one who labelled you lesbian, darling, that was all you.'

Dad looks at me. 'She's got a point there, love.'

I let out an exasperated sigh. 'Fine. Here's my label now. I'm a queer woman who happens to be seeing a man because I like him. Okay? Everyone happy?'

Sophie reaches across the table and gives my hand a squeeze. Josh is quiet, and I'm glad to see him hang his head guiltily.

'I reckon you've said enough, Helen. Give it a rest, ay,' Dad says.

Mum sniffs and hops up to make her usual after-roast cheeseboard. If only she'd shown this much interest in my sexuality years ago.

'So, how's Maddie and Caroline?' Dad says. 'It'll be good to see them tomorrow.'

'They're well. They say hi.'

'Real shame they broke up,' he says for about the tenth time since the split.

'Yeah, it is.'

'So, who's this woman on Caroline's date card?'

Date card. Jesus. What's with these two?

I knock back the remainder of my wine and slosh another helping into my glass. 'No one serious.'

Chapter Twelve

The fridge door slams shut, and I peer through the open bifold doors to see Jenna dressed to go out. Her long, black hair is straight and sleek; her make-up is all sultry eyes and glossy pink lips. She's wearing skinny black jeans and a tiny red T-shirt. I'm worried she'll get cold, and I have an urge to take off my cardigan and wrap it around her.

Luke jumps up and strides into the house. 'Where are you going?'

'Out,' she says, unplugging her phone from the charger on the kitchen bench.

'Out where?'

'With friends.'

'What friends?'

She ignores him.

'Jenna! What friends?'

She whips around and fixes him with a defiant glare. 'Kate and Emma. That okay?'

'No, it's not bloody okay. Not after the way you acted today.'

'The way I acted? What about the way your *girlfriend* acted?'

She can see me sitting on the deck; obviously she doesn't care. I met Jenna for the second time last weekend, but she didn't speak to me. Not verbally anyway – her death stares said plenty. Today she decided to talk. Luke was asking what I'd like to do this evening when she interjected with, 'What the hell are you doing with Dad if you're a lesbian?' I suspect Ben told her that because I can't imagine Luke having that conversation with her. I clenched my teeth to stop a catty retort flying out and walked away, Luke's voice telling her off in my wake.

Luke crosses his arms. 'You were out of line. I'm not surprised she ignored you.'

She grunts. 'I'm leaving.'

'You're goin' nowhere.' He walks to the fridge and grabs himself another beer.

Her eyes instantly water.

I silently scoff. *Oh, she's good.*

'Dad, please. We're going to that gig in the Valley. I told you about it. We've had tickets for months.'

He eyes her suspiciously. 'What gig?'

Amazingly, she's able to stick her fingers into the pocket of those tight jeans to pull out three tickets. 'This one. You told me ages ago I could go. It's not fair if I can't now.' He pushes up his glasses and peers at the tickets. 'I'm sorry I said that to Amy. You're right, I was out of line. I'm sorry, Amy,' she calls to me.

'It's okay, Jenna.' My reply is delivered with a touch of insincerity that I don't anticipate, and hope Luke doesn't notice.

'Fine.' He jabs his finger at her. 'But if you pull a stunt like that again, I won't care that you have plans. You'll be goin' nowhere.'

'Whatever. I've gotta go.' She heads for the door.

'Wait. How are you getting there and when does it finish? Do you need me to pick you up?'

'I'll call a ride share. It finishes at midnight or something. I'll come home with Emma.'

He places his beer on the bench. 'Well, I'll stop drinking now and come and get you. I've only had one—'

'No, Dad! God, don't smother me. I'm seventeen. I'm capable of getting a cab with my friend.'

Concern, mixed with a little bit of hurt, replaces his irritation and the crease in his brow deepens. 'I'm not trying to smother you, Jen. I just worry. Okay, share a ride home with Emma. Keep your phone handy, please. And I'll have mine close by if you need me.'

Her face softens, sadness and vulnerability peeking out from behind that angry wall. 'Okay,' she says quietly. She looks as though she wants to give him a hug, or is waiting for a hug, but she says, 'See ya then,' and walks out.

My heart squeezes and now I feel like a bitch for being so judgy. I promise myself I'll try harder with her.

Luke comes back out to the deck and sits beside me. He twists his wedding ring as he watches her on the footpath.

As the car pulls away, I rub his shoulder to bring him back from wherever it is he's gone. 'You okay?'

He stares at the spot where she was standing. 'Hey?' He turns to me and blinks. 'Sorry. Yeah.'

'Wanna talk about anything?'

He releases a long, slow breath. 'Can't help think I'm messing this up. I don't know how to handle her. What to do.'

'You're not messing things up, Luke. You're doing your best.'

'You reckon?'

'Yeah, I do. Have you talked to Dr Garcia about this? She might have some good advice.'

'Um...'

The wind picks up, bringing with it a faint stench of seaweed. I remove a strand of hair that blows across my face. 'You went this week, didn't you? You've been going?'

He frowns.

'Luke?'

'Not this week.'

'What? Why?'

A flicker of agitation crosses his face. 'Because I didn't.'

'But why?' I ask more firmly.

He swigs his beer.

'Luke?'

'I don't have time to go every week. I've got a business to run, all this shit with the kids. And it's out of my way in the city.'

'You have to go. We both have to go. Neither of us are well enough to give it up.'

He faces me, a hardness in his eyes. 'Don't tell me what I have to do. I don't have the fucking time.'

I flinch.

He groans. 'Shit. I'm sorry.' He reaches for my hand. 'I didn't mean that. I know you're just trying to help. I've only missed one week. I won't make a habit of it.'

I nod but I'm shaken, not just from the way he snapped, but because he thinks he can miss sessions. 'I don't like them either, Luke, but they help.'

He gives a single nod and looks away.

We sit for a few minutes longer, the uncomfortable silence broken by squealing bats flying overhead and the odd car driving along the parade, until Luke says he's going to order Cody some pizza for dinner and heads inside.

*

I'm woken by Luke's phone vibrating on his side table. He switches on the lamp and quickly reaches for his glasses before answering. 'Hello?'

I glance at the clock beside him – 1:00 a.m.

'What's happened?' He sits up. 'What drugs?'

My pulse quickens.

'Ecstasy? Are you sure?'

I take slow, deep breaths.

'Right. I'll be there as soon as I can.' He hangs up and looks at me, his eyes wide with confusion and fear. 'That was the Royal Brisbane. It's Jenna. She... she's had some sort of turn taking ecstasy.'

I swallow. 'Did they say if she's okay?'

He nods. 'She is, but I have to get to the hospital.'

I exhale loudly. 'Thank goodness.'

He taps the screen on his phone. 'I'll call Ben to come over.'

'No, don't. I'll stay here with Cody.'

'Are you sure?'

'Of course.'

'I should tell him where I'm going though, right?'

'Yeah. He'll want to know.' I swing my legs out of bed. 'I'll come with you.'

We dress and head into Cody's room.

Luke shakes him gently. 'Cody,' he whispers. 'Codes.'

'Mmm.'

'Wake up,' Luke says.

His room is dark, but a stream of light from the hallway shines through and highlights his face scrunched with sleep. 'Dad? What's wrong?' he says, rubbing his eyes. 'What time is it?'

'It's early. Listen, I've gotta go to the hospital.'

He sits up and brushes the hair from his face. 'Why? Is it Grandma or Grandad?'

'It's your sister. She's had some drugs and the ambulance had to take her to the hospital.'

Cody's eyes widen. 'Is she alright?'

'Course she is. They just want me to go and get her. Amy's going to stay here with you.'

I give what I hope is a supportive smile.

He nods, but his eyes dampen. 'Will she really be okay, Dad?'

Luke clears his throat. 'Yeah, mate. You know how strong she is.

She'll be fine.' Luke hugs him. 'Try and go back to sleep, ay?'

Cody holds him tight. 'Don't be long.'

'I won't. Be back before you know it. I've got my phone if you wanna call.'

He nods and curls up on his side.

'I'll be downstairs if you can't sleep, Cody,' I say.

Luke leaves the door ajar behind him. He's dazed as he walks downstairs, and I know he'll be thinking about Sarah. Blaming himself for the accident, thinking this wouldn't have happened if he didn't make her go to that party. He grabs his wallet and car keys from the coffee table and gives me a quick kiss at the front door.

'Thanks for staying with Cody; I appreciate it.'

I pull him into a hug. 'Let me know what's happening. Not sure I'll get back to sleep anyway.'

Once he's driven off, I make tea, grab a slice of cold pizza, and settle on the couch, pulling a blanket over my legs. I flick on the TV, scroll through the channels, and stop on a music channel playing old dance tracks. Dance music and ecstasy. Probably what Jenna was doing tonight, just like Mel and Maddie when I met them. I wasn't into drugs that much, but they pushed themselves to the edge most weekends, and every now and then I joined them. Mel was even high the first time she told me she loved me.

We'd been together three months and were at a club in Melbourne. Bass and drums thumped from the speakers, working in rhythm with my heartbeat. People were crammed on the dance floor, flesh on display, sweating, hands in the air. The ecstasy I'd taken began to peak, making my legs buckle, and I leant against a rail separating the dance floor from the bar. Mel was in front of me within seconds, hands either side of my body resting on the handrail. Her eyes bore into me, intense and resolute, the beautiful blue almost hidden by her dilated pupils. She put her lips to my ear and said, 'I love you so much. There will never be anyone else for me.' She didn't wait for me to respond before she devastated me with a kiss just as the effects of the pill rushed through my body. Her silky lips on mine. Her warm tongue in my mouth. Her strong hands around my waist. Every cell in my body danced, my skin erupted, my heart exploded. Love, lust and ecstasy raced through my veins as music and bodies pulsed around us.

A light film of sweat has broken out on my forehead at the memory and my hand trembles as I wipe it away. I lie down and prop a cushion under my head. I'm tired, but I don't want to go back upstairs. An eeriness lurks in Luke's bedroom, particularly with all of Sarah's belongings still there. My eyes drift to the wedding photo at the bottom of the stairwell. Sarah looks as though she's staring straight into my soul, judging me for taking her place.

I shiver, pull the blanket up around my neck and focus on the TV. I could use a friend right now. I distract myself by flicking through the channels again and settle on a home renovation program. It reminds me of Caroline. I glance at the time on my phone – 1:45 a.m. She'll be asleep, but she'll have her phone beside her. I shoot off a text.

Hey. What are you up to?

And then it occurs to me that she's probably with Rachel. An image of them pops into my mind – their naked bodies fused together as they sleep, their legs intertwined. Or maybe they're awake, talking quietly as Caroline strokes her hair. How well do they know each other? Does Rachel know that the freckle a few centimetres below Caroline's right ear is exactly where she likes to be kissed? There's a sharp barb in my chest and I shake my head as though the action will dissolve the image.

My phone buzzes.

It's 2.00am. What do you think I'm up to?

I call her.

'Mmm,' she says after two rings. 'Has something happened?'

I close my eyes and push the phone harder against my ear. We've barely spoken this week, both busy getting on with our differing lives, and I've missed her voice. 'Luke's gone to the hospital. Jenna's had a bad turn with an E. I'm here with Cody.'

'Shit, Ames. That's awful. Is she okay?'

'I think so, but Luke's not.'

'I bet.' She's silent for a beat. 'And you? Are you alright?'

'A little shaky.'

'Oh, hun. Wish I could give you a hug.'

'I'd like that,' I say. 'Sorry I woke you. There's a home reno show on and I thought of you.'

'Which one? Bet I've seen it.'

'Don't know. A rundown shack somewhere in Sydney that's about to sell for two million bucks.'

'I won't turn it on. I'll get too angry about the housing market.' She yawns.

'Better let you get back to sleep. Just wanted to say hi.'

'Don't go. I'm awake now.'

The barb diffuses knowing Rachel mustn't be there. 'Maybe we can do something tomorrow? The French Film Festival is on. We could go to a movie, have some lunch?' I say before I realise that Luke might need me tomorrow for support.

'That sounds good.' She yawns again.

'I'll let you go. I'll call you tomorrow, hey?'

'You going to be alright?'

I want to ask her to come over. Tell her I'd be better with that hug and with her sitting beside me, but I say, 'Course. I'll be fine. Night.'

*

Cody and I have been awake for an hour or so, and my neck is stiff from sleeping on the couch. I've been helping him with his lines for the school play when Luke and Jenna arrive home.

Luke gives an exhausted smile when he walks in. 'You're both up,' he says, squeezing my shoulder over the top of the couch. He has dark rings under his eyes, his lids are heavy, and that worry frown is back.

He ruffles Cody's hair. 'Hey, Codes.'

'Hi, Dad,' Cody says and stands to walk over to Jenna.

She sets down a couple of takeaway cups and fast-food bags on the coffee table and wraps her arms around him. Her hair is tied back, she's pale and her eyelids droop as she speaks. 'We got you both some breaky.'

I smile. 'Thanks, Jenna.'

'Starvin',' Cody says, although he's already had two pieces of toast.

Jenna goes upstairs for a shower and straight to bed. Cody takes his breakfast to his room, which already smells like dirty washing and fast food, and Luke updates me on what happened. After the gig, Jenna and her friends went to a club where Kate managed to find some pills. After Jenna took one, she panicked and collapsed. She told Luke that her throat felt tight and she was sweating. The hospital doctor said he thought she'd had a panic attack, rather than the collapse being associated with the drugs.

I sit close to him and listen quietly as he talks. His voice is husky from tiredness and heavy with stress. He looks at me with bloodshot eyes. 'Thanks for staying with Cody. Was everything okay?'

'Yeah. He slept. I watched telly and ate cold pizza. Called Caz.'

His brows shoot up. 'You called Caz?'

'I just wanted someone to talk to.'

He nods and I see him processing what I've said. 'Shit, Amy. I didn't think how this might make you feel.' He puts his coffee down and drapes his arm around me. 'And I left you here on your own. I'm sorry.'

I pat his thigh. 'I was fine, and you needed to be with Jenna.'

He shakes his head. 'I couldn't think when I got that call. It scared me so much.'

I curl my legs up onto the couch and wait for him to talk more, want him to talk more.

'If I lost her...' He closes his eyes. 'If I lost either of them, I couldn't survive.'

I understand that fear always stirring underneath – the fear of what will become of you if more people you love are ripped away.

He removes his glasses and pinches the bridge of his nose. I wrap my arms around him, and he pushes his head into the crook of my neck. And then I feel his tears on my skin. I hold him tight and let him cry. And I cry, too, for everything we've both lost.

Chapter Thirteen

'Hi, Mum.'

'Hello, darling, how are you?'

'Good. Busy today.' I cradle the phone between my ear and shoulder while I tap out a reply to an email.

'I won't keep you. I wanted to know if you and Luke would like to come for lunch on Sunday.'

I stop typing and grasp the phone. 'What?'

'Lunch. On Sunday. We'd like to meet Luke.'

She has never wanted to meet one of my new partners this quickly before. 'Why the interest? Because he's a man?' I snap.

She tuts. 'Don't be silly. For goodness' sake, you're so touchy about your sexuality.'

I roll my eyes. That's a new one.

'I wouldn't care if you were seeing an alien with two heads. We've been worried about you, and it's nice that you have someone in your life again.'

'Oh. Sorry.' I gaze out over the rooftops.

'So, you'll come on Sunday?'

'I'm not sure, Mum.'

The truth is Luke hasn't had a good week following the drug situation with Jenna. He at least went to his session on Tuesday afternoon and said that he spoke to Dr Garcia about it, but of course he didn't give me any details.

'Why not? You're seeing each other, aren't you? It's just lunch.'

'Well, yeah, but it's only been six weeks or something. It's a bit soon.' I swig the now cold coffee I bought over an hour ago.

'Just thought I'd ask,' she says stiffly.

I sigh. 'I'll ask him. But no promises.' A knock sounds on my office door and I swivel around to find Paul standing in the doorway. My stomach plummets. 'I have to go. Someone is here.'

'Okay, darling, see you Sunday. Look forward to meeting Luke.'

'I said no promises.' I hang up and turn to Paul.

'Amy,' he says, not waiting for an invite before he walks in.

I want to practise my breathing exercises but he's standing there, staring at me with his dead eyes.

'Paul. How can I help?'

He motions to the meeting table. 'Do you have a few minutes?'

'Sure,' I say tartly.

The bright sunshine that filters into my office highlights the grey patches around his hairline that he missed with the black dye. 'Listen, Amy, I'm not sure how to say this.'

That statement tells me exactly where this discussion is headed. I've had enough of his crap over the past few months, and I'm not playing this game anymore. 'You're the head of HR, Paul, you should know exactly how to have difficult conversations with staff members.'

His already narrow eyes narrow even further. 'Fine. Your absence has become an issue, along with the declining quality of your work.'

I cross my arms. 'Bit of a delayed conversation, isn't it? I haven't had a sick day for about a month, and the quality of my work is getting back to what it was.'

'Agreed you haven't had a sick day in a few weeks, but prior to that you barely did a five-day week in six months. Not to mention all the time off you had at the beginning of last year. Your absence has affected the team. And I don't agree your work is back to its usual standard.'

'Well, don't hold back.'

His mouth forms into a tight line and he spreads his hands, palms up.

'Has there been complaints from my team? From other people in the department? Because if there has, I think I would've heard them by now.'

His eyes harden. 'Amy, I don't want to sound harsh—'

'Then don't.'

'But Mel passed away, what? Two years ago or something like that?'

I stiffen. *Fifteen months, one week and two days, you heartless prick.* My eyes sting. I squint and clench my jaw to stop the tears.

He's oblivious to the impact of his comment and prattles on. 'I don't for a minute think it's been easy for you, but I've been accommodating and understanding for a long time now, and I need your buy-in. You're a senior manager in the organisation and the expectations are high, you know that.' He sighs his usual patronising sigh. 'Look, what can we do to get you back to core competency?'

Now he's pissing me off with his wanky corporate jargon that makes no sense. He has no interest in helping me get back to where I was. He's just going through the motions to cover himself, so that when he gets pulled up for trying to sack me, he can say he tried.

I fix him with a wintery stare. 'Back to my old self? Are you serious? Do you *ever* think I'll be back to my old self?' He's nudged my angry inner beast and I want to attack. 'You might not give a crap about your wife, but I loved mine.'

His nostrils flare. 'No need to get personal.'

I raise a brow. 'When you have an affair in the workplace it's not personal though, is it?'

His jaw tightens and I'm amazed to see some emotion in his emotionless eyes – even if it is contempt.

'Is that what this is about?' I say. 'You're worried I'm going to tell people what you've been up to?'

He shakes his head and tugs on his earlobe. 'I have no idea what you're talking about. All I meant was how can we get you focussed on your job again. Like you were before.'

Like I was before. That means doing most of his job for him. Caroline was right. He's had to do things himself for over a year now and he's not up to it because he's inept. Caroline should be doing his job. She applied for it a few years ago when it was vacant, but Greg didn't think she was ready. Paul must've turned on the charm in the interview because Caroline's skills, experience and personality far outweigh his. Although he has the personality of a dead fish, so that's not hard.

'Or what?' I sit up straight.

He purses his lips. 'You've worked in HR a long time, Amy, you know how things operate.'

I give an incredulous laugh. 'Oh, that's rich. You're going to sack me?'

'I'm hoping it won't come to that.'

'Unbelievable. After everything I've given this organisation over the past ten years.'

'I've been more than fair. I'm happy for you to have the time for any therapy sessions and appointments you need during the week, but from this point forward, you need to up your game.'

My door is slightly ajar and Daniel peers in as he passes in the corridor. He double takes and tilts his head. I give a tiny nod and he walks on.

'What's the matter, Paul? You don't have anyone to do your work anymore? Are you being exposed? Not meeting your KPIs? Is that it?'

A surly expression settles on his face. 'I'll let that comment slide.'

'Or maybe since I can't complain to myself or my boss, I'll go to employee relations or the CEO and show them the bullying emails you've sent me over the past few months.'

He flinches at the 'b' word. 'Asking someone to do their job isn't bullying.'

'No, it's not. But putting undue pressure on them, constantly shifting the goalposts, sending them relentless demands, and criticising their good work is. Particularly when that staff member has had a life-changing, traumatic, personal tragedy.'

His face reddens. 'The bottom line is this position isn't really needed. It has nothing to do with you. It's just departmental restructure.'

I know he's said this on the fly, but it doesn't stop a massive lump forming in my stomach. 'Not needed? And who will do all of this?' I motion my hand around the office.

He breaks eye contact. 'I'm... I'm thinking of elevating one of the other managerial positions and having higher level support under that.'

I consider him a moment. 'Well, this sounds like a substantial change that hasn't been discussed with any employees. Because if it had, I'd be one of the first to know.'

He glares at me, his mouth a tight line.

I want to make him squirm. See what else he comes out with. 'And what position will you be elevating?' It can only be one. 'Caroline's?'

He doesn't respond.

'Is she aware of this?'

'The matter hasn't been discussed with key stakeholders yet.'

'What does that mean? This is a little plan you've come up with yourself? I bet you haven't even spoken to Greg, have you?'

Greg and I have always had a good relationship – even better since Mel died. He drove me back to my place the day the police turned up to tell me about Mel. And he arranged to have Mel's body flown up from Melbourne so that I could have her funeral here. If anyone goes to Greg about a restructure or managerial performance matter, he comes straight to me.

Paul stands, his crotch close to eye level. He's wearing the same style of skinny jeans my nephews thirty-five years his junior wear, and they're outlining way more of him than I want to see. My gut churns. How Vanessa can go there, I don't know.

'It's the way it is, Amy. We'll circle back on this soon,' he says and storms out.

I grip the edge of the meeting table and take some deep breaths. Then I jump up and check my computer to see if Caroline's online. She is, so I head down to her office.

'Fucking Paul, that wanker,' I say as I barge in. I stop short when I see Rachel. 'Oh, Rachel.'

She throws me a saccharin smile. 'Amy.'

Her dull brown is tied up in a top knot, showing off her cat-like grey eyes and exposing that dewy skin. She looks fresh and bright, particularly in that cute aqua dress she's wearing. Part of me wants to say, 'ooh, where'd you get that?' but the comment can't get past that massive wall of dislike.

I give my hair a flick. 'Nice to see you again, Rachel.'

'Hey, Ames,' Caroline says. She points to Rachel. 'Rach just dropped by. We're going out for lunch.'

Rach? I swallow. 'Right. Sorry to interrupt. I wanted a word about an urgent work matter.'

'No problem. Is it a quick one or do you need longer?'

'It's quick.' I turn to Rachel expecting her to leave, but she stays put. I raise my brows at her.

'Oh, you want me to go? I thought it might be something you need a union rep for,' she says, with a touch of superiority.

'No,' I say.

She gives me a strained smile and steps towards Caroline. Then she kisses her. On the lips. Open-mouthed. Right in front of me. Once she's finished pawing Caroline, she says, 'I'll wait outside.' She throws me some bitchy side-eye as she saunters past.

Caroline awkwardly tucks a strand of hair behind her ear, her cheeks flushed.

'What the fuck was that?' I say as soon as Rachel shuts the door. 'You've been seeing each other five minutes.'

'Don't give me a hard time. I cop enough shit from Maddie.' She crosses her arms. 'What's up?'

I collapse into a chair at the small meeting table. 'Paul just tried to sack me.'

'What?' She pulls out the chair opposite and sits.

I recall the conversation for her.

She shakes her head. 'He can't sack you.'

'He can make the position redundant though, can't he?'

'Well, he can try, but that position is needed. It would be stupid to get rid of it. Greg won't approve it; you know how much he values you. Besides, who would do your job? Daniel can't take it on.'

'He reckons he'd elevate one of the other manager positions and put in higher level support underneath.'

Caroline scoffs. 'Who the hell would take that on?'

'Who do you think?'

She points to herself. 'Me?'

I shrug.

'Amy, I know nothing about this. As if I would do anything to put your job at risk.'

I sigh and drop my head into my hands. 'I know you wouldn't. I didn't want to do this, but I'm going to have to lodge a bullying complaint.' I look up. 'It's the only way I can stall him pushing ahead.'

She nods. 'Good. I've been telling you for weeks that his demands are unacceptable. Regardless of whether he tries to make the position redundant or not, you need to complain.'

'But it's another thing I have to deal with. I haven't been able to think about it with everything else.'

She tilts her head, her eyes filling with concern. 'I know it's tough. But you can't hold off now.'

I nod.

'Greg will give the complaint to my team since yours can't do it. I can't handle this either. We're too conflicted. And I'm conflicted with that position. I'll get Sian on it, though. I've taught her everything she knows. She's great; she'll sort this out for you.'

Sian is her assistant manager and is excellent at her job.

'Thanks.' I rest my head back against the wall. 'The worst thing is that he did all this while he had his casual Friday "check out my massive dick" jeans on.'

Caroline snorts. 'That's why I never book meetings with him on Fridays.'

I laugh too, but it subsides quickly. 'I can't lose my job, Caz. I'm on my own now. I've got a mortgage and—'

'Hey, come on.' She reaches across the table and rubs my forearm. 'It won't come to that.'

Normally her support would calm me, but my brain feels like a pressure cooker ready to explode.

*

I spent the afternoon digging out all the emails Paul has sent me over the past few months, compiling information on my sick leave and any impact on the team, reviewing previous work to check the quality and reading through the enterprise agreement. Daniel appeared armed with flat whites and chocolate donuts and helped me work through everything as I recalled what happened. I left out Paul's affair, but office gossip is rife because Daniel alluded to it, peering at me for confirmation. I shoved half a donut in my mouth and winked. He grinned and muttered, 'I knew it.'

By the time I arrived at Luke's, Jenna and Cody were both out, so Luke and I had a few hours to ourselves. I probed him about his session with Dr Garcia, but he gave me a quick smile and said he was fine.

Now we're in bed, and although I've been complaining about work most of the night, I'm still stewing. Luke is making responsive noises as though he's listening, but he's been cuddling and kissing me for about ten minutes.

I carry on talking. 'And he reckons my absence means others in the team have had to pick up my slack,' I say.

Luke brushes his lips against my cheek as his hand glides up my thigh. 'Uh huh. So you said.'

'But that's crap because they haven't. I did a whole assessment of it this arvo with Daniel.'

His hand moves across my stomach as he nuzzles my neck. 'Right.'

'And he reckons Caz can take on my job. My entire job!'

'No way.' His hand travels up to my breast and his hardness presses against my hip as he kisses the edge of my mouth.

'Are you listening to me?'

'Course I am. Your boss is a prick. I get it.'

'And my job is at risk.'

'Yeah, you said earlier.' He gives me a suggestive grin. 'You need to relax.'

I roll onto my side and run my finger down his chest. 'You reckon?'

He kisses me, firm and intense, his hand gripping the back of my neck. 'Mmhmm. And the kids won't be home for ages, so we don't need to, you know, keep the noise down.'

I smile. He says he can let loose when the house is empty. I push him onto his back and straddle him. If I'm going to relax, then I'm going to relax completely.

He groans and slides his hands down my back as I get into position. As we move together, my tension melts and my mind empties. He kisses me hard, one hand on my arse, the other on the back of my head. He's different tonight, less self-conscious, more open, and I like his firm grasp. I sit back and he peers up at me, his face flushed but relaxed. We're in a nice rhythm – our breathing becomes more rapid, our pace quickens, our moans louder. I sense him getting close and bend forward so that he's hitting the perfect spot for me. The tingling starts in my legs and quickly travels north. My torso is flat against his, his grip tightens on my arse, and his breath is hot against my ear.

He thrusts underneath me and says, 'Oh, Sarah.'

My eyelids fly open. I want to jump off him, but my shuddering body won't let me.

'Fuck,' he says breathlessly. 'Fuck.'

'Whoa,' I say. It's the only word that comes to mind. My body stills, and I roll off him putting some distance between us. A chilling presence takes hold and I pull the doona over me. I can almost see Sarah standing at the end of the bed with a smug grin.

He scoots closer. 'I'm so sorry.'

'Um. I... um.' I blink at the ceiling.

'Amy, look at me.' He gently holds my chin and turns my face towards him. 'I can't believe I did that. I am so, so sorry.'

'You didn't mean it,' I say, but it's unsettled something, like a whirlwind of debris from the bottom of a lake when it's disturbed.

A door bangs and our eyes widen at each other.

'Shit. They said they wouldn't be home until eleven or something,' Luke whispers.

'Oh, god. We were so loud,' I whisper back. I peer over at the doorway. 'The door isn't closed properly either.'

Luke grimaces. He hops out of bed, throws on his jeans and T-shirt and leaves the room. There's muffled voices between him and Jenna in the hallway, and he returns within a couple of minutes.

'Please tell me she didn't hear anything?' I say quietly.

He undresses and hops back into bed. 'Cody isn't home yet, but yep, she heard.' He winces. 'You should've seen the look of disgust.'

'Fucking hell.' I throw the pillow over my head. This day could not get any worse.

*

The following afternoon, we're by the pool making the most of the higher-than-average April temperature. The sky is a clear cornflower blue, dotted only by an occasional plane flying overhead or a random flock of birds. Normally, a day like today would lift my mood, but threads of awkwardness hang heavy in the air, sticking to me like I've walked through a giant cobweb.

Cody is on a lounger on the other side of the pool with his headphones on, singing loudly. Jenna's been in the water for most of the afternoon, but is throwing filthy looks at Luke and me every chance she gets. Luke's mind is somewhere else entirely, and I'm pretending last night never happened, so she's not receiving whatever reaction it is she's after.

I eventually fell asleep last night despite my brain being crowded with thoughts all fighting to take centre stage. Luke mustn't have had the same problem, because his soft snores began soon after he switched off the lamp. This morning I decided it was pointless being annoyed at him. It's not like I haven't thought about Mel during sex; I've just managed to stop myself calling her name during an orgasm. As soon as we woke up, he rolled over and said, 'I'm so sorry.' I reassured him it was fine. He seemed happy with that, but as the day's progressed, he's become more distant, so I can only assume that Sarah is weighing heavy on his mind. I considered going home to give him some space, but we'd already planned to go to Cody's basketball game at lunchtime. Cody was so excited about Luke having a Saturday off work and going to his game that I wanted to stick around to make sure Luke actually went.

Jenna jumps out of the pool, wraps a towel around her waist and sits across from me. She takes a long drink of water, watching me with fiery dark eyes as she tilts her head back. She screws the lid back on the bottle, licks her lips and fixes me with some fierce attitude. 'Do you want me and Cody to leave so you can fuck?' She enunciates the 'f' and 'k' sharply.

'Jenna!' Luke scolds.

I've been patient so far. Ignoring her snide comments and resentful glares. Staying reticent for Luke's benefit, and because losing someone you love can affect your behaviour. But that pressure cooker is still boiling from yesterday and the release valve is whistling.

I give her a deathly cold stare, and it must work because she visibly shrinks in her seat. 'Yeah, I would, because I could really use a fuck.' I enunciate my 'f' and 'k' to copy hers.

'Amy!' Luke says. 'Jesus!'

Jenna's eyes grow huge with shock. 'Oh my god, Dad! No!' She jumps up and runs upstairs.

Cody's still singing loudly, playing air drums, oblivious to what's going on.

Luke glares at me. 'Did you have to say that?'

'She started it,' I sniff.

'She started it? How old are you? Be the fucking adult, Amy,' he says, following Jenna upstairs.

'Be the fucking adult, Amy,' I mimic. But it only takes a minute for me to realise how childish I've been and my face burns with shame. After about ten minutes when Luke still hasn't returned, I stand to head upstairs and he appears on the stairwell, glowering at me.

'I'm so sorry. I just snapped.'

'She's seventeen and she's lost her mum.'

The fact that he's not willing to hear my apology sets me off again. 'So, she gets to be a bitch for the rest of her life because she lost her mum over a year ago?' My hand flies to my mouth and I screw my eyes shut. When I open them, Luke is staring at me open mouthed.

'I'm sorry, that was—'

He shakes his head. 'I can't believe you said that.'

'I didn't mean it, I—'

'I think you should leave.'

'What? No. I don't need to leave. You know how stressed I am at the moment. I'm truly sorry.'

He holds up a hand. 'I'm not in the mood for this.'

That ignites my anger again. 'Shouldn't I be the one to be pissed off after last night? It's okay to call me Sarah during sex, but it's not okay for me to slip up and say something I regret?'

He holds his head with one hand like he can't handle what's going on in there. 'I need some space. This is too much for me.'

'What the hell does that mean?' I put my hands on my hips. 'We're done?'

His eyes flick to Cody, who's pulled off his headphones and is staring at us. Luke lowers his voice. 'I don't know. But you're right. You should be angry about last night, so why aren't you? Are you that needy you're okay with that?'

Pressure builds behind my eyes. 'It's not about being needy. I care about you, and I know you didn't mean it. Like I didn't mean what I just said.'

'You need to go,' he says and heads back upstairs.

'Luke, please don't do this.' But he doesn't turn back.

I go upstairs and grab my bag. I hear Luke through Jenna's closed door calming her. By the time I get back downstairs, Cody's moved to the kitchen.

'Bye, Cody. I'm heading home.'

He brushes the damp hair from his eyes. 'Why? I thought you were staying tonight. We were gonna watch a movie.'

I place my bag on the table and give him a hug. His lanky arms wrap around me. 'I'm sorry. Something came up, and I need to get home.' I pull away. 'I'll see you soon though and we'll do it then, hey?'

He looks puzzled but nods. 'Okay, Bye.'

My heart squeezes for this beautiful, sensitive kid. I give his arm a rub, grab my bag and rush out before the tears fall.

Chapter Fourteen

It's dusk by the time I arrive home. My face is blotchy, and my body odour is chlorine from the afternoon in the pool. Embarrassment simmers under my skin, warming my neck and face. I'm angry at myself for taking Jenna's bait and crushed about what I said to Luke. I take a long, hot shower and wash my hair vigorously. I shave, buff and rub like I'm trying to remove a layer of myself, like if that layer doesn't exist, nothing that happened before now exists either.

Afterwards, I make a cup of tea to delay opening a bottle of wine and check my phone. Nothing. I dial while I pace the lounge room. My call goes to voicemail. 'Luke, it's me. Please call.' I text the same message. Whatever happens between us – if this is it – I at least want him to know how sorry I am.

I take Mel's ashes to the couch and grasp my wedding ring. Like Dr Sachdev advised, I sit quietly and wait for the mass of angst in my chest to ease. This is the ritual I've developed that keeps Mel close, as though she's beside me.

She loved this room; it was her sanctuary. She put in an offer for the house based purely on this room, taken by the high ceiling, the intricate patterns carved into the wooden beams, the polished floorboards and the stained-glass windows that open to the jacaranda tree in the front yard, which was in full bloom at the time. The striking contrast of the vivid lavender flowers against the pastel blue sky spoke to her.

'Babe, look how beautiful that tree is,' she'd said, standing in the middle of the lounge. 'The couch can go right here, and we can sit and take in those amazing colours.'

I wrapped my arms around her from behind. 'They only bloom for a couple of months.'

She faced me with her adorable nose crinkle. 'Really?'

'Mmhmm.'

She turned back to the view and pulled my arms tighter around her. 'Well, I still love it, and it'll give us something to look forward to each year.'

I sigh at the memory, carefully place her ashes back and walk over to the window to open it. I lean against the frame and stare at the jacaranda, which has started its autumn shed. I let the painful longing roll through my body and remember Dr Sachdev's words – *feel it, don't squash it down; it can't leave you if you keep it buried.*

I stay like that for a while before I wipe my face and fall back onto the couch. I flick through channels and settle on a movie – guns, a car chase, explosions. I try to focus, but it reminds me of the plans I had with Cody this evening, so I switch it off and move out to the back deck. It's dark now, and the glow of the full moon illuminates the piles of soil and ripped up pavers from the work Luke started, but probably won't finish.

My mind drifts to last weekend when I was alone downstairs at his place. How much I missed my old life, my home, my friends. How much spending the afternoon with Caroline the next day fed my soul. I was so satiated that evening. But the high slowly melted through the week from constantly talking to Luke about issues with the kids, my session with Dr Sachdev on Wednesday, the run-in with Paul yesterday, and what happened with Luke last night all served to shorten my fuse and make me snap today.

I check my phone again. Still nothing. I remember Caroline saying she wasn't doing much tonight because Rachel had other plans, so I shoot off a text.

Hey, Caz. What's happening?

I sip my tea trying to convince myself it's hitting the spot and alternate between staring at the yard and checking for messages. After about ten minutes, I decide to open a bottle of wine and find something for dinner when my phone pings with a reply.

At pub with Maddie. About to grab takeaway. Where are you?

I reply. *Home. Come over?*

On our way. Assume you need dinner?

I respond with a smiley face. While I wait, I sift through the strange emotions that are clouding me about Luke. I feel like some sort of protection and new purpose has been taken away, a safeguard against my grief. But shouldn't I feel more than that? Shouldn't my heart be sore that things didn't work out? Shouldn't I want to listen to sad love songs and pine for what could've been? Or am I not capable of ever experiencing heartbreak again because my heart is already shattered?

'Hel-lo,' Caroline's voice calling through the screen door spares me from having to think any longer.

I walk through the house and un-snib the lock. 'Hi,' I say, holding the door open.

Maddie holds up a large bag full of takeaway containers as she steps inside. 'We went for Indian.'

'Excellent. I had nothing for dinner,' I say.

Caroline grins. 'Of course you didn't.'

We head through to the kitchen where I switch on some music, grab some glasses and a bottle of white wine, while Caroline organises plates and Maddie sets the food out on the table outside.

'How'd you go yesterday?' Caroline asks. 'Get everything together?'

'I think so.' I place some ice in a steel chiller bucket. 'Daniel helped.'

'Good. I've got you a meeting with Sian at ten on Monday.'

'Oh, right. So soon.'

She pauses mid taking cutlery from the drawer and stares at me. 'You can't stall on this, Ames. You'll give Paul too much room. You need to get the complaint in.'

I nod. 'Yep, you're right. Monday at ten. Got it.'

We join Maddie at the table, the rich aroma of sweet, buttery sauces and spices rising from the containers, and I pour wine for the three of us.

'Where are your new girlfriends?' I ask, rolling my eyes and stressing 'girlfriends' like I'm an eight-year-old boy who thinks girls are yucky. The comment also sparks a desire I don't expect – to have my own new girlfriend to talk about.

'I wouldn't say Billie's my girlfriend, but she's at work. She's coming to my place afterwards,' Maddie says. She met Billie three weeks ago through mutual friends at a party, and she's been in a dream-like trance ever since.

'That sounds girlfriendy to me,' I say, serving myself a large portion of rice, chicken tikka and vegetable Madras.

Caroline nods. 'It does.'

Maddie smiles, a loved-up glimmer in her eye.

'Rachel's out with friends,' Caroline offers.

No reference to Rachel not being her girlfriend, I notice.

'I'm surprised she isn't texting you every five seconds,' Maddie says.

Caroline grunts. 'Shut up, Maddie. You're such a pain in the arse sometimes.' The look Caroline shoots her stops me asking what that's about. She turns back to me. 'And where's Luke? You were heading there last night after work.'

I shrug. 'I stayed last night, spent the day.' I shove a huge forkful of food into my mouth.

'Why?' Maddie asks.

'Why what?' I ask, still chewing.

'Why did you come home? You sometimes stay Saturdays, too.'

'No reason. Just thought I'd give him some time with the kids after what happened with Jenna last weekend. Thought they might want some space.' I rip off a piece of Peshwari naan and shovel it in.

Caroline's eyes roam my face curiously. I focus on my plate. She'll know something is up if look at her.

'Something's up,' she says.

Damn her. 'What?' I screw up my face. 'No, it's not.'

Caroline nods slowly and waves her fork at me. 'Yeah, it is. You stayed there last night and spent the day with him, but you're sitting home alone on a Saturday night. And you're being weird – talking fast with that high voice thing you do when something's wrong.'

I look at her intently and lower my voice. 'I'm not.'

'You are,' Maddie says.

I sigh. 'We had a small argument. A tiny disagreement. It was nothing really.' Now I'm waving my fork around. 'More a case of words being exchanged with Jenna and he... ah... he took her side and asked me to leave.' I drain the remainder of my wine and pour myself another one.

'Shit,' Maddie says. 'That sounds a bit more serious than a tiny disagreement.'

Caroline watches me closely and continues to eat.

I groan and slide down in my chair. 'I've been trying with Jenna, I really have. But the pressure of work yesterday, and...' I stop. I haven't told them about Sarah joining us for a threesome. 'And I snapped.'

'What happened?' Maddie asks.

'Some stuff happened last night and it kind of carried over to today.'

They exchange a glance and turn back to me.

'That sounds interesting,' Caroline says, relaxing back in her chair, glass of wine in one hand, samosa in the other.

I mop up the last bit of tikka sauce with a chunk of naan and pop it in my mouth, like I need it for energy to regale my story. 'I was stressed last night about what happened at work yesterday. I was already on edge. Last night, the kids were out, so Luke and I thought we'd take advantage of them not being there. And he... erm... he called me Sarah.' I gulp my wine.

'What, when you were chatting?' Maddie asks, with genuine confusion.

'Um, no.' I pause. 'While we were having sex.'

Maddie chokes on the forkful of rice she's just put in her mouth.

Caroline covers her mouth, but her eyes are smiling. She pulls her hand away. 'Ooh, not good,' she says, before pressing her lips together.

Maddie winces to disguise her laugh. 'Oops.'

Seeing their response makes me smile. 'Can you fucking believe that?'

Maddie is still laughing. 'I'm sure he didn't mean it.'

'That's not all. Straight after that, we heard a door bang. It was Jenna. Home early. She heard us.'

They both grimace.

'The kids were supposed to be out until late.' I drop my head into my hands. 'And we were so loud.'

They both crack up.

I knock back my last mouthful of wine and top up our glasses. 'Anyway, I tried to forget about everything this morning. Told Luke the Sarah thing wasn't an issue, and I thought he was okay with that. But he was weird today.' I then tell them about the events that unfolded at the pool, including exactly what Jenna said to me about wanting a fuck and how I responded.

Maddie snorts. 'Bloody hell, Ames.'

Caroline is grinning. 'I can see why he's pissed off. That's not the most mature reaction.'

I place my palms on my cheeks. They're cool against my warm skin. 'That's not the worst of it. When he told me to be the adult because she's only seventeen and has lost her mum, I said...' I close my eyes, the regret thick. 'So she gets to be a bitch for the rest of her life because she lost her mum over a year ago.' I open my eyes and they're both gaping at me.

'Ames, no,' Caroline says.

'I feel so awful about it. I tried to apologise. I've sent Luke messages, called him, but he hasn't replied.' I shake my head. 'How could I say that? How could I even think it?'

'He'll understand you didn't mean it,' Maddie says. 'He knows what you've been through.'

'All the more reason I shouldn't have said it. I regretted it as soon as it came out of my mouth. He said he can't deal with this, with us, and that he wants space. And he called me *needy*.' I throw up my hands.

Caroline is sitting back in her chair, twisting the diamond stud in her ear and peering at me with narrowed eyes. I know that look. She's preparing to fight my corner. 'Some space? Too needy? What's that mean? You're done?' There's a touch of outrage in her voice.

I glance out over the yard. A possum scuttles along the top of the fence and jumps into the neighbour's tree. 'Sounds that way.'

'Because of a couple of comments?' Maddie says. 'He fucked up, too.'

'They were pretty awful comments, Mads. And, no, I don't think it's that. They were the just the catalyst. He's started skipping his sessions. He's stressed. And I don't think he can handle a relationship.'

'How do you feel about that?' Caroline asks softly.

I shrug. I can't articulate it to myself, let alone them. All I know is that I liked being with someone who understood, and I liked being there for someone again. 'I just want him to know how sorry I am.'

'I know you were a good support for each other and that you care about him,' Caroline says, with genuine compassion. 'I'm sorry it hasn't worked out.'

'Yeah, me too,' Maddie says.

'Thanks.'

We're interrupted by her phone buzzing on the table. 'It's Zoe,' she says, picking it up. 'She's asking what we're doing?'

My stomach clenches. 'Nothing! We're doing nothing!'

Maddie cocks her head. 'Oh, come on. She's a friend, and she's only up the road.'

I look at Caroline.

She dishes herself up some more curry. 'I'm staying out if it.'

'Can't she come over for a drink?' Maddie asks.

'No, she bloody can't!' I say, my voice screechy. 'I can't deal with that tonight, too.'

'You can't completely avoid her. Besides, I thought you'd moved on. It's been months since you hooked up,' Maddie says.

I swig my wine.

'Or is it that you don't trust yourself around her?' Caroline says.

Maddie's eyes flick up from her phone.

'No, Caz, you're wrong.' Her innate ability to understand how I tick really pisses me off sometimes.

'I don't believe you. Seeing a man doesn't mean your attraction to women automatically switches off – particularly when it comes to Zoe.' She takes a bite of curry, watching for my reaction while she chews.

A smile spreads across Maddie's face. 'I think Caz might be on to something.'

Caroline doesn't take her eyes off me. 'I know I am.'

I glance between them. 'Okay, maybe I might miss women a bit. So what?'

Caroline leans across the table and grabs the bottle from the ice bucket. 'Nothing. I'm just saying that was a strong reaction to the possibility of Zoe coming over.'

'Come on, Ames. You broke it off with her ages ago. You need to learn to be friends again at some point,' Maddie says.

I let out a defeated sigh.

Maddie holds up her phone. 'Can I tell her she can come over?'

'Whatever. I don't care.'

Maddie sends a reply and picks up her glass. 'So, you miss women. Does that mean man sex isn't doing it for you?'

Caroline smirks.

'It is. Other than being referred to as his late wife and his daughter hearing us. I like it.'

Caroline leans forward. 'Does it blow your mind? Are your orgasms off the scale? Do you come every time you have sex?' She sits back. 'Because that's how you talk about sex with women.'

'I've had orgasms with him,' I say. Not many, but they don't need to know that.

'How's the oral?' Maddie says.

'It's… it's early days. We haven't got 'round to that yet.'

'Fucking hell, if he hasn't gone down yet, count your blessings it's over,' Maddie says grinning.

Although I know she's joking, I say, 'Sex isn't all about oral, Mads. I don't only like that.'

She snorts. 'You were with my best friend for nine years. I know exactly what you like.'

I try to ignore them, but I can't help smiling. 'Anyway, it works both ways, and I'm not ready for his dick in my mouth.'

They both laugh.

We finish the wine, pick at the food and hear all about Billie while we wait for Zoe to arrive. When she does, I peer at her through the window that separates the kitchen from the deck as she and Maddie make vodka lime sodas for all of us. She's wearing skinny blue jeans and a thin jumper that clings to every curve. A vision of me peeling them off pops into my head and I moan.

Caroline kicks me under the table.

'Ow,' I blurt and glare at her.

She raises a brow.

'What?'

'She's only been here two minutes and you're already undressing her.'

I groan. 'Well, why does she have to look so good? Jesus.'

Caroline shakes her head, picks up her phone and starts tapping at the screen.

I glance sideways. *'Rach?'*

'Hmm?' She looks up, smiling. 'Yeah, she wants to stop by later.'

I focus my attention back on Zoe. Desire is already racing through me. This isn't good. Not good at all.

'I need to call the police,' I say.

'What?'

'I need to report a weapon of mass destruction in the house.'

'Oh my god, you are so corny sometimes,' Caroline says, shaking her head.

Zoe and Maddie come outside and pass around the drinks. Zoe is oozing attitude, which is bold considering she's in my house.

'Hey, Zo.' I don't expect the sultriness in my voice to be so syrupy thick, and by the way Caroline and Maddie look at me, neither do they.

Zoe must also pick up on it because she adopts a quizzical expression and tilts her head ever so slightly. 'Amy. It's been a while.'

There's a frostiness to her voice that I'm not used to, and it sends a current of electricity straight to my groin. I cross my legs and pick up my vodka. 'How are you?'

'Good, thanks. How's the boyfriend?' she adds sarcastically.

I like this side of her, but I'm not discussing Luke. I sip my drink. I haven't felt this sexually charged in months. She must pick up on my vibe because a satisfied smile pulls at the edge of her lips. I flick my eyes to Maddie who's giving me a 'what the fuck are you doing' shake of her head.

For the next couple of hours, we chat, laugh and gossip about who's sleeping with who among our group of friends, and they break through the stress that's built over the past week. I sneak occasional glances at my phone. Luke hasn't responded despite me messaging him another couple of times. But the more I drink, the less I care. Eventually, it becomes too cool on the deck, so we head inside.

Caroline picks up her bag. 'I have to go. Rachel's on her way over.' Her eyes flick between Zoe and me. 'Are you sticking around, Mads?'

'Yeah. Until I hear from Billie.'

'Right,' Caroline says, hesitating for a few seconds before she grabs Maddie's arm. 'Lock the door behind me.'

I head into the kitchen to make more drinks and see them talking by the doorway. Their voices are low and I can't catch the conversation. Caroline's back is to me, and Maddie's eyes are heated as she speaks, like she's telling Caroline off. I shake my head. Always at each other. Then I hear the door shut and Maddie is back on the couch when I return.

I've only taken one sip of my drink when Maddie's phone pings and she jumps up. 'That's Billie. Share a cab, Zo?'

'Oh, um… no, I'm good.' She points to her glass. 'I'll finish my drink. Might have another.' She looks at me. 'If Amy's still up for drinking.'

I shrug. 'Sure.'

Maddie's eyes dart between us. 'If you're—'

I hop up and give her a hug. 'See you Monday for our run.'

'Wow. Sounds like you're looking forward to it,' she says.

I poke my finger in her chest. 'I'm not. Just trying to be positive,' I slur.

I see her out and drop back down onto the couch. I hold my phone up to Zoe. 'Nothing.' I throw it on the coffee table. She kept asking about Luke earlier, so I told her what happened.

'Oh, well,' she says. She's sitting close to me. Too close. 'Why didn't he reply?'

She shrugs. 'Men.' She strokes my hair. When I don't pull away, she inches closer and slides her arm around me.

'I've fucked it up with him.' I lie my head on her shoulder, breathe in the citrus of her perfume. It takes me straight back to the last time she was here, and that electricity that's been humming since she arrived ramps up several volts.

She runs a fingertip down the side of my face, and my pulse quickens. 'He wasn't right for you anyway.'

I look up, my gaze drifting to her mouth. 'Sometimes he was.'

She trails her finger under my chin. 'I don't think he was,' she whispers.

My chest is rising up and down, and I can tell by the satisfaction in her eyes she knows she has me. She kisses me; I kiss her back. Her sweet tongue moves inside my mouth, and her gentle hands cup my face. I sigh at the deliciousness of her lips rubbing against mine. The hunger takes over then, and I kiss her more urgently, shifting position to straddle her. Our shirts come off and she's quick to unhook my bra. I moan against her mouth as her hands move to my breasts and I fumble to undo her jeans. The rest of our clothes fly off, landing on the coffee table, the floor, the armrest of the couch. I lie back and pull her on top of me, running my hands down the soft skin on her back and over the curve of her arse.

I need this. I need the familiarity. And I need an orgasm where I don't have to try so hard to have one. I shudder as she kisses my neck, glides her tongue over my nipple and continues south. Her thick hair falls loose and brushes my stomach.

My skin is on fire, my cells are throbbing, her head is between my legs and... *Oh, god.*

Chapter Fifteen

It's late morning and I'm absent-mindedly scrolling through my phone while I listen to Zoe's slow, steady breaths.

She stirs and her eyes flutter open. 'Morning,' she says, stretching.

'Hey, Zo,' I say, hoping she doesn't pick up on the remorse in my voice.

She hops out of bed and heads down the hallway to the bathroom, her luscious nakedness on display, the lovely roundness of her arse gently swaying side to side.

After the couch last night, we moved to the bedroom where the sex went on and on. Hands, tongues, toys. I couldn't get enough. Luke was a distant memory. Another lifetime. But this morning, in the harsh light of reality, guilt about sleeping with her is whittling away at me and I'm thinking about him again.

'You want a coffee? Something to eat?' I ask when she returns.

She slips back into bed and slides her arm across my waist. 'You're cooking for me?'

'I'll cook you some toast.'

'That'll do,' she says, and then kisses me with a tenderness that suggests she thinks this can go further.

I find some clothes and head to the kitchen. It's a cool, drizzly day, and the fresh earthy scent of wet soil floats through the open windows. Zoe appears wearing my dressing gown and sits at the bench. I listen to her talk about her job as we eat toast and drink coffee, the fizz and chemistry from last night gone. She tries to drag me into the shower with her, but I decline. I need to think, and I can't do that when she's naked in front of me.

I'm at the sink when she emerges dressed in her clothes from last night. She wraps her arms around me and presses her lips to my cheek. I jerk my head away and she drops her grip. I turn to face her.

'You're kidding me. You're seriously going cold on me?' she says.

'I need some—'

'You need? What about what I need?'

'I can't give you that, Zoe.'

She shrugs. 'You haven't even tried. How can you go from last night to this? I don't get how you can be like that.'

I stare at her. She knows why. 'We have tried; it didn't work.'

'So, you can have a relationship with Luke but not with me? You are capable of being with someone then?'

'That's different.'

'How?'

I can't explain that, and even if I could, she wouldn't listen, so I give her the same reason I always do. 'You want too much from me. It drains me. You indulge me and let me wallow.'

Hurt and confusion creep into her eyes. 'That's because I care about you. I can be tougher if that's what you want.'

I brush a strand of hair from her lovely face. 'You can't, Zo. It's not you and I don't want you to change for me. You need to be with someone who will love you the way you want to be loved. That's not me. I'm sorry.'

She takes a step back, anger igniting in her dark eyes. 'Then why did you do that last night? Why didn't you walk away? Make me leave?'

If I remember correctly, she initiated the physical contact. Sure, I wanted it, but she went in first. 'You came here last night. I didn't call you.'

Her brows pull together. 'And you had sex with me.'

I close my eyes and release a frustrated sigh. 'Yes, I did, and that was wrong.'

'Is it because of Luke? Because it sounds like things are done with him.'

'This has nothing to do with Luke.'

She considers me for a long moment. 'If I walk out of here now, that's it. There's no more.'

I nod. 'I know.'

She crosses her arms. 'You can't tell me after last night that Luke gives you what you want.'

I peer out the window and hope she doesn't notice my nostrils flare. I hate that she's right. Sexually, Luke doesn't give me what I want. But emotionally, at this point in my life, he gives me exactly what I want. I won't ever find both again, so I'm going to have to choose, and the latter will be better for me in the long term.

'Guess I'll leave then.' She reaches for her phone and taps the screen, presumably for a cab. She slips on her shoes and grabs her bag from the kitchen table.

I give her one last kiss at the front door. If things were different. She races down the stairs in the rain, and I wait to see if she looks back, but she jumps in the back of the car with her head down.

I slump on the couch. Mel's face stares back at me from the row of photos. The first time I hooked up with Zoe, we had sex right here. It wasn't until the following day that I realised I might've done that intentionally, hoping Mel could see. She was always jealous of the attention Zoe gave me. It felt like I was getting even. After Zoe left that day, I glared at Mel's photo and said, 'That's what you get for leaving me'. It only took a few minutes for the guilt to consume me before I was hugging her photo and sobbing.

And now I've done it again. But things are different this time. I'm not as fragile as I was a year ago, and there's Luke. Is there a part of me that did that last night to claw back control? To have the upper hand over him? Over Zoe? Over Mel?

I lie my head against the back of the couch, listen to the rain softly falling on the roof, and close my eyes. When I open them, I see it. The blank panther. It creeps across the floorboards. Taps my toes with its paws. A warning. I try to move, but it's too late. It pounces and swallows me whole.

I grab Mel's ashes, my phone and slink back to bed. I curl up, prop the urn beside me and go to the Mel folder in my phone to watch clips of our wedding. Her beautiful face smiles back at me. The sunshine lights up her hair and golden skin, and the turquoise sea glistens in the background. It rips my chest apart and I sob.

After the tears subside, I jump out of bed, grab a bottle of wine and a glass and move back to the couch. I put on one of Mel's favourite old movies – *Sideways*, which ironically is about wine and fucked-up relationships. I call Luke again. I text Zoe to say sorry. Neither reply. I guzzle more wine and watch the rest of the film.

As the credits roll, my phone rings. I snatch it up.

'Hi, Mads,' I say.

'What the hell, Amy? Could you destroy Zoe any more? She's been at my place in tears all morning.'

'For fuck's sake. You invited her here. I didn't call her.'

'You didn't have to fuck her all night and then break her heart.'

'She knows the score,' I say coldly.

'Jesus. And what about Luke? I thought you liked him?'

'I do like him, but we're done.' My voice is rising now.

'Have you tried to call him?'

'I haven't fucking stopped trying to call him. What else can I do?' I yell.

She sighs. 'Christ, Amy. I'll see you in the morning for our run.'

'Don't bother. I'm not going.'

'Don't start this shit with me. I'll be there at seven. If you don't answer, I'm letting myself in with the spare key, so don't think you can hide.' She hangs up.

I pour more wine, flick to the Lifestyle channel and squint at some reality show I don't recognise. I switch my attention to Instagram and end up on Rachel's profile. She's posted a photo of herself and Caroline out for breakfast this morning. Through my haze, they look happy. I do a dramatic fake spew, throw my phone down and go back to the TV.

Half an hour later, my phone rings again. I glimpse the name flashing on the screen and roll my eyes. How good of Caroline to break away from domestic harmony to contact me.

'Yep,' I say.

There's a lull and then, 'You slept with Zoe? Seriously?'

'Jesus. Yes. So fucking what? What did you think was going to happen when we were left alone?'

'Oh, so you're a lesbian again?'

'I was never not a lesbian, Caz. Don't be so pathetic.'

'Me, pathetic? That's a fucking joke. So because you're done with Luke you rush straight back to Zoe? It's back on with her?'

'No, it's not.'

'So you completely used her again?'

'She came here. I didn't call her.'

'And that makes it okay? You couldn't control yourself?'

The anger that's been sparked by Maddie's call and seeing Caroline all loved up on Insta turns brittle. 'What's it matter to you anyway? You're all cosy with *Rach*.'

There's a heavy pause. 'Is that an issue for you? Would you rather I not be with Rachel?' Her voice is gentle, and there's something unspoken there that unnerves me.

'I don't give a fuck what you do,' I slur.

'Are you drunk?'

'No.'

'It's 3:30 on a Sunday afternoon. Please tell me you're not drunk.'

'Fuck off, Caz. Go back to your *girlfriend*.'

'You've got a meeting tomorrow. You know, that meeting I arranged for you. The one to save your job.'

'I said. Fuck. Off.'

'Fine,' she spits and hangs up.

I hold the cushion to my face and scream, then pick up the wine bottle and hurl it against the wall, followed by the glass. White wine rolls down the paintwork and drips onto the broken glass below. The acidic stench hits me, but I don't care. I don't care about anything because nothing can ever destroy me as much as losing Mel did. I grab the bottle of vodka that Zoe left from the kitchen, fall back onto the couch and throw my phone across the room. I put crap on TV and cling to Mel's ashes. The panther sits beside me, purring, its tail flicking, and we drink until late into the night. Until everything in front of me is doubled. Until I can't stand up.

*

'Amy, wake up.'

Someone is shaking me.

'Amy.'

'What?' My head spins and a wave of nausea hits me. I squint at Maddie leaning over me. I groan and put my hand to my head. 'Oh, god.'

'Jesus, Ames.' She prises Mel's ashes from me and puts them back on the bookshelf, her hand lingering on the urn. She glances at the broken glass across the room, the empty vodka bottle on the coffee table, and a half-eaten pizza that I don't remember ordering on the floor. Her forehead creases. 'What happened?'

My mouth is a festering pit of stale alcohol. I throw my forearm across my eyes. 'I don't know,' I whisper. 'I'm such a fucking mess.'

She pulls me up and I fall against her chest. 'I've fucked up everything. With Luke. With Zoe. Caz. Work. Everything.' I clutch her tight as she rubs my back. I can't let go; she's all I have left.

She peels my arms off, grips my face and wipes my cheeks with her thumbs. 'You haven't. You can't think like that.'

'It's so hard,' I say. 'I hurt so much.'

'I know you do.'

'You're so together. You're happy and healthy, and you've met Billie.'

Her mouth twists in a pained expression. 'You think my heart doesn't ache for Mel? It kills me, Amy. I spoke to her almost every day since I was ten. It tears me apart to never hear her voice, to never see her face.'

I know that, but it's hard to remember sometimes – hard to break through my own pain to see others'.

She clutches my shoulders. 'But she's not coming back. No amount of crying or drinking or fucking up your life will bring her back.'

I fall into her arms again, my shoulders shuddering as I sob. She leans her head on mine and her torso shakes as she cries, too. After a few minutes, we pull apart and she wipes her cheek with the back of her hand.

'We need to get it together,' she says. 'I'm going to make you some food and you're going to have a shower.' She heads into the kitchen, returning with a glass of water and two painkillers.

I swallow them, drag myself to the shower and scrub my body, like I'm scrubbing all the alcohol out of my system. But it doesn't work; my dehydrated organs are screaming. When I emerge, Maddie is serving up scrambled eggs on toast for both of us.

'Thanks,' I say, the cutlery trembling as I lift it. 'Don't know what I'd do without you.'

She gives me a sad smile. 'Always promised Mel I'd look out for you if anything happened to her.'

'I made that promise to her about you, but I'm not doing a very good job.'

'I'll need you in the same way one day.' She scoops up a forkful of scrambled egg. 'I take it you're not going to work?'

I shake my head. 'I can't. And I just got my period. My stomach is cramping.'

'Then I can't leave you alone.'

'I'll be fine, Mads.' I spread the egg on my toast and take a bite.

'No, you won't. I'll duck home and pick up my laptop. I can work from here. I'm not meeting any clients today anyway.'

My heart swells because if there's one thing I don't want right now, it's to be alone. 'Thank you.' I wrap my hands around the warm mug of tea. 'How's Zoe?'

Maddie swallows her bite. 'Upset.'

'I can't be the person she wants me to be.'

'She knows that, deep down.'

I sip the sweet milky tea. 'Have you spoken to Caz?'

She puts down her fork and presses her lips together.

I close my eyes and recall our conversation. 'Should I call her?'

'Maybe give her a day or so, hey?'

I nod.

She jumps up and grabs the toast from her plate. 'I'm popping home to get my work stuff. I'll be quick. Will you be okay?'

'I'll be fine.'

I finish my breakfast, then clean up the broken glass, dried-up wine and pizza, the stench causing me to retch. I make myself more tea and settle on the couch with a blanket. It's still raining, and the house is cool. I want Mel's ashes beside me, but Maddie will take them away the minute she returns, so I resist. Still nothing from Luke. I try him once more and tell myself this is the last time I'll contact him. The call goes straight to voicemail. I don't leave a message. I sip my tea and try to refrain from texting Caroline, but I can't. I need her to know that I'm sorry, even if she doesn't want to speak to me.

I'm so sorry Caz. Please call xxxx

The reply doesn't come for fifteen minutes and all I get is an 'x'. That means she can't talk to me at the moment, but hasn't completely written me off. All I want to do is hug her and know that we're okay, but I feel like the tectonic plates have shifted and an earthquake has dislodged our foundation.

Maddie lets herself in and sets herself up at the kitchen table. I drift in and out of sleep with daytime TV humming in the background. Maddie wakes me just before ten. Caroline had messaged her about my meeting. Sian calls and I tell her about Friday – how it's added to my fragile state over the weekend. I email her the file I compiled to support my complaint and drift back to sleep. Maddie brings me water and more painkillers through the day and serves me tomato soup for lunch.

At 5:30, she closes her laptop and moves into the lounge. 'Right, that'll do for today. I'm cooking dinner and staying the night.'

'You don't need to do that, Mads,' I say, pulling my legs up to make room. I'm about to say that I can look after myself, but clearly I can't.

She sits at the end of the couch and pats my shin. 'I want to.'

I give her a grateful smile. 'Do you want Billie to come over? She's welcome. I'd love to meet her.'

'We're not at the seeing each other every night stage. You'll meet her soon.'

I swing my legs off the couch and force myself up. 'I'll make the spare bed for you.'

'And I'll find something for dinner.'

I put clean sheets on the spare bed, while Maddie cooks an impressive pasta dish from the scant ingredients in my kitchen. I ask questions about her work and Billie so that we can't talk about Luke, Caroline or Zoe.

After dinner I say, 'You want to watch a movie?'

'Sure.'

'Can we watch *The Breakfast Club*?'

She smiles. It was one of Mel's favourites. 'You know there's been a heap of good movies made since the mid-eighties, right?'

'I like that one.'

'*St Elmo's Fire* is better, but okay.'

Those two films are how Maddie and Mel became best friends.

I clear the plates from the table. 'Tell me the story again,' I say as I stack the dishwasher.

Maddie grabs a container of chocolate ice-cream from the freezer. 'We were in grade four, and our homework over the weekend was to find things from the eighties that we liked.' She scoops ice-cream into two bowls. 'Mel showed up raving about two movies she'd watched with her big sister. All the other kids were staring at her with no idea what she was talking about. But I thought she was the coolest kid in the class because I didn't know anyone else my age who'd seen them. As soon as she sat down, I passed her a note asking if she wanted to come to my place that weekend to watch them.'

'She kept that note,' I say, moving to the lounge.

Maddie smiles wistfully and drops onto the couch. 'I know she did.'

We eat the entire tub of ice-cream and watch *The Breakfast Club* with Mel's ashes watching over us – the two most important people in her life.

Chapter Sixteen

I'm busy writing a change management plan Greg has asked me to do when my phone rings. I don't bother to check the caller ID. I'm focussed on the job at hand, proving myself to Greg – be the person I once was at work. Besides, it's Thursday and I've given up hope of Luke or Caroline returning my calls. Caroline's also been avoiding me at work by either being in back-to-back meetings or basing herself in the airport office. Not speaking to her whenever I want feels like part of my being has been torn and hangs by a thread.

I returned to work on Tuesday, still as broken as that bottle I smashed against the wall. I wanted to stay home another day, but Maddie forced me out of the house. She stayed again that night, which meant we had to go running yesterday morning, and she's been constantly checking in. I don't ever want to fall back into that place I was on Sunday, so I follow her orders. I suspect she's been in touch with Josh and my parents, too, because they're in contact more than usual. I told her she's like a pesky mosquito that pisses me off by buzzing around my head. She laughed because she knows the truth – that I think she's like an adorable pet dog – loyal, protective, intuitive, and I love her dearly.

Yesterday I had my session with Dr Sachdev and told him every detail about the weekend. I don't think I've ever been that open with him. He directed me to additional support resources and reminded me of the coping strategies I can use. He also revisited a topic he's brought up previously – my motivations for the relationship with Luke, or former relationship, which made me question his motivations for asking. He smiled and said, 'How about you leave the questions to me.' He prescribed a mild anti-depressant, but I don't trust myself not to mix them with alcohol, so I threw the script in the bin. Afterwards, I went to Mum and Dad's to make up for Sunday, but I haven't told them it's over with Luke yet.

So, after three days of 'actively making better choices', to use Dr Sachdev's term, I'm functioning and have thrown myself into work. Greg called a meeting with me first thing Tuesday morning to change my reporting line to him while my complaint against Paul is investigated, and I have another meeting with Sian tomorrow. Paul has been moved to the floor below, so it should be easier to avoid him for a while.

My phone vibrates again. I sneak a glance at the screen and my stomach knots when I see the name flashing. It stops, then rings again a second later. I hit the call answer icon. 'Luke. Hi.'

'I'm sorry to call you at work, it's just that... um...'

The knot tightens. 'Is something wrong? What's the matter?'

'It's Jenna. She's... she's pregnant. I don't know what to do.' His voice is a shaky whisper.

I slump back into my chair. 'Shit.'

'Can you come over after work? What time do you finish?'

'Oh. I suppose,' I say hesitantly. Is it possible I misread 'you're too needy', 'I need space' and 'I can't deal with this'? Or maybe he can't process anything else right now. I check the time in the corner of my monitor – 4:00 p.m. 'Be there as soon as I can.'

'Thanks. And Amy...'

'Yeah?'

'I'm sorry. I've been meaning to call, but it's been chaos.'

I breathe out some tension. 'I'm sorry too. We'll talk about it later. See you soon.'

I hang up and attempt to finish what I'm doing, but I can't get Jenna out of my head – how frightened she'll be and how much she'll be missing her mum. I have a strong urge to bundle her up and protect her. I shoot off a quick email to Greg with a work update and switch off my computer. I turn to leave and inhale sharply as Caroline steps into my office, closing the door behind her. I guess the law of attraction works because she and Luke are all I've thought about this week.

'Hi,' she says. When I don't speak – can't speak – she says, 'I'm sorry.'

I drop my bag and pull her into a hug. And there it is. The needle and thread begin stitching and I start to feel whole again. I step back. 'You've got nothing to be sorry for. I was such a moll.'

She shakes her head. 'So was I. It's none of my business what you do. And I'm sorry I wasn't there for you on Monday.'

We sit down at my meeting table. 'It's not your job to look after me, Caz. And Maddie was amazing – is amazing. She's keeping me in check.' I shrug. 'I've missed you, that's all.'

She nods, a sadness surrounding her. 'I've missed you, too.'

'And Zoe...' I let out a puff of air. 'I'm done. I told her on Sunday and then I spiralled. Everything was too much last week.'

Worry lines form across her forehead. 'I should've noticed you were stressed, that things were too much—'

'No. You can't always do that for me. I've got to sort out this stuff myself.'

She nods again. After a beat, she says, 'Maddie said you haven't heard from Luke?'

'Well, I hadn't, but he just called. I'm going over there now.'

'Oh. Right,' she says, a note of surprise in her voice.

'He sounds like he's in a bad way because Jenna is pregnant.' I grimace.

Caroline's eyes widen. 'Holy shit. That's a bombshell.' She pauses and gives a half-smile. 'And he called you?'

I laugh. 'I know. I can't even look after myself. How does he think I'm going to help with a pregnant teenager?'

She turns serious again. 'Does he know about you?'

She's talking about my own pregnancy when I was eighteen. A few weeks ago when Luke confessed how worried he was about Jenna and something like this happening, I encouraged him to talk to her about birth control because I had been careless with that and there had been consequences, but I doubt he ever got round to that conversation.

'He does. I'm not sure he has many women around him he feels comfortable talking to about this stuff,' I say. 'His mum's in Perth. I'm not sure how close he is with his step mum. He has plenty of married friends, but I don't think he's that friendly with any of their wives.'

'Sounds like he could use your help then.' A wistfulness appears on her face – that look she gets whenever someone is pregnant.

I reach for her hand. The time she spent trying to get pregnant was the beginning of the end for her and Maddie. They tried for a year, Caroline finally falling pregnant two years ago. I'd never seen her so happy. But it was short-lived, ending in miscarriage at twelve weeks, and it broke her. She was starting to accept it when Mel died and her world collapsed again. She coped by throwing herself into caring for Maddie and me. She doesn't talk about having children much anymore, but it's still something she desperately wants.

She takes a deep breath and retracts her hand. 'Well, you'd better get over there.' She stands. 'Let me grab my bag. I'll catch the train home with you.'

*

It's dark by the time I arrive in Sandgate, and the sea breeze nips at my skin. I pull the sleeves of my cardigan down and button it. Luke opens the door before I reach the bottom step and he comes out to greet me.

The security light flicks on and highlights his heavy eyelids.

'Hi,' he says.

'Hey.'

He wraps his arms around me. He smells fresh, as though he's just stepped out of the shower. I press my face into his neck and breathe in his earthy bodywash. I've missed him.

'I've fucked up,' he says, still holding me.

I think about the times I've nursed friends through difficulties and search for the strength and resilience I used to have. He needs me, and I can do this for him. I place my hand against his cheek, his stubble prickly against my palm. 'You look shattered. Have you slept?'

He shakes his head. 'Not much.'

'Come on. We can't sort anything standing out here.' I link my arm in his and lead him up the steps.

Inside, the house is oddly quiet. 'Where are Cody and Jenna?'

'Upstairs. Jenna hasn't stopped crying since she told me yesterday. And Cody doesn't know what to do, so he's staying out of the way. He tried consoling her, but he's not much better than me.'

I walk towards the kitchen, past the school bags and books spread across the dining table. 'You want a cuppa?'

'Coffee would be great, thanks.'

I gesture to the lounge. 'Go and sit down. I'll bring it over.' As I slip a pod into the machine, I watch him walk to the couch like he has a block of concrete on each foot. I wish I could fix him, fix both of us, but how do you mend something that not even a miracle super glue could hold? This is both of our lives now, rattling around because we're broken inside. At least we can be broken together.

'Here you go.' I hand him a mug and sink into the couch beside him.

'Ta.' He takes a sip then gives a drawn-out sigh. 'What am I going to do?'

I scoot closer to him. 'You can start by telling me what happened.'

He runs through the events of the past five days – Cody giving him a hard time because he's always at work, Jenna's panic attacks, appointments with teachers, and what happened between us playing on his mind the whole time.

Although the guilt about Zoe is eroding my insides, I'm bruised he didn't call me earlier if I was on his mind. Why has he waited until today? Am I just a female fill-in? A necessity? Did he try and get through the week on his own and suddenly realise today that he can't?

'You know that kid Noah,' he continues. 'The one whose house she's been going over to study *biology*.' His eyes flash with anger.

I nod slowly. 'Ah. Noah.'

'I've asked her about him before and she swore nothing was going on, but I saw stuff on TikTok that made it very clear something was.'

I grimace. 'Does he know?'

Luke shakes his head. 'Apparently not. And she doesn't want to tell him.'

'How did you find out?'

He takes another sip of his coffee. 'She's been sick, and I could tell she wasn't bungin' it on 'cause she looked so washed out. She didn't want to go to school this week either, so I kept pushing her and she broke down.'

'She must be so scared.'

'She is.'

'Does she know how far along?'

'She thinks about two months. She said they asked questions at the hospital about whether she could be pregnant. She said no, but it made her realise she could be, so she bought a test. And we've been to the doctor.'

He places his mug on the coffee table and rubs his chin. 'How could I let this happen?'

I take his hands. 'You didn't let this happen. Seventeen-year-olds have sex. You can't blame yourself.'

'I feel like I've failed.' He swallows. 'Like I've let Sarah down,' he adds quietly.

'Oh, Luke. You haven't failed. I had both my parents, no issues in my life, and it still happened to me. It's got nothing to do with your parenting. Has she said what she wants to do?'

He nods. 'She thinks she wants an abortion.'

'And what do you want her to do?'

'Doesn't matter what I think. She needs to make the decision.'

'It does matter. She'll want her dad's support, whatever she decides.'

'Course I'll support her, but I'd be lying if I said I wanted her to keep it. She's too young.' He looks at me intently. The lines around his eyes are deep today, like he's aged years since Saturday. 'What do you think?'

'Me? Oh, well, I agree with you. If she were my daughter, I don't think I would want her to have a child this young either.'

'Can you talk to her? You understand this more than I ever could. You were around the same age, weren't you?'

I don't know whether to be flattered because he trusts me enough to have such a personal conversation with his daughter, or whether to be annoyed because he's possibly only asked me to come over to sort this out for him. 'I was, but I'm not sure that's a good idea. She's not my biggest fan.'

'That's not true. She just can't deal with stuff at the moment. And this is something that needs... well, she needs a woman to talk to, especially someone who's been through it.' His lovely brown eyes are pleading. 'Please, Amy. I don't know what else to do.'

And that confirms I'm right. I'm a need rather than a want. But does that matter if he also serves a need for me? 'If you think it will help.'

'Thank you.'

I hold his face with both hands. 'And then I think we should talk.'

He closes his eyes and leans his forehead against mine. 'Yep.'

'Let's do this.' I stand and hold my hand out for him. 'You should probably come with me. And then maybe you can check on Cody?'

He takes my hand and hoists himself up.

Upstairs, he knocks on Jenna's door before opening it. 'Jen?'

She's lying on the bed with her back to the door. Music is softly playing from her phone on the desk, and the lit-up screen casts a white light along her body. A pillow is between her knees and a box of tissues sit on another pillow beside her. Luke switches on her lamp and sits down.

'Sweetheart?' He places his hand gently on her shoulder.

She turns, her face red and patchy, and her eyes flick to me. There's a brief look of confusion, but it passes, like she's too exhausted to fight it. 'Oh, hi, Amy.'

'Hi, Jenna.'

'Dad told you then?' She sits up and pulls her knees to her chest.

'Is that okay?' I say.

She nods and holds a tissue to her nose.

Luke shifts so that I can sit between them. I tentatively put my hand on her shoulder. 'How are you feeling?'

To my surprise, she falls into my arms. 'I don't know what to do. And I miss Mum.'

The anguish I carry for their loss crashes with mine, causing my throat to burn. A desperate longing will be racing around inside her right now, and nothing can take that away at a time like this. I stroke her hair as her tears wet my neck.

Luke stands and mouths, 'I'll leave you alone.'

After a few minutes, Jenna pulls away and dabs at her face with the sleeve of her jumper. 'How much did Dad tell you?'

'I think he told me most of it. About Noah. That you think you might be a couple of months along.'

She nods.

'He also said you think you want an abortion. Is that everything?'

'Pretty much,' she says.

'Nothing you've kept from your dad?'

She shakes her head.

'Is that what you want?'

'I… I think so.' She looks at me, the attitude and fire that's blazed all these weeks replaced by fear and vulnerability. 'Is that wrong?'

'No. But you need to do what's right for you, not for anyone else.'

'Dad wants me to get rid of it, doesn't he?'

'He wants you to be happy and to have a good life. He doesn't want to make this decision for you.'

'What would you do?' Her brows draw together. 'Oh, have you had boyfriends before Dad?' she asks innocently.

I smile. 'I've had one. And I've been exactly where you are now.'

Her eyes widen. 'What did you do?'

'I had an abortion. I thought I was pretty cool having sex with a boy who was a year older and had a car.'

'Lots of people still think like that.'

'I ended up telling him, and he dumped me straight away.'

She tuts. 'Arsehole.'

'He sure was. I thought about it for a while but decided to go through with it in the end.'

'Do you regret it?'

I shake my head. 'Not really. It would've changed my life, and probably not for the better. There's no way I could've been a good parent back then. I made the right decision – for me.' I brush a strand of hair from her wet face and pull another tissue from the box for her. 'That doesn't mean it's the right decision for everyone, though.'

She takes the tissue and holds it under her nose.

'Are you going to talk to Noah?'

She shrugs. 'We're not going out. He's a bit of a dick, actually. I don't even like him that much. He's just hot and popular, and he pays me a lot of attention.'

'I get it, and you don't have to rush your decision. You can talk to other people about it. A counsellor, if you think that will help.'

'Maybe.'

'Why don't you come downstairs for some dinner. I don't think your dad has eaten all day, and I bet you haven't either, so I might need to take charge of the food situation tonight. Which is scary because my speciality is toast.'

She smiles through her tears. 'Dad can only cook steak.'

I rub her arm. 'I might need my friends to give us some cooking lessons.' A rush of empathy hits me for this beautiful girl who's been struggling all these months but had no idea how to handle her emotions. I, more than most, should've recognised what she was going through. Deep regret for not making more of an effort weighs on me. 'And hey, I'm sorry about Saturday. That was a stupid thing for me to say.'

'It's okay. I shouldn't have said that either. I know Dad likes you being here.'

'I like being here, too. You want to come downstairs?'

She nods. 'Soon.'

I stand and head for the door.

'Amy?'

'Yeah?' I say, facing her.

'If... if I have an abortion, can you be there? For me and for Dad?' She pulls her knees up and wraps her arms around her legs.

My chest is so tight right now. I walk back over and kiss the top of her head. 'Of course.' I have no idea what will happen between Luke and me, but I'm certain I can commit to that.

When I get downstairs, Cody's watching TV and Luke's at the kitchen table on his laptop.

'Hi, Cody,' I say as I walk past.

'Hi.' He waves, not taking his eyes off the screen.

'Hey. How'd you go?' Luke asks, hope filling his tired eyes.

I lower my voice so Cody can't overhear. 'She seemed to open up. She's worried about what you want her to do.'

He sighs. 'I just want her to be happy and to think about things.'

'She's smart enough to do that. Especially now that you know. And the fact you're supporting her rather than losing your shit helps.'

He shakes his head. 'Oh, I lost it yesterday. I was so bloody angry with her. And I was ready to murder Noah. I calmed down overnight, though, realised it wasn't helping.'

I rub his shoulder. 'There you go, sign of a good dad right there.'

He smiles weakly. 'Thank you for talking to her. For rushing over here. For being in our lives.' He leans forward to kiss me. It's gentle and lingering. 'I'm not sure what I would've done without you right now.'

Those are loving words, followed by a loving kiss, and now my head is foggy with confusion and my heart is heavy with guilt. I give a tight smile. 'No problem. Right. You need to eat and so does Jenna. Cody is probably starving, too.'

'Yeah, I am!' Cody shouts over the TV.

Luke raises his eyebrows and shakes his head. 'Amazing.'

I laugh. 'Okay, Cody. I'm on it.' I turn back to Luke. 'You know if I'm in charge of dinner, it's takeaway, right?'

He grins. 'Yep.'

'I'll nip down to that nice Thai place in Shorncliffe,' I say.

'Yes, Thai!' Cody says, punching his fist in the air.

'Have you heard this whole conversation, Cody?' Luke asks.

'Nuh. Just the food bit.'

I pick up my bag as Jenna comes downstairs. 'Hi, Jenna. I'm going out for some Thai. Anything you want?'

'Um... fried noodles? And maybe chicken satay?'

'Hey, Jen.' Luke holds out his arm for her, and she hugs him.

'Back soon,' I say.

'Thank you,' he mouths over Jenna's head.

I watch them for a few seconds, their bond palpable, and ask myself whether that's something I can be a part of – whether it's something Luke wants me to be part of – before heading outside and jumping in my car. I pull out my phone to find a text from Caroline and another from Maddie. I plug into the car play, and reverse.

Everything okay? My car reads Caroline's text.

This is one of Caroline's special qualities – regardless of her feelings on something or someone, she always cares about other people.

Yep fill you in tomorrow I'm sorting out dinner

She replies within seconds.

Hope they enjoy their toast

I chuckle and play Maddie's text.

Caz told me about Jenna. Fuck. Make sure you look after yourself too. We still running in morning?

I smile because I still get a kick out of my car having to swear from reading a message, and her commitment to making me human again is everything.

We are. see you at seven

Half an hour later, I'm back at Luke's with the nutty scent of satay and fresh coriander seeping from the containers. For the first time since I've been seeing him, we all eat together at the kitchen table. School bags and books have been pushed to the side, the conversation is awkward, and that discussion Luke and I need to have about the weekend hangs between us, but I'll take all of that over Jenna's snide comments any day.

Jenna and Luke pick at their food, while Cody and I demolish huge platefuls of chicken satays, pad Thai and Massaman curry. Luke has a beer and offers me one, but I still can't face alcohol after Sunday. Also,

I want to be fresh for my run and my meeting with Sian tomorrow, so I opt for lemonade with the kids instead.

After dinner, Cody and Jenna head to their rooms, and Luke and I settle on the couch.

I face him and take his hand; it's rough and dry. 'I'm sorry about what I said to Jenna. I was so angry at myself. I know it's been hard for her, and I should've supported her, not acted like a teenager myself.'

He gives my hand a squeeze before releasing it and reaching for his beer. 'I don't blame you for snapping. I let her get away with treating you like that.' He sighs. 'Because of what they've been through, I'm wary about coming down too hard on them, but I should've been tougher with her.' His voice wobbles and he takes a quick swig of his beer. 'And I'm sorry about that whole calling you Sarah thing—'

I wave away his comment. 'Let's forget that.'

He nods. 'I was confused and embarrassed, and I didn't know how to be around you after that, if that makes sense.'

'It does. I would've felt the same.'

'I don't think you're needy either. That was a stupid thing to say.'

I shrug. 'I can be sometimes.'

'Reckon I need you more than you need me.'

I smile. 'Let's agree we're equally as needy.'

He grins. 'Righto.'

We're quiet for a long moment, until I say, 'You said you also needed space, a break…'

His eyes meet mine and he gives a single nod. 'I might've got that part right.'

My chest stings a little. 'I see.'

'Last weekend, I mean. I needed to sort out my head, and…' He shakes his head. 'Never mind.'

'No, go on.'

He crosses his ankle over his knee and picks at the hem of his jeans.

'I could tell by your messages that you were upset, but I couldn't see us working out, and I didn't want to deal with it.' He looks at me. 'I'm sorry I ignored your calls, but it was too much for me. I knew you'd have people around you all weekend, so you would've been okay.'

I try not to scoff at that comment. 'I had a bad weekend actually.'

His eyes widen. 'Shit.'

'I completely unravelled. Drank a lot. Had a big argument with Caz.' Heat rises in my cheeks and I look away quickly, deciding to leave out one minor detail. Or major, depending how you look at it. I mean, Luke and I were done, so what happened with Zoe doesn't technically count, right? And what would telling him achieve anyway?

He lets out a remorseful sigh and peers up at the ceiling. 'Fuck, Amy. I'm sorry.'

I shake my head. 'No, it's not your fault. It was me not dealing with stuff, and I should've given you the space you needed and not kept calling. Maddie sorted me out. Got me back on track. I had a session with Dr Sachdev yesterday and that helped.'

He nods. 'Good.'

I wait to see if he offers anything more about his own sessions or how this situation with Jenna has affected him, but he picks up his beer and downs the last mouthful. 'Did you get to Dr Garcia this week?' I ask gently.

He places his empty bottle on the coffee table. 'Nah, too much going on. I feel alright though.'

I doubt that's true, but there's a finality to his words that tells me this topic is closed.

He yawns. 'Long day. Need to be up early for work.'

'Oh.' I stand. 'I'll get going then.'

He stands too and after a beat he says, 'Oh, did you want to stay? You can.'

As much as I don't want to leave him alone, it doesn't feel right to stay, and I'm slighted by the afterthought. Besides, I'm still shaky after the weekend and need Mel around me. 'I think I'll go home. I'll call tomorrow to see how Jenna is.'

He walks me to the door. 'Maybe we could spend some time together this weekend? If you're free?'

I nod. 'I'd like that.'

We exchange a hug goodbye, and I give him a wave as I drive off with that confusing fog clouding my vision.

Chapter Seventeen

The Spring Hill family planning clinic's bright white walls and faint smell of disinfectant take me back to when I sat in a similar waiting room. Although I was eighteen, my parents insisted on being with me. Their reservation and sadness told me their true feelings, but they never tried to persuade me otherwise. They just made sure I was armed with as much information as possible and took the time I needed to decide. The benefits of having a GP dad and a medical receptionist mum, I guess. Almost immediately after my termination, Josh and Sophie announced they were pregnant with their second. It was a bittersweet moment that shifted the focus from me.

It's different for Jenna. She's a year younger than I was and doesn't have her mum, which will be ripping her apart – Luke, too. They don't need to say it; their pain is obvious from their downcast mouths, their tormented eyes and the heaviness in their steps. Despite Luke's torment, I watch him comforting and supporting Jenna, being the best dad he can be, and it's beautiful to watch. I wish he could see what I see instead of constantly blaming himself for what happened.

When he hasn't been supporting the kids, the past week is the worst I've seen him. He hasn't slept or eaten properly, and he didn't see Dr Garcia on Tuesday. In fact, he hasn't seen her for weeks, he finally admitted to me. I encouraged him to go, even offered to collect the kids from school, drive Cody to basketball training and sort out dinner so that he could. But his irritability told me to drop it.

Now he stares blankly at the wall-mounted TV playing a twenty-four-hour news channel, holding Jenna's small hand in his large one while she jiggles one leg up and down by the ball of her foot.

A soft voice sounds. 'Jenna Harris?'

Jenna looks at Luke, her face tight with angst.

'This is Jenna,' Luke says, standing.

The nurse smiles warmly, an air of calm emanating from her. 'Hi, Jenna. I'm Simone. I'm going to look after you today.'

'Hi,' Jenna says meekly.

'We'll have a chat first. Is that okay?'

Jenna nods.

Luke rests his hand on Jenna's back as we follow Simone down a wide corridor to a small office. She takes a seat at a desk, and we occupy the three seats opposite.

'Jenna, I want to talk to you about the procedure and run through everything that happens today,' Simone says before launching into the details.

The day following my talk with Jenna, she went to a counsellor at a local health centre and decided to proceed with the abortion. I had to take charge then because Luke couldn't. Not that I minded. It took my mind off the pressures at work and gave me something to focus on. It also helped Jenna and I discover that we like each other. We're maybe even a little bit similar with our attitudes and phone obsessions and dry sense of humour. Luke relaxed slightly, for a couple of days at least, knowing a decision had been made and that it was all in hand, and we were able to have a nice weekend together. He was attentive and caring, and the make-up sex was pretty good.

'I'm sorry Mr and Mrs Harris—'

Simone's voice cuts through my thoughts and it takes a moment to register what she's said. I'm annoyed she assumes we're married, then I remember Luke and I still have our wedding rings on display. 'Oh, I'm not Mrs Harris, I'm...' I'm not sure what I am.

Luke jumps in. 'This is my... this is Amy. My wife, she...' He pauses. 'You can call me Luke.'

I'm just Amy. I glance at Luke, but he's focussed on Simone. I'm not sure what I expected him to say – partner or girlfriend might've been nice.

Simone smiles. 'Okay, Amy and Luke. I'm sorry, I'm going to have to ask you to leave while I chat with Jenna.'

Jenna looks at both of us, her eyes wide.

'Why?' Luke asks.

Simone laces her fingers together over the desk. 'We need to understand Jenna's own thoughts about this. We need to know that she's made this decision for herself.' She holds her hands up. 'That's not to say I think you've forced her. She's seventeen, and you're both clearly very supportive, but it's protocol that we speak to all clients alone.'

Luke nods and turns to Jenna. 'Alright, Jen?'

She stares down at her feet. 'Yeah.'

Luke and I head back to the waiting room, and I make tea from the drinks station. 'Here you go.' I hand him a cup and sit beside him. 'I don't think we've shared a horrible polystyrene cup of tea since group therapy.'

He gives a weak smile. 'No, we haven't.' He takes a sip and looks directly into my eyes. 'I'm glad I went to therapy that day.'

This is Luke, I've come to realise, distant one minute, sweet the next. I pat his thigh. 'Me, too.'

He leans his head against the wall and releases a long, exhaustive sigh. 'This is horrible. Seeing her here, going through this. And I feel judged. Like the nurse is thinking what sort of father lets his seventeen-year-old get pregnant.'

'No one here will be judging you. Teenagers do what they want sometimes. You can't control them.'

His head is still resting on the wall, and he shifts his eyes to me. 'It's hard not to feel responsible.'

I lean in and he drapes his arm around my shoulder. 'You need to not be so tough on yourself. You're a great dad. The kids know that.'

'Thanks,' he murmurs, his lips brushing my temple, but he's up in a shot when Jenna and Simone emerge from the corridor.

'I'm going to take Jenna through to get gowned up,' Simone says. 'You won't be able to see her until she's in recovery.'

Luke pulls Jenna close. 'It'll be okay, sweetheart.' She clings to him, her eyes watery. He kisses her forehead and releases her.

'We'll be right here when you wake up. Everything will be fine,' I say, giving her a hug.

She dabs the corner of her eye, and Simone places a maternal arm around her. 'Time to go.'

'Love you,' Luke says and reaches out to squeeze Jenna's hand.

'Love you, too,' she says.

He stands in the middle of the waiting room staring after her until she disappears, and it makes me ache for him. I link my finger through the belt loop in the back of his jeans. 'Come on. We'll go for a walk and get some decent coffee. They'll call you when she's in recovery.'

*

By the time we arrive back at Luke's, the sun is setting over the bay. The late afternoon joggers and dog walkers look minuscule against the expanse of azure sky and lilac cloud. There's a crisp autumnal air, so Ben, Chris and Cody are in the lounge with the bifold doors to both decks closed. Cody's sitting cross-legged on the rug with his laptop on the coffee table, and Chris and Ben are slumped on the couch drinking wine and yelling answers to a quiz show that's on TV.

Ben jumps up and opens his arms wide for Jenna. 'Baby girl, come here. How are you?' He squeezes her before pulling away and holding her at arm's length.

'I'm fine, thanks, Uncle Ben,' she says, with a tired smile.

Chris embraces her next. 'We were worried about you.'

Cody stands and gives her an awkward hug, his long arms wrapping around her small body. 'Glad you're home.'

She returns the hug. 'Don't tell anyone at school about this. Don't tell Noah!'

He rolls his eyes and plonks back down on the rug. 'I'm not an idiot. I don't talk to him anyway. He's a fucking dickhead.'

Luke drops onto the couch. 'Oi, language.'

'Hey, Amy,' Ben says, giving me a peck on the cheek. 'Grab a glass and come have a wine.'

I've barely drunk since my Sunday bender almost two weeks ago, but it's a Friday, it's been a long day, and I'm a little wound up from absorbing Luke's stress all week. 'That sounds good. Do you want something, Luke?'

'I'll have a beer, thanks.'

'I'm going to lie down, Dad,' Jenna says.

Luke holds his hand out and she takes it. 'I'll come and get you when dinner's ready.'

She nods and heads upstairs. Cody picks up his laptop and ventures towards the kitchen.

I hand Luke his beer, he takes a swig and lies his head back on the couch. 'Jesus Christ. What a fucking day. What a fucking week.'

'Language, Dad,' Cody says, popping back to grab his phone from the coffee table.

I can't help but laugh.

'Everything go smoothly?' Chris asks once Cody is out of earshot.

'I think so. She was okay, right?' Luke asks me.

'Yeah, she was fine. Really brave.'

'That's good,' Ben says. 'She must be feeling pretty down.'

Luke nods, that sadness he carries around with him coming to the fore. I give his leg a supportive rub.

'Hey, what are you two doing for dinner?' he says to Ben and Chris 'Why don't you stick around? Have something to eat, a few drinks?'

I glance at him, trying to keep my disappointment under wraps. As much as I like Ben and Chris, I'm drained, and I want to spend time with Luke. He must be a mess inside.

'Oh, if we're not intruding?' Chris says, looking between us.

'Nah, course not,' Luke says.

I smile politely. 'Not at all.'

Luke moves off the topic of Jenna and talks about more general things – his business, what Ben and Chris have been up to, Cody's school play, and the clips he's discovered on TikTok forgetting why he created an account in the first place. As the time slips by, the beer slides down his neck way too fast. I can see the stress and sorrow being pushed further into that emotional safe he keeps stored away. I drop a few hints about him working tomorrow, and me going to Maddie's for her birthday, but the alcohol has taken effect and he doesn't care. And who am I to lecture when I'm hooking into the wine just as much?

*

I wake the next morning with a dry mouth, a splitting head, and an overwhelming sense of disappointment. I promised Dr Sachdev and Maddie I would ease up on the alcohol. The late morning sun penetrates the windows making the room too warm, and the stench of day-old body odour fills my nostrils. Luke lies on his stomach with the sheet covering his bottom half. What time we came to bed, I can't remember. I throw off the doona, sit up and drain the glass of water beside me.

Luke stirs. 'Ugh,' he groans.

'How much did we drink?' I put my hand to my forehead.

'A lot.' He grabs a packet of painkillers from the drawer in the side table. He hands me two and takes out a couple for himself. 'Here you go.'

'What time did we stop?' I ask, swallowing the tablets.

'Dunno. I don't think they left until one or something. I don't want to know how many empty bottles are downstairs.'

'I feel disgusting.' I swing my legs out of bed. 'I need a shower.'

'Want me to come with you?' He gives me a sly grin.

'Don't even think about it,' I say, walking into the ensuite. He knows my thoughts on couples showering – that it's suffocating rather than sexy. It doesn't stop him trying to encroach on my space in there any chance he gets, though.

He laughs. 'I'll go and assess the damage.'

When I get downstairs twenty minutes later, Cody's in the pool, Jenna's lying in the shade and Luke's in the kitchen staring into the fridge.

'Hi, Jenna,' I say, stepping out to the back deck. 'How are you?'

She looks up and shades her eyes from the glare with her phone. 'I'm good. Feel better.' She points to the kitchen. 'How much did you all drink? Have you seen how many empty bottles are in the kitchen?'

I wince. 'We got a bit carried away.'

She tuts and jumps off the lounger to follow me into the kitchen. 'Are you okay, Dad?'

A row of empty wine and beer bottles are lined up on the bench, along with dirty plates and cutlery.

'Yeah. Why?' He opens the cupboard door to place the bottles in the recycle.

'You don't normally drink so much. I thought that maybe...' She shakes her head. 'Nothing.'

'Maybe what?' he says, facing her.

'That maybe it was a bit much for you yesterday.' She looks at me briefly before turning her attention back to Luke. 'Without Mum there,' she adds softly.

He focusses on stacking the plates by the sink. 'I'm fine, Jen.' He gives her a reassuring smile. 'Just cut a bit loose, that's all.'

'Hmm. If you say so,' she says before going back outside.

I walk around to the other side of the bench. 'You sure you're okay?'

'I'm fine,' he snaps.

I narrow my eyes at him, but I let it go and glance around the kitchen. 'What a mess. Looks like we enjoyed ourselves.'

'We did,' he says, his voice softening. 'Now I feel like shit. I've got a job this arvo as well.' He opens the fridge and guzzles from the water bottle.

Cody walks in with a towel wrapped around his waist, wet hair stuck to his forehead. 'Don't drink straight from the water bottle, Dad.' He sits on the stool. 'What's for lunch?'

'I'll make you something, Cody,' I say. 'What do you want? A toasted sandwich?'

'Yeah, cool, thanks.' He heads back to the pool.

'He's got some form, that kid,' Luke says. He hugs me from behind. 'Sorry. I didn't mean to snap.' He pushes my hair to the side and kisses my shoulder.

'You can't keep things bottled up.' I spin around. 'We talked about this. You need to make an appointment with Dr Garcia. There's too much stuff going on for you.'

He wraps his arms around my waist. 'I'll do it first thing Monday.' His voice is muffled as he buries his face into my neck.

'Yuck, Luke, you stink.' I push him away. 'Go and have a shower while I clean up and make some sandwiches.'

I watch him plod upstairs, like he's filled with lead. I wonder if he was closed off like this with Sarah, or if he's like this because of Sarah. I make a mental note to chat with Ben about it next time I see him.

I tidy up and make lunch for Jenna, Cody and me, popping Luke's sandwich in the press when I hear the water from his shower switch off.

'Better?' I ask when he appears.

He ruffles his damp hair. 'Yep.'

I hand him his sandwich and sit beside him. 'I've got to go after this.'

He looks sideways at me, his mouth half full. 'Where are you going?'

'It's Maddie's birthday. She's having a party at her place. And I need to go shopping for her present.'

He nods. 'I remember now,' he says and takes another bite.

'Maddie invited you, but you said you were working today and that you wanted to catch up with Nick afterwards.'

'No worries. I've got plenty to do.'

I look outside. Cody's hands are flying around as he tells Jenna a story, and she's in fits of giggles.

'They seem good today,' I say.

He twists his head to glance at them, then turns back to me. 'They do, don't they?'

'Maybe after you see Nick you can do something with them. Go for dinner or the movies?'

'Yeah. Maybe.'

'I'm going to clean my teeth and grab my stuff.' I lean across the bench to put my plate by the sink and head for the staircase.

After a few seconds, he calls, 'I'll miss you.'

Distant one minute, sweet the next. 'You'll see me soon,' I call back.

When I get back downstairs, Luke's outside talking to the kids. 'I've got a job on this arvo. I won't be long though. What are you two doing?'

Cody swims over to the side of the pool. 'I'm going to the movies with my friends.'

'Oh, right. Did you tell me about this?' Luke asks.

Cody pushes away from the side with his feet and floats on his back. 'Yes, Dad,' he says, with the tone of a bored fifteen-year-old.

Jenna looks up, squinting into the sun. 'I'm going to Emma's.'

'Is Emma the one that got the drugs?' Luke asks, crossing his arms.

She rolls her eyes. 'That was Kate. And we're not going to take drugs, don't worry.'

He relaxes. 'Alright then.'

'I've gotta go,' I say to him before looking down at Jenna. 'You take it easy the next couple of days, hey?'

She gives me a small smile. 'I will. And, um, thanks.'

I bend down and give her a hug. 'No problem. Bye, Cody,' I call into the pool.

'See ya!' he shouts before diving under the water.

Luke walks me to my car. 'Have fun at the party.' Then he leans through the window and kisses me, deep and intense with plenty of tongue. It's kind of hot, and I have an urge to drag him upstairs for ten minutes. Maybe five would do.

I pull my head back. 'Jesus. What was that?'

He smirks. 'Just saying goodbye. Will, er, will Zoe and Caz be there tonight?'

My cheeks warm and I pray my skin hasn't turned pink. 'Caz, definitely. I suppose Zoe will. Why?'

'Just curious. You were seeing Zoe for a while. You said she was still keen. And Caz...' He shrugs.

I peer at him, confused about where this is coming from, then a hazy memory of a conversation late last night drifts into my mind. Ben and Chris asked about my sexuality, my partner history, my friends, how I identify – not distrustfully, just with a genuine curiosity. I remember saying, with the free tongue that wine always gifts me with, that I'm still attracted to women, but I'm also attracted to Luke. And I told them about my history with Caroline. All of it. *Shit.* I recall a bemused Luke peering at me across the coffee table and a realisation spreading across his face. It was as though he'd forgotten my former life existed, and that he'd just grasped that my sexuality is part of who I am – that the attraction to women doesn't switch off because he's in my life.

I'm also madly racing through other conversations from last night to make sure I didn't inadvertently talk about what happened with Zoe recently. When I'm confident I haven't, I say, 'Zoe's moved on. She and Maddie have had a thing since, and she sees other people and we hardly speak anymore...' I wave my hand around as I ramble.

He smiles. 'I'm just muckin' 'round.'

'Oh. Right.' I click in my seatbelt and start the engine. 'Come here.' I motion him towards me with my index finger and give him a much less heated kiss. 'I'll call you tomorrow.'

He taps the bottom of the window frame. 'Go on, get out of here.'

I reverse and see him in the rear-view mirror watch me drive off. I pull at my shirt, which suddenly feels like it's choking me, and step on the accelerator.

Chapter Eighteen

I drive straight to Chermside Shopping Centre and spend a few solitary hours browsing for Maddie's gift and something to wear to her party. She didn't celebrate last year because it was the first birthday without Mel since they'd met, but she's in a better place now and has been looking forward to today. She's also finished some renovations, so it's a housewarming of sorts, too.

I buy her a set of cast-iron cookware she's had her eye on for a housewarming gift and a white gold chain with a tiny diamond 'M' for her birthday – to symbolise both her and Mel. Extravagant, but she's worth it. I search for an outfit and settle on an emerald green, knee-length Georgette dress that's covered in a pattern of tiny white leaves, which the sales assistant says is 'made for me'. I inwardly roll my eyes, but I do love the dress – and the comment. And her sales patter of 'look how well it blends with your gorgeous green eyes and chestnut hair' absolutely works. Because I'm in a spending mood, on impulse, I buy a pair of tan ankle boots to team with it on the way out.

At home, with an hour to spare, I make an effort with my hair, running some irons through to tame my waves, and go for an evening look with smoky eye make-up and thick black mascara. I'm excited about the party, to spend time with Maddie and Caroline, to meet Billie and to catch up with Maddie's sisters who are visiting from Melbourne. Zoe will be there, and I'm a little queasy at the thought of seeing her, but she's part of our circle so I need to be a normal functioning adult around her. I grab a lightweight jacket, Maddie's gifts, and jump in the car for the short drive to her place.

I park in the driveway and walk along the side of the house to the backyard, following the sound of chatter and music. A large marquee sits in the middle of the lawn decorated with strands of white lights that hang loosely from the frame. It looks magical against the twilight sky. The garden beds that run the length of the fence are lined with solar lights and filled with new plants. Maddie and Zoe's work colleagues and our mutual friends are scattered around, along with Maddie's two younger sisters. Maddie is talking to Caroline and a woman with sandy blonde shoulder-length hair who I recognise as Billie from the photos Maddie has shown me.

'Hey, you made it,' Maddie says, approaching me with open arms. 'Wow, look at you. You look gorgeous.'

I smile. 'Thanks. Thought you were worth the effort.' I place the gifts on a table beside her and pull her into a hug, catching a delicate spicy fragrance. 'Ooh, you smell good. What's that?' She offers me her neck and I bend down for another sniff.

'It's the new Tom Ford. Like it?'

'Yeah. Sexy.' I point to her gifts. 'There's your pressies. Happy birthday. Happy housewarming.' I gesture to the larger one. 'That's your housewarming.' And then to the small box. 'And that's your birthday.'

She holds up her birthday present. 'I'll open this now.' She unwraps it and opens the box, then peers at me. 'Oh, Ames, it's beautiful.'

I give her another squeeze. 'Happy birthday.'

She pulls the chain out and holds it up. 'Put it on me.'

I clasp it around her neck and turn her back around pressing my finger against the 'M'. 'Perfect.'

She grasps the pendant. 'I love it, thank you.'

The woman with the sandy coloured hair appears next to her, and

Maddie slides her arm across her shoulders. She's small like Maddie and quite beautiful with dark eyebrows and a coating of freckles covering otherwise flawless skin. Her eyes are unusual, kind of a cinnamon colour with flecks of hazel.

'Ames, this is Billie.'

Billie beams at me. 'Hi, Amy. I've heard so much about you.'

'Ha. I bet!' I grin.

She gives a one-shoulder shrug and a faux catty brow raise. 'It's mostly good,' she says, with a jokey tone.

I point at her. 'You're cheeky. I like it.' I gently rub her upper arm. 'It's nice to meet you. I've also heard plenty about you.'

She blushes and looks coyly at Maddie who winks at her. Sweet.

'Hey, Caz,' I say, stepping to the side.

'Hi.' Her eyes flick over me. 'Cute outfit. New?'

I hold out the skirt of my dress. 'Yeah, do you like it? The shop assistant said it matches my eyes.'

She smiles warmly. 'She's right, it does. It's lovely.'

I fall into place beside her and glance in Zoe's direction. She looks incredible as always, but I'm determined to keep my eyes firmly on her face. NFA – Normal Functioning Adult. That's who I am now. 'Who's that with Zoe?'

Caroline leans in. 'That is Taylor.'

'Who's Taylor?'

'Her new partner, apparently.'

I turn to Caroline, open-mouthed. 'Her what? How is that possible? There's only been a couple of weeks between... oh, hang on, unless she was already seeing her.'

She shrugs. 'Probably.'

'Huh, and she had the cheek to give me a hard time.' I size up the alleged partner. She has short black hair, which is a sharp contrast against her white skin. I can't tell what colour her eyes are from here, although I can see the fire behind them. 'She looks fierce.'

Caroline grins. 'She does.'

Taylor's eyes cut to me. I gasp and face Caroline. 'Shit. Did you see that?'

Caroline chuckles and nods. 'Maddie's had a few of those looks, too. It's fascinating. I know exactly who Zoe's slept with here by the looks Taylor is throwing out. Which means Zoe's told her.'

'Well, Zo's always been a fuck-and-tell kind of person,' I mutter, watching Taylor to see who else she's spearing with her eyes. 'I need to patch things up with Zoe. I'm going over.'

'You're brave.' She gestures to a bottle of wine on the table. 'You might want a drink first for courage.'

'Yuck, no thanks. We drank way too much last night. I might grab one later.' I take a deep breath. 'Here I go.'

'Good luck. I'm going to chat to Priya,' she says, pointing the neck of her sparkling water bottle towards Maddie's sister.

Zoe watches me cautiously as I approach. So does Taylor.

'Hey, Zo,' I say in my best casual voice.

'Hello,' she says warily.

'How are you?'

'Fine.' She points to her left. 'This is Taylor. Taylor, this is Amy.'

Did I hear some emphasis on *this* is Amy? 'Hi, Taylor.' I flash a smile.

She does an upward nod. 'Hey.' Her eyes are dark and intense, and they burn me.

I turn back to Zoe. 'So, how are you?'

'You've already asked me that.' She necks the last mouthful of her wine.

'Oh, right.' There's an awkward pause before I wave my finger between them. 'Caz said you two...'

Zoe looks at Taylor and smiles then turns back to me. 'Yeah.'

Taylor stares at me with a satisfied smirk, like she's beaten me in a competition for Zoe's heart.

'That's great,' I say. 'I'm happy for you.'

Zoe tilts her head. 'Are you?'

'Of course I am, Zo.'

The ice melts, just a little. 'Okay, thanks. I guess.'

Taylor puts her hand on Zoe's lower back. 'You want another drink, babe?'

Babe? How long have these two been seeing each other?

'Yeah, thanks,' Zoe says, all syrupy sweet.

Taylor plants one on her lips while giving me a bit of side-eye and struts off.

Once she's out of earshot, I say, 'I'm sorry about the other weekend, Zo. I wasn't in a good place.'

She crosses her arms. 'Maddie said you weren't good afterwards either.'

'No. I wasn't.'

'She also said it's back on with Luke.'

I nod. 'It is.'

'And did you tell him about that night?' she asks with a judgemental lift of her brow.

'Did you tell Taylor?' I shoot back.

She sniffs. 'Taylor knows about you.'

'Does she know about me two weeks ago? I assume you haven't just met.'

'Thanks for your apology and I hope things work out with Luke.'

'I'll take that as a no, so don't give me a hard time about not telling him. Besides, I thought Luke and I were done at the time.' I sigh and reach for her hand, yanking it away when Taylor shoots me a glare from the other side of the marquee. 'Come on, Zo, we were good friends before. I'd like us to keep being friends. And I'm pleased you're making a go of it with someone.'

She stares at me a moment before she gives a defeated grunt. 'Apology accepted.'

I smile. 'That's good enough for me.' I lean forward. 'Taylor's scaring the shit out of me.'

She smirks. 'I know. She's full on; I love it.'

I laugh. 'I think she might be good for you.'

She glances in Taylor's direction, her eyes soft and a tiny, dreamy smile on her lips. We never looked at each other like that, and I feel vindicated because it proves that I was right about us.

'I think so, too,' she says.

Taylor appears as I'm about to walk away. 'Nice to meet you, Taylor,' I say in my friendliest voice. 'Maybe I'll see you again soon.'

She narrows her eyes. 'Yeah. Maybe.'

I give an uncertain nod and head back to Caroline who's ditched the water and is pouring herself a pinot.

'How'd it go?' she asks.

'Okay, I suppose. Taylor made my soul shrivel and die.'

Caroline laughs and takes a sip of her wine. 'How's things with Jenna? No issues yesterday?'

'It all went well, and she's good today. Luke on the other hand... I'm worried about him. He's stopped seeing his psychologist.'

Caroline frowns. 'Hmm, that's not good.'

'He gets shitty every time I bring it up. I can't force him to talk or to go back to therapy.' I shake my head. 'And all this stuff with Jenna. He's really stressed. Not eating or sleeping properly.'

'Maybe he doesn't know how to open up. Men can be like that, can't they? You have to keep trying, I guess.' She gives me a wry smile. 'It's not easy getting someone to go to therapy when they need it.'

'Okay, don't rub it in.' I dig out a bottle of water from the ice bucket behind me. 'How's things with you? I'm sorry I haven't had much time to catch up this week. Greg's got me doing a million things, and I've had all those meetings with Sian and then sorting stuff for Jenna.'

She gives a half smile, but there's a discontent behind her eyes. 'No worries. It's great you're getting into work again.'

'Yeah, it feels good,' I say, watching her closely. 'Sure you're okay?'

'Uh huh.' She sips her drink.

I follow her gaze across the marquee where Maddie and Billie are sharing a tender kiss. 'Those two are well suited.'

Caroline nods. 'They are.'

'You alright with that?'

She fixes me with a deadpan expression. 'It's been nine months since we split. I'm fine with it. Billie's lovely. It's great for Maddie.'

So that's not it. 'And how's things with Rachel?'

She sips her wine and looks away. 'That kind of stopped during the week.'

Bingo. 'What? Why didn't you call me?'

She shrugs. 'It's not a big deal.'

'Oh. Right. Well, I'm still sorry to hear that.'

She gives me some sceptical side-eye.

'Caz, don't be like that.' I nudge her with my shoulder. 'I would've warmed to her eventually.'

'No, you wouldn't.'

'Course I would. What happened?' I try again.

'It just fizzled out.' She points to one of Maddie's colleagues. 'Oh, I want to catch Terri. They've bought a new house and done all this work on it,' she says and walks away.

Maddie will tell me what's going on, but Caroline will be suss if I go straight to her, so I do the rounds. I chat to Maddie's sisters for a while before moving on to some of our mutual friends.

An hour later, I sidle up beside Maddie and Billie. Maddie has a large glass of white wine in one hand and her other arm is around Billie's waist. A strand of lights sways in the breeze above their heads, and they gaze at each other, talking quietly between kisses.

'You two are very cute,' I say.

'Hey, Ames,' Maddie says.

'Having a nice time?' I ask.

'Sure am.' Maddie grabs the bottle of wine from the table and splashes a good measure in her glass. 'Although I'd better slow down after this one; it's still early.'

'You're not drinking?' Billie asks me.

'Not yet. We had a big one last night with Luke's brother. I'll have some food first.'

'Caterers will be here very soon,' Maddie says.

I glance over to Caroline to make sure she's occupied. 'So, things haven't worked out for Rachel and Caz?'

'Nope,' Maddie says.

'Why not?'

'Probably because Rachel's possessive and stalkerish,' Maddie says.

I look at her briefly before turning back to check Caroline isn't on to me. 'Is she really that bad?'

She sighs. 'Maybe not that bad, but she's full on. I don't know why they split; whatever the reason, I'm not surprised. No one can compare to you.'

I whip my head to face her. Her cheeks flush, and Billie winces.

'What did you just say?'

Maddie plays with the pendant on her necklace. 'Nothing. I meant... she's been worried about you and—'

'You're lying. What do you mean?'

She looks at Billie, who awkwardly sips her drink, before turning back to me. 'Fuck. She's going to kill me.'

The anxiety that's become a permanent fixture of my being ignites, like flammable liquid, and my entire body burns. I stare at Maddie waiting for an answer.

'What do you think it means?'

'I don't know; that's why I'm asking.' Now I sound like my mother.

Her brows draw together. 'Serious, Amy? It's so obvious and you can't see it?'

'See what?' I rapidly unscrew the top off the water bottle and take a swig.

'You think a relationship with someone else is going to work for her when she's completely in love with you?'

I shake my head, which makes me dizzier than I already am. 'She isn't.'

'She is,' Billie says. 'Even I noticed before Maddie told me.'

Maddie tilts her head towards Billie. 'See.'

My eyes cut to Caroline. She's laughing with a group of our friends – that smile and those dimples that make her face come alive on display. Her gaze drifts to Maddie and me, but from the shock that's probably plastered to my face and the guilt on Maddie's, she must sense something is wrong because her smile fades and her eyes dart suspiciously to Maddie.

'Please tell me this isn't true,' I whisper.

'I shouldn't have told you. Caz is going to go spare.'

'How could I not see this? How could she not tell me?'

Maddie's head pulls back and her brows knit, as though she can't believe I'm asking such a stupid question. 'You've kind of had a lot going on, Ames. This has been really tough for her. And you have been seeing someone.'

I drop the water bottle into my handbag and press my fingers to my temples, screwing my eyes shut. My mind flashes back to the phone call we had that Sunday afternoon and her saying, 'Would you rather I not be with Rachel, is that what you want?' And that night at the Wickham. How angry she was when she found out about Luke. How pissed off I was about Rachel. And that moment outside afterwards. That tremor of electricity that passed between us when our lips were only inches apart. How I could've tilted my head forward and kissed her. How I wanted to tilt my head forward. The air around me becomes heavy. I need to get away from here. I open my eyes to catch Maddie mouthing 'sorry' to Caroline.

Caroline looks at me with those eyes that always remind me of the sky on a perfect cloudless day and are so warm and soulful and wise. *Oh, god. No, no, no.* 'I need… a bit a space.' I head for the driveway, stopping to lean against a pillar because my pulse has gone into overdrive, and I need to gulp for air.

'Amy?' Caroline's voice sounds behind me.

I take off, and hear her footsteps gather pace on the pebbles.

'Amy, stop.' She catches up to me as I unlock the car door. 'Please look at me.' When I don't turn around, she gently grabs my shoulder and turns me to face her.

'Why didn't you tell me?' I ask.

'How could I tell you? *When* could I tell you?'

'Are you kidding? All the conversations we've had about relationships lately. Me and Zoe. Me and Luke. You and Maddie. You and Rachel. Zoe and Maddie. Maddie and Billie…' I'm waffling because my brain can't process this. 'You didn't think to throw a you and me in there?'

She cups my cheek. Her palm is soft and warm. 'I didn't think you were ready to hear it. You seemed happy with Luke, and I didn't think you'd want… I… I didn't want to risk losing our friendship.'

'You wouldn't have.' I go to pull her hand away, but my fingers melt into hers, and I don't ever want to let that hand go.

'Really?' She takes a step closer. 'Then I'll tell you now. My feelings for you have changed and I love you more than a friend.'

I open my mouth to respond, but the words catch in my throat and all I can think about is how perfect she is. Her smooth skin and heart-shaped face. Her lips that turn up ever so slightly at the corners. The space between us pulses with heat and love and the hammering of my heart. That magnetic force that is so strong between us draws me in and before I can stop myself my mouth is on hers. I feel like I'm twenty again and exploring her sweet lips for the first time because I'd forgotten how lovely her mouth is and how she tastes like salted caramel.

I'm pressed up against my car, my arms around her waist holding her tight while she gently grips my face. I moan as the kiss becomes more intense. Our tongues intertwine, and our breathing becomes heavier. My stomach swoops and my soul shines, like the lights have been switched on after a long blackout, and I can see again. But what am I doing? I don't want to see this. I put my hand on her chest and push her away. 'Stop. This is wrong,'

She's still holding my face. 'You know it's not wrong.'

I pull her hands away and shake my head. 'I can't do this, Caz.'

My phone rings in my bag.

Caroline stares down at my bag, then back to me. 'Please don't answer it.'

I quickly grab for it, welcoming the distraction. Jenna's name flashes on the screen. She doesn't call me. She only had my number in case she needed me last week. The phone rings again, and I answer. 'Jenna?'

Caroline throws her hands up.

I hear crying.

'Hello?' I say.

'Amy?'

'Is that you, Jenna?'

'Yes,' she says, sniffling.

My grip tightens on the phone. 'Jenna, what's the matter?' I automatically reach for Caroline and she steps closer to me.

'It's Dad...'

'What's happened?' I don't want to frighten her, but I'm struggling to keep the panic out of my voice.

'We've just come home. Dad's not here. And his car's gone. And there's empty beer bottles,' Jenna cries.

Deep breaths. Think. 'Maybe he's gone to a friend's house. He said he wanted to see Nick. Maybe he's there.'

'He's not. I called.' She lets out a sob. 'And he's left a note. It says, "I'm sorry."'

I clench Caroline's hand and lean against the car to steady myself. 'Have you called anyone else to check? Your family? Luke's friends?'

'Yes, he's not anywhere. Ben and Chris went to Bryon Bay this morning and they're not answering.'

'Listen to me,' I say, adrenaline forcing me into action. 'Hang up, call triple zero straight away. I'm on my way. I'll be there in twenty minutes or so.'

'Okay,' she says and hangs up.

My hand trembles as I press the call end icon. 'I have to go,' I say through jagged breaths.

'You can't drive in this state.'

'I have to.'

'Well, I'm coming with you. I'll drive.'

I wipe my face. 'No. Stay here.'

She shakes her head. 'Amy, you're a mess, you can't drive like this—'

I jump in my car. 'Stay here for Maddie and tell her what's happened.' The sadness in her eyes claws at my chest. 'They need me.'

I see the conflict on her face between wanting me to stay and knowing that Luke might be in trouble. 'I need you, too,' she says quietly.

'Caz, I…' But words can't get past the wedge in my throat. 'I'll call you,' I whisper.

She doesn't respond, just nods and walks away.

Chapter Nineteen

I race through North Brisbane, weaving in and out of side streets, pushing amber light boundaries and driving at least ten kilometres over the speed limit. I attempt to take calming breaths and to stop the flow of tears, but I struggle to do either because I have Luke in my head and Caroline under my skin.

I'm at Sandgate within fifteen minutes, and the second I pull up Cody and Jenna run out to me. 'Did you call triple zero?' I ask, jumping out of the car. 'What did they say?'

Jenna nods. 'They've put calls out to police everywhere. They took the number plate and are trying to track his phone.'

'Will he be alright?' Cody's voice cracks. 'Where's he gone?'

I throw my arms around him. 'They'll find him.' Of course, I have no idea if that's true, but what else can I say? I grab both their hands. 'Come on, let's go inside.'

In the lounge, Jenna hands me Luke's note. It's a messy scrawl in black ink and says exactly what she told me on the phone – *I'm sorry*. I quickly fold it and pass it back to her. I can't think about that; I need to stay focussed. I run through the list of family members and Luke's friends with them. They've called and messaged the people they know he's still in contact with. No one has seen or heard from him.

I walk over to the bi-fold doors and peer through the glass to the darkness. Sarah's ashes being scattered in the ocean and Luke sitting on the deck alone filters into my mind. 'Did you check the beach?' I ask, facing Jenna and Cody.

They both shake their head.

'I'm going over there,' I say.

'I'm coming with you,' Cody says.

I zip up my jacket and strip off my boots. 'You stay here, Jenna, in case your dad turns up.'

She clutches her phone to her chest. 'Okay.'

'Do you have a torch?' I ask.

'Yeah.' Cody races to the kitchen pantry and grabs one from the top shelf.

'We won't be long,' I say to Jenna, shoving my phone into my pocket. 'Call me if you hear anything.'

Her eyes are wide with fear, but she nods.

Cody and I run across the road, through the grassed picnic area and hop over the stone wall that separates the walkway from the beach. The full moon, dull behind a hazy cloud, casts a haunting glow across the rough, angry sea. It's high tide and the ocean swallows most of the sandy bank. The white noise of the waves is loud in my ears, and flecks of salty water spray my face. The thought of Luke being out here with a combination of alcohol and suicidal thoughts in his system makes my blood run as cold as the wind whipping my skin and the water lapping my feet. In the distance, the lights of the Ted Smout Bridge glimmer to the north, and the Shorncliffe Pier sparkles to the south. Cody is running the torch along the length of the beach, but there's nothing to see except the water splashing violently over the wave breakers.

'No one's here,' he says.

'No, let's go.'

Once we're back on the grass, Cody shines the torch along the walkway and over the row of picnic tables. Apart from a group of teenagers gathered further along, it's empty. We also check the parked cars along the parade, but don't see Luke's.

Jenna jumps up from the table when we walk in.

'Nothing,' I say. 'No one's called?'

She shakes her head.

Cody grabs some towels to wipe our feet, and I'm grateful for the warmth of my socks and boots again. The adrenaline pumping through my body prevents me from sitting still. I pace the lounge, my heels smacking against the concrete floor and echoing in the silence.

I eventually fall onto the couch and we try to think of places Luke could be. Other than friends, family or the beach, nowhere comes to mind. We constantly call his phone; it goes straight to voicemail. We go upstairs to check if he's taken anything; nothing is missing. We leave a message for Ben and Chris, and Jenna calls their grandparents to let them know what's happened. We switch on the TV in case something is reported on the local news and keep peering at our phones as though doing so will make them ring.

I'm staring at the TV when Jenna begins to take ragged breaths and clasps her throat. 'Jen, what's the matter?' I shift closer.

'Can't... breathe.'

Cody rushes to her other side.

A film of sweat covers Jenna's upper lip. I put the back on my hand against her forehead, and it burns. 'Cody, can you get an ice-pack?'

He dashes to the kitchen.

I drop to my knees in front of her. 'Jen, listen to me. You need to try and slow your breathing.'

She gives a tiny nod but continues to grasp her throat and take laboured breaths.

I gently remove her hands. 'It's a panic attack.' Cody returns with the icepack wrapped in a tea-towel. 'Put that on the back of her neck, Cody.'

He pushes her hair aside and holds it in place.

'Jenna, try and take deeper breaths,' I say. 'We're right here with you.'

The rise and fall of her chest begins to slow.

'That's it.' I want to tell her not to worry, that Luke will be fine, just to calm her, but I can't tell her something that might not be true. 'That's good. Slower again.' I hop on the couch and lean her back so I can move the icepack to her forehead.

'It's… easing,' she says.

Cody buries his face in his hands. I rush to his side and pull him to me. He clings tight, his shoulders jerking. Jenna reaches out to rub his back, while she holds the icepack against her forehead with her other hand. We stay like that for several minutes until the shrill sound of a ringtone makes us all jump.

Jenna throws down the icepack and snatches up her phone. 'Hello?' After a few seconds, she says, 'Hang on.' She hands the phone to me. 'Can you talk to them?'

'Hello?' I listen as a woman from emergency services says that someone has reported a man matching Luke's description and his number plate on Ted Smout Bridge. I hang up. 'He's at the bridge.'

'Is he okay?' Jenna asks.

I nod, although I have no idea if that's true. All I know is that he's alive and isn't far away. 'The police and ambulance are there. They want us to come. Let's go.'

We drive in silence, and it gives me the space to process what's happened. I know why Luke's chosen that bridge. It's the highest point over the bay and crosses the body of water where Sarah's ashes are scattered. I imagine him alone on the deck earlier, drinking and staring at the angry sea, thinking about Sarah's scream being the last time he heard her voice. The panther on his lap, whispering in his ear to join her. The blackness robbing him of his ability to form rational thoughts and understand what he was about to do.

I pull up where two police cars have barricaded the entrance of the southbound lanes. We explain who we are and an officer drives us towards the vivid blue and red sirens that slowly spin in the centre of the bridge, relaying information down the radio to her colleagues.

Another police officer approaches when we hop out. The wind is stronger up here and bites hard on my bare legs.

'Amy? Officer Carlson.' She offers me her hand.

I shake it and point to the kids. 'These are Luke's children – Cody and Jenna.'

She gives them a business like nod and says, 'Your dad's fine.'

Jenna puts her hand to her mouth and lets out a strangled cry. Cody and I slump against the police car.

'He's down on the fishing platform talking to another officer. We plan to have him up here very soon.'

The platform is a few metres below the surface of the bridge and extends out over the ocean.

She continues. 'Two people who turned up to fish recognised Luke might be in trouble. They called emergency and kept him talking until we arrived.'

'Is he in any danger now?' I ask.

Officer Carlson shakes her head. 'We don't think so. He's being cooperative. We just have to be careful.'

Tears pool in my eyes and I blink fast to contain them. I won't break down in front of the kids. I put an arm around each of them as we stand and watch and wait.

Around fifteen minutes later, Luke appears at the top of the platform wrapped in a silver emergency blanket and a police officer close to his side. Jenna and Cody both release their grip on me and step forward, but Officer Carlson puts her hand out to stop them.

'Give them a moment,' she says.

Jenna stays where she is and yells, 'Dad!'

Luke looks up and his face crumples. They race to him, and he breaks down as he clings to them, the silver blanket falling to the ground.

I start towards them, but the adrenaline comedown turns my legs weak and I freeze. Luke moves to me instead. Blue and red lights flash across his face, highlighting his remorse and distress. I throw my arms around him, my fingers digging into his back as I sob into his neck.

'I'm sorry,' he says in my ear. 'I'm so sorry.'

A paramedic interrupts. 'Luke, we're going to need to take you to the hospital.'

He releases me and wipes his face.

'Can we go in the ambulance with Dad?' Cody asks the paramedic.

'Sure you can,' he responds.

I rub Jenna's shoulder. 'You go in the ambulance, too, Jen. I'll meet you there.'

'Are you sure? Will you be okay on your own?' she asks.

'Yeah. Go with your dad. I won't be far behind.'

I reach for Luke's hand. 'I'll come straight to the hospital.'

I watch them bundle into the ambulance before a police officer gently touches my elbow. 'I'll drive you back to your car, Amy. Officer Carlson will return Luke's vehicle to his place.'

As soon as I'm in the safety of my car, I collapse against the steering wheel and sob again – loud, violent convulsions. After a few minutes, my tears ease and I sit back. Deep breaths. Slow, deep breaths. I start the engine so that I can blast the heater and pull the visor down to check my face in the mirror. I'd forgotten about the thick mascara I'd applied for the party and black streaks stain my cheeks. I grab the bottle of water from my handbag, tip some water onto a tissue and rub my skin. My hand trembles as I pour more water onto the tissue and rub again, but I can't shake the triggered memories. The police could've been telling me that Luke was dead, like they did when they came to my office that day. *Amy Campbell? We're so sorry to tell you...*

'Fucking get it together,' I mutter as I flip up the visor and plug my phone in. Two messages. A slurred voicemail from Maddie to check on Luke and a text from Caroline asking the same thing. I close my eyes. I crave her support right now. To feel her arms around me, holding me up. But I can't think about that. Luke needs me. I send the same reply to both of them.

Luke ok going hospital talk tomorrow.

Chapter Twenty

The nurse behind the emergency counter at the Royal Brisbane buzzes me through the security doors and directs me to a small cubicle where another nurse is taking Luke's blood pressure. Jenna is perched on the edge of the bed, and Cody is sitting on a chair off to the side.

'Everything looks good.' The nurse removes the arm band and scribbles on the clipboard attached to the end of the bed. 'The doctor won't be long,' he says and pulls the curtain across on his way out.

Jenna and Cody have been waiting for me to arrive so they can leave to find the toilets and a vending machine. Once they've gone, I stroke Luke's cheek. 'Hey,' I say.

He's pale and his eyes are heavy. 'How could I do that to them?'

I hop onto the bed and gather him in my arms.

He burrows into my chest for a minute, then pulls away and roughly wipes his face. 'I can't explain it,' he says. 'These thoughts in my head took over. I was convinced they'd be better off without me. And now I can't believe I'd put them through that.'

'I understand,' I say. I've lost count of the number of times I've thought about joining Mel. Not so much this year since I've been back in therapy, but last year when I fell into that dark well, the thoughts were always there simmering underneath.

'I'm sorry I did this to you, too. After everything you've been through.'

I shake my head. 'It's not your fault.'

His eyes water. 'When I got to the bridge, I sat on the edge, drinking, looking out over the ocean. I needed to feel close to her. Nothing else was in my head except being with her. Until those two blokes started talking to me.' His chins quivers and his voice cracks. 'Asked about my family and my life – it snapped me back to reality.'

I cup his cheek. 'I'm so glad they were there.'

'What if they weren't and I jumped? What would've that done to the kids?' He drops his face into his hands, his shoulders jerking.

'The important thing is you're here and you can get help now.'

He looks up and I pass him a tissue from the side. He takes it and dabs at his eye.

The curtain slides back, and Jenna and Cody appear with soft drinks and chips. Jenna looks between Luke and me. 'Everything okay?'

I hop off the bed. 'Yeah. We were just talking.'

Jenna glances at Luke, uncertain.

'Yeah, sweetheart. Come here.' He holds out his arm. She puts her vending machine dinner on the end of the bed and snuggles into him, lying her head on his chest. He places his head on hers and breathes her in, his face anguished. He releases his grip and holds his arm out for Cody. 'Come here, Codes,' he says and gives Cody the same embrace.

A tall woman with grey hair pulled back off her face walks into the cubicle. 'Evening, everyone. I'm Dr Blackwood.'

We all mumble hello and Luke attempts to sit up.

'Hello, Luke. You've had a difficult night,' Dr Blackwood says softly.

Luke nods, and his neck flames red.

'You're in the right place now, and we can send you home with some help.'

Luke nods again.

'We've been monitoring you and physically everything looks fine, so we have no concerns there. But we need to put a mental health plan in place and monitor you a while longer. You mentioned you have a psychologist in the city?'

'Yeah. Dr Garcia at The Psychology Centre on Adelaide Street.'

'I'd like you to get back there as soon as possible. We'll call them first thing Monday to request an emergency appointment.'

'Oh, I don't need a—'

She gives a curt shake of her head. 'We can't let you out of here unless we know you've got a professional appointment lined up and you've got people at home to stay with you.' She glances at the kids and me. 'And it looks like you have a supportive family, so that part shouldn't be an issue.'

He sighs and lies back against the pillow. 'The best. I'll go back to Dr Garcia. No worries.'

'Good to hear. I'm sorry to tell you this, but we're going to have to keep you in overnight at least. We need to make sure you're actually okay and not telling us what you think we want to hear. If everything goes well, then you can go home tomorrow – only if you have someone there with you, otherwise we'll need to move you to another facility.'

'I have to stay here? It's just that I have the kids—'

'I'll stay with them.' I address Dr Blackwood. 'I can stay with him when he gets out, too. And I know The Psychology Centre well, so I'll make sure he gets there.'

'We can sort things out at school next week to be home more,' Jenna says.

Dr Blackwood smiles. 'Excellent. I'll go and organise a room.'

Once she leaves, Luke says to me, 'You don't need to stay. You've got all that stuff at work going on. I can get Dad to—'

I gently place my finger against his lips. 'That's not important.'

He grabs my hand and kisses it. 'Thank you.'

We wait while the staff find Luke a ward. Ben calls and wants to leave Byron Bay straight away, but Luke insists he and Chris stay until the morning. He messages his parents to say he's fine and that he'll contact them tomorrow. He promises the kids he'll talk to them more about what happened as soon as he's home – right now he wants to sleep. When a nurse arrives to take him to the ward, we say our goodbyes and head off with a detour to my place so I can pack a bag.

*

When we arrive back in Sandgate after collecting Luke from the hospital the next day, the esplanade buzzes with people enjoying the perfect autumn weather – no humidity, mid-twenties and sunshine. The kite surfers and jet skiers are out on the water, small groups gather around picnic blankets and public barbeques, and bike riders glide along the paths. The smell of sausages and onions mixed with light laughter and voices carry across the road as we hop out of the car. I stay close to Luke and watch him carefully as we move inside, although I'm not certain what I'm looking for.

'Are you hungry?' I ask as he collapses onto the couch.

'Nah, just tired. Reckon I could sleep for days.'

'You can, if you want. We've done everything. We even did a huge grocery shop and bought food for dinner.'

He gives me a weak smile. 'You gonna cook?'

'Yep. It'll be basic, but better than eating takeaway all week.'

He extends his arm and I cuddle into him, his whiskers brushing against my forehead. 'Thank you,' he says.

'You're welcome.' I kiss him softly. His lips are chapped from the harsh wind last night, and the stark difference between his and Caroline's makes me pull away quickly as the guilt ripples through me.

'You know what I'd love?' he says.

'What?'

'A strong, black coffee. That hospital coffee is shit.'

I jump up, grateful for the distraction. 'I'm on it.'

Jenna and Cody slump on the couch with him and I join them a few minutes later.

Luke sips his coffee and groans. 'That's what I needed.' Then he takes a deep breath and rubs his hands up and down his thighs – like he used to in the group – and explains what happened yesterday. He started drinking when the kids were out and watched the tide and fierce winds roll in. His mind went over everything that had happened during the past few months – issues with the kids, all the ugly feelings he'd kept buried, unable to handle them and thinking they'd go away if he ignored them, and the excruciating pain he felt over losing Sarah. Everything surged, crashed over him and he snapped. He grabbed some beer, his keys, wrote the note and drove to the bridge. He said it was like something else had control over his body and his mind.

Jenna and Cody sit either side of him, listening quietly.

'The mental health nurse told me that widowed fathers are the highest risk group for intense and prolonged symptoms of grief.' He looks between the three of us. 'Who knew, ay?'

I shake my head. 'Not me.' I wish I had; I would have pushed him harder to get help.

He grabs the kids' hands. 'I'm so sorry I did that to you. I promise I'll put everything into dealing with this. I won't ever put you through that again.'

'You mean you'll get proper help though?' Jenna asks. 'Like, go every week to therapy and groups and stuff?'

He slides his arm across her shoulders. 'Course. Whatever it takes.'

Cody brushes the hair from his eyes. 'We'll help you, Dad.'

Luke ruffles Cody's hair. 'Thanks, mate.'

I watch the three of them, their bond stronger than any of them realise, and my heart expands. That talk would've been hard for Luke. I'm proud of him.

We spend a lazy afternoon together on the couch. Luke drifts in and out of sleep. Cody and Jenna flit between their phones and homework, until Jenna heads upstairs and I scroll through the movie channels landing on an old black and white film that instantly calms me.

Cody's eyes drift to the TV. He's engrossed for several minutes until he hears me reciting some lines. 'You know a movie this old?' he asks.

'Yeah, Mel and I watched old movies all the time,' I say, my voice low so I don't wake Luke, who's snoring softly on the other sofa. 'This is *The Seven Year Itch.*' I point to the screen. 'That's Marilyn Monroe. Mel loved this film. Every summer, whenever it was a really hot day, she'd act out the "undies in the icebox" scene.' I give him a sad smile.

He returns the expression and says, 'Mum liked movies. We went to the cinema a lot together. And she always wanted me to be in school plays.'

'That's nice,' I say. 'You like to act?'

He nods. 'I like being someone else sometimes. It kinda takes my mind off things.'

I swallow. *Oh.*

'We don't mind if you talk about Mel. I don't think Dad talks about Mum enough and they told us at school when it first happened that we should talk.'

God. This kid. I nod and reach across to squeeze his hand because I'm too choked to speak.

'Sorry,' he says.

'It's okay,' I manage. 'Thanks.'

He smiles shyly and goes back to flitting between his phone and the movie, while I curl up and watch the rest of the film.

When Maddie calls, I go outside to talk to her. After I explain about Luke, I ask about the party, but all she wants to talk about is what happened with Caroline.

Caroline has left me voicemails, and I feel sick about calling her, but I take a deep breath and dial her number.

'Hey,' she says.

'Hi.' There's a tense pause before I launch into what happened after I left Maddie's. Once I'm finished, she doesn't give me her usual comment of 'wish I could give you a hug' or ask if I'm alright. Instead, she says, 'I'm relieved the worst didn't happen and that he's open to getting proper help now.' It's genuine, but there's an edge to her voice.

We both fall silent. She'll want to talk about other events, but I can't do that. Not here and not now.

'I have to go,' I say.

'What? We're not going to talk about last night?'

'I can't talk about it here.'

'Fair enough. When can you?'

'I don't know, Caz. I can't think with all this going on.'

'And how do you think I feel?'

'I'm sorry. It's too much right now. I'll… I'll call you.'

'When?'

'I don't know! When I can.'

'Whatever,' she grunts and hangs up.

I stare at my screen in shock. She seriously whatever'd me? I head back inside.

Luke's awake and brightens when he sees me. 'Everything okay?'

I feel like such an arse. 'Um, yeah, just Maddie telling me about the party.'

'Oh, shit, the party. I ruined it.'

'Don't be silly. Maddie will have more parties.' I quickly change the subject. 'Suppose I better cook something for dinner.'

'Righto. Jen, Codes, can you help Amy to make sure she doesn't poison us?'

'I'm not that bad,' I say, heading to the kitchen.

After a basic dinner of steak, salad and jacket potatoes that everyone is impressed with, I take Luke's hand and lead him upstairs. He's weak and vulnerable. It gives me a glimpse of what he must've been like when Sarah died.

He heads straight for the ensuite. 'I need a shower.'

'Leave that door open,' I call after him.

'I'm not going to drown in the shower,' he calls back.

I sit cross-legged on the bed, scrolling through social media and listening to the water run. I'm glad he's home. I struggled being in this room alone last night. Sarah's belongings everywhere, the fierce wind shaking the windows, the roof creaking. It was like being on a ghost train, except this ride lasted all night.

'Better?' I ask as he emerges with a towel wrapped around his waist.

'Yep.' He digs out some boxers from the drawer, slips them on and crawls into bed. He lies on his side facing me. There's a deep sadness in his eyes and they start to water.

My heart aches for him, for both of us, and a tear rolls down my cheek.

He gently wipes it away. 'It fucking hurts, hey,' he whispers.

My tears fall harder. 'Yep.'

'I'm glad I found you to share it with,' he says.

My chest swells with affection. 'Me too. You're so special to me.'

'And you,' he says, his eyes closing.

I stroke his hair as he drifts off. Only when I hear him breathing deeply do I leave the room and head back downstairs to Jenna and Cody.

Chapter Twenty-One

The crisp, dry air fills my lungs as Maddie and I do some warm-up stretches then set off on a fast walk. The sun beats onto the Southbank boardwalk and casts a silver sheen across the river. A City Cat glides past and disappears under a bridge, while other runners and walkers pass by.

The last two weeks have been a blur. Work, therapy, living between two houses, helping Luke set new routines and attend his appointments, and finding the right support for Jenna and Cody. Luke didn't question anything or push back – just let me take charge. He said he was too frightened of what the outcome might be if he didn't. Dr Garcia set up a regular weekly time for him that works with his business and the kids' schooling and put him into a program for widowed fathers that's in North Brisbane in the evenings, so he has no excuse not to attend.

He's trying to be more open but finds it difficult to articulate his grief. He's cried at least and talks about Sarah more than he did, so that's something. He's spent his days dozing and has slept solidly every night. Ben and Chris have visited constantly, the kids have alternated days off from school, and his parents have moved between his place and Ben's. I even got to meet a couple of his mates who stopped by.

Maddie and Billie came over one night, too. Maddie cooked her amazing vegetarian curry and homemade chapati bread, plus a huge batch of beef and ale stew to freeze especially for Luke. I think he fell in love with her then. She lined him up to sort out her front yard when he's up to it, while Billie not-so-subtly put her nursing hat on and asked Luke a stack of mental health questions. I could tell they both genuinely liked Luke, but I also knew Maddie visited to support me – to let me know she was okay with my choice.

This weekend he has his family around him, so I'm spending some time at home and persuaded Maddie to come for a Sunday morning run.

After a good stint of a steady pace together, I stride ahead of Maddie, relishing the pounding in my muscles. Sweat builds along my hairline and drips down my back. My lungs expand with oxygen and my thighs throb. I push through the pain and forge ahead.

'Whoa, slow down.' Maddie grabs my arm.

I slow to a swift walking pace. 'What?' I say breathlessly.

'What's gotten into you?' she gasps, trotting to keep up.

'Nothing. I just want to run.'

She clutches her side. 'You're killing me.'

'Big night?' I poke her in the ribs. 'Too much wine? Too much sex?' She grins. 'Both.'

I laugh and take off again. She groans but picks up her pace. When we reach the end of the boardwalk, just past the Gallery of Modern Art, we circle back towards where we've parked. My body wants to slow, but I push myself hoping the burn in my muscles will detract from the jumble in my head. It doesn't, and Caroline won't shift from my thoughts. I woke every couple of hours last night sick at the thought of seeing her later, and I need to get it out my system. Get her out of my system.

We still haven't spoken about what happened at the party. I've sent a few texts making excuses about why I can't meet, and she kept calling last week, but I didn't reply. By Thursday, she sent me a message that said, 'stop fucking avoiding me,' so I told her I needed more time to think. Work took over then with team issues, the bullying complaint, jobs Greg gave me, and I lapped it all up knowing it would keep me too busy to see her.

Now that some time has passed since 'the kiss', I thought I should try and get back to being friends, now that I'm a normal functioning adult again. I was on my way to her office on Tuesday when she emerged from the adjacent meeting room with colleagues and clocked me watching from further down the corridor. The hurt in her eyes caused such a vice-like grip around my torso that I fled through the fire exit to the stairwell.

The next day, she was in the kitchen when I went to grab a cup of tea. The hurt was still there, but I averted my gaze and chatted like I usually would – asking how she was, what had been going on, that sort of thing. After a few minutes of a largely one-way conversation, she said, 'This isn't going to work for me, Amy.'

I drew my head back in surprise. 'What isn't?'

She pointed between us. 'This. Pretending nothing happened. Acting like we can go on like before.' She shook her head. 'No.'

I clenched my jaw to stop the flow of indignation spreading across my face. 'That's not fair.'

Her eyes grew wide. 'Fair? Fuck you,' she said and strode off.

'Caz,' I called after her, but she kept walking, leaving me with an open mouth and flaming cheeks.

That was three days ago.

Of course it's played on my mind that if Luke had been okay the night of Maddie's party and I hadn't received that phone call, I would've ended things with him because of that kiss, or at least cooled them. Except things are different now. He's fragile and needs support from someone who understands. But I can't let Caroline's friendship go either. It's everything to me, and I need to do whatever it takes to fix it. That means talking about what happened. So, this morning I messaged to ask if we can catch up later, to which she replied with a simple, 'I'll be home from six.'

As we approach Maddie's car, we slow to a walk. I groan and fall against the boot.

Maddie doubles over and rests her hands on her knees. 'That was hell. No more Sunday morning runs,' she gasps.

We stretch, scull from our water bottles and grab our jackets and phones from the car.

'I'm starved,' Maddie says, locking up. She points to a café down by the water. 'Let's go there.'

We find a table outside and order. I go for baked eggs and bacon, while Maddie orders the big vegetarian breakfast – eggs, avocado, haloumi, hash browns, toast, tomato and mushrooms.

'Bloody hell, you really are hungover,' I say, repositioning my chair and stretching my legs out so they're exposed to the autumn sun.

'Yep. So is Billie and she had to go to work.' Maddie tosses her sunglasses on the table and ruffles her cropped hair. 'I feel like shit.'

'I had an alcohol-free Saturday night.'

She shakes her head like she can't believe what she's hearing. 'You stay at your place last night?'

'Yeah. Luke's family were with him, and I needed to be home.'

'How is he?'

'Good. Seeing his psych again and started a new program for widowed dads. He's going back to work next week. Said he'll contact you about your front yard.'

She moves her hand off the table as our coffees are delivered. 'That's great. And Jenna and Cody?'

'They're good. They're seeing a counsellor at school, and Jenna's getting some extra support through a local place.'

She nods and peers at me while she sips her long black.

I peer back. 'I know that look, Maddie. What do you want to ask me?' I swing my legs back under the table, rip open a couple of sugar packets and pour them into my coffee.

'And you? Are you okay?'

'Yeah.' I sip my coffee. 'Mmm, that's good.'

'Uh huh. Talking about your coffee isn't going to throw me. You talk to Caz?'

I stare into my flat white, sensing Maddie's eyes drilling through the top of my head. 'We've chatted.'

'Liar.'

I raise my head. 'I'm not lying,' I lie.

'You spoke to her the day after the party, ignored her for a week and then when you did speak to her, you acted like nothing happened.'

I roll my eyes. 'If you know, why are you asking?'

She smiles. 'Wanted to see if you'd lie to me.'

'I always lie to you.'

She laughs.

I glance across the river and take in the scene. 'Don't you love the city from this angle? The beauty of the buildings you don't get to appreciate from the CBD. The way they sparkle as the sun bounces off them.'

'Amy,' Maddie says. 'I'll keep hounding you until you talk about it.'

I sigh. 'Fine. I don't know what to say to her, how to act around her now. But I've arranged to catch up with her later, so...' I shrug.

'To talk about what happened at the party.' It's a mix between a question and an order.

'I guess. I want to forget about it and go back to how we were.'

She scoffs. 'Are you kidding?'

'No.' I move my mug aside as our meals are delivered.

'You don't seriously think Caz can go back to being friends after what she told you?' she says, sprinkling a stack of salt over her food. 'Not to mention the pash.'

'Yeah. I do. And it was just a kiss. She'll realise she doesn't feel that way and we can get back to normal.' I almost say *like we've done before* but stop myself.

Maddie's brows rise. 'It was *just* a kiss? I might believe that if you were talking about some random at a club, but this is Caz we're talking about. And you feel nothing? Nothing at all?' She watches me as she takes a huge bite of hash brown and groans. 'Oh my god, so hungry.'

I cut into my baked eggs. It doesn't matter what I feel because it can't happen. And I can be happy with Luke because we have a nice, sensible affection for each other. No crazy head over heels stuff. It's safe. It's a good, safe relationship. 'I love her as a friend and that's what I'll tell her later.'

'I don't believe you.'

'Believe what you want. It's the truth.' I shrug and take a bite.

'Um, didn't you kiss her?'

I screw up my face. 'It was a mutual kiss. No one kissed anyone first.'

She spears a finger of haloumi and points it at me. 'That's not what Caz said.'

I drop my cutlery. 'For fuck's sake, does she tell you every little detail about everything?'

'Touchy. Now I know it's true.'

'You cow. I should've known you were fishing.'

She grins. 'Not really. Caz did give me some details – once she was talking to me again, that is.'

'I was caught up in the moment. She was right there.' I hold my hand in front of my face. 'She looked sooo good, and I... I don't know.' I pick up my fork. 'It was a mistake. Me and Caz...' I shake my head. 'It wouldn't work.'

'Why not?'

'It just wouldn't. And I'm with Luke now.'

She narrows her eyes while she chews. 'Ames. You know I'll always support you, and as long as the person you're with treats you well and you're happy, I'm happy for you. But I'm going to say it as I see it. I don't think you and Luke are in love.'

I stiffen. 'Well, no, we're not. But we care about each other. We don't have to be in love to have a good relationship. Besides, true love grows over time.'

She gives a brief nod. 'It does. But there needs to be a very special seed there to make it grow.'

I push the eggs around the dish and bite my bottom lip.

'Anyway,' Maddie says. 'Caz said it felt like more than *just* a kiss. She said it was "hot and heavy."'

I throw her a questioning look. 'Caz would not use the phrase "hot and heavy". That's your talk.'

She chuckles. 'Okay, she didn't say that. She did say it was heated.'

My face warms because that's true. It was scorching, in fact.

A smile pulls at Maddie's lips. 'You're blushing.'

'Get lost. I'm red from the sun and from outrunning you because you're too tired and hungover from rooting and drinking all night.'

'Ha. You sound jealous.' She takes a sip of coffee and turns serious. 'You will sort this out later, won't you? One way or the other?'

'Yes. Get off my case.'

'Because this has really cut her up.'

I close my eyes and moan. 'Don't say that to me, Mads. It kills me she feels like that.'

'Then fucking fix it.'

'Okay, I'll try. Can we drop it?'

'Fine,' Maddie says and bites down on a piece of buttery toast.

I jump up. 'I need the bathroom. You want another coffee while I'm up?'

'Sure.'

I head inside to the toilets and splash my face with cool water. What I don't want to tell Maddie is how fragile I feel about the whole Caroline thing and how that angst of loving and losing gives me chest pains. That sensation was never part of my fabric before, and I remember exactly when it started – a month after Mel's accident.

She'd fallen down the stairs at work and dislodged her back and hip. The only thing that helped was the opioid painkillers the hospital prescribed, and I saw her love of substances return.

One Saturday afternoon I came home to find her passed out on the couch and gently shook her. 'I'm home.' She didn't stir. I nudged her again. 'Mel.' I spotted an empty blister packet on the floor and grabbed her by both shoulders and shook. 'Mel, wake up!'

Her eyelids fluttered open. 'What are you doing?' she slurred.

I held the blister packet up to her. 'How much have you taken?' I started pacing. 'How much have you fucking taken?'

Her dark eyebrows pulled together in confusion, and she brushed the hair from her face. 'Babe, no, I haven't taken that much.'

'Then why are you out of it? Why are you slurring? Why couldn't I wake you?' I held up the packet. 'This is empty.'

She wiped her mouth with the back of her hand. 'I didn't take the whole packet. There were only a couple left.'

'Bullshit. This is the packet you started yesterday.'

She stared at me knowing she'd been caught out. 'There were four left.'

My stomach clenched. 'Four? You've taken four since I've been gone? I've been out three hours, Mel!'

A darkness crossed her face. 'You don't understand the pain I'm in. It's the only thing that helps.'

'That's crap and you know it.'

She glared at me, a sulky pout forming.

'You have to fucking stop,' I yelled. 'You have to find another way.'

I sank down onto the couch. 'I can't lose you.'

She pulled me close. 'You're not going to lose me. It's just some painkillers.'

'I will.' I gazed into her dark-blue eyes. 'If you keep doing this, I will. You always need more.'

She cupped my face. 'You're right. I need to stop. I'll see someone.'

I pushed my face into her neck. 'I need you here with me.'

She stroked my hair and kissed my forehead. 'I'll always be here with you. I'll do anything for you.'

I clung to those words and tried to ignore the niggling in my gut. For the next few months, we slowly weaned her off until she was down to one small dose a day. That's why when she went to Melbourne, I trusted her. But in the end, her need for that constant high was too strong. It overrode our love, and my fear was justified.

And if I've lost true love once, who's to say I won't lose it again?

Chapter Twenty-Two

I press the doorbell and zip up my jacket. Winter is only a couple of weeks away and there's a cool shift in the evening air. The minute Caroline opens the door, I regret coming here because seeing her makes something weird happen inside me. Her hair is messy and casual, her blue T-shirt complements her eyes, and her skin is clear and fresh. I've always thought she looked better out of work gear and make-up. I go all melty, like my limbs have liquified, and have a vision of burying my face into her warm neck, breathing in her coconut soap, feeling her soft skin under my fingertips...

'Hi,' she says.

'What?'

She screws up her face. 'Hey? I said hi.'

'Oh. Hi.' I step inside and follow her through to the kitchen. One of her favourite old songs blasts through the house – it's *Untouched* by The Veronicas.

She turns down the volume. 'Do you want something? Tea? Wine?'

My tongue sticks to the roof of my mouth. 'Just water. Thanks.'

She pours a glass of cold water from the fridge and places it on the bench in front of where I've taken a seat. She doesn't sit with me. Instead, she leans against the bench on the other side of the kitchen, crossing her legs at the ankle. A faint scowl marks her brow and a strange, tense vibe pulses between us.

'It seriously took you two weeks to talk to me about this?' she says.

I gulp the water. I guess we're skipping the pleasantries. 'I'm sorry. I've had so much going on.'

The scowl disappears and is replaced by the hurt I saw in the office on Tuesday. 'And you couldn't spare even a little bit of time for me? Do you know how that makes me feel?'

I stare into the glass because I know exactly how that makes her feel. I know her better than I know myself sometimes. 'I'm sorry,' I repeat. 'I needed to think, and I didn't want to talk about this at work.' The electronic intro for *This Love* starts and my heart jumps. This is our song, and no one knows that except us – not even Mel and Maddie. I lift my head, and the look on her face tells me she's thinking about the same thing.

It was around six months before we met them, and I'd returned to Brisbane for a holiday. It was one of those rare moments in our friendship that Caroline and I were both single. We'd been at a party and stumbled into her house afterwards giggling, full of champagne. She switched on The Veronicas while we continued to drink. A few songs in, she came back from the kitchen. Her hair was longer, and it swished against her shoulders as she danced. She looked so beautiful, and I remember the tug on my heart because I had feelings for her then. She fell onto the couch as *This Love* started, her leg landing across mine. When I gazed at her, she reached out to brush a strand of hair from my face, her fingertips feathering my cheek. I hesitantly leant forward and when she didn't pull back, I pressed my lips to hers. She responded and we kissed for the entire song before taking it to the bedroom.

In the morning, she was awkward and remorseful. I wanted to take things further, tried to take thing further, and she pushed me away – said that she didn't want to risk our friendship for a relationship that might not work, and that it couldn't work with us living in different cities anyway. Things were strained between us for a few months afterwards while I recovered from the hurt and rejection, but we moved past it. And then I met Mel and no longer thought about Caroline in that way. Mel and Maddie knew about my history with Caroline at uni, but I didn't want to tell Mel about that one night, or my feelings at the time, because I never wanted her to have a reason to question my commitment to her, or my friendship with Caroline.

Caroline's voice cuts through my memory. 'I get that you didn't want to talk about it at work. You're here now. Talk.'

Everything I planned to say about how much she means to me, how important our friendship is, won't form. The words are caught in my throat and instead I blurt out, 'I was confused that night. I shouldn't have kissed you. I don't feel the same way.'

'I don't believe you,' she shoots back.

'Why is that so hard to believe?'

She shakes her head slowly. 'That was some kiss, Amy. You don't kiss someone like that when you don't feel anything. You've kissed me like that before. You felt something then, too. Remember that?'

I peer outside to the glow of the pool lights. 'And you weren't interested.' I face her. 'Remember that? And that was a long time ago.'

'So, that's it? We forget about what happened and go back to being friends?'

'I think that's for the best.'

'Don't you think we've gone past that? That our relationship is a bit different now?'

'No, I don't.'

'So you're going to ignore your feelings and carry on this thing with Luke?'

Anger rises in my body and my jaw tightens. 'There's nothing to ignore. I care about Luke, it's not a thing.'

She scoffs. 'Yeah, right.'

'Can't you support me? Why do you have such an issue with me seeing a man?'

She screws up her face. 'What? It has nothing to do with you seeing a man and everything to do with you not being honest about your feelings for me. You think I haven't been jealous of Zoe all this time?'

I open my mouth to respond, but I can't make sense of it all and stand to leave. 'I was hoping we could put this behind us.'

She walks around to my side of the bench. 'I can't do that.'

I tuck my hair behind my ear and shift my gaze to the tiles. 'Well, you'll have to if you want this friendship to continue.'

She takes a step closer; I take one back. I'm starting to feel way too warm in this jacket.

'Don't think I haven't noticed things over the past few months,' she says, inching even closer.

'I don't know what you're talking about.'

'The way you watch me. The look in your eyes when I told you how I felt. How you sighed when you kissed me.'

I shake my head. 'No. You've got that wrong.'

'How jealous you are of Rachel.'

I grunt. 'I am *not* jealous of Rachel.'

'So, me being this close makes you feel nothing?' She places her hands on the bench either side of my hips.

My mouth is dry again, but I can't reach the glass of water. 'Nope.'

She runs the edge of her finger down my cheek. 'And me touching you does nothing?'

My skin erupts in goosebumps. 'No,' I whisper.

She inches even closer, and I swear a fire ignites between us. 'And I can stand this close and you still feel nothing?'

My eyes drift to her lips. I shake my head and shift my gaze back to hers, and then it happens. Our mouths collide, fast and hungry and urgent, moans escaping from both of us. Her hands grip my face, and my fingers slip beneath the waistband of her jeans, digging into her hips.

'I want you so bad, it's killing me,' she murmurs, her lips still pressed against mine.

And I want her so bad it's killing me. My soul has lit up again, like it did at Maddie's party, but the feeling doesn't last long, because the fear and guilt floor me. I fall against her chest and cry.

'Hey.' She strokes my hair. 'What's the matter?'

My tears seep into her shirt as I cling to her. I would lose myself in her. I know I would. And if I did that and lost her, too, I wouldn't survive.

She gently places her fingertip under my chin, tilts my head up and kisses me. It's tender and loving, and I let it happen because there is something magical about the touch of her lips. It makes me feel like everything I'll ever need is right here, with her. But it can't go on. I can't expose myself again. And Luke, he needs me. I push her away and wipe my face. 'That shouldn't have happened.'

'What? How can you say that?'

'No. That was... no. I have to go.'

'You can't go,' she says, grabbing my arm.

I brush it off, pick up my bag and rush to the front door.

'Will you stop? Amy, we need to talk about this.'

I can't turn around, because if I do, I will never want to leave. 'I'm sorry.' I race to my car and start the engine, then drop my head into my hands and scream. When I look up, Caroline is leaning against the doorframe, arms folded, watching me. I can still feel the heat of her lips on mine, the silkiness of her skin on my fingertips.

I put the car in reverse, drive off and don't look back.

*

'Hey, Mads,' I sniff as she opens the door.

'Hey.' Her forehead creases. 'You're supposed to be at Caz's place sorting thing—'

'Um...' I step inside.

'Oh, you've been. It didn't go well?'

I shake my head.

She sighs and throws her arm around me. 'Come on.'

I walk into the lounge and drop onto the couch while she fetches me some water, joining me a minute later. She listens as I tell her what happened, but as always, she's on to me.

'What are you so afraid of?'

I dab my eyes with the tissue she's given me. 'I'm not.'

'It sounds to me like you feel the same way.'

'No. I just got caught up—'

'In the moment? That's what you said this morning about the last kiss. How many moments will it take for you to realise what's going on?'

'But... Luke's good for me. He's... he's safe and he gets my grief.'

She brushes a strand of hair that's stuck to my wet cheek. 'I agree he's good for you, but you need to be with someone for the right reasons. Besides, you think Caz doesn't understand grief?'

Caroline's had more grief in her life than anyone should have at her age, and she's always understood mine. 'No. I guess I don't think that.'

'I know you and Luke get each other's grief, but that's not a reason to be a couple.'

'I'm not unhappy being with him. I care about him. A lot.'

'Of course you do. It's obvious you care about each other, and that you help each other, but don't you want to be with someone you're in love with? Doesn't Luke deserve that, too?'

I sip the water and place it down on the side table. 'We both had that. True love, the whole package. I don't think either of us can ever find it again.'

'But you might've found it and you're pushing it away.'

I want to believe that, but all I can see is Caroline and I being happy and then her being ripped away from me. 'I can't lose someone I love again,' I whisper.

Maddie scoots closer and puts her arm around me. 'Is that what this is about? You think you'll lose her?'

I nod, the tears starting again.

'Oh, Ames.' She rests her head on mine.

I reach for my wedding ring. 'I might drive her away.'

Maddie draws away from me. 'What?'

'Like I did with Mel.'

She holds my shoulders and looks at me intently. 'You didn't drive Mel away. We've talked about this so many times. There is no way she took her own life. It was an accident. A horrible, tragic accident.'

'I feel disloyal to her.'

'Disloyal? To Mel?'

I nod. 'I loved her so much. I was committed to her. Made vows.'

Her brows furrow. 'Do you mean you feel unfaithful if you fall in love with a woman who isn't Mel?'

I dab my eye and nod.

She presses her lips together. 'Mel wouldn't be upset with you finding love again. Don't you think she'd want you to be happy?'

I shrug.

She rubs my arm. 'I promise you, she'd want that.'

'And then there's you.'

She points to herself. 'Me? What do you mean?'

'You and Caz were together for years, and you're still so close.'

'As friends. We were over a long time before we split. I don't have any hang ups about you being with her. Besides you two had plenty of history before I came along.'

'I wouldn't say plenty,' I sniff.

Her eyebrows shoot up.

'What? We didn't.'

'I know about what happened before you met Mel and me.'

'Yeah, at uni. But we were young—'

She shakes her head. 'No, I mean years after that.'

I swallow. 'Caz told you?'

She nods. 'Only last week.'

I drop my head and sigh. 'I wasn't trying to hide anything from you or Mel, but you know how jealous Mel was.' I look up. 'And there was nothing between me and Caz when we met you two.'

'I believe you. Caz said you wanted more then?'

I pull my legs up onto the couch. 'I did. She didn't and I had to accept that. Then Mel came along, and I didn't want anyone else. So, see, we've been here before and have moved past it. We can do that again.'

'Things are different now, Ames.'

I wipe my nose. 'They don't have to be.'

She sighs. 'I'm not going to argue with you. You'll do what you want anyway.' She nudges me. 'Wanna have a sleepover? I'll cook dinner. We can watch a funny movie. Go for a run in the morning before work. Billie's on nightshift. I'll be lonely on my own.'

I nod. 'Thanks.'

Her phone buzzes. We both look down to see Caroline's name flash on the screen.

'Wondered when she'd call.' Maddie jumps up and waves her phone. 'I'm definitely taking this – I need to hear the other side of the story.' She moves out to the back deck and closes the door.

I grab myself more water and try to read Maddie's face through the glass, but she clocks me and turns away. When she eventually comes back inside, I ask, 'Is Caz okay?'

She rolls her eyes, like she can't be bothered with either of us. 'Come and talk to me while I find something for dinner.' She rustles around in the pantry and plonks a tin of tomatoes on the counter. 'Of course she's not.' She grabs some vegetables from the fridge and dumps them onto the chopping board. 'I know you've got feelings for her, but I'm not going to hassle you about it. You need to figure this out yourself and you need to make a decision. If you want to see if something can work with Caz, then end it with Luke and give it a proper go with her. If you want to be with Luke, then commit to him and let Caz know so she can get on with her life.'

'I did let her know and she won't believe me. I was just at her house telling her that.'

She makes a face. 'Erm, maybe 'cause you followed it up with a hot and heavy pash. You can't say you're not interested and then do that.'

'She kissed me first,' I say sulkily.

She tuts and shakes her head.

'It's so hard to talk to her at the moment. She's so angry.'

'Of course she is!' Maddie's voice rises. 'Think about it. She's watched on while you've had relationships with two other people. She's hurting and she's jealous because she wants to be that person, and she doesn't understand why you can be with them and not her.'

I drop my head into my hands and let out a frustrated groan. The taste of Caroline's lips lingers, but I can't risk the potential agony that comes with being in love.

Chapter Twenty-Three

Today is my thirty-sixth birthday. Like Maddie, I didn't celebrate last year. Mel had only been gone five months then, and Caroline and Maddie were on the verge of splitting. The three of us sat on their couch in the house that is now Caroline's, reminiscing and drinking heavily. I didn't want to do much this year either – although I wasn't inclined to drink myself stupid, so that's progress – but Luke insisted we celebrate. He wanted to do something special for me to say thanks for everything I've done for him, and now a group of our friends and family are gathered on his front deck.

The sun has almost disappeared, leaving a strip of flame orange stretching across the horizon. The light ocean breeze has a bite to it, so Luke has set up heat lamps and placed blankets on the backs of chairs. Drinks and chat flow easily, while Jenna and Cody buzz around with trays of food. Luke's bright and animated, the lines on his face crinkling as he laughs with his mates on the other side of the deck.

Josh and Sophie are talking to Ben, while Dad chats with Luke's parents. Zoe and Taylor are here, too, getting on well with Chris, and Mum has bailed up Maddie and Billie. I can tell by the confused crease in Maddie's brow and Billie's tiny smile that Mum is probably regaling them with PFLAG stories and her newly acquired knowledge of all things queer. Caroline hasn't arrived yet. I'm not sure I expect her to arrive at all, but the emptiness I feel about our friendship falling apart tells me I desperately want her to.

A month has passed since that day in her kitchen, and we've barely spoken. I called her in the days following and admitted I had feelings for her but said that taking things further couldn't work, and that I wanted to be with Luke. I couldn't answer her question why at the time. Now I could tell her that he and I being together has helped us find ourselves again – that we can talk for hours about our pasts without the other one wishing we'd shut up and move on, and how the longing for what we've lost can be so crushing some days that we can barely breathe, but we don't need to explain that to each other either.

I tried to keep our friendship together, but Caroline said she couldn't be around me – she'd let me know when she could. I invited her today of course, to which I received a dismissive, 'I'll try and make it.' That took the wind from me because we haven't missed each other's birthdays since we met.

Luke's noticed something is up, too. He's asked why Caroline and I aren't close like we were. I shrugged it off and said we're both busy with work and getting on with our lives, which is true. He didn't look convinced, but he didn't push it.

Other than that, Luke and I have found a nice flow. We see each other a couple times during the week and again on the weekends. Although we're affectionate, we've definitely fallen into friends territory. It took him a few weeks to want to have sex again after the bridge incident, and it was nice, although I'd be lying if I said it rocked my world. And I'm certain it doesn't rock his. But we have a special bond now and we hold each other up. He's sticking with his therapy sessions and likes the widowed father's group. We've talked constantly about Mel and Sarah, which has been cathartic for both of us, and he's more open with Jenna and Cody about his grief.

Maddie pulls up a chair beside me. 'Hi, birthday girl.'

'Hey, Mads. You escaped Mum then.'

She laughs. 'Yeah. Billie can't get away, though. Your mum's like a different person with this PFLAG stuff.'

I roll my eyes. 'I know. She wants to take Cody to a meeting so he can get tips to support his trans friend at school.'

'I reckon Cody's probably got that covered,' Maddie says, leaning forward to peer at the plates of food in front of her. She grabs a cracker, spreads on some dip, pops it in her mouth and groans. 'This food is amazing.' She points at the dip. 'What's that?'

'That is walnut beet caviar spread. I chose it because it sounded fancy, and I knew you'd love it.'

She takes another. 'I do.' She waves her hand around. 'Luke and the kids have done a great job with all of this.'

Darkness has fallen now, and the red glow of the heat lamps blends with the flicker of candles scattered on the tables and the fairy lights affixed to the railings. 'They have. It's lovely,' I say, a sad note to my voice.

Maddie leans in. 'You wondering where Caz is?'

I frown. 'I thought she'd come.'

She pats my thigh. 'She'll be here.'

'You think so?'

'She said she was. But...' She plays with the mint sticking out the top of her mojito. 'There's something you should know.'

My brows knit. 'What?'

'Rachel's back on the scene.'

'Oh.' If it's possible to feel colour drain from your face, that's what I'm experiencing right now. 'I've seen Caz at work. She hasn't said anything.'

'Probably because you barely speak,' Maddie says.

The disappointment over Caroline not being here is quickly replaced by that fire that flares every time I think about her and Rachel being together. 'Why can't she fucking talk to me like she used to?'

Maddie tilts her head. 'You know the answer to that. She can't wait around forever. She needs to move on, not that I think Rachel's good for her.'

I take a few deep breaths to extinguish the flames. 'Why are you telling me this now?'

She grimaces. 'Because she's bringing her.'

I stare at Maddie, dumbfounded. '*Rach*,' I spit. 'Wasn't fucking invited.'

Maddie stifles a laugh. 'Jesus, and I was actually starting to believe that you didn't have feelings for Caz after all.'

'I don't,' I hiss.

'You clearly do.'

I huff. 'Well, I can't believe she hasn't told me. Just lump it on me.' I'm overreacting, but I can't keep it in.

Maddie laughs again and I shoot her a glare.

'Sorry. But bit of a severe reaction. You're allowed to have a partner and she's not?'

I sigh and shake my head. 'I didn't mean it. I've no right to be angry. It's none of my—' Her gaze shifts behind me. I spin around to see Caroline. And Rachel.

Maddie places her hand on my shoulder. 'Be nice,' she whispers.

I jump up. 'You made it,' I say, giving Caroline a hug.

She squeezes me. 'Of course. Happy birthday.'

I inhale as she holds me, hoping to breathe in some familiarity, but I don't catch the jasmine from her Chanel. I feel slighted, like she's worn a different perfume deliberately.

I release her and face Rachel. 'Hi, Rachel.'

'Happy birthday,' she says in the usual saccharin tone that she greets me with.

A bitchy retort is ready to launch from my tongue, but I refrain for Caroline's sake and flash my most genuine smile. 'Thanks.'

Luke appears beside me, placing his hand on my back. 'Hi, Caz, you made it.'

I slide my arm around his waist.

Caroline's gaze drops to my hold on him and flicks back to my face before she brightens and turns to him. 'Hi, Luke. Nice to see you again.' She points to her right. 'This is Rachel. Rachel – Luke.'

I fetch them drinks and leave them with Maddie. I spend time mingling with different groups, eating mascarpone fennel puffs and lemon crab bites, and drinking mojitos until eventually I find myself alone leaning against the deck railing. My eyes drift to Caroline. She's laughing with Dad, her face lively and beautiful. My gaze drifts down. Her jeans cling to her long legs and a soft aqua jumper hugs her upper body. My heart cracks. I have so much I want to say and so many questions. Things I couldn't process weeks ago, but now I've had time, I want to sort them out.

She catches my eye and I turn away quickly. A minute later, she's at my side.

'Hi.' She leans her hip against the rail.

'Hello,' I say stiffly, peering across to the ocean.

'You're pissed off at me.'

I face her. 'No.'

She crosses her arms. 'Yes.'

I keep my voice low. 'You don't tell me you're seeing Rachel again and then you bring her here?'

Her eyes widen, but she also keeps her voice low. 'Wow. Okay. Are you annoyed because I'm seeing her again or because I didn't tell you?'

'Because you didn't tell me. You tell me everything.'

'No, Amy. I used to tell you everything. Things are very different now,' she says, with a bitter edge.

'Why? Why do they have to be different?'

The glow from the heat lamp turns her eyes a deeper shade of blue, and they fill with hurt. 'You know why.'

'Did you bring her to rub my nose in it?' I bite my bottom lip. *Shit.*

Her eyes narrow. She'll be dissecting that comment, but she doesn't react. Instead, she sighs. 'No. It was a spur of the moment decision. She was at my place today and I mentioned the party. She assumed I invited her. I couldn't really say no. I should've contacted you first to tell you I was bringing someone. Sorry.'

Across the deck, Luke watches us curiously. 'Enjoy the party,' I say and walk over to him.

He tilts his head towards Caroline. 'Everything alright?'

'With me and Caz? Yeah, course, why?'

He shakes his head. 'No reason.' He grins. 'Having fun?'

'I am. I'm glad you talked me into it.' I point to his empty glass. 'You want me to make you a cocktail?'

He perks up even more. 'Sure.'

I make us both mojitos and do the rounds again, talking, laughing, drinking and eating. I stay close to Luke, and I'm pleased that my friends and family like him so much. I'm pleasant with Caroline and Rachel when I need to be and do my best not to focus on them, but find myself sneaking glances their way through the evening. They seem happy – holding hands, loving looks, casual kisses. I don't want to see it, but like a horror film, I can't look away. I catch Caroline glimpsing my way, and every so often our eyes meet and linger. When she looks at me does she see a reflection of what I see? A yearning for each other? A desire for things to be different?

*

It's midnight by the time everyone leaves, and Jenna and Cody have gone to bed. I watch Luke as he clears up. He looks good tonight in his tight blue jeans and black T-shirt. Sexy, too, with his glasses and stubble. I get an urge I haven't felt for a while. I walk around to the other side of the kitchen bench, run my hands up his back and kiss his neck.

'Hey,' he says, stacking some glasses by the sink.

I turn him to face me and press against him. 'Thank you for the party.'

He eyes me curiously. 'You're welcome.'

I kiss him hard. His mouth is warm, and his whiskers graze my lips and chin. He wraps an arm around my waist, and I reach down to undo his jeans, slip my hand in and move my palm against him.

He groans softly. 'I think we'd better go upstairs,' he says, his voice low and throaty.

I grab his hand and pull him upstairs as quickly as I can. As soon as he shuts the bedroom door, we pull at each other's clothes until we're naked. I push him onto the bed, straddling him, and he grips my thighs as I lower onto him. I try to force my mind to empty, but all I can see is Caroline. Her face, her smile, her body.

An electric current fizzes through me, and Luke's fingers dig into my hips as his breathing increases. I push Caroline from my mind and focus on what is happening right now, but she bounces straight back. Those scorching kisses float into my memory – the salty sweet of her mouth, the heat of her skin under my fingertips. I moan as my body sparks even more and grab the top of the headboard. What's she doing now? Having sex with Rachel? Does she see my face when Rachel goes down on her? Does she want to call my name when Rachel makes her come?

Luke grips my arse and thrusts harder against me.

I imagine Rachel working her way down Caroline's body, running her tongue over Caroline's breast, across the soft skin on her stomach, kissing her inner thigh. Except it's not Rachel; it's me.

I'm too loud now and Luke clamps a hand over my mouth. I'm grateful because I might have called out Caroline's name as my body and brain explode. Luke tenses underneath me and groans. My pulse is off the grid, my skin tingling. I slump down, my torso pressed against his.

'Holy shit,' I say, breathless.

'Bloody hell,' he says, his chest rapidly rising and falling. 'You'll give me a heart attack.'

I roll off him and lie my head against him. 'Sorry.'

He laughs softly. 'Wouldn't be a bad way to go.'

I smile; he's lovely. I slide my arm across his waist and bury my face into his neck hoping it will somehow make me only think of him, but Caroline's still there. My eyes sting and my shoulders jerk as the tears fall.

'Amy?' Luke reaches to turn on the lamp. 'What's up?'

I keep my face buried.

'I know that was good, but I'm not sure it was a move you to tears performance,' he says, placing his finger under my chin and tilting my head up. 'But I don't think that's why you're upset.'

I stare into his deep brown eyes. Eyes that spoke to me the first time we met. What do I say? *I just had the most amazing orgasm because I was thinking about Caroline? I know you and I aren't in love, but we help each other be okay, so we keep this thing going?* No, I can't say any of that. 'I'm fine. Just being my normal emotional self.' I press the back of my hand to my cheek.

'Something you want to talk about?'

I shake my head.

He strokes my hair and searches my face. 'Maybe there's something you want to tell me?'

'No. I just need to sleep. It's been a long day.'

He stares at me for a few seconds before he kisses me. 'Night.'

'Night.'

He shifts onto to his side facing outward like he always does. I spoon him and he pulls my hand to his lips before his body relaxes and his breathing deepens. I roll onto my back, but sleep doesn't come. I stare at a sliver of light that filters through a gap in the curtain and beams across the ceiling, thinking about how much Caroline means to me. How much I love her and need her in my life. And how she's with another woman right now that's not me. Does she stare at the ceiling and think of me while Rachel sleeps beside her? Or has she moved on already? Found her rhythm with Rachel and realised she doesn't love me after all?

Luke is snoring softly now. I hop out of bed to find my jeans and dig out my phone. I tap out a message.

Thanks for coming over tonight x

I tap back, delete x. No, add x. Send. I stare at the screen willing the three dots to appear, and they do. A minute later, a message arrives.

Would never miss your birthday x

I close my eyes and hold the phone to my forehead.

Damn her.

Chapter Twenty-Four

Luke's side of the bed is empty when I wake. The room's dark and I can hear the soft drizzle of rain against the windows. It takes a moment to orient myself and process the night before, and then I remember. Heated words and longing glances with Caroline. Hot sex with Luke while thinking about her. Him knowing something was up, and probably suspecting what. I groan and throw my arm across my eyes.

After a shower, I head downstairs. Luke's at the kitchen table tapping away at his laptop, while Cody and Jenna laze on the couch scrolling through their phones, a music channel playing on TV.

'Morning, you two,' I say.

'Hi,' they both mumble, eyes glued to their screens.

'Hey,' Luke says, with a warm smile.

I rub his shoulder as I pass. 'You've cleared up already?'

'Yeah. I woke early.'

I head round to the other side of the kitchen bench and drop a pod into the coffee machine. 'You want a coffee?'

'Sure,' he says, following me.

I turn to hug him. 'Thanks for the party. I had a great time.'

'You deserve it.' He squeezes me in return. 'Want something to eat? I was about to make bacon and egg sandwiches.'

The receptors in my brain awaken in response to the woody aroma of coffee and the mention of food. 'Yes, please. That sounds good.' I hand him a coffee and stick another pod in the machine for me.

After greasy breakfast sandwiches, Luke pats my hand. 'Rain's stopped. Tide's out. Wanna go for a walk on the beach?' There's a serious tone to his voice that tells me he doesn't just want fresh air.

'Oh. Sure.'

'Back soon,' he says to Jenna and Cody, grabbing his jacket off the back of the chair and slipping his arms through the sleeves.

I zip up my hoodie as we head outside and cross the road. The wind is cool, and the sky is dense with heavy, grey clouds. Apart from a few Sunday morning dog walkers and a lone kite surfer in the distance, the beach is deserted. We hop over the stone wall, roll up our jeans and drop onto the wet grains before moving onto the hard, uneven sand. The wind is sending my hair in all directions, so I dig into my pocket for a hairband and secure it into a top knot. Once I'm done, I put my arm around Luke's waist, and he drapes his across my shoulder.

'Think we might need a chat, ay?' he says.

I keep my head down so that I can dodge the soldier crabs and jelly fish, and his eyes. 'Yep.'

'Something's going on with you.'

I gaze ahead to the ocean, trying to figure out what to say and how to say it. All I come out with is, 'I guess.'

After a few moments of silence, he says, 'Are you going to tell me what it is?'

I peer at him. 'I'm not sure how to explain it.'

He tilts his head. 'You wanna have a go?'

I release my grip on him, and we navigate around shallow pools of water and seaweed. 'You know that you're really special to me.'

He nods. 'Yeah.'

'And that I care about you.'

'I know that, too. I feel the same.'

I swallow. 'Being around you, Jenna and Cody has forced me to get out of my head and think about other people again. Think about life again. I forgot how to do that after Mel died.'

'You've done the same for us. Don't know how we would've got through the past few months without you.' He runs his rough palm across the back of my neck. 'But you've been distracted the past few weeks and... troubled. Not a grief sort of troubled. More of a life troubled – like things are going on right now that are bugging you.'

'I guess you could say that.'

'Okay. Anything in particular?'

'Um... I...' I fall silent and pull him close again as we continue to walk. We need to let go of each other for our own happiness, but it's not easy to cut loose such a strong foundation. I feel like a boat that's been anchored to a pier for months, and now it needs to return to the water and sail alone.

'Are you going to make me state the obvious?' he says.

I pull the hood of my jumper over my head and look at him.

'I'll take that as a yes. I'll say how I feel, and you can tell me if you agree.'

I nod.

'We help each other function, but this probably won't work long-term because I don't think I'm what you're looking for, and I'm not sure what I want.'

I glance out towards the waves. 'Something like that.'

'You don't need to worry about me, Amy. I'll be alright. You need to do what's right for you.'

'It's not that I worry. It's more that I like this.' I wave my hand between us. 'This bond we have.'

'I like it, too. But you have to admit we're probably more like good friends.'

We reach the edge of the ocean and I stick my foot out to drag a shell along the sand with my big toe. 'We're more than friends sometimes.

We were more than friends last night.'

'That's because we're trying to be a couple. We don't have to do that. We can just be friends.'

I wrap my arms around him and lie my head against his chest. 'I think I'd like that.'

'I'd like that too,' he says, rubbing my back.

I peer up at him. 'What you said before, that you're not sure what you want, what did you mean?'

He frowns. 'I don't know what I'm looking for. Not in a relationship anyway. I feel like I've been living under a black cloud since Sarah died, like I died with her. It's only been the past six weeks or so that I've felt a bit lighter. I thought I was okay before. Now I realise I was far from okay. I just want to find some peace and fix things with Jenna and Cody. I can't get my head around committing to a relationship. Not at the moment.' His eyes search my face. 'And even if I was ready, I'm not sure I'm what you're looking for. Maybe that had something to do with why you were upset last night?'

My cheeks warms. 'Maybe.'

He kisses my forehead.

'So that's it then? We're calling a day on this?' I say.

'That's what you want, isn't it? What we both want?'

'Yeah,' I say sadly.

'Then, yeah. But just the relationship? Not the friendship?'

'No way.' I cup his cheek.

He grabs my hand, and we head back to the shore. 'Good. I remember you telling me that's what happens in your world. You stay friends with your exes. So, this can work for us, right?'

I smile. 'That's right. You're an honorary lesbian now. Got your own thread on our queer spiderweb. Amy's web – once you're caught, you can't get out. You have to be my best mate. It's a rule.'

He laughs. 'The queer spiderweb. Ben will be proud.'

'He will.'

'How many threads on this web?' he asks.

'Ha. You have no idea. It's a minefield.'

He nods slowly and his eyes flit around as though he's processing a complex thought. 'So... does that mean I get to make my own threads?'

'That's usually how it works.' I throw him some suspicious side-eye. 'Why?'

'Because...' He smiles slyly. 'Zoe.' He lets out a slow wolf whistle. 'Wow. I can see why you struggled.'

I laugh. 'I saw you eyeing her up last night. You definitely have a type, and I'm not it.'

His eyebrows shoot up. 'Do I?'

'Yeah. Sarah, Zoe. Women you make comments about on telly. Dark-haired, dark-eyed beauties with killer curves. Sarah and Zoe are like a mix between JLo and Beyoncé. I'm more...' I look up at the grey sky while I think of a suitable comparison who Luke will know. 'Emma Stone.'

'Emma Stone is beautiful.'

I shove him. 'Good response. Good luck getting past Taylor.'

He grins. 'She's all Taylor's. I'll settle for one thread.'

'Cody's English teacher was checking you out when we went to meet the counsellor.'

'You reckon?'

'Defo. She was into you.'

'Huh. She's... very attractive.'

'She's a dark-haired, dark-eyed beauty. And no wedding ring. I checked. Not that that means anything. But no wedding ring and eyeing you up – that might mean something.'

A wicked grin spreads across his face. 'Don't reckon the kids would be too pleased if I had it going on with a teacher from Sandgate High.'

I laugh. 'Definitely not.'

We walk a few more minutes, the soldier crabs parting and scurrying into their holes as we step onto their territory.

'Anything else you want to tell me?' he says.

I glance at him briefly before shifting my gaze back to the sand. 'About what?'

'About whatever's going on with you and Caz.'

I'm quiet for a beat. 'Why would you think that?'

'Well, you haven't been in each other's pockets for ages. No calls or texts for I don't know how long. You never mention her when you talk about work, and you only do stuff with Maddie now. It looked like you had words last night, when you were standing by the railing.'

'Oh...'

He shakes his head slowly. 'And the way you two look at each other.'

Despite the cool wind, my cheeks flame.

'You've got history. Doesn't take a genius to work it out.'

I sigh, dropping my head and pinching the bridge of my nose. 'Things have gone very wrong between us.'

And then I tell him the whole story, starting from that night at the Wickham Hotel and how clear it is now why we both acted the way we did. I tell him what happened at Maddie's party and in her kitchen two weeks later, and that we've drifted apart over the past month, until last night, where I found out she was seeing Rachel again and how hard that hit me.

He listens quietly, his face impassive. When I'm finished, he says, 'Shit, Amy. This has been going on all this time and you've been focussing on me? Why? You must've been a mess inside.'

I pull my hand from my pocket and hook my arm through his. 'No. it wasn't like that. I wanted to be there for you. And now I realise that I needed that for me, too. This time we've had together has been so good for me. For both of us. I'm stronger because of it. And for the first time since Mel died, I'm starting to feel like me again.'

He nods. 'I'm glad to hear that.'

'I've needed time to process these thoughts and feelings about Caz. Seeing her last night with Rachel was a slap in the face. I'm sorry I couldn't tell you this before. It wasn't clear like it is now. It's taken me a while to figure it out, and you had so much going on, it didn't seem important in comparison.'

'So, now you've told me, how do you really feel about her?'

I gaze ahead to the approaching shore. 'I love her.'

'And what are you going to do about it?'

'What can I do? She's back with Rachel.'

'You're giving up that easily?'

I shrug. 'They like each other. They might even love each other. Look how they were last night. I've got no right to break that up. I'm not even sure Caz feels anything for me anymore. But she's the missing link now – I can't fully be me again without her, so if that means friendship while she's with Rachel, then I'll take it.'

'I saw how they were, but I also saw how she watched you. Amy, if you've got another shot for a new life with someone after what you've been through, you need to take it.'

'You think so?'

'No question.'

We step over a pile of washed-up shells and debris before he launches himself onto the stone wall, holding his hand out for me.

'We should tell Jenna and Cody, hey?' I swing my legs over the wall and onto the walkway.

'Yep.'

We clean our feet on the deck and strip off our jackets once we're back inside. The house is quiet.

'Jenna, Cody,' Luke calls.

'There's a note,' I say. 'They've gone to the movies with Emma. They tried to call; you left your phone here.'

Luke pats his jeans pockets. 'Guess I did.' He walks into the kitchen and points to the space beside the toaster. 'There it is.' He checks the screen.

'Oh. I wanted to talk to them,' I say.

'They'll understand.'

'I can hang around until they get back?'

'Nah, they'll be hours. Call them later if you like.'

'You'll be alright on your own?'

He smiles. 'I'll be fine. I've got plenty of things to keep me occupied.'

'Okay. I'll go grab my stuff.'

I head upstairs and throw my belongings into my bag. I sit on the end of the bed, absorbing the memories of the past few months and the strange, haunting presence in here. 'See ya, Sarah,' I whisper. 'Watch over him. Be great if you could send him another true love when he's ready. Give Mel a kiss from me. Wait, no, you're too hot. A hug, give her a hug.' Despite the heaviness in my chest, I chuckle and shake my head at my own absurdity.

Back downstairs, Luke walks me to my car. I place my bag onto the passenger seat and lean against the door.

'So, I was thinking it's probably time I packed up Sarah's stuff,' he says, rubbing his hand across his chin.

'You're ready for that?'

He nods. 'I think it's time. I was hoping that you'd help, maybe? A bit of emotional support?'

I wrap my arms around him. 'Of course.'

He squeezes me. 'Thank you.'

I tilt my head up and plant my lips on his one last time, then pull away and clear my throat.

'Hey, come on. None of that.'

'I'll miss you.'

'We'll see each other soon. You're only up the road,' he says, but his eyes are glassy.

I nod, hop in the driver's seat and buckle my seatbelt. 'Bye.'

He holds his hand up. 'See ya.'

I wave as I drive off and decide to head to Mum and Dad's. They were elated last night seeing me coupled with someone again, so it's best to let them down in person. And part of me needs them right now.

I call out as I let myself in. 'Mum? Dad? Only me.'

'In here, love,' Dad calls from the kitchen.

They're sitting at the kitchen table working on a jigsaw.

'Hello, darling. This is a nice surprise,' Mum says, peering over the top of her glasses.

'Hi,' I say, taking a seat.

'Not spending the day with Luke?' Dad asks.

I pick up a random jigsaw piece and try to slot it in somewhere. 'No. That's why I'm here actually.' When I look up, they're both staring at me.

'Oh, dear. This doesn't sound good,' Mum says, standing. 'Think I'd better make you a cup of tea.'

'Thanks, Mum.'

She switches the jug on and clatters about with mugs and spoons.

Dad hops up and squeezes my shoulder. 'You probably need a bickie, too. Mint Slice or Kingston?'

Mint Slice or Kingston; Caroline or Luke. Too many choices today. 'That's a hard decision, Dad. You better give me one of each.'

'What's going on, love?' Dad asks, placing the biscuits in front of me, followed by Mum with the tea.

I grab a Kingston and dunk it in my tea. 'Luke and I have decided it's not going to work.'

'Oh,' Mum says. 'You seemed so happy and comfortable with each other last night.'

I nod. 'Yeah, but we're not couple material. We're better friends.

He's getting himself together again after what happened on the bridge. He needs to focus on himself and the kids. And me, well...' I shrug.

Dad frowns and pats my hand.

Mum leans over and rubs my shoulder. 'He's a lovely man, but some couples aren't meant to be, and there's no point being with someone for the sake of it.'

I give her a small smile. Every now and then she gets it.

'Well, you'll meet someone again.' She rustles in the packet for a Mint Slice. 'Oh, Joan at PFLAG, her daughter's single and—'

'Helen,' Dad warns. 'I don't think Amy wants to be set up.'

She holds her hand up. 'Just trying to help.'

'Thanks, Mum. I'm good. I'll let you know if I want you to hook me up.'

She waves the half-eaten biscuit around, the crumbs falling to the table. 'I'm sorry. I know you don't need my help. I just worry.'

'I know you do. I'll be okay.'

She smiles and clutches my hand.

The doorbell rings and we hear Josh call, 'Hello?'

'In the kitchen,' Dad yells.

'They're here for lunch. Why don't you stay?' Mum says.

I nod. 'That'll be nice.'

Josh and Sophie appear with a bowl of salad and some bread rolls.

'G'day, Ames,' Josh says, rustling the top of my head.

'Hey, Josh. Soph,' I say.

'Luke not with you?' Sophie asks.

I tell them what I've just told Mum and Dad, and they both say they're sorry and comment how much they liked him.

I dig out a Mint Slice and bite into it, washing it down with a gulp of sweet tea. 'Anyway, we're still good friends, so I'm sure you'll see him again. Did you all enjoy the party?'

'Wonderful,' Dad says. 'Luke's got a lovely family.'

I nod. 'They're great.'

'Maddie and Billie are adorable together,' Mum says.

I smile. 'They are.'

'Rachel seems nice. I'm glad Caz has met someone,' Dad says.

I stare into my mug. I need to get past these uncomfortable feelings every time Rachel's name is mentioned. I need to do that for Caroline. I clear my throat and look up. 'Yeah, they look happy. I… I hope it works out for them.'

Dad nods and focusses on the jigsaw. Mum follows suit, but Sophie narrows her eyes at me, and a tiny smile pulls on Josh's lips.

I curl my top lip. 'What's up with you two losers?'

Josh shrugs. 'We didn't say anything.'

I shake my head. 'Shut up.'

Chapter Twenty-Five

'Hey, Evan,' I say, my mouth watering from the smell of fried onions wafting from the kitchen.

He beams. 'Amy, hi. You don't usually come in on a Wednesday. Mixing it up this week?'

'You know me. I live on the edge.'

He grins and faces Daniel. 'G'day, Daniel. Working lunch?'

'If catching up on office gossip for an hour counts as a working lunch, sure,' he replies, flicking me a knowing look.

'I'm a great boss,' I say.

Evan laughs. 'What can I get you both?'

We place our order and head for the last free table in the middle of the café. I allow myself a fleeting glance at my regular spot and follow Dr Sachdev's advice – let myself feel the pang of longing, know that it will pass, and focus on the present. I close my eyes for a second, breathe through it, and sit facing the counter so that I can't see the other table. I turn my attention to Daniel, and we launch into the latest work drama – Paul and Vanessa being caught out by Vanessa's husband.

Evan eavesdrops with a smirk as he delivers our coffee. When he walks away, I freeze mid-sentence and stare at the counter. Rachel peers at the menu board, while Caroline glances around the café, presumably for a table. She double takes when she sees me, and a faint smile appears as our eyes lock. It's an olive branch smile that makes my heart sing. It also makes me want to walk up to her and say, 'I love you. Choose me.' Our moment is broken when Rachel turns to her and mouths something, then follows Caroline's gaze to me, and her face darkens. I quickly turn to Daniel who's staring at me with a stupid big grin on his face.

'What's going on with you two?' he asks.

'Me and Rachel? I don't like her.'

He rests his arms on the table and leans forward. 'You know I'm not talking about Rachel.'

'Caz?' I sip my flat white. 'Nothing.'

'Come on, Amy. For years you're in and out of each other's offices, out for coffee, lunches, best mates, and then overnight you stop speaking?'

I blink at him. 'Oh. Um...'

He lowers his voice. 'And I can feel the tension from here. Whatever's happened, you need to get a room and set the date.'

I screw up my face. 'What?'

'Yes. *That's* obvious too.'

I sigh. I don't have the energy to hide it anymore. 'Well, Dull Brown over there's in the way.'

Evan appears and places our burgers and chips on the table.

'Cheers,' I say.

Daniel takes a sweet potato chip from the shared bowl and peeks towards the counter. 'Who's Dull Brown?' he whispers. 'Rachel?'

'Yep.'

'Oh-kaay. Why?'

'That's her hair colour,' I say, through a mouthful of chicken burger.

He sneaks another look and then squints at me with a bewildered frown. 'It's the same colour as yours.'

I scoff, drop my burger and hold out a chunk of my hair. 'This. Is chestnut.' I release my hair, pick up a chip and point it at him. 'Not just any chestnut. *Rich* chestnut.'

He winces. 'Sorry.'

'And of course I don't call her that in front of anyone. Only you now you're in on the secret.'

He sniggers. 'The secret? Are you kidding? The whole department has bets on how long it will take you and Caz to get it together.'

'Shut up. They have not.'

He nods and dunks a couple of chips into a pot of chili sauce. 'Have.'

I tut. 'Bloody hell.'

He shrugs. 'We've got to do something to spice up our workdays.'

'You could do some work. How about that?'

'Bor-ing,' he sing-songs.

I shake my head and take a huge bite of burger, watching Caroline as she waits for her order. She's wearing a navy suit and mint green blouse that I haven't seen before. She looks good. Amazing, actually. Apparently, she's been doing hot yoga for the past month. I can see the benefits from the way her pants cling to her toned legs and skim her stomach. She's chatting to Rachel but keeps glancing my way. Maddie would've told her it's over with Luke, although I made Maddie promise that 'Luke' was the only four-letter word starting with L she'd mention to Caroline. I haven't spoken to Caroline since that midnight text the night of my party. I want to, but I've been busy trying to be a functioning adult – and work out how I'm going to salvage this friendship.

'Amy…' Daniel says.

'Hmm?' I say, still gazing as I bite and chew.

'Amy?'

'What?' I whine.

He lifts his finger to the corner of his mouth and wipes. 'You've got sauce dripping from the side of your mouth and down your chin.'

'Shit.' I drop my burger, quickly grab a napkin and dab at my mouth. My phone flashes with a message. I gasp when I see it's from Caroline.

You've got sauce all over your face

I flick my eyes to her. She smiles wider this time, enough to show her dimples, before collecting her order and leaving.

*

Eight days have passed since that day in Evan's, with nothing improving between Caroline and me. I took her smile and that text as a peace offering, and messaged her to ask how she was, but she didn't reply. Monday, as soon as I woke, I messaged to ask if we could meet for lunch, to talk. Again, no reply. I saw her on Tuesday in the office and said hi. She gave me a stiff hello and raced off. She wasn't at work on Wednesday, so I called her in the evening – no answer. Yesterday, I decided to back off for a day, but I'm not ready to give up. We've been here before; we can fix this.

I head downstairs to her office to see if she wants coffee with a plan to have a casual chat about my HR meeting this morning. Her office is empty, her computer is off, and her chair is pushed against the desk.

I wander out to Sian. 'Is Caz off today? Is she sick?'

Sian's brow creases. 'She's in Sydney.'

'Sydney? Is she on leave?'

She tilts her head. 'No, she's there for the head of HR interview. The one Greg recommended her for. She's been back and forth all week.'

I swallow.

Sian puts her hand to her mouth. 'Shit. I probably wasn't supposed to say. I assumed you'd—'

'Oh.' I shake my head. 'The interview. Of course. I knew that. I forgot it was today.' I give a forced smile. 'A lot on my mind.'

She relaxes. 'Phew. Thought I'd put my foot in it then.'

'No. You're good.' I hold my stomach. The chocolate croissant I've not long eaten swirls in my stomach, threatening to come up.

'Are you alright?' Sian asks.

'Yeah, just a bit...'

She wrinkles her nose. 'Stressed about the meeting this morning?'

I nod. 'Have I got time to grab a coffee first?'

She glances at her watch. 'You've got half an hour.'

I rush to the lift and press the button for the ground floor. When I get to the foyer, I burst through the glass doors to Edward Street and gulp in the fresh, cool air, then dig out my phone and call Maddie.

'Hey, Ames.'

'Caz is in Sydney. For an interview.'

'Whoa! Slow down. What are you talking about?'

'You didn't know?'

'No, I had no idea.'

'I just went to see her, and Sian told me she's in Sydney for an interview.' I choke back a sob. 'She's been back and forth all week.'

'Shit, what's she playing at?' Maddie says.

'Why wouldn't she tell you at least?'

'Because she knows I'd try and stop her. And that I'd tell you.'

'I can't lose her, Mads. And she'll get this job for sure if Greg sent her.'

'Then fucking do something about it.'

'I've tried. She doesn't respond. And she's with Rachel.'

'Rachel can't be that important if she's planning to leave.'

'Unless she's going with her,' I say, the queasiness in my gut intensifying. 'Oh god. They're going to move there together, aren't they?'

'No way. Caz wouldn't make a move that fast. Ames, you've got to tell her how you feel.'

'She knows and—'

'She doesn't! How could she?'

'She knows it's over with Luke.'

'Yes, but she doesn't know how you feel about her. I haven't told her. It's not my place.'

'But she gives me nothing. She hardly responds to my messages. And when I talk to her, she's frosty.'

'And why do you think that is?'

I close my eyes and lean my head back against the wall. 'I don't know what to do.'

'Talk to her. Tell her.'

I push my fingers against my temple. 'I can't think. I've got this HR meeting now. I'll call you later.'

'Shit, your meeting. I forgot. And Caz isn't there.'

'No.'

'Ames, you two can't go on like this. You need to sort it out.'

'Okay, I'll deal with it later. Speak soon.' I hang up and walk to the hole in the wall café on the corner and grab a strong black coffee. I plan a conversation with Caroline in my head. I'll be honest. Tell her that I love her and that my life can't work if she's not in it. Simple. But the minute my brain forms the words, the fear that I could lose her too takes hold. *You're losing her anyway,* a voice in my head tells me. *Yes, but this way I don't carry the risk of my love being blown apart,* I argue back.

Back in the office, I seat myself in the boardroom. Sian and Greg arrive a few minutes afterwards.

'Greg, I didn't realise you'd be at this meeting,' I say.

'Last minute decision.' He smiles and slides into the chair opposite me.

Sian clicks the door shut and takes a seat next to him.

'So, Amy, as you know,' Greg says. 'Paul was presented with your complaint and was provided an opportunity to respond.'

I nod and fiddle with my hands under the table.

'It will come as no surprise that he doesn't view his behaviour as bullying. He claims he was simply giving you directives as your manager.'

'I assumed that would be his response,' I say.

Greg links his fingers together on the desk. 'Look. You know how these things go. Unless you have witnesses and a lot of strong documentary evidence, it's hard to prove.'

I sigh and drop my head.

'A lot of time was spent going through your information and talking to Paul,' Sian says. 'There's no question there's borderline bullying behaviour, but it's mixed with requests that form part of your role. It's difficult to separate. Nevertheless, many of his requests were outside your remit and at times he put too much pressure on you, and he'll be informed of that.'

I nod. 'That's something, I guess. What happens now? I keep reporting to him like nothing's happened?'

'Well, no. That's why I'm here,' Greg says. 'I'm about to tell Paul that he won't be at work the next few weeks. The reason I'm telling you is because your team will need to be involved.'

'Right,' I say warily.

'We've received other bullying and harassment complaints against Paul, so he's about to be suspended while those matters are being investigated.'

I glance between the two of them. 'They must be quite serious if he's being suspended.'

Greg gives a curt nod. 'Under the circumstances, you can't investigate those complaints – let Daniel handle them. If we move into a dispute, then Sian can act on Caroline's behalf. Caroline's too conflicted.'

'Wow. Okay. I'm surprised and not surprised at the same time.'

He smiles. 'You did the right thing by speaking up, Amy. And there will be no restructure. Your job is safe.'

My shoulders drop. 'Thanks, Greg.'

'I know things have been tough for you, but you've always given so much to this company, and you do a great job. I've seen a difference in you the last few months. Seeing a bit more of the old you. I'm pleased about that.'

'I feel a bit stronger every day.'

'Glad to hear it.' He stands. 'I have a meeting with Paul now.'

As soon as he leaves, Sian and I race back to her desk, which has a clear view of Paul's office. We pretend to look at her monitor and wait for Greg to re-emerge.

'Did you know about any of this?' I whisper.

'I'd heard a few rumblings around the place, but nothing definite. Greg called me while you were out for coffee to tell me.'

'Paul's such a fucking creep,' I say. 'I bet he's tried it on with someone.'

'That's the rumour,' Sian says.

Paul's office door swings open. Greg strides out, and I catch his smirk before he heads in the opposite direction.

Paul emerges a few minutes later and glares at Sian and me.

'Don't worry about it,' Sian mutters. 'He'll be in the shit if he says anything.'

He walks towards us, oozing bitterness and enters the lift.

*

The next day, I open my front door to find Maddie standing there with takeaway coffees and salad containers.

'I bought you lunch,' she says, not waiting for an invite before she barges in.

'That's nice of you. Hello.' I close the door behind her.

She places everything on my kitchen table and faces me, hands on her hips.

'Ta,' I say, picking up one of the coffees.

'I've just spoken to Caz about this Sydney thing. She's seriously thinking about taking that job.'

I drop onto one of the dining chairs and Maddie sits opposite. 'What can I do? I messaged her this morning as soon as I woke up. I've texted and called since that day I saw her at Evan's, and she's replied to two messages or something.' I open a container and dig around with the fork.

'And was your message this morning, "I love you, Caz, please don't leave?" Or did you tell her you hope she gets the job?' She spears a tomato with so much force I worry she'll break the container and leave a permanent scar in my very expensive oak dining table.

'I asked what was going on, what's the job, that sort of stuff.'

Maddie rolls her eyes, but luckily her gob is full of salad so she can't reply.

'I can't bare my soul over text. I was hoping she'd reply and then I could take it from there.' I nod trying to convince myself.

'You know Caz doesn't operate like that. It's not enough.' She sighs and slumps back against the chair.

'She's seeing someone. I don't want to ruin that if it's what she wants.'

Maddie shakes her head. 'No. They're done. That's what I've come to tell you. Caz told me this morning. She ended it during the week.'

My stomach flutters. 'Why?'

Maddie shoves a large cube of fried tofu in her mouth and starts talking. 'Caz caught Rachel going through her phone.'

'No!'

Maddie nods. 'Mmhmm.' She swallows. 'She started telling me something else about deleted messages, then just said Rachel was too intense. I asked more questions, but you know what Caz is like – said she didn't want to talk about it.'

'Deleted messages? Do you think that's what happened to my messages? Why Caz hasn't replied?'

Maddie's face scrunches as she considers my question. 'Fuck. Yeah. Maybe.'

'That's messed up.'

She shakes her head. 'Anyway, she's out of the picture.' She jabs her fork at me. 'So you can't use that as an excuse.' She softens. 'Look, sorry I'm pissed off. It's so hard being messenger between the two of you. You love her. She loves you. Simple.'

I push my salad to the side. 'It's not simple. I've been trying to fix it.'

'She doesn't just want a friendship. This has broken her, Amy.'

My being is screaming out for Caroline – to have her in my life again, to hold her, to tell her that I love her.

'You love her, don't you?' Maddie asks.

I nod.

'Then do something before she packs up and moves to Sydney.'

'Okay. I'll call her. Go and see her.'

'Today?'

'Yeah,' I say, but my heart is heavy because if I'm going to fully give myself to Caroline, then there is something I have to do first.

We pick at our salads, making small talk about our week, and I fill her in about what happened at work yesterday with Paul.

'He deserves everything he gets,' she says once I'm finished. She stands. 'Sorry to run off. I need to pick up Billie from work.'

'No worries. Thanks for lunch.'

She tilts her head. 'You will go and see Caz, won't you?'

'I will. I just need to...' I circle my hand around my head. 'Think.'

She hugs me. 'Don't think too long, ay?'

I shake my head, the ache in my throat preventing me from speaking.

She jogs down the stairs and jumps in the car, giving me a toot as she drives off.

I close the door and lean my forehead against the wood, counting my breaths in an attempt to slow my heart rate. I head back to the lounge room, pick up a wedding photo and Mel's ashes and sit cross-legged on the couch, propping the urn in my lap. I run my finger over Mel's still image, my eyes filling. We had just exchanged rings, grinning at each other, looking forward to the rest of our lives together.

I grip my wedding ring and close my eyes. My chest stings, like a million pinpricks jab me all at once. *I love you so much. You gave me the most amazing nine years.* Warm tears glide down my cheeks and my sobs become audible. *I have to stop wearing your ring now. It doesn't mean I won't always remember you.* I reach back to unclasp the chain, hold the ring to my lips and let myself wail.

Chapter Twenty-Six

'Hey, Mads,' I say when she answers the phone, my voice low.

'Hi. What's up?'

'Do you know what Caz is doing tonight?' I ask, peering at Caroline's house through the darkness from my stake-out position across the road.

Maddie's silent for a moment. 'Why?'

'Thought I'd stop by and say hi.'

'Then why don't you ask her yourself?'

'Because I haven't asked her what she's doing on a Saturday night for ages. She'll think it's weird.'

'It is weird.'

I squint as headlights from a passing car cross my vision. 'Can you find out?' I ask, almost a whisper.

'Why are you talking so quiet? Where are you?'

'In my car.'

'Where in your car?'

'In the driver's seat.'

She tuts. 'That's not what I mean.'

I chuckle. 'Erm… just out. Driving around.'

'You're not driving around, I can tell.' A pause. 'Shit, Amy, you're not parked outside her house, are you?'

'Maybe.'

'Get out of your car and ring the doorbell. She'll be home.'

'How do you know?'

'Stop whispering, she can't hear you.'

'Right. Sorry. How do you know?' I ask again, louder.

'I spoke to her earlier. She said all she's doing tonight is cooking herself a nice dinner and drinking wine.'

I assess the house. Light peeks through the upturned shutters in the lounge. 'Lights are on, so I guess she's there.'

'She is.'

'What if she isn't alone?'

'She will be.'

'*Rach* might be there.'

'I told you; they're done.'

'Or someone else. Maybe she's got an online date or something.'

Maddie laughs. 'You know she's not into that.'

'Can you find out for me? Please.'

She sighs. 'Fine. Give me a minute.'

I end the call and stare at a couple of flying foxes hanging in an overhead tree while I wait, bouncing my leg up and down by the ball of my foot.

I jump as my phone rings. 'Hey.'

'She's there and she's alone.'

I lie my head back against the seat and exhale. 'Thanks.'

'So... what's going on?'

'Hi, Amy,' Billie calls in the background.

'Hi, Billie,' I call back, then answer Maddie's question. 'Nothing. I just wanted to catch up with her, that's all.'

'Uh huh. You seem very nervous for someone who just wants to catch up. Billie – Amy's in her car outside Caz's house. Putting you on speaker, Ames.'

'You didn't tell her I asked you to ring, did you?'

'I'm not an idiot,' Maddie says.

'Maybe not, but you do have foot in mouth disease.'

She chuckles. 'I promise I'm not suffering from that tonight.'

I release a puff of nervous energy. 'Oh, god. I feel sick.'

'Well don't bloody throw up on her. That's not sexy.'

'I'll try not to. Okay. I'm going over there.'

'Call me later, please. I won't be able to sleep until I know what's going on.'

'*We* won't be able to sleep,' Billie shouts.

I hang up and drive across the road to park in Caroline's driveway. The familiar evening sounds of crickets and frogs surround me as I hop out of the car and venture along the steppingstones leading to the front door. A crisp breeze rustles the leaves of the fig tree outside the front gate and nips at my exposed skin. I pull my jacket tight across my chest. My gut jumps with nerves, but there's hope in there, too, and the promise of something new. I shake my arms to release the adrenaline and press the doorbell. A few moments later the outside light flicks on, and I see Caroline approach through the frosted glass.

The door opens, and music, the smell of cooking and a blast of warmth from the heating rush out and embrace me. A glow emanates from the lamp behind Caroline giving her a golden halo. Her hair is shiny, like it's just been washed, and she's wearing an old pair of jeans and a plain red T-shirt. She's perfect.

Her brows knit. 'Amy.'

'Hi.'

She blinks at me.

'Can… can I come in?'

'Um…' She steps aside. 'Yeah.'

I catch the scent of her vanilla shampoo as I pass, and as always, the minute I'm inside, calm works its way into my muscles. I feel something else tonight, too – like I've arrived home and will never leave. The music becomes louder as we walk through the lounge to the kitchen.

'What are you doing?' I ask. 'Getting drunk and listening to The Veronicas?'

'I always get drunk and listen to The Veronicas,' she says, walking over to the speaker to turn down the volume.

'Are you alone?' I glance around for evidence of a visitor.

'Uh huh.' She gestures to the stove. 'I was just making dinner.'

A familiar garlic and basil scent fill the kitchen and I spot a tray of gnocchi on the bench. 'You're making that gnocchi dish I love.' I remove my jacket and drape it over the back of a chair.

'I am.' She gives me a sideways glance as she stirs. 'You're dressed up. You going out?'

'Oh. I was with Josh and Sophie. They're having a thing at their place, but Josh was being his normal pain in the arse self, so I left.'

Her lips twitch. 'He's good at that.'

'Yep. Hey, I've got something for you.' I pull a bottle from my bag and hand it to her.

Her eyes rest on my face for a second, before she takes it from me and unwraps the tissue paper. She stares at the label and then at me. 'Penfolds? This is a very, very good wine.'

I shrug. 'You've always wanted to try it.'

Her eyes narrow suspiciously. 'Okay. Why?'

I walk back around the bench to the stool and take a seat. 'To... say sorry.'

'For what?'

'Everything.'

Her gaze lingers for a moment. 'I guess you have put me through some shit worthy of an expensive Penfolds.' Her face softens. 'Thanks. I'll save this. You can have a pinot if you like.' She nods towards the bottle. 'Since you're here.'

A drink offer. This is good. 'Sure.'

She grabs a glass from an overhead cupboard, pours, and pushes it across the bench. I take a sip and try to formulate what I planned to say, but my brain is a scramble. 'Not hanging out with Rachel tonight?' I blurt out.

She fixes me with a deadpan expression. 'You've already asked if I'm alone.'

Shit. Very uncool. 'Oh, have I? Just wondering how things are going, that's all.' I take another sip.

'Going with what? With me and Rachel?'

'Mmhmm.'

'Well, they're not. But you'd know that because Maddie would've told you.'

I shrug. 'She didn't say much.'

She raises a doubtful brow. 'And you? Not hanging out with Luke?'

I return her deadpan look. 'I'm not seeing him anymore. But you'd know that because Maddie would've told you.'

She shrugs. 'She didn't say much.'

I smile and peer into my glass, twirling it slowly by the stem. The space between us is tense and frosty, but something else is trying to cut through – it's desire and love and hope. She must feel it, too.

'Why are you here, Amy?' She watches me and takes a slow sip of wine.

I point to myself. 'Me? I wanted to say...' I swallow. 'To say hi. See how you are.'

'You're lying. And you have that nice dress on that I like. You'd never wear that just to pop over and say hi.'

I smooth my hands over the material. 'You like this?'

'You know that I do.' She places her glass down and rests her palms back on the bench.

'Well, like I said, I was at Josh and Sophie's, so thought I'd make an effort.'

'Uh huh.' She stares at me.

'How did it go yesterday? In Sydney.'

She shakes her head. 'Sian shouldn't have told you that. I'll be having words wi—'

'Don't blame Sian. She assumed I knew.'

She rolls her eyes and snatches up her glass.

'Why didn't you tell me, Caz? Sydney? That's huge.'

Her brow creases in irritation. 'Why would I tell you? What does it matter to you?'

'Of course it matters to me.' My tongue sticks to the roof of my mouth. 'You… you matter to me.'

She picks up the wooden spoon and stirs the contents of the pan, her back to me. And now I know she's rattled because she's controlling the eye contact, like she always does. 'I haven't mattered to you much the past couple of months though, have I?' She drops the spoon and faces me again.

'You have. I just couldn't…' I shake my head.

'Couldn't what? Be honest with yourself?'

I slip off the stool and walk towards her. She doesn't flinch, just watches me get closer, her beautiful eyes filled with confusion. And hurt, so much hurt. 'Maybe. I guess.' I stop in front of her. 'Please don't leave.'

'Why would I stay here?'

'Your house. Your family and friends. Me.'

She scoffs. 'You? We barely speak.'

'Jesus, Caz. I'm trying here. I've been trying to fix this. You're giving me nothing.'

'You haven't tried very hard.'

'I have. I've called and messaged and asked to meet. You haven't replied.'

'You've sent a couple of casual texts and some work emails. That's it.

That day I saw you at Evan's, I reached out to you. I thought you knew me well enough to know what that meant.'

'I do. I tried.'

Her brows pull together in confusion. She puts her head down and rubs her forehead. 'Do you have any idea how much you've hurt me?' She looks up. 'How devastated I was that you knew how I felt, that you felt the same, but you chose to have a relationship with someone else?'

'I didn't choose... it wasn't like that. I couldn't deal with things. I couldn't figure it all out.'

She crosses her arms. 'And now? You're single again, so why do you want me to stay now?'

'I... I just don't want you to go.'

She stares at me before she grunts and turns to top up her wine. 'Still can't be honest with yourself,' she mutters. 'Just leave, Amy.'

But I can't. I can't walk out of here knowing that this is it. That our relationship is over and that she'll be out of my life. I take a few steps closer and gently place my hand on her back.

'I asked you to leave,' she says, her voice cracking.

'Please look at me.' I turn her to face me.

She drops her face into her hands, but not before I notice her damp eyes.

'Please stay.'

She shakes her head. 'I can't be around you. It's breaking me.'

I remove her hands, and she looks so fragile and vulnerable. I take a step closer, and her gaze moves to my mouth. I tilt my face to hers and feel her soft breath on my lips. My pulse quickens as I tentatively touch my lips to hers. She stiffens for a beat before she relaxes and responds, sliding her arm around my waist.

'I can't be without you,' I say, cupping her face. 'I'm sorry I pushed you away.'

She dabs at her eye. 'You broke me.'

'I was confused and scared,' I say.

'And now?'

'I'm still scared. But I'm not confused.'

'You sure about that?' She shakes her head. 'Because I can't play these gam—'

I kiss her again.

She chokes back a sob and rests her hand on my chest, then breaks the kiss and flicks her eyes downward. She touches my neck and pulls the neckline of my dress down slightly. 'Your wedding ring…'

I place my hand over hers. 'I've put it away.'

She gapes at me.

'I love you,' I say. 'You're everything to me.'

She nods, another tear falling. She runs her hands up my arms, their warmth penetrating the sheer fabric of my sleeves.

'Don't cry.' I wipe my thumb across her cheek.

She wraps her arms around my waist and kisses me. I melt into her, my soul alive and bright and lost in hers. That flame that ignited the last time we kissed crackles and spreads through my body. Except this time, I don't need to stop.

She rests her forehead against mine. 'We have so much to talk about.'

'Mmm,' I say, kissing her again.

She sighs. 'I guess we can talk anytime.'

'You weren't having dinner soon, were you?'

'It can wait,' she breathes.

I moan at the delicious sweetness of her lips, and the heat of her tongue sends a current through me. I slip my hands under her T-shirt so that I can feel her skin, be closer to her. It bumps under my touch, and she sighs against my mouth.

She turns the dial on the stove and takes the pan off the heat. 'I'm going to turn that off for a little while.'

I link my fingers through hers and lead her down the hallway.

It's warm in her bedroom and smells like fresh sheets. The glow from the front door lamp shines along the hall, and the lights from the back deck filter through the partially open shutters.

Caroline pulls the covers back and I perch on the end of the bed. She kneels in front of me and strips off my boots before standing and peeling off her shirt. I draw her closer and touch my mouth to her stomach. Her skin is silky against my lips, and she releases a breathy sigh as my tongue makes contact. I unzip her jeans and help her wiggle out of them, then slowly pull down her underwear, my face warming as my eyes roam her body. I stand to remove my dress, but she does it for me, running her hands up my thighs and over my hips as she does so.

She wraps an arm around my waist and pulls me tight against her naked body, kissing me deeply. My heart pounds against my chest, and if she didn't have such a firm grip on me I'd sink to the floor. Her finger slides under my bra strap, and it slips off my shoulder. I push it back up. She stops kissing me.

'I'm not allowed to take this off?' she asks.

'Not yet.'

'I'm naked. This isn't fair.'

'This set was expensive. And it's new. I bought it for you, so you need to appreciate it a bit longer.' I turn and stick my arse out slightly to show off the lace that's only half covering my cheeks, watching her over my shoulder.

She casts her eyes downward. 'Cute.' She pulls me in so my back is pressed against her and brushes my hair to the side to kiss my neck. Her other hand snakes down my stomach and slips into the front of my underwear. 'But it's coming off,' she says in my ear, her voice thick with want.

Heat pools between my legs and I release a tiny whimper.

She unhooks my bra and slips it off. Her hands move over my hips, slide inside my underwear and she tugs them off. She guides me back to the bed, and I drape myself over her kissing that exact spot below her right ear.

'Oh, I love that,' she says, with a tiny shudder.

'I remember,' I murmur against her throat.

Our bodies melt into each other as our mouths join and then part to explore necks and breasts. She moans and gazes down at me, her eyes heated, as my tongue finds her nipple. I trail my lips down her stomach, her skin is soft against my face, until my tongue slides between her legs and she gasps.

My body throbs, and I groan as desire, love and memories of our past race through me. Our rhythm together is perfect, her breaths steadily becoming more rapid as her pelvis rocks against my mouth. She moves slowly at first, but her pleasure quickly peaks, and she clutches a fistful of my hair as her heel presses into my back. Her moans become louder and my fingers sink into the flesh on her thighs as her body jerks and she gasps my name. After a long moment, she releases a contented sigh as her grip loosens on my hair and her body slumps.

I lie my cheek against her inner thigh. There's a strange sensation in my chest – like my heart is slowly being glued back together and is filling with a new love. It doesn't replace my love for Mel because nothing can replace that, but there's room for Caroline now. And my love for her is equally as strong, but in a new and different way that's just ours.

She strokes my head. 'Sorry, I think I pulled your hair,' she says, still breathless.

I crawl up and snuggle into her. A shard of light from outside falls across her face. Her eyes are half closed, and a satisfied smile plays on her lips. She rolls onto her side and drapes her arm over me, pressing her face into my chest.

I kiss the top of her head. 'You okay?'

She nods. 'Just lots of feels going on.'

'Me, too.'

She peers up at me. 'Are you sure about that? You can't mess me around, Ames.'

'I'm sure.'

'You promise?'

I give a small laugh. 'I promise.'

She runs her finger down my spine, causing my skin to erupt, then kisses me hard and rolls me onto my back. She's strong and her grip is firm, and my body fires up again. Her mouth moves to my breast, her teeth graze my nipple and I groan. She moves down my torso, slips her arms under my thighs and her mouth is on me, her tongue pressing against the perfect spot. I lace my fingers through her hair as her lips and tongue move between my legs.

I try to prolong the pleasure and gently push her head away, but she peers up at me with a slow smile and presses her mouth to me again. I'm too charged and groan through shallow breaths, my back arching, and my head sinking back into the pillow as I push against her. Her tongue presses harder in response, and I gasp as the pleasure fills every space in my body. My moans become louder, and my thighs clasp her shoulders as I grip the back of her head with one hand and scrunch a fistful of sheet with the other, letting out a loud 'holy fuck' as my body convulses and finally erupts.

Once my body has fully stilled, she moves back up to me. 'I'm glad those windows are closed,' she murmurs against my cheek.

'Me too,' I say, with a breathless laugh.

She hooks her leg over mine. 'I am so content right now,' she says. 'And you're not running away, so that's a win.'

I wrap my arm around her shoulder. 'I'm not going anywhere.'

'Good.' She kisses me and lies her head on my chest. 'Your heart is racing.'

'Uh huh. And it's doing other weird stuff.'

She peers up at me. 'Love stuff?'

I nod, and she smiles.

Once my breath has stabilised, I say, 'So, there's something I've wanted to ask you for a while now.'

'Mmm.'

'When did your feelings change?'

She props herself up on her elbow, resting her head in her palm. 'We're talking about this now?'

I nod.

She's quiet for a moment. 'After you had that fling with Zoe, I watched you fall into a bad place and it made me realise how much you mean to me. How much I wanted you to be okay, and everything became more confusing.'

My brows draw together. 'You were still with Maddie then.'

'Living together, but I knew we'd finished, and I was so messed up about everything.' She lies her head on the pillow. 'I was confused for a long time until Luke came along, and it hit me. I tried to push it to the side, told myself I didn't love you by seeing Rachel.' She runs a strand of my hair through her fingers. 'I could see you getting well with Luke. I liked seeing that. It gave me hope. And Maddie told me you were in a good place.'

'Luke and I needed each other. Just not in the way we thought.'

She nods. 'He's a good guy.'

'The best. We're mates. You're okay with that, right?'

She kisses my collarbone. 'Of course. You're a good support for each other. And I really want to see his house again.'

I laugh. 'I knew you'd love that house.'

'It's amazing. I had serious house envy.'

'And Rachel? Will you be staying friends?' I ask tentatively.

She narrows her eyes. 'I don't think you'd like that.'

'I am *so* not jealous of her. I can handle it.'

'You're such a liar,' she says, sliding her hand under the sheet and slipping it across my waist. 'Don't worry. I hope to never see her again.'

'Maddie told me about the phone thing.'

'Yep.'

'She said something about her deleting stuff?'

She props her head up again. 'I caught her at the beginning of the week. I'd gone for a shower and found her in the kitchen going through my phone when I came out. We had a massive argument, and she said she'd deleted messages from you. She took so much glee in it too. I fucking lost it. I wasn't sure if she was telling me the truth, or she said it to get at me.'

'Is that what happened to my voicemails, too?'

'Probably.' She tuts. 'I shouldn't have got involved with her.' She cuddles into me. 'Let's not talk about her, hey?'

'Yes. Sorry I brought her up.' I press my face into the crook of her neck and breathe in her coconut soap. 'You smell nice.'

'So do you. You've got that mint body lotion on I like. Speaking of nice smells, I've got dinner to finish,' she says. 'You're staying for dinner, I take it?'

I smile. 'You know it's my favourite.'

'I do.' She rolls away.

I pull her back and cling to her. 'Don't go.' I run my hands up the soft skin on her back and nuzzle her neck. 'It feels so good to hold you.'

She brushes the hair from my face. 'I'm just going to the kitchen. You can cuddle me out there. I assume you're staying the night?'

'Yes.'

'Then we've got the rest of the night for this.' She kisses me. 'You know how upset I'll be if my gnocchi sauce is ruined. And I'm starving.' She jumps up, throws on her T-shirt and does a little jump as she wiggles into her jeans. She tosses my clothes to me. 'See you out there.'

I lie in bed soaking up the warmth and contentment until I hear *This Love* blast through the house. I take it as my cue to move, but I don't want to put my dress back on. Caroline's right, I would never normally dress up to come and visit her, so I dig out a pair of her tracksuit pants and a T-shirt.

She hands me my wine when I emerge, looking me up and down. 'Didn't take you long to make yourself at home.'

'The dress was a seduction tool. This is the real me.'

'My clothes are the real you?'

'Yeah.' I wrap my arms around her, and I can feel the dreamy smile on my face. 'This is our song.'

'It is.' She tucks my hair behind my ear and gazes at me. 'I've always regretted pushing you away then.'

I shrug. 'It wasn't our time.'

Her phone buzzes and she reaches around me to grab it off the bench, a smile spreading across her face as she reads the message. 'You tell Maddie you were coming here?'

'Maybe.'

'I wondered why I got that weird phone call asking me if I was home alone and then hanging up.'

'What does she say?'

Caroline holds her phone up so I can read it. It simply says, 'so?'

I walk over to the island bench to grab my phone from my bag and see two missed calls. I hold it up. 'She's keen. How long do we keep her waiting?'

She shrugs as she throws the gnocchi into boiling water. 'She's waited this long; she can wait a bit longer.' Her phone rings and Maddie's name flashes on the screen.

I pick it up from the bench and answer. 'Hi, Maddie. Caz is busy.'

'Oh, Amy. Hi. You're there. Out of your car and inside the house. And answering Caz's phone.'

'Yep. I made it inside.'

Caroline tilts her head at me, puzzled.

'So... how's it all going? I've been calling. You must've been *busy*. And why is the music so loud?'

I walk over to the speakers and turn down the volume. 'Everything's good.' I gaze at Caroline. 'Very good.'

'That's it? That's all you're giving me?' Maddie says.

Caroline sets out two plates and mouths, 'Dinner's almost ready.'

'Well, I can tell you that we're going to have dinner now and we'll call you tomorrow.' I walk over to the dining table.

'*We'll* call you tomorrow? Billie – *they'll* call us tomorrow.'

'Aww,' Billie coos in the background.

'This is so great, Ames. I think I might actually cry,' Maddie says.

I laugh. 'You're so soft. Thanks, Mads. For everything.'

'No worries. I can sleep easy now. Talk tomorrow,' she says and hangs up.

Caroline brings two plates to the table. 'Here you go.' She drags her chair closer to me before picking up her cutlery.

I bite into the soft texture of the gnocchi and groan as the rich creamy sauce melts on my tongue. 'Oh my god, amazing.'

She grins. 'It's fairly basic, but glad you like it.'

'You were cooking this just for yourself?' I take another bite.

She finishes chewing. 'That's what you do when you're single. Cook for yourself.'

'No, not like this,' I say, pointing to my plate.

Her face softens. 'Plenty more dishes like this if you stick around.'

I run my hand up her thigh. 'I'm sticking around. You don't even need to bribe me with food. But... Sydney... you might not be?'

She peers at her plate, then sheepishly up at me. 'I don't actually want that job. Greg was trying to help me out, and I thought it would be good for me to go to the interview...'

'You let me believe you were going?' I say, with a wry smile.

'Well, you didn't really ask me about it, and you seemed upset, so...' She shrugs. 'I might have taken it though. And I meant it when I said it was hard to be around you.'

'And now?'

'If you're serious about us, then no, I don't want to go anywhere.'

'I'll follow you to Sydney if that's what it takes.'

She strokes my cheek. 'I'd rather stay here. Besides, Paul will get the boot soon and I'll go for his job.'

My hand freezes half-way to my mouth. 'Will he? You know about all of that?'

'Of course I do. Greg needed to discuss the complaints with someone. That's how I knew you'd be fine yesterday.'

I stare at her.

'I didn't forget about your meeting. I'm sorry I wasn't there for you.'

I shrug. 'It wasn't a big deal in the end.' I pick up my fork. 'This is turning out to be a good night.'

We finish dinner and take our wine to the lounge. I sink down into the couch and stretch my legs out. 'I am sooo chill.'

She drops down beside. 'Same.'

I slide my arm across her waist and lie my head against her shoulder.

'So, we going to give this a proper go?' she says.

I gaze up into her lovely face. 'Definitely. I love you. I'm ready for this.' I press my lips to hers and know I'll never grow tired of her kiss.

She touches the spot on my chest where my ring used to be. 'You think Mel would be happy for us?'

There is still so much hurt inside me, but each day the sharp edge of pain loses a bit of sting as it quietly shifts to the background, and a re-worked version of the old me emerges. 'Yep. She adored you and she would want us to be happy.' I tuck the loose hair behind her ear. 'Thank you for not giving up on me.'

She smiles. 'Now you're stuck with me.'

'Good.' I close my eyes and breathe her in. The leaves of the flytrap fuse together. I have caught my fly.

Epilogue

It's almost Christmas and the stifling summer heat is back. Caroline and I are in the back seat of Maddie's RAV travelling north to the Sunshine Coast. Today would've been my third wedding anniversary, and to mark the day we're going to scatter Mel's ashes on the beach where we were married. I would've chosen a different day, but Maddie said it's what Mel would've wanted. The anxiety has been high this week, the flytrap leaves creaking open for the first time in a while. Caroline and Maddie felt the same, and by extension, Billie.

Apart from this week, the past six months have been good. I couldn't ever imagine my life being good again. I still have bad days, but I no longer hit bottom. It's more like I'm sailing on still seas with the occasional swell, and very occasional tidal wave.

Caroline's home is now also mine. I moved in almost two months ago and put my house up for rent. That was a tidal wave day. Packing up, saying goodbye to that part of my life with Mel. Maddie and Caroline were in pieces, too. They became a couple in that house. Luke helped me pack and offered another set of arms to hold me while I cried, like I did for him when he packed up Sarah's belongings.

I've been getting back to my old self at work. Although I'm currently on long service leave, which I took after the complaints against Paul were finalised and I got to witness the satisfaction of his sacking. But I won't be returning to that job. I've found a new one heading up HR at a small hotel chain that I'll start at the end of January. Caroline secured Paul's job, Sian got hers, and I've already found something for Daniel at my new company, so he's handed in his notice and will be coming with me. Greg tried his hardest to change my mind, but Caroline and I agreed living and working together wasn't ideal, particularly as she'd be my new boss. She's bossy enough at home, and I love it.

I asked her to marry me, too. It's not like we need longer to get to know each other or work out if we're meant to be. I took advantage of my heavily discounted staff flights for the last time and took Caroline, Maddie and Billie to Hawaii. Billie wove some sort of spell over Maddie to shut her up about the proposal, and Jenna helped me pick the ring. It's a single solitaire diamond in white gold. It's beautiful and elegant without being flashy – just like Caroline. The proposal didn't quite go to plan, but it was still perfect.

The four of us went for dinner at a restaurant in Kona that was on Caroline and Maddie's must-go-to list – not only for the food, but for the incredible views of the cliffs and Pacific Ocean. Somehow, the restaurant messed up the booking for the table I'd chosen that offered us privacy and the best view. We stood on the balcony where Caroline argued with the manager while I tried to pacify her.

'Caz, don't worry about it. This is fine, we can have dinner out here,' I said, gesturing to the lounge set up.

'We're worrying about it. You went to a lot of trouble to book this, and we can't have dinner on a couch! With a coffee table! That has a fire pit in the middle of it!' Her voice rose, and she jabbed the air with each exclamation. 'Nor do they serve a full menu out here!'

I reached for her hand. 'We don't need the full menu. It's okay.'

'It's not okay,' she snapped and continued to argue with the manager.

I shot an exasperated look at Maddie and Billie who were watching on with bemused expressions. Then I noticed the most beautiful setting behind them. The full moon shone in the inky black sky. A stream of light beamed across the ocean in its shadow highlighting the swell of the sea and surrounding cliffs, and the sound of the waves crashing against the rocks below carried with the breeze. The manager had left to sort something out, leaving Caroline with an adorable angry crease in her brow and a sulky pout. The wind gently blew her hair and the glow from the fire pit flickered across her face. I cupped her cheeks and touched my lips to hers as she started to complain again.

'What was that for?' she said when I pulled away.

'I need you to shut up.'

'Oh.'

'I love you,' I said.

She smiled. 'Love you, too.'

'Shh. I... um...' I turned to Billie and Maddie who both gave me an encouraging nod.

'You're being weird now. You're scaring me,' Caroline said, looking between the three of us.

I dug into my pocket for the ring and held open the box. Before I had a chance to ask the question, her hand flew to her mouth and she nodded.

'I haven't asked you anything yet.'

She pulled me to her and kissed me. It was gentle and tender – the soft, cool breeze on my skin mixing with her sweet lips. When she stopped, she said, 'You can ask me now.'

'I want to marry you.'

She stuck her hand out and splayed her fingers. 'Yes.'

I slipped the ring on with Maddie and Billie's 'awws' in the background, along with a few turned heads from other customers and an open-mouthed manager who had reappeared. The four of us took the lounge seats and were given complimentary champagne and offered whatever we wanted on the menu, while the fire pit kept us warm, and the full moon smiled down on us. I was definitely rewarded when we finally returned to our room in a way that kept me satisfied for days. Mum cried when I told her and Dad even had a tear in his eye.

The rest of my time has been spent throwing myself further into recovery, to do everything I can to live a good life, focus on my new relationship and be me again. I'm down to one session a month with Dr Sachdev, and I'm involved in some other support groups. I meet Trish often and have run into Steve and Kylie at the centre a few times. I even went to Melbourne one weekend to visit Mel's sister and give her a piece of jewellery I had made for her from Mel's ashes. I saw her parents, too, who broke down and talked about how much they miss Mel and regret not being closer with her. It's heartbreaking that it took Mel losing her life for them to accept her. That's all she ever wanted from them.

Luke, Jenna and Cody are a close part of our friendship circle now. Luke's sessions with Dr Garcia have also reduced to once a month. He spends a lot of time with the other dads from the widowed father's group and has made some great friends. He's been seeing Cody's English teacher, and it's going well. Caroline and I persuaded Luke to speak to her the night of Cody's school play.

We were milling around in the school hall foyer when Ms Fay, as Cody called her, sauntered past throwing Luke some serious sexy vibes.

'Ooh, did you see that? She's still into you,' I said.

Luke flashed his gappy-toothed smile. 'Is that what that was?'

'Definitely,' Caroline said. 'We know a look like that when we see it.'

Jenna screwed up her face. 'Oh my god, Dad. You are not getting it on with one of the teachers.'

'Not yet I'm not,' he said, his gaze following Ms Fay across the hall.

Jenna rolled her eyes. 'Gross.'

'You need to ask her out,' I said. 'Or at least go and speak to her.'

'No. He doesn't,' Jenna said, folding her arms across her chest.

'He does,' Caroline said.

Jenna groaned. 'Dad. I cannot hear you having sex with one of our teachers.' She looked between Luke and me. 'I'm still scarred from last time.'

'It's alright, sweetheart. I'll go to her house. You won't need to hear it,' Luke said, smirking.

Caroline and I both laughed.

Jenna stuck her tongue out like she'd drunk off milk. 'Yuck. You're like forty-two or something really old. I don't think you should be doing that at your age. You're likely to hurt something.'

'Go on, Luke,' I said. 'She keeps looking over this way. Go and talk to her or ask her out or something.' I pointed to Jenna, who'd covered her eyes like she couldn't bear to witness any more. 'Madam here and Cody can stay with us for a night so you can have the house to yourself.'

Cody appeared to tell us he was going backstage. 'What are you doing, Jenna?'

She dropped her hand. 'Dad's eyeing up Ms Fay.'

'Well, to be fair to your dad, she's eyeing him up,' Caroline said.

Cody looked at Luke, mouth open in disgust. 'Gross, Dad.'

Luke laughed. 'Right, I'm going over there to talk to her.'

'Dad, noooo,' Cody whined.

I turned Cody in the direction of the stage door. 'Go on, get backstage. Leave your dad alone.'

And Luke did ask her, and Ms Fay, Grace, said yes. That was a couple of months ago and they're going strong. She's funny and kind, and she adores Luke. And Cody's finished year ten now, so she's no longer his teacher.

I glance across the back seat at Caroline. Her eyes are closed, a stream of sunshine touching her face. I'm so lucky to have her. Especially today. I reach out and run my finger along her jawline. She opens her eyes and gives me a lazy smile.

'You okay?' she asks.

I nod but a tear falls. She unhooks her seatbelt, slides to the middle seat and hooks herself in there. She drapes her arm around my shoulder and kisses my temple. Billie glances at me in the rear-view mirror, and Maddie twists in the passenger seat to reach for my hand.

When we arrive at the coast, we dump our bags at the apartment and head down to Sunrise Beach. It's hot, but the humidity isn't yet at its worst. A handful of people laze on the sand, swim, or surf. We walk further along, white foam lapping our feet, until we reach the spot where Mel and I had our ceremony.

I drop onto the sand, my chest pounding. Caroline and Maddie sit either side of me and drape their arms around me. Billie slides in next to Maddie, who pulls her into the fold. I place Mel's urn and four lilies in front of us. Maddie's hand trembles as she reaches out to touch the stalk of a lily. She's struggled this week. Losing your closest friend is up there with losing your partner of almost ten.

I rest my chin on her shoulder. 'Mel loved you, Mads. Truly loved you, like her own sister.'

She nods, tears falling. 'I miss her so much.'

Billie nuzzles her face. 'I've got you, babe.'

I turn to Caroline, who's wiping her eyes, and press my lips against her cheek. 'Okay?'

She rests her forehead against mine. 'Yeah. You?'

I swallow. 'As long as I have you, I will be.' I take a deep breath. 'Let's do this.'

We stand and walk towards the ocean, wading in until the water reaches our thighs. I remove the urn lid, slide it into the pocket of my boardshorts and gently tip the urn, watching some of Mel's ashes delicately scatter into the sea. My chest cramps as I say, 'I love you.' Caroline passes me a lily, and I place it in the water, watching it drift in the direction of the ashes.

Maddie scatters some ashes next. 'Love you, Mel. See you again one day.' She hands the urn to Caroline, releases a lily and falls to her knees, her face anguished.

I keep my hand on Caroline's back as she takes her turn. 'Love you, Mel,' she says. 'I promise to look after Amy.' She tips the ashes, then places a lily in the water. She looks upward. 'My god, this hurts.'

Billie swims over to us and takes the urn, and I pull Caroline to me. We hold each other tight and let the tears that have built over the past week escape.

Once they ease, I wade over to Maddie and wrap my arms around her. She falls against my chest and breaks down. I'm in so much pain right now, but I have to do this for her. I promised Mel I would look after her. We cry together for a few minutes before Maddie gently pulls away.

'This is so fucked,' she says.

I laugh through my tears. 'Yeah.'

Caroline takes my place and throws her arms around Maddie. They cling to each other and cry for a long time. They were still together when Mel died and shared that shock and torment with each other.

Maddie paddles back to Billie. 'Hey, babe,' she says, kissing her softly. Billie drops the fourth lily into the water and cuddles into her, the urn nestled between them.

I smile. They are so right for each other. Mel would approve.

'I am so proud of you,' Caroline says, swimming up behind me.

'Why?'

'For doing this. For supporting Maddie. For doing everything you can to get well.'

I kiss her. She tastes salty from the ocean and her tears. 'I'd do anything for you and Maddie.'

I stretch my legs out and lie on my back, Caroline holding my hand so that I don't float away. The sunshine warms my skin and sinks through to my bones. The waves washing over me bring with them a sense of calm, and I can almost see Mel hovering above smiling down on us. I come out of the float position and look around at the others. 'I think we deserve a night out.'

'Good idea,' Maddie says, grabbing Billie's hand.

I hold my hand out for Caroline; she takes it and follows me to shore.

We gaze at the ocean as we dry off, the four lilies bobbing up and down drifting further out to sea.

I close my eyes and breathe in the salty air. I can hear Mel's voice in my head, the day of our wedding and now saying, 'I love you.' I swallow. 'Let's go.'

Caroline and I put our arms around each other as we wander along the sand, Maddie and Billie hand in hand beside us.

I'm overwhelmed with the beauty of our surroundings, the tranquillity of the ocean, and the deep love and respect we all have for each other.

And the peace it gives me is incredible.

Acknowledgements

From first having the idea of two grieving people meeting in a group therapy situation to *Normal Functioning Adult* being published, the following people have helped me along the way. .

Thank you to the Shawline Publishing team, especially Alana Lambert for her support and quick responses to my endless questions and to my editor Daniel Car for patiently helping me work through certain scenes.

Thank you to my extended family, friends and colleagues who have listened to me talking about writing this story for the past few years. (I can't list you all, but you know who you are!) Fiction is my passion, and I appreciate the interest you all took in my writing and your excitement about this book being published.

Thank you to a special group of people I met through a writing course that I decided to take on a whim while in lockdown in 2020. Not only did they read and comment on every chapter I sent them over the years (from this story and others), but they have been a constant source of support, positivity and reassurance, and have always understood Amy. Kellie Smith, Priscilla Hocking, Sam Leah and Claire Furniss, thank you and I can't wait to read your published novels.

To my beta readers for taking the time to read my manuscript, for their insights and positive feedback – Priscilla Hocking and Kristy Eulenstein. To Lucy Bexley for reviewing early drafts of the beginning chapters and for providing helpful feedback and support.

To Roz Bellamy for the manuscript assessment (through Writers Victoria), for giving me such positive and helpful feedback. Roz – you were the first person outside of my writing circle to read this; sending it out into the world for a professional critique was daunting, but your encouraging comments and belief in my story was a huge boost for my confidence and made the whole experience enjoyable.

A special thanks to my writing bestie, Sam Leah. Sam, your daily support on messenger, your amazing feedback and story suggestions, listening to me moan about negative feedback and rejections, reading the same chapters over and over, having faith in me and my writing, being my number one fan (who isn't related or married to me), for keeping me focussed, for making me laugh, for loving Amy and her crew as much as I do (I think?) and for believing in this story. Your friendship has made this novel writing business so much more enjoyable. This story wouldn't be what it is without you, and entire chapters are the way they are because of you. How lucky we were to sign up to the same course at the same time to find each other!

To my family (Lani, Brian, Hannah, Georgie, Mum and Keith) who've supported me and listened to me talk about this book for years (sorry I wouldn't let you read it, but you can read it now if you really want to). Thanks to my mum (and my grandparents) for introducing me to books at such a young age by always reading me bedtime stories and never limiting the fiction I had access to as I grew up (within reason) – from fairy tales, picture books and Dreamtime stories to Archie Andrews comics to Enid Blyton and CS Lewis, Australian fiction, teenage romances and adult commercial fiction – I read as widely and as much as I could. Reading, libraries, book exchanges, school book clubs and lying on my bed reading novel after novel are a huge part of my childhood memories, and I don't think I'd be a writer now if it wasn't for that exposure to fiction as a child.

And finally, the biggest thanks to Kirstie Valentine-Stuart. My wife, my soulmate, my life partner, my best friend, my confidante, my biggest fan, my reader, and the person who has been behind the scenes encouraging me, supporting me, believing in me, listening to me, loving everything I write (even when it's bad), letting me spend my evenings and weekends writing, and never questioning all the images of strangers on my computer (inspiration for my characters) or my suspect search history (all research). Thank you for everything you do. I love you.

Shawline Publishing Group Pty Ltd
www.shawlinepublishing.com.au

SHAWLINE
PUBLISHING
GROUP

More great Shawline titles can be found by scanning the QR code below.
New titles also available through Books@Home Pty Ltd.
Subscribe today at www.booksathome.com.au or scan the QR code below.